Great British Fictional Villains

For my wife Jill who,
for over a year,
has had to put up with
a house full of villains.

Great British Fictional Villains

by
Russell James

First published in Great Britain in 2009 by
REMEMBER WHEN
an imprint of
Pen & Sword Books Ltd
47 Church Street
Barnsley
South Yorkshire
S70 2AS

Printed and bound in Thailand
by Kyodo Nation Printing Services Co., Ltd.

Pen & Sword Books Ltd incorporates the imprints of
Pen & Sword Aviation, Pen & Sword Maritime, Pen & Sword Military,
Wharncliffe Local History, Pen & Sword Select, Pen & Sword Military Classics,
Leo Cooper, Remember When, Seaforth Publishing and Frontline Publishing

For a complete list of Pen & Sword titles please contact
PEN & SWORD BOOKS LIMITED
47 Church Street, Barnsley, South Yorkshire, S70 2AS, England
E-mail: enquiries@pen-and-sword.co.uk
Website: www.pen-and-sword.co.uk

'In an age abandoned to dissipation, and when the ties of religion and morality fail to have their accustomed influence on the mind, the publication of a New Work of this nature makes its appearance with peculiar propriety.'

from the original Preface to
The Malefactor's Register or New Newgate and Tyburn Calendar

CONTENTS

Further Evidence:

FOREWORD

By JOHN HARVEY

VILLAINS. Don't you just love 'em?

Well, love 'em and hate 'em – especially at the other end of somebody else's pen or camera lens.

And the British do seem to have a particular way with villains. Maybe not the five hundred plus pages of closely written dissection of anguish and moral arm wrestling that a Russian would so lovingly afford such a character as Rashkolnikov in *Crime and Punishment*, but the brilliant, unforgetable stamp of character that you find in Shakespeare or Dickens, where the villains outshine the heroes almost every time.

I mean, who can recall, without difficulty, anything interesting that happens to Pip in *Great Expectations* after he hits puberty? Whereas the image of the convict, Magwitch, suddenly appearing out of the marshes, is inescapably etched in the minds of anyone who has read the book or seen David Lean's film.

(The actor, Finlay Currie, who played Magwitch, incidentally, used to live in the same block of council flats as me in Camden. As did Laurie Gold, saxophone playing brother of the Harry Gold of *Pieces of Eight* fame, and Ken Richmond, the Olympic wrestler who became the second man to bang Arthur Rank's gong. But I digress ..)

Who do you remember most clearly from *Oliver Twist*; the poor put-upon Oliver and the saintly Mr Brownlow, or Fagin and Bill Sykes? And Shakespeare. It's all too easy, I always find, to lose patience with Hamlet as he shilly-shallies about, incapable of making up his mind about sticking it to Claudius for poisoning his

father, seducing his mother and usurping the throne. How much more does he want by way of motivation?

Whereas the family Macbeth……. According to Duke Ellington, Lady M had a little ragtime in her soul, but I think there was more to her than that. A sliver of evil, cold as the first light of a winter's day. Like more than a few admirable villains (admirable for the skill with which they achieve their ends) she excels at persuading others to do her dirty work. Think of Iago, so tellingly planting the seeds of suspicion in Othello's increasingly addled brain.

The mention of Iago makes me think of another malcontented underling, Daniel de Bosola in John Webster's blood-soaked Jacobean tragedy, *The Duchess of Malfi*. I read this first as an impressionable teenager when it was part of my A level syllabus and it has never left me. (What do they study now I wonder? Harry Potter?)

Released from prison, where he has been serving time for murder, Bosola becomes involved in what these days would be called an 'honour killing'. Unable to forgive the Duchess for the shame she has brought to the family by marrying below her, her two brothers (one of whom harbours incestuous feelings for her anyway) hire Bosola to wreak vengeance. But after the Duchess and two of her children are dead, Bosola turns against the brothers, killing them and dying himself in the protest.

> *"Do you not weep?*
> *Other sins only speak; murder shrieks out.*
> *The element of water moistens the earth,*
> *But blood flies upwards and bedews the heavens."*

Great stuff!

More recent British villains seem to fall into one of three camps. First off, there is the masterful protagonist of so much romantic fiction and melodrama. Frequently dark-haired and dark-skinned, he cuts a dashing figure as he bestrides the landscape, oft-times on horseback and wearing tight-fitting breeches; the kind that James Mason made his name playing in those Gainsborough dramas of the '40s, such as *The Wicked Lady*, all curled lip and lascivious glances. Enough to make any nicely brought up virginal girl, alone and palely loitering, go all of a dither.

Think of Rebecca, cowering in the lee of the powerful Maxim de Winter; or Hardy's poor Tess, in thrall to the contemptible Alec d'Urberville …

'He had an almost swarthy complexion, with full lips, badly moulded, though red and smooth, above which was a well-groomed black moustache with curled points, though his age could be no more than three- or four-and-twenty. Despite the touches of barbarism in his contours, there was a singular force in the gentleman's face, and in his bold rolling eye'.

Heathcliff, mind you, more than met his match up on those rolling, windswept moors; but heroines like Catherine Earnshaw don't, unfortunately, come around too often.

Next there is that creature of the fifties, rising up on a tide of public hysteria in the face of a perceived breakdown in the social order – the teenage tearaway. Feral child of the war years, brought up without proper control and left to run wild (his father too long overseas and perhaps never returned). This is Pinkie in Graham Greene's *Brighton Rock.*

'From behind he looked younger than he was in his dark thin ready-made suit a little too big for him at the hips, but when you met him face to face he looked older, the slatey eyes were touched with the annihilating eternity from which he had come and to which he went'

Pinkie is the Artful Dodger of the Welfare State, amoral and brimming with resentment; lacking a true family, he adheres to Kite and Kite's gang much as the Dodger does to Fagin and his team of pickpockets and thieves.

Chillingly portrayed by Richard Attenborough in John Boulting's 1947 film – all nervous tics, cold sweats and teenage angst – he has a close cousin in the character of Tom Riley, played by Dirk Bogarde in Basil Dearden's film, *The Blue Lamp*, made three years later. When Riley panicked in the face of PC George Dixon's implacable advance and shot him dead, a whole nation held its breath – and released it with a howl of protest at something that should never have been given credence and should never have been shown: a young hoodlum gunning down an unarmed British bobbie. What was the world coming to? What indeed?

In fact, we were coming to Marcus Harvey's huge monochrome portrait of Myra Hindley, controversially shown as part of the *Sensation* exhibition at the Royal Academy in 1997, and rendered using the tiny hand prints of a child.

We were also coming to Morrisey's *Suffer Little Children*, written for The Smiths, and *Very Friendly* by the band Throbbing Gristle, which describes the last Moors murder in detail, to Carol Ann Duffy's poem, *The Devil's Wife* and Rupert Thompson's recent novel, *Death of a Murderer*. We were coming too, to David Peace's *Red Riding Quartet* based around the police investigation into the murders committed by Peter Sutcliffe, the so-called Yorkshire Ripper, the hundred and hundreds of columns of newsprint devoted to the Soham murders and to Fred and Rosemary West and the Gloucester House of Horrors.

We British love murder. We are fascinated by murderers. Perhaps these are our favourite villains. Why else do we write songs and so many novels and plays about them? Why do we incant their names till they become a part of our shared folklore? They are our bogey men. Jack the Ripper. Sweeney Todd. They are names with which to frighten the children. Myra Hindley's coming to get you, so watch out....

John Harvey

INTRODUCTION

'I must now discover to your strangely abused ears the most prodigious and most frontless piece of solid impudence and treachery that ever vicious nature yet brought forth ... '

from Volpone Act IV scene V

W HEN YOU READ a book or watch a film, do you always root for the good guys? Don't you sometimes want the bad guy to win? (There are some films, indeed, where I'd have preferred almost anybody other than the so-called hero to win.) In this book we bring villains centre-stage while heroes stay in the background. In fiction, villains bring blood and fibre to the story – *they* more than heroes do the things we dream of, albeit guiltily. Villains, male and female, seize the gold, pull themselves up from the gutter, seduce the object of their desire. Villains get the funniest lines. Even Dracula, one of our favourite villains, warns his guest Jonathan Harker: 'Take care how you cut yourself. It is more dangerous than you think in this country.' Villains have a clear-sighted, if outrageous, logic. When De Flores in *The Changeling* is asked to bring back his victim's ring to prove that he has killed him, he hacks off the entire finger to save time. He is asked how he could do that. 'Is that worse than killing the entire man?' he replies – genuinely puzzled at his employer's scruples.

In this book we meet – and sometimes, perhaps, you'll meet them for the first time – a host of British fiction's greatest villains, ranging from the earliest (Grendel, say, from *Beowulf*) to TV's latest. Interestingly, when we look at today's TV we find that the most memorable villains are not the serial killers and one-off baddies of modern drama, but the revived villains of classic literature. Frankenstein, Dracula and Doctor Jekyll have all recently returned to the small screen, and Fagin was brought back one Christmas by Timothy Spall. Fagin is perhaps the supreme Dickensian villain, but there are enough superb Dickensian villains for them to have a section of their own in this book. After all, as well as Fagin, Dickens brought us such memorable characters as Ebenezer Scrooge, Uriah Heep, the dwarf Daniel Quilp and Bill Sikes. It took TV to reveal to us the full horror of Mr Tulkinghorn. Shakespeare also has his own section. His finest include The Macbeths, Goneril and Regan, Shylock, Iago and Richard III.

These, though, are villains that you know. Less well-known are The Scottish family who dined off the bodies of its victims[1], the villain with springs in his heels, devil's horns, and a coat of hair running down his back[2]; and the villain who could remould his face as if it were made of clay[3]. This book includes real-life villains who went on to an afterlife in fiction – such as Dick Turpin, William Corder and Jack the Ripper. You'll find comic villains too, from Blackadder to 'Del Boy' Trotter, and from the aptly-named Horner to 'the greatest fornicator of all time'.[4]

They're all here. Some of the villains in the A to Z section may warrant only a line or two, but the more interesting have several pages, with quotes from books, illustrations and a wealth of background information. There are extra stand-alone chapters covering topics such as Censorship, Gothic Thrills, Villains from Jacobean and Nineteenth Century Drama, TV Villains and Villains Against James Bond.

12

This is a reference book, so dip into it anywhere and any time you will. By all means read through in sequence, but why not skip straight to the sections that interest you most, perhaps a particular villain, a TV programme, or any of the essays shown in the *Contents* page? This book is for keeping at your bedside or, if you'd prefer not to entertain such evil persons in your bed, why not place the book in a sunlit corner of your library? Wherever you read it, you'd be advised to keep the light shining brightly and the door bolted against intruders.

[1] Sawney Beane
[2] Spring-heeled Jack
[3] Colonel Clay
[4] Uncle Oswald

Exhibit One

Root Causes

Acts Of Villainy

MANY AN AUTHOR has decided that it's not enough to have their villain simply murder or rob an unlucky victim. To pep up the story the writer looks for something more. Critics – especially those who don't actually read such stories – are much given to tut-tutting over this tendency. 'Don't put ideas into impressionable young heads,' they plead. 'Stories weren't like this in the old days.' Well, yes, they were and probably they were worse. Gory deaths and devious villainy are found in the earliest stories. Back before man had learnt how to write he knew how to create a memorable villain. Those were less sensitive days, when life, as Hobbes defined it, was 'nasty, brutish and short.' If, as people saw, inhumanity in real life knew no bounds, it was fiction's mission to keep up. Here are a few tastes of villainy to whet your appetite:

Villain	Knavish Trick
Alice and Mosbie	They planned to have a painter poison his artworks in such a way that whoever looked on the painting would inhale the venom and die.
Sawney Beane	(Based on a real character) Beane and his family kidnapped lost travellers and dined off their carcases – some of which were smoked and pickled so the flesh would keep.
The Cardinal	Mortally wounded, he offered Rosaura an antidote to poison, which he drank before her to prove that it was harmless – but he was already dying, and the antidote was deadly.
Comus	Sorcerer who transformed his captives' faces to those of animals.
Elisabeth Kane	Innocent-seeming and convincing teenager who persuaded almost everyone of her incredible charges against two respectable women.
Basil Seal	Inadvertently dined on his current girlfriend.
Sweeney Todd	Slit his customers' throats and sold their bodies for meat.

Fairy Tale and Myth

Dramatically heartless villains (of either gender) enliven many fairy stories, but the original tales are seldom British. Germany, Scandinavia and, to a lesser extent, France contribute more than Britain. But the tales have been collected and studied meticulously by British scholars and have, of course, meant more to British children (and sometimes adults) than any other tales.

RAPUNZEL

"O RAPUNZEL, RAPUNZEL! LET DOWN THINE HAIR."

They have become a much-loved tradition of our childhood. Now, when we glance back at some of the fairy tale villains below, we realise that these full-blooded and black-hearted monsters may have inspired many of the finest villains of adult fiction.

Fairy stories pre-date the printed word. British examples can be found in fourteenth century Chaucer and fifteenth century Malory, while among the larger fairy story collections is that of Thomas Percy whose *Reliques of Ancient English Poetry* (containing fairy stories among folk tales, ballads and much more) was published in three volumes in 1765. Much of Percy's notable British collection was gathered a century before from an important handwritten manuscript belonging to Humphrey Pitt of Shifnal. That document, re-titled *The Percy Folio*, was printed in full in 1867-8 and now resides in the British Library.

Other early collections borrowed heavily from continental and Arabian sources, and include many of the tales we love most today. Arabian tales reached these shores as early as 1570 (Sir Thomas North's *Fables of Bidpai*), although we had to wait until the early eighteenth century for *Arabian Nights*. These were hardly children's tales; *Arabian Nights* in its original form (versions of which are still available, though not in children's editions) is a spicy saga containing plenty of gently erotic scenes. Perrault's French tales arrived a little later, translated as *Mother Goose Tales* by Robert Samber in 1729, and included such classic stories as *Cinderella, Sleeping Beauty, Bluebeard, Puss in Boots* and *Little Red Riding Hood.*

Joseph Ritson published several important collections of children's tales later that century (before he went insane), and in the nineteenth century we were brought the major works of the Brothers Grimm, translated by Edgar Taylor in 1823, and Hans Christian Andersen (various translations from 1846). More Norse myths came from Sir George Dasent (*Popular Tales From the Norse*, 1859, published in both expurgated and explicit forms) and from the Keary sisters (*The Heroes of Asgard*, 1857). There were also Celtic tales from T. C. Croker (*Fairy Legends and Traditions in the South of Ireland*, 1825-8) and Sir John Rhys (*Celtic Folklore, Welsh and Manx*, 1901). Throughout the twentieth century and still today, traditional fairy tales have been studied by psychoanalysts including Freud and Jung and have been revisited and revised by countless authors including Angela Carter, Maureen Duffy, Marina Warner, A S Byatt and Salman Rushdie.

Here are some of our favourite fairy tale villains:

Rumpelstiltskin: The king has told a miller's daughter he will marry her if she can spin straw into gold. Trapped with an impossible task and a floor strewn with straw, she accepts an offer of help from a deformed dwarf who says he will spin the gold if she will give him her first child. (The obvious sexual connotation has been stripped from practically every later version of this story.) The girl agrees, the dwarf spins the gold, and she becomes queen. But, as in many fairy stories, she has made a terrible bond. Rumpelstiltskin returns for the baby and, when the girl weeps, he agrees to relent if, and only if, she can guess his name. He gives her three days during which she searches for anyone who might know his name. On the third day as she wanders desolate in a wood, she passes his cottage and overhears him muttering to himself that she won't be able to guess because no one knows 'that Rumpelstiltskin is my name'. She confronts him with his name and earns the right to keep her baby. Rumpelstiltskin is so furious that he stamps his feet and destroys himself in his rage.

The wicked step-mother: To a child the scariest of all villains is the loving mother who has been transformed. (Given the high rate of maternal death from childbirth in early times, it was by no means rare for children to be 'taken over' by a new wife. They wondered if the new mother would treat them as lovingly as did the old. This was a genuine childhood fear.) The step-mother might prefer her own children to any left over from before – as is the case in *Cinderella* and *Sleeping Beauty* – or she might have no maternal instincts at all, as in many versions of *Snow White*.

The wicked uncle: Competing with, and often losing out to, the wicked step-mother as a dispenser of monstrous villainy, the uncle takes the blame for child abuse in the earliest British versions of *Babes in the Wood* in both Thomas Percy's and Joseph Ritson's collections, where the tale is titled *The Children in the Wood*. These early British versions place the tale in Norfolk, and have a gentleman consign his son and daughter to their uncle's care. The uncle, with his eyes set on his brother's legacy, hires two ruffians to do away with the children in a wood, but the more tender-hearted of the ruffians abandons the children to whatever fate may bring. Here the story differs from the one we know today – the tender-hearted ruffian is not so gentle. For his own protection he kills his rogue companion. And the children die! A robin covers their corpses with leaves (in contrast to the current version, where a flock of birds lays a blanket of leaves across the sleeping children). Then, as so often in early tales, the ruffian confesses, and the wicked uncle meets his doom.

The Wicked Stranger: If one's relatives could not be trusted, how much more dangerous were mysterious strangers met far from home? Here was an essential warning to all children – beware of strangers. We easily forget that until recent times few people travelled any distance from their homes. They knew their family, their village and the fields around, but nothing more. They rarely went to the next town. Most people spent their entire lives within thirty miles of where they were born but they knew the world around them intimately; every lane, every field, and every person in the neighbourhood. A stranger was utterly unknown. You couldn't be sure where the stranger came from, why they'd come or what their history was. You couldn't even be sure the stranger was of the human kind. The stranger might smile, might offer money or sweets, or might even offer to tell your fortune – but your wise course, at all times, was to remain vigilant. Certainly, the stranger might not be bad. They might be simply passing through, but it was still wisest to be vigilant. They might claim to have magical powers which they could use to transform your life – but would the change be for the better? Even when it was, as in the many versions of the *Three Wishes* story, there was every chance that, by your own foolishness or mischance, you would turn a potential benefit to misfortune. It was best then, to have nothing to do with strangers. Far better to remain as you were than to take a risk and to suffer a terrible fate.

One should not forget that in the original fairy tales, villains were far nastier and more frightening than in the bowdlerised versions we know today. When concerned parents – and even more concerned moralists – of the nineteenth century stumbled across the translated tales they quickly moved to censor, change, and even suppress them as being far too terrifying for young readers. Translators and defenders of the tales fought back but were defeated by the fierce puritanism of the time. One of the early translators, Sir George Dasent, was forced to reissue his *Norse Tales* in a version 'For The Use Of Children' in 1862 and added a bitter preface castigating those who 'uttered woe on him who wounds the feelings "of one of these little ones".' He had changed his selection, he said, 'to meet the scruples of those good people who thought some of *The Norse Tales* too outspoken for their children.' He listed several deleted titles by name and reassured his critics sarcastically that 'other naughty stories are blotted out, and no doubt the rest feel glad to be rid of such bad company, and proud to be raised to the rank of "moral tales". The beautiful illustrations and bright bindings will make them vain too. They had best beware. Pride and vanity hand in hand can hardly fail to trip. But if any little readers before whose eyes either of the earlier editions may have come should chance to miss some of their old friends, and ask why they have been left out of this volume, it is hoped that their mothers will be better able to answer the question than the writer of these lines can ever be, for he still sees no harm in them.'

Exhibit Two

IN OLDEN DAYS

Enter A Villain

THE GREAT AGE for villains, on stage if not in real life, was the Jacobean, the reign of James I of England (James IV of Scotland), which encompassed the latter days of Shakespeare and extended through the first three decades of the seventeenth century – though historical periods seldom coincide with dates, and theatre's 'Jacobean' age did not exactly coincide with that of the Anglo-Scottish king. (In the same way, the nineteenth century truly ended in 1914, and that fabulous decade, the 1960s, probably ended in 1968.) It has been suggested that the turbulence of the Jacobean stage reflected a turbulence widespread in a population unhappy with its king, a dour Scot with none of the charisma of his predecessor Elizabeth I – though James was a keen patron of the theatre and a writer himself: 'the wisest fool in Christendom,' as he was unkindly called. It was an age of violent contrasts. In his first years in the throne the Gunpowder Plot was foiled. Throughout his reign, anti-Catholicism scoured the land, science and astronomy challenged religion while, at the same time, scholars worked to produce the new King James Authorised Version of the Bible, improved versions of which are still in use today.

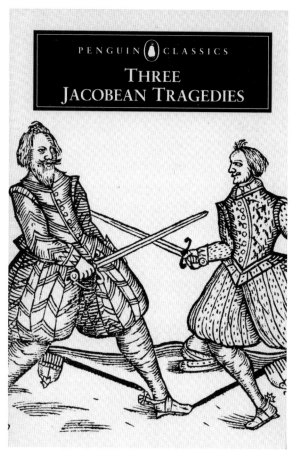

Jacobean plays combined knock-about violence with equally knockabout humour. They had their origins in the earliest theatre (think of Aeschylus) and the development of what we now call the Jacobean style can be seen in the preceding Elizabethan age. Shakespeare is not always thought of as a Jacobean, though he lived and worked under both Elizabeth and James, but many of his plays with that familiar mix of violence and humour are supreme examples of what Jacobean drama was about. Jacobean plays were clear-cut, black and white, visceral. Dealing with the most horrendous crimes and villainy, they nevertheless display a clear sense of moral justice. The anonymous play *Arden of Feversham*, published in 1592 but performed earlier, advertised itself on first publication (in Jacobean spelling and punctuation) as the

Lamentable and True Tragedie of M. Arden of Feversham in Kent.

Who was most wickedly murdered, by the meanes of his disloyall and wanton wife, who for the love she bare to one Mosbie, hyred two desperate ruffians Blackwill and Shakbag, to kill him.

Wherein is shewed the great malice and discimulation of a wicked woman, the unsatiable desire of the filthie lust and the shameful end of all murderers.

The description 'lamentable and true tragedy' has led many to read the play as a serious period drama, whereas in fact it is a rumbustious black comedy, based on a true story (a real-life murder from forty years before, reported in Holinshed's *Chronicle*, a source plundered by several dramatists for ideas). Its use of a real-life crime, suitably decorated and enlivened, is a precursor to the lurid ballad sheets and chapbooks of the eighteenth century. Many

Jacobean dramas (those written between 1602 and, say, 1635, ten years after James's death) display the same mix of blood and buffoonery, albeit enhanced with more poetry than in *Arden*.

The poetry was supreme in William Shakespeare. He blazed an exciting path in the London theatres of the 1590s (despite their closure from June 1592 to April 1594 because of the Plague). His plays brought a new vigour and freedom to the theatre, despite resistance from the authorities, and his success encouraged rival playwrights to experiment. Drama broadened its scope to include on the one side fantastic humour and on the other side bloodthirsty violence and scenes of breathtaking rapacity – often within the same play. Holinshed's *Chronicle* was a common source, as was Chaucer, together with classical authors such as Seneca, Plutarch, Livy and Ovid. Writers of the time plundered freely, often from each other, and it isn't always clear where some of their ideas originated. *Arden of Feversham* includes an exchange which could be thought to anticipate Lady Macbeth's famous 'Out, damned spot' soliloquy. See what you think. Alice has just collaborated in the murder of her husband. She turns in anguish to her lover's sister Susan:

Alice: *And, Susan, fetch water and wash away this blood.*
Susan: *The blood cleaveth to the ground and will not out.*
Alice: *But with my nails I'll scrape away the blood.*
          The more I strive, the more the blood appears!
Susan: *What's the reason, Mistress, can you tell?*
Alice: *Because I blush not at my husband's death.*

Blood and inescapable retribution are the themes of Jacobean drama. Another husband-slayer, Vittoria in *The White Devil*, laments:

Oh, my greatest sin lay in my blood.
Now my blood pays for it.

Such lines will be found in many Jacobean plays, underpinned as they are by blood, lust, revenge and the supernatural. Of the many classic dramas dating from that time, some notable examples include:

The Alchemist	Ben Jonson
The Changeling	Middleton & Rowley
The Duchess of Malfi	John Webster
The Jew of Malta	Christopher Marlowe
The Malcontent	John Marston
The Revenger's Tragedy	Cyril Tourneur, Thomas Middleton
The Spanish Tragedy	Thomas Kyd
The White Devil	John Webster
Tis Pity She's A Whore	John Ford
Volpone	Ben Jonson

Hiss the Villain

No Medieval Mystery Play was complete without its villain. How else would a restless and largely peasant audience sit through two hours of moral harangue? Judas, Herod and the devil himself were the most common. But for Theatre's finest larger-than-life, barnstorming villains look no further than the Jacobean stage, where blood, guts and treachery reached nightly climax. (Our modern day sympathetic treatment of Shakespeare's villains – Shakespeare himself was Jacobean – would have surprised and disappointed sixteenth and seventeenth century audiences.) After this golden period (late sixteenth and first half of the seventeenth century) villains continued to hog the stage in pantomime, masquerade and Punch and Judy. Punch, a rogue rather than a villain, appeared in France around 1650, but settled into 'Punch and Judy' in England around 1800. Pantomime, in its earlier form of Mime, can be dated back to Ancient Greek and Roman times, though its current British form stems from roots put down in the eighteenth century. It has long been a given among actors that the villain is much the most attractive part. The audience may hiss him throughout the play but will cheer him loudest in the curtain call, while the poor clean-shaven hero can expect only perfunctory applause.

Here are some pre-nineteenth century villains that actors give their eye teeth to play:

Play	Villain	Main Traits
Arden of Feversham	Alice & Mosbie	Lovers who scheme to murder Alice's husband.

The Atheist's Tragedy	D'Amville	Wants his son to marry the wealthy Castabella; then tries to get her for himself. In attempting to execute her ex fiancée, he dashed out his own brains.
The Beggar's Opera	MacHeath (Mack the Knife)	Highwayman anti-hero of this 1728 musical drama.
The Changeling	De Flores	Possibly the most attractive role of them all. A scheming but witty servant who blackmails the heroine into sleeping with him
Doctor Faustus	Mephistopheles	The Devil's emissary.
The Duchess of Malfi	Bosola	Duplicitous servant, eventually killed by an insane wolf-man.
The Fatal Marriage	Carlos	Sexual manipulator and murderer of his own brother, for the sake of an inheritance.

The Jew of Malta	Barabas	Anti-Semitic portrait of a Jewish merchant.
The Monk	Ambrosio	Young, over-sexed Spanish monk.
The Revenger's Tragedy	Vindice	Avenges the murder of his mistress as ruthlessly as only Jacobeans can.
The Roaring Girl	Moll Cutpurse	Sword-wielding thief and forger
Sforza, The Duke of Milan	Francisco	Revenge-seeking favourite of the Duke of Milan.
The White Devil	Flamineo	Violently over-ambitious brother.

Shakespeare's Villians

Shakespeare is often thought of as being separate from the Jacobean dramatists though he is, in fact, very much a part of them. He was one of the earlier as his plays began in the preceding reign (Elizabeth I) but he lived and worked on for a further decade into the Jacobean reign (that of James I of England). In many ways Shakespeare helped set the tone of that uproarious era – bawdy, violent, darkly comic and rich in earthy poetry. The Jacobeans loved their villains (some plays were stuffed with them) and although Shakespeare would never have claimed to have invented the vigorous villain or even to have reshaped him, he certainly did invent some of the greatest the stage has seen. For example:

MACBETH

Play	Character	Main Traits
Cymbeline	Iachimo	Ruins the good name of innocent Imogen.
Hamlet	Claudius	Murdered Hamlet's father then married Hamlet's mother.
Julius Caesar	Cassius	Leader of the murderers.
King Lear	Edmund	An evil bastard – literally.
	Goneril and Regan	Murderously self-seeking sisters.
Macbeth	Lord and Lady Macbeth	Seek the crown of Scotland. Nothing less will do.
Measure for Measure	Angelo	Hypocritical puritan who closes down the brothels while seeking to seduce a novice nun.
The Merchant of Venice	Shylock	Moneylender who demands that his debtor honours his contract.
Othello	Iago	Racist and duplicitous. Poor Othello thought he was his friend.
Richard III	King Richard	According to Shakepeare, an utterly unscrupulous hunchback who'll have young princes murdered to secure the throne.
The Winter's Tale	Autolocus	A travelling thief.

Broadsides and Ballads

Today the internet is so widespread, cheap and easy to use that it has inevitably become cluttered with tacky content. Much the same happened back in the late Sixteenth Century when print – a technology invented the century before – became similarly widespread, cheap and easy to use. The easiest thing to print was a single sheet of paper, upon which ballads, poems, advertisements, short news reports and sensational journalism of many kinds appeared. These popular sheets were called Broadsides (occasionally Broadsheets) – and often it was a broadside they delivered: an attack or polemic, usually unsigned, quickly printed and as quickly sold. They often contained nothing more than words – not always in a consistent typeface – though sometimes they were embellished with a crude woodcut picture to increase their attractiveness and, more importantly, to increase sales. The sheets were ephemeral but popular. Books were not cheap at this time, nor later were newspapers, because the government taxed them. But pamphlets and song sheets were cheaply produced and cheap to buy (at a penny a time) and most people could afford them. Their content swung from the sentimental to the lurid. In the seventeenth century, single sheets of paper, blotchily printed and often as not containing one crudely drawn woodcut, were rushed out from the press when murderers were hanged. Sheets sold by hawkers spread the news of sensational killings, abductions, freakish births and curious events. Songs and stories in popular broadsides became famous – and some remain so today. They include:

Song or Story	Villain	Main Traits
Barbara (or Barbary) Allen	Barbara Allen	Cruelly uncaring.
Sawney Beane in various spin-offs from Lloyd's serial	Sawney Beane	Leader of a family of cannibal Scots.
Jonathan Bradford, or The Murder at the Roadside Inn	Jonathan Bradford	Later found innocent of the murder for which he'd been hanged.
Captain MacHeath	MacHeath	Highwayman.
Peeping Tom	Peeping Tom	Curiosity.
Robin Hood ballads	Sheriff of Nottingham	Imposing the law.
Spring-Heeled Jack, the Terror of London & other Penny Dreadfuls	Spring-Heeled Jack	Supernatural highwayman cum bogeyman cum thief.

In the Eighteenth and early Nineteenth Century, ballads and broadsides were the preferred reading for the ordinary low reader, and made a fortune

for publishers such as James Catnach and John Pitts. By the middle of the nineteenth century the taste of the respectable classes had narrowed and become more puritanical, while with growing literacy and cheaper print the availability of affordable literature had widened and, to the puritanical, its content seemed even more lurid. Broadsheets continued to be hawked through city streets: 'There's nothing beats a good murder, after all,' as a ballad seller told Henry Mayhew in the 1850s. 'Penny Dreadfuls' were singled out for particular opprobrium:

It is generally conceded that some of the finest fruits of the finest minds are found in this field of literature, encumbered it is true, with ponderous heaps of the most vile trash. One in a thousand of these volumes may, perhaps, be read with some profit and no serious injury, while four hundred and ninety-nine of the residue are frivolous, as to render their perusal a criminal waste of time. The other five hundred will be found positively injurious.

from *The Christian Miscellany and Family Visitor*, 1853

But it was too late. For a great proportion of the population Penny Dreadfuls had become the main form of reading. Gothic tales and adventures, xenophobia and sex won out over fine literature and 'Improving Reading' in respectable Sunday Magazines and tracts. Why was anyone surprised?

Gothic Thrills

After a century-and-a-half of blood and gutsy violence begotten in the Jacobean era (see **Enter A Villain**), tastes began to change. Even if the public was happy with a diet of gore and sensationalism, writers had had surfeit. And the public, too, was changing: the raucous theatre audiences and semi-literate broadside sheet buyers were being supplemented by a growing market of book readers (among whom a significant number was female). Not that women didn't like a spot of violence, but for them 'slash and curse 'em' was not enough. They wanted romance too. And what the public wants, the market eventually supplies. Probably the first of the 'new genre' Gothic novels was Horace Walpole's *Castle of Otranto* (1764) with its fanciful storyline and romantic heroine Isabella who survived tribulation to marry her handsome and rich saviour. (In Jacobean dramas the virtuous heroine seldom survived.) Soon there were more stories of haunted castles, thwarted legacies, mad monks and struggling heroines.

The wind was high, and as it whistled through the desolate apartment and shook the feeble doors, she often started, and sometimes even thought she heard sighs between the pauses of the gust; but she checked these illusions, which the hour of the night and her own melancholy imagination conspired to raise. As she sat musing, her eyes fixed on the opposite wall, she perceived the arras, with which the room was hung, wave backwards and forwards; she continued to observe it for some minutes, and then rose to examine it farther. It was moved by the wind; and she blushed at the momentary fear it had excited: but she observed that the tapestry was more strongly agitated in one particular place than elsewhere, and a noise that seemed something more than that of the wind issued thence. The old bedstead, which La Motte had found in this apartment, had been removed to accommodate Adeline, and it was behind the place where this had stood that the wind seemed to rush with particular force: curiosity prompted her to

examine still farther; she felt about the tapestry, and perceiving the wall behind shake under her hand, she lifted the arras, and discovered a small door, whose loosened hinges admitted the wind, and occasioned the noise she had heard.

The door was held only by a bolt, having undrawn which, and brought the light, she descended by a few steps into another chamber ..

from *Romance of the Forest* by Ann Radcliffe.

Ann Radcliffe (born in 1764, the year *Otranto* was published) became supreme in the field with five melodramatic page-turners including *A Sicilian Romance* (1790), *The Romance of the Forest* (1791), *The Mysteries of Udolpho* (1794 and her greatest success) and *The Confessional of the Black Penitents* (1797). The supernatural plays a large part in Radcliffe's and Gothic stories (even if it is sometimes explained away in a naturalistic solution). Gothic novels merged into the standard canon in the nineteenth century but have remained with us today.

Gothic classics include:

Book Title	Villain	Author
The Castle of Otranto (1764)	**Manfred**, Prince of Otranto.	Horace Walpole
The Italian, or The Confessional of the Black Penitents (1797)	**Schedoni**, the wicked monk.	Ann Radcliffe
Melmoth the Wanderer (1820)	**The Devil** himself, who has bought Melmoth's soul – unless Melmoth can find someone else to take on the dubious bargain.	Charles Maturin
The Monk (1795)	**Ambrosio**, a Capuchin Abbot who becomes besotted with a young noblewoman **Matilda**, the wickedly seductive Devil's emissary who leads Ambrosio far astray.	Matthew Lewis
The Mysteries of Udolpho (1794)	**Montoni**, castle-owning adventurer who lusts after his niece.	Ann Radcliffe
The Old English Baron (1777)	**Lord Lovel**, disguised usurper of property.	Clara Reeve

The Romance of the Forest (1791)	**Phillipe de Montalt**, licentious Marquis, who lives deep in the forest.	Ann Radcliffe
Uncle Silas (1864)	**Uncle Silas** is the last person one should put in charge of a seventeen-year-old niece.	Sheridan le Fanu
Vathek, An Arabian Tale (1786)	**Vathek**, 9th Caliph of the Abbaside dynasty.	William Beckford
The best-known satire on the Gothic novel is *Northanger Abbey* (1818)	**General Tilney**, more cussed than villainous	Jane Austen
The greatest American Gothic writer is		Edgar Allan Poe

Fans of Gothic fiction in the first half of the nineteenth century were catered for by periodicals such as *The Calendar of Horrors* and *Terrific Tales*. Gothic fiction left its mark in other kinds of fiction too – notably in vampire and horror stories, but also in novels such as William Godwin's *Caleb Williams*, Mary Shelley's *Frankenstein*, Charlotte Bronte's *Villette*, Wilkie Collins's *The Woman In White* and Charles Dickens' *Bleak House, Little Dorrit* and *Great Expectations*. Daphne du Maurier's *Rebecca* gently led the way towards Twentieth Century Gothic (heroine trapped by menacing male), while more modern purveyors of Gothic (Americans being supreme) include Stephen King, Patrick McGrath and especially Anne Rice. Britain's Sarah Waters, particularly in *Fingersmith*, has made effective use of Gothic too. Gothic literature, like Gothic architecture, remains part of our twenty-first century world.

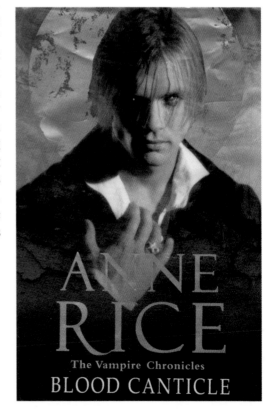

ANNE RICE
The Vampire Chronicles
BLOOD CANTICLE

Exhibit Three

Nineteenth Century Villains

T HE NINETEENTH was a great century for villains. It was a great century for books, which became far more plentiful and far more a part of everyday living and ordinary lives. Among all the fine, high-minded and good literature came, for the first time, a wide selection of books designed principally for enjoyment, books that told stories. A good story, to paraphrase Aristotle, must have a beginning, a middle and an end. But it must also have progression – it must move – and it must have conflict. A romance is a conflict between lovers or potential lovers and the obstacles between them. An adventure is a conflict, more often than not, between good and evil. Good is represented by the hero, and evil by the villain.

Nineteenth century stories resonated with strong heroes and wicked villains. The books built on, and developed, the foundations laid down in ballads, broadsides and melodramas. Gothic tales, the wildfire of the previous century, were trimmed and redrawn – the Bronte sisters being notable in domesticating Gothic – while melo-dramas were made more believable. Nineteenth century readers of Dickens and Bulwer Lytton wouldn't have felt they were reading melodrama – and indeed they weren't. For although the stories might have been based on melodrama and have used melodramatic tricks, they were fleshed out with thought and allegory, political argument, and all the novelistic paraphernalia of Richardson, Smollett and Henry Fielding. But at heart they were stories, and as stories they needed conflict. For conflict they needed villains.

We will see (in **Modern Villains**) how, in the twentieth century, writers became less capable of creating satisfying villains (the villains may have been satisfactory, but they were less capable of satisfying readers). In the rumbustious and thrusting nineteenth century, writers seemed better able to create villains that pulsed with life and vigour. It was as if they knew those villains, as if they shared the streets with them and met them every day. Perhaps they did. We'll never know. All that matters is that they wrote as if they did – and we believed them.

In a table of nineteenth century villains those of Charles Dickens are all too liable to dominate, so I have listed his separately. First, here's a selection of notable villains by other hands (fuller details can be found in the main alphabetical section):

Book	Character	Main Traits
Barry Lyndon	Barry Lyndon	Unreliable narrator, a rogue who amuses the reader if no one else.
Doctor Nikola series	Doctor Nikola	One of the weirdest late-Victorian villains.
The Egoist	Sir Willoughby Patterne	Arrogant and egotistical, he jilts his fiancée, gets jilted himself, and ends up where he started.

Book	Character	Main Traits
The Eustace Diamonds	Lizzie Eustace	Gold-digging wife, widow and mistress.
The Final Solution and other stories	Professor James Moriarty	'The Napoleon of crime,' and therefore main adversary of Sherlock Holmes.
Frankenstein	Doctor Victor Frankenstein	Unthinking creator of the world's favourite monster.
Lady Audley's Secret	Lady Audley	Apparently respectable bigamist and murderer.
Lorna Doone	The entire Doone family – apart from Lorna	The terrorisers of Exmoor.
The Picture of Dorian Gray	Dorian Gray	Having effectively sold his soul, Dorian can sin and sin and never grow old – but meanwhile, up in the attic ...
The Prince of Swindlers	Simon Carne	Probably fiction's first gentleman thief.
The Prisoner of Zenda	Rupert of Hentzau	Pretender for the Ruritanian throne.
The Ring and the Book	Count Guido Franceschini	Marries for money but when he discovers his wife has none he treats her cruelly and murders her parents.
Rob Roy	Rashleigh	Seducer and embezzler.
The Strange Case of Dr Jekyll and Mr Hyde	Mr Hyde	Evil alter ego of Dr Jekyll.
Trilby	Svengali	Mesmerist
Vanity Fair	Becky Sharp	Scheming little minx – though hardly a villainess in the eyes of many gentlemen.
The Way We Live Now	Auguste Melmotte	Successful financier whose investment advice can surely be relied upon.
The Woman in White	Count Fosco	Portly Italian gentleman, less affable than he seems.

No author has created as many memorable villains as **Charles Dickens**; villains from the high-minded Thomas Gradgrind to the irredeemably vicious Bill Sikes. Here are the main 'baddies' from his books:

Book	Character	Main Traits
Barnaby Rudge	Mr Rudge	Father to Barnaby and later revealed as a murderer.
	Sir John Chester	Schemes to thwart the romance between his son and Emma Haredale, then again between Joe Willet and Dolly Varden.
Bleak House	Mr Tulkinghorn	Meticulous, unshakeable solicitor, seeing himself as the nemesis of Lady Dedlock.
	Harold Skimpole	Feckless and ungrateful scrounger.
A Christmas Carol	Ebenezer Scrooge	Fiction's most famous miser until he's miraculously transformed.
Martin Chuzzlewit	Jonas Chuzzlewit	Mean, murderous cousin to Martin.
	Seth Pecksniff	The most hypocritical character in Dickens, which is saying a lot.
David Copperfield	Uriah Heep	Creepy clerk who is 'ever so 'umble.'
	The Murdstones	Nasty Jane moves in after her creepy brother marries David's trusting mother.
Dombey and Son	James Carker	Failed lover and crooked business manager who meets his end in a spectacular train crash.
Hard Times	Mr Bounderby	Cold, unsympathetic businessman – but not too cold to lust after Louisa.

Book	Character	Main Traits
	Thomas Gradgrind (Louisa's father)	Another hard-hearted businessman and a keen proponent of utilitarianism.
Little Dorrit	Mrs Clenham	Shrivelled and crippled property owner who tries to trick Little Dorrit out of her inheritance.
	The Flintwinch brothers	Terrifying if half-mad family of extortioners.
	Mr Merdle	Financier who causes thousands to lose their savings.
Nicholas Nickleby	Ralph Nickleby	Miserly money-lender and uncle to Nicholas.
	Wackford Squeers	Horrible schoolmaster.
The Old Curiosity Shop	Quilp	Villainous money-lending dwarf in pursuit of Little Nell and her grandfather.
Oliver Twist	Fagin	Fence and leader of a gang of thieves.
	Bill Sikes	Murderer and thief.
	Artful Dodger	Likeable young thief.
	Monks	Oliver's evil half-brother.
Our Mutual Friend	Rogue Riderhood	Riverside workman who turns to blackmail on the side.
	Silas Wegg	One-legged illiterate stall-holder turned blackmailer.

Exhibit Four

Villains Various

Modern Villains

T HE BESETTING SIN of many modern villains is that one cannot warm to them. They may be more like real-life villains (in so far as we law-abiding folk can tell from lurid stories in the newspapers) but they are not the sort of people we enjoy snuggling down with in our beds. We may find them acceptable companions on train journeys to and from work when we jostle with fellow passengers and engage less with what we're reading. At such times, we'll tolerate thin characters. On screen too, we're prepared to sit back and study these distasteful types dispassionately, but on the page we find them less enjoyable than villains of yesteryear. The books they inhabit may be more exciting than those older ones but we are less enamoured of the people in them – and ultimately, perhaps, we are less enamoured of the books. Certainly we remember them less distinctly.

Our forefathers loved to hiss the villains of melodrama and cheer their portrayers at the curtain call. They shivered and railed at the villains of Gothic literature, and although they didn't believe in them any more than they believed in the villains of fairy tales, they truly relished them. Those villains were fun. Stage villains stormed and ranted, ignoring laughs and catcalls, while those in books delighted readers with their wit and ingenuity.

Today's villains are too often simply nasty; there's nothing to relish about them. Such villains may be excused on the grounds of their being more realistic, but what happened to the author's creativity? A writer knows, as the reader perhaps does not, that such characters are easier to write. They're thin, they're one-dimensional. It's an adolescent trait in authors to pile on the nastiness and to swamp the pages with violence and blood. It's quite another thing, a more adult skill, to make a character as rounded, subtle, humorous and multi-faceted as they used to be. Perhaps there are too many unsubtle authors writing today. Perhaps books are affected by the simpler media of screen. We can't shrug it off by saying we live in a more violent age – we live in a softer, safer one – but we do seem to have lost the knack of creating a really lip-smackingly splendid villain. Not convinced? Check the villains in this book. See how few, comparatively, come from the last fifty years. They simply don't make 'em like they used to do.

Real-life Villains Fictionalised

ATTEMPTED WIFE MURDER AT BRIGHTON

Life is stranger than fiction, they say, so perhaps it is no surprise if writers struggling for ideas sometimes feel that nothing their pens can create can compare with the awfulness, or at times the audacity, of real-life villains. Until the Great Train Robbery actually happened, such a scheme would have seemed pure melodrama (it was, in fact, one of cinema's earliest films). Until we learned of Harold Shipman or Ian Brady and Myra Hindley, we might have disbelieved such stories if they'd been presented to us as fiction. The stories went too far. But as newspapers fill page after page with revelations (or sometimes mere speculation) about the extraordinary doings of real-life criminals, so writers turn to those same stories for inspiration. Real life can inspire a story – the writer, as writers always have, taking a single event or character and using it as a springboard for ideas. Sometimes the writer will take real-life characters and place them, with varying degrees of authenticity but using real names, into their book. Listed below are some of the more successful fictionalisations of real events:

Real-life Villain	Fictionalised in:
Walter Calverley	*A Yorkshire Tragedy*: a 1606 play by Thomas Middleton.
William Corder	*Maria Marten*, the girl who in the play was murdered in the Red Barn.
Buster Edwards	Real-life *Great Train Robber* featured in the film *Buster* (1988) where he was played by singer Phil Collins.
Mary Frith (Moll Cutpurse)	*The Roaring Girl*, a comedy of 1610 by Middleton and Dekker.
Baron Albert Grant	Presumed to be the financier that Auguste Melmotte was based on in *The Way We Live Now*. He too cheated investors out of millions.
Catherine Hayes	*Catherine*, a short novel by Thackeray.
The Krays	Film, 1990, directed by Peter Medak, starring Martin and Gary Kemp.

Real-life Villain	Fictionalised in
Jack the Ripper	Countless adaptations starting with *The Curse Upon Mitre Square.*
Charles Peace	Sundry Penny Parts of which the longest was *Charles Peace,* or the *Adventures of a Notorious Burglar.*
Jack Sheppard	*The Life and Adventures of Jack Sheppard* (1840) and others.
Dick Turpin	*Rookwood,* and later, *Black Bess, or The Knight of the Road,* etc.
Jack Wild	*Jonathan Wild,* then *The Life of Mr Jonathan Wild the Great* etc.

The State of Villainy

'There is a tradition in criminal circles that even the humblest of detective officers is a man of wealth and substance, and that his secret hoard was secured by thieving, bribery and blackmail.It is the gossip of the fields, the quarries, the tailor's shop, the laundry and the bakehouse of fifty county prisons and of every convict establishment, that all highly placed detectives have by nefarious means laid up for

themselves sufficient earthly treasures to make work a hobby, and their official pittance is the most inconsiderable portion of their incomes.'

from *The Treasure Hunt*,
a story in Edgar Wallace's *The Mind of J G Reeder*

In most crime stories, as in most thrillers, adventures and stage dramas, the villain is outside and against society. But sometimes a story sets society itself as the villain. In such a story the villain may be a dictator or a despot, or the police themselves may be the villains. 'Bent coppers' may be presented lightly, as in Bill James's **Harpur and Iles** novels, starring a pair of (sometimes justifiably) amoral detective officers, or as a fully-fledged villain, as is **Merrick** in Paul Scott's *Raj Quartet*. Despots were particularly common villains in Jacobean drama and Gothic novels, though in other, more subtle stories, the villain is society itself in the form of its condemnatory mores. Interesting examples are George Orwell's *1984*, where the state has personified itself as an all-knowing Big Brother, and Anthony Burgess' *A Clockwork Orange* in which the young über-hooligan Alex is as much evil as he is malformed by the society he keeps and in which he lives. But that's an excuse villains have used since society first apprehended them.

Foreign Influences

This is a book of *British* villains but there are some cads from foreign shores who are so memorable that they have insinuated themselves into the British canon. Unique as they may have been when conceived, they have been absorbed, assimilated and adapted into the universal villains' genes. No study of British villainy should ignore them.

NORMAN BATES (created by Robert Bloch)
The creepily charismatic central character of Hitchcock's masterpiece *Psycho*, Bates is a lonely orphan motel-keeper who comes to believe (look away now if you don't know the ending) that he is his own dead mother and that the sexually attractive young visitor to his motel is out to get him. (Or simply using the shower at the wrong time of day!) A preposterous story which was transformed into one of the most exciting and memorable movies of all time. The stabbing in the shower is the most famous scene, but movie fans have a long list of their own favourite moments. **Anthony Perkins'** portrayal of Bates was the high-spot of his career and, although Perkins was a fine actor, the Bates persona kept intruding into anything else he did until, in the end, all that was left for him were the sequels, *Psycho 2* (1982) and *Psycho 3* (the more imaginative sequel, in 1983). Few psycho-murderers have left such a mark as Norman Bates, often parodied, often copied. How the

motel industry survived him is a mystery.

Although everyone knows the films (at least the first one), it should be remembered that Robert Bloch wrote the books upon which the films were based: *Psycho* and *Psycho 2*.

DON VITO CORLEONE (created by Mario Puzo)

New York Mafia boss whose son Michael will take over from him, and instigator of a reawakened interest in the world's greatest criminal organisation, albeit in a glamorised form. Puzo charts the progress of the family in a series of monumental novels, beginning with Don Corleone's death, continuing into Michael's stewardship, but taking time out to return to the time when the patriarch first arrived penniless from Sicily. The books were already a success when the all-conquering film trilogy began, and they eventually went on to sell well over twenty million copies. The book series comprises *The Godfather* (1969), *The Sicilian* (1984), *The Last Don* (1996) and *Omerta* (2000).

The Godfather (1972) was directed by Francis Ford Coppola and starred **Marlon Brando** (with an extraordinary amount of cotton wool padding in his cheeks) and a magnificent cast that included Al Pacino, James Caan, Richard Castellano, Robert Duvall and Diana Keaton among many others. *Part II* (1974) surprised almost everyone by being, if anything, better than its predecessor. **Robert De Niro** took over the Brando role for the extended sequence covering the young Don Corleone's life in and departure from Sicily. The vigour and colour of that time was contrasted with the more melancholy present presided over by his son Michael (**Al Pacino**). *Part III* (1990) was good but couldn't match the earlier pair. Meanwhile, the first two were stitched together to make a six-and-a-half-hour television epic (an epic indeed, called *Godfather: The Complete Epic, 1902 - 1958)* in 1981.

DOCTOR FU MANCHU (created by Sax Rohmer)

The original and greatest – though to modern tastes, politically unacceptable – oriental villain. An unscrupulous and, at times, all-powerful master criminal, whose wily tentacles stretch all around the globe. For those readers with a taste for the non-PC, here's a good place to begin.

GUTMAN (created by Dashiell Hammett)

The villainous Fat Man in the novel and film *The Maltese Falcon* – and memorable in both, particularly for his dialogue, full of barely hidden threat: 'Talking's something you can't do judiciously unless you keep in practice. Now, sir, we'll talk if you like. I'll tell you right out: I'm a man who likes talking to a man who likes to talk.' Memorable too, for the unmatchable on-screen menace of **Sidney Greenstreet**, whose performance in the film showed that it was not necessary for a villain to be physically tough for him to intimidate.

THE JOKER (drawn by Bob Kane, written by Bill Finger)
Indestructible opponent to Batman, he 'smiles a smile without mirth, a smile of death' so, when the 1989 big-budget film was made, **Jack Nicholson** was the obvious choice. *Batman* began in *Detective Comics* in 1939, was given his own comic book the following year, and his first film serial in 1943. His TV series came in 1966, along with a missable feature film directed by Leslie Marinson, but in the cinema it was director Tim Burton's 1989 take on the story that built the franchise.

HANNIBAL LECTER (created by Thomas Harris)
Oscar Wilde's 'the unspeakable in chase of the uneatable' might have been meant for the fox-hunter but would better suit this cannibalistic criminal first introduced in *Red Dragon* (1981), then in *Silence of the Lambs* (1988), *Hannibal* (1999) and returned, although we thought we'd seen the end of him, in the appropriately titled *Hannibal Rising* (2005). Successful as the first two books were, their success was nothing compared to the film, in which **Anthony Hopkins** played Lecter (acting for most of the film from behind an iron muzzle) and **Jodie Foster** played the detective Clarice Starling. Lecter is a serial killer who flays the skin from his victims and eats choice titbits from the corpses. He is so violent in confinement that he has to

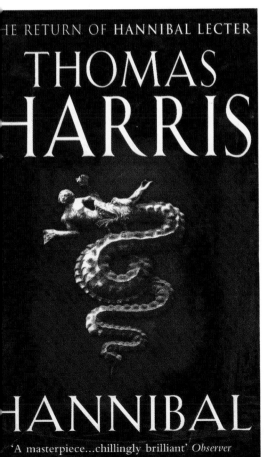

be kept in restraint in an underground reinforced and adapted cell. No human contact can be allowed as it is rightly feared that he will exploit any opportunity to kill or make his escape. Despite all safeguards, Lecter manages both to mastermind a series of copycat killings from behind bars and inevitably, to escape. There are no limits beyond which he will not go. He fashions a lock pick from a mislaid ballpoint pen, and to effect his escape, kills a guard and peels off the skin from the dead man's face to make a mask across his own. Once free, he indulges his appetite for fried human liver served with fava beans and a nice Chianti. (Actually, in the book, the wine was 'a big Amarone'. That was a bit too specialist for Hollywood.) The third and fourth books change tone. Stephen King thought they were even better but many fans felt let down.

MONSIEUR ARSÈNE LUPIN (created by Maurice Leblanc)

A French gentleman crook who later became a detective and master of disguise. These witty tales continued to be read for years and had a great impact on fellow crime writers, for some of whom Lupin seemed the quintessential Englishman. His first appearance was in *Arsène Lupin, Gentleman Cambrioleur* (1907), and in English in *The Seven of Hearts* (also known as *The Exploits of Arsène Lupin*) that same year. For some, Leblanc went too far with *Arsène Lupin Versus Holmlock Shears* (1909). Other books included *The Fair-Haired Lady* (1909), *The Confessions of Arsène Lupin* (1913) and *The Teeth of the Tiger* (1914). *Les Trois Crimes d'Arsène Lupin* (1910) contained exactly what it said on the cover. His career revived in the 1980s in the hands of the French writers Pierre Boileau and Thomas Narcejac.

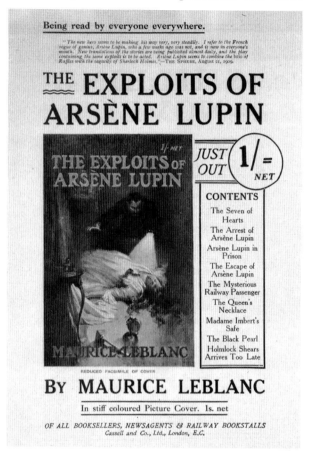

Being read by everyone everywhere.

"*The new hero seems to be making his way very, very steadily. I refer to the French rogue of genius, Arsène Lupin, who a few weeks ago was not, and is now in everyone's mouth. New translations of the stories are being published almost daily, and the play containing the same exploits is to be acted. Arsène Lupin seems to combine the brio of Raffles with the sagacity of Sherlock Holmes.*"—THE SPHERE, August 21, 1909.

THE **EXPLOITS OF ARSÈNE LUPIN**

JUST OUT **1/=** NET

CONTENTS
The Seven of Hearts
The Arrest of Arsène Lupin
Arsène Lupin in Prison
The Escape of Arsène Lupin
The Mysterious Railway Passenger
The Queen's Necklace
Madame Imbert's Safe
The Black Pearl
Holmlock Shears Arrives Too Late

REDUCED FACSIMILE OF COVER

BY **MAURICE LEBLANC**

In stiff coloured Picture Cover. 1s. net

OF ALL BOOKSELLERS, NEWSAGENTS & RAILWAY BOOKSTALLS
Cassell and Co., Ltd., London, E.C.

Paul Otto was the first screen Lupin in the German-made *Arsène Lupin Contra Sherlock Holmes* (1911). **Earle Williams** played him in 1917 and the first talking Lupin was **John Barrymore** in *Arsène Lupin* of 1932. Several other actors played him in later films.

PARKER (created by 'Richard Stark' aka Donald E Westlake)

A cold, impersonal and amoral sociopath, for whom crime is a profession to be performed with cool efficiency and without conscience. Stark gives no background or justification for Parker and his crimes. The books are as brutal and pared down in prose as is Parker's mindset, yet they are among the finest and most addictive American crime tales in which, for no reason other than that one lives almost exclusively with the criminal, one cannot help but root for him and wish him well. Despite the cold beauty of their prose, the books might have been overlooked and forgotten were it not for the film made of one of them: *Point Blank*, directed by John Boorman and starring **Lee Marvin**. The film is included in many a masterclass of film direction and drew attention to the neglected books.

THE PHANTOM OF THE OPERA (created by Gaston Leroux)
The Phantom, whose real name is the mildly comic Erik, has a horribly scarred face which he will not reveal in public. Consequently (or for the sake of a good story) he ekes out a living in the bowels of an old Parisian opera house. He compounds his problems by falling in love with a singer, masking his face, and embarking on a spate of murders to dissuade rivals and help achieve his hopeless aims. Leroux's novel came out in 1911, and has been a gift to dramatists.

Lon Chaney, hiding his own less than handsome face behind a skull-like mask, played him in a silent film of 1925. He was followed by **Claude Rains** in 1943, **Herbert Lom** in 1962, **Paul Williams** in a rock version in 1974 (needlessly re-titled *The Phantom of the Paradise*), **Maximilian Schell** in a TV film of 1983, **Robert Englund** (more famous as Freddy Krueger) in 1989, **Charles Dance** in a TV movie of 1990 and **Julian Sands** in 1999. All but the 1974 film were called *The Phantom of the Opera* but each remake strayed a little further from the original story. Out-gunning them all has been the Andrew Lloyd Webber stage musical which first appeared back in 1986.

THE RIDDLER (drawn by Bob Kane, written by Bill Finger)
Recurring opponent to comic hero Batman (see The **Joker**), he was played in the 1995 film *Batman Forever* by **Jim Carrey** .

TOM RIPLEY (created by Patricia Highsmith)
The amoral psychopathic anti-hero of a series of five extraordinary books by 'The Mistress of Unease', Patricia Highsmith, beginning with *The Talented Mr Ripley* (1955) and continuing, after a long gap, with *Ripley Under Ground* (1970), *Ripley's Game* (1974), *The Boy Who Followed Ripley* (1980), and finally *Ripley Under Water* (1992). When we first meet Ripley he is young, inexperienced and almost cowardly, but as the books progress and he grows older his creator softens her attitude towards him: he becomes increasingly urbane and successful and – as can happen with real-life psychopaths – he gains better control of his murderous tendencies. Highsmith invented nothing new in making her anti-hero a villain but she broke new ground in making no excuses. In the first book he had no justification for taking his companion's life. His playboy friend had done him no harm and in fact was generous to him. But Ripley was a psychopath. In that first book (though not in later ones) he wasn't even clever: his attempts to cover up his crime were feeble, his alibis non-existent, and any half-decent police investigation should have caught him. But the police were incompetent and their investigation was botched. Ripley escaped more by luck than by anything else (a recurrent Highsmith theme) and only as he aged and gained experience (in the later books) did he develop into a genuinely skilled criminal. At the same time, peversely, he became more likeable. This realistic portrait of a not-uncommon criminal type would surprise few who have spent their lives in

real-life crime (from whichever standpoint) but was fresh in fiction.

The Talented Mr Ripley was a Rene Clement French/Italian film of 1960 called *Pleine Solei* (aka *Purple Noon*) starring **Alain Delon**, and was filmed again in 1999 (not quite so well) by Anthony Minghella with **Matt Damon** as Ripley. *Ripley's Game* (retitled *The American Friend*) was filmed by Wim Wenders in 1977 with **Dennis Hopper** as a chilling Ripley.

DARTH VADER (created by George Lucas)
Enigmatic and rightly threatening, this dark-garbed and midnight-voiced villain of the *Star Wars* series is the servant – unlikely as it seems for him to serve anyone – of the **Evil Emperor**. He and his immediate boss **Grand Moff Tarkin** (played by **Peter Cushing** in the films) tour the known universe and beyond in their **Death Star**, a vast inter-galactic battleship that can blast planets into oblivion. At one time in his grim past, or in a film prequel yet to come, Vader was both father to the series hero **Luke Skywalker** and a **Knight of the Jedi**, traces of which austere discipline remain with him. Despite, or perhaps because of the fact that no-one could see the man behind the mask, Darth Vader was one of cinema's most charismatic, if scary, villains. He appeared in *Star Wars* (1977), *The Empire Strikes Back* (1980), and *Return of the Jedi* (1983). Played on screen by tall stuntman **David Prowse**, he was voiced by **James Earl Jones**. *Star Wars* without him could never be the same.

a to Z

ALEX in *A Clockwork Orange* (1962) by Anthony Burgess
Anti-hero of a sensational first-person novel set in a dystopian
near future where, since he was fifteen, Alex has led a gang of
violent thrill-seeking thugs. He tells his story in an extraordinary
but exuberant slang invented by Burgess, called 'nadsat'. The
tale begins with Alex released from a corrective institution
where he underwent a partially successful aversion therapy
which has left him unable to truly enjoy his earlier vices –
though he is unwilling to forsake them and sees the treatment as
having made *him* a victim. The deliberate violence and
amorality of Alex and his gang is set against the cold
dispassionate attitudes of the State, and leads to a shockingly
cynical conclusion.

The sensational film *A Clockwork Orange* made in 1971 by
Stanley Kubrick caused an outcry, with many demands that it be
banned before Kubrick, to everyone's surprise, withdrew the
film from British distribution. His decision was thought by many
at first to be a marketing ploy until it became clear that he no
longer felt the film conveyed the message he had intended. Alex
was portrayed (in iconic make-up) by **Malcolm McDowell**.

ALICE & MOSBIE in *Arden of Feversham* (1592) Anonymous
In this late-Elizabethan drama Alice Arden and her lover Mosbie
conceive a series of wonderfully unlikely schemes to get rid of
her husband. Arden strongly suspects his wife's infidelity
(though not her murderous intent) and belittles Mosbie as 'a
botcher' who 'crept into service of a nobleman and by his servile
flattery and fawning is now become the steward of his house.' In
Alice's first scene as she sees her husband off to London she
confides to the audience: 'O, that some airy spirit would in the
shape and likeness of a horse gallop with Arden 'cross the
ocean, and throw him from his back into the waves!'

Alice and Mosbie's ideas for murder include engaging a
painter who can poison his artworks in such a way that whoever
looks on the painting will inhale the venom and die. 'But Mosbie,
that is dangerous,' Alice points out reasonably. 'For thou, or I, or
any other else coming into the chamber where it hangs, must
die.' Mosbie's response is that he'll cover the picture with a
curtain. A corrupt servant more sensibly suggests that a poison
be put in Arden's drink. Arden tastes it, grimaces, and asks:
'Didst thou make it, Alice?' In a fit of petulance she throws the
pot to the ground, crying: 'There's nothing that I do can please
your taste!'

We normally find *Arden of Feversham* solemnly described as a domestic tragedy, but it's actually a hilarious comedy, full of the black humour that would, a few years later, underpin Jacobean drama. Though it has been suggested that Shakespeare himself wrote this wondrous tosh of a play, the idea is as ludicrous as were Alice and Mosbie's crackpot ventures.

BARBARA (or BARBARY) ALLEN (or ALLAN) (*traditional*)
The hard-hearted object of Sweet William's affections in one of Britain's best-known folk songs. Both lived in Scarlet Town with William, perhaps, the higher born since 'he sent his servants to the town, he sent them to her dwelling.' As for Barbara, when told 'he's sick, he's very sick' she slowly rose and came to him. But all she said, when she got there was: 'Young man, I think you're dying.' One imagines a stern Puritan Miss frowning disapprovingly at the love-sick young swain – whose illness may have been more than love-sickness, for his next action was to 'turn his pale face to the wall'. Even as she wandered her way home, 'she heard the death bell knelling.' Most versions of the song have Barbara repent too late, after which she 'begged to be buried nigh him'.

> *They buried her in the old churchyard*
> *And he was buried nigh her.*
> *From William's grave grew a red rose;*
> *From Barbara's a green briar.*
>
> *They grew as high as the church top;*
> *They could not grow no higher.*
> *And there they tied a true love's knot*
> *For all true lovers to admire.*
> *(Red rose wrapped round the green briar.)*

The story's earliest written form is in *Reliques of Ancient English Poetry* (1765) by Thomas Percy, where it appears twice, both as a Scottish ballad about Barbara Allan and her unrequited lover Sir John Grehme, and as the unpitying heroine of *Barbara Allan's Cruelty*.

AMBROSIO in *The Monk* (1796) by Matthew G Lewis
The young Spanish monk took the title role in one of the eighteenth century's most notorious books which mixed anti-clericalism with lashings of sex and sado-masochism to produce

a story which was still offered from beneath the counter until the late twentieth century, when practically all pornography was made legitimate. Expect lots of dirty old monks, some less than virtuous nuns, and sensationally innocent novitiates. Wicked as Ambrosio learns to be, his induction comes at the skilful hands of **Matilda** who enters the monastery in the guise of a nun, but who is actually the Devil's agent. The denouement is suitably gruesome, because no one, not even the monk, expected the Spanish Inquisition.

THE ANCIENT MARINER in *The Rime of the Ancient Mariner* by Samuel Taylor Coleridge
The unwitting villain at the heart of Coleridge's most famous poem (first published in *Lyrical Ballads* in 1798). Told by the mariner himself, the poem recounts the story of his dreadful voyage in the icy regions around the South Pole, during which he deliberately but unthinkingly shoots an albatross, a bird of good omen, after which everything goes wrong. The ship is driven by winds into tropic seas and becalmed; the water runs out, a ghost ship passes and the other crew members die. Only when the mariner finally prays to God does the much-needed rain return, but by then it is far too late. Though the mariner survives, his penance is that for the rest of his life he must relate his terrible story to every casual passer-by and try to persuade them to revere God's creatures (not that God showed much reverence for the mariner's fellow crew members).

ANGELO in *Measure For Measure* by William Shakespeare (first performed 1604)
The less than puritanical puritan who becomes master of a Vienna which is too lively for his avowed tastes. He sets about closing brothels, inveigling against lechery and imprisoning young Claudio and sentencing him to death for getting his fiancée pregnant. Claudio, no shining saint himself, implores his sister Isabella to obtain his release by sleeping with Angelo. Isabella has no intention of doing this (she is, after all, a novice nun) and while seeking a way out learns that Angelo has previously jilted Mariana (when she lost her dowry) but that the broken-hearted Mariana would gladly take Isabella's place in bed on the specified night. Mariana thus sleeps with Angelo but the blackguard goes back on his promise and orders Claudio's execution. A typical round of Shakespearian mistaken identities and surprise revelations brings this 'comedy' to an uneasy close.

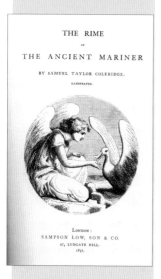

THE RIME
OF
THE ANCIENT MARINER

BY SAMUEL TAYLOR COLERIDGE.

ILLUSTRATED.

LONDON:
SAMPSON LOW, SON & CO.
47, LUDGATE HILL.
1857.

THE ARTFUL DODGER in *Oliver Twist* (1838)
by Charles Dickens
The leader of a gang of young thieves in one of Dickens' most popular stories. The Dodger is a rogue, but a likeable one, first drawing Oliver into Fagin's gang (on Fagin's instructions) and later helping him to find his freedom.

> *He was a snub-nosed, flat-browed, common-faced boy enough, and as dirty a juvenile as one would wish to see; but he had about him all the airs and manners of a man. He was short of his age, with rather bow-legs, and little, sharp, ugly eyes. His hat was stuck on the top of his head so lightly that it threatened to fall off every moment – and would have done so very often, if the wearer had not a knack of every now and then giving his head a sudden twitch, which brought it back to its old place again. He wore a man's coat, which reached nearly to his heels. He had turned the cuffs back, half way up his arm, to get his hands out of the sleeves, apparently with the ultimate view of thrusting them into the pockets of his corduroy trousers, for there he kept them. He was, altogether, as roistering and swaggering a young gentleman as ever stood four feet six, or something less, in his bluchers.*

> from *Oliver Twist* by Charles Dickens

According to Harry Furniss, Dodger was played in Dickens' time by the actor Johnny Toole who wore 'the very worst trousers that ever appeared on stage. They were really old, had never been patched up.' Dickens saw the production and remarked gravely that he 'admired the trousers'. It then turned out that Toole had borrowed them from another actor, Murray, who had worn them for some years on stage in a

"Johnny Toole" by
Harry Furniss

production of Sir Walter Scott's *The Heart of Midlothian*. Scott, it seems, saw that production and, like Dickens, 'was particularly struck by the trousers'.

Dodger was played in the splendid David Lean film of 1948 by the erstwhile pop singer **Anthony Newley**. There had been earlier versions; a silent film directed by Frank Lloyd in 1922 and a forgettable 1933 movie directed by William Cowen. Dodger was entertainingly portrayed by **Jack Wild** in the 1968 Carol Reed film of the Lionel Bart musical *Oliver*. Later, *Oliver Twist* was needlessly remade in 1982 (the film directed by Clive Donner) and there was a Disney cartoon version, *Oliver and Company*, in 1988 in which he was played by **Billy Joel**. (Well, he provided the voice-over and sang the songs). **Alex Crowley** played Dodger in Alan Bleasdale's fine adaptation for ITV in 1999.

LADY AUDLEY

in *Lady Audley's Secret* (1862) by Mary Elizabeth Braddon

The anti-heroine of a mid-nineteenth century three-decker shocker (initially a serial begun in the *Sixpenny Magazine*, but not completed there, as the magazine collapsed). Lady Audley confounds all the expectations of a respectable Victorian housewife by being a scheming stop-at-nothing who deliberately contracts a bigamous marriage with the unsuspecting, but wealthy, Sir Michael Audley. Thus she sheds her original name of Helen Maldon, together with her first married name of Mrs Tallboys *and* her assumed name of Lucy Graham. (She's that kind of girl). But her first husband George Tallboys inconveniently returns from Australia – then disappears. When Sir Michael's nephew Robert Audley endeavours to find out what happened to Tallboy she tries to kill him by burning down the inn in which he is staying. Eventually Lady Audley confesses that she has killed Tallboys and shoved him down a well. (Though there is a final twist ...)

Lady Audley's Secret sold in vast numbers in the nineteenth century and retained a foothold in the twentieth, being particularly popular with downtrodden wives. Several silent films were made of it, including one in 1915 which starred the legendary vamp **Theda Bara**.

AUTOLYCUS in *The Winter's Tale* (c.1610)
by William Shakespeare
Likeable rogue who enlivens the latter stages of the play. Autolycus is a travelling thief, pedlar and occasional troubadour who famously describes himself as a 'snapper-up of ill-considered trifles'.

MR B in *Pamela* (1740) by Samuel Richardson
In the first of Richardson's three long novels (written entirely in the form of letters and scraps from journals) fifteen year-old Pamela is left to the mercy of the lustful Mr B after his mother, Mrs B, dies. Pamela is attracted to the rogue but defends her chastity. Impatient at her antics, Mr B eventually locks her up in his Hall in Lincolnshire, under the stern guardianship of **Mrs Jewkes**. After a while, he follows her there, attempts to rape her, and sets up a bogus marriage. Still Pamela resists, causing an exasperated Mr B to do the decent thing and marry her for real. (Her private correspondence suggests this may have always been her aim.)

The book was so successful that Richardson produced *Pamela, Part II* the following year (my, how that man could write), getting it out just in time to fight off a parody, *Shamela*, believed to have been written by Henry Fielding (of *Tom Jones* fame). He returned to the plot in 1748 with a less scrupulous villain, **Lovelace** in *Clarissa*.

MR BADMAN in *The Life and Death of Mr Badman* (1680)
by John Bunyan
With such a name how could he not be a villain? Mr Badman is the subject of an allegorical dialogue by the author of *Pilgrim's Progress* (but a livelier tome than that) with his moral tale related by Mr Wiseman and Mr Attentive. Badman tricks a rich young lady into marriage, squanders her money, goes into trade, swindles his customers and suppliers, drinks too much, sees his wife die of despair – and blithely marries again. Unfortunately for him, his second wife is as bad as he is and their marriage ends in poverty, upon which Badman succumbs to a combination of diseases and dies unlamented.

BALTHAZAR (Thomas Kyd) see **LORENZO & BALTHAZAR**

BARABAS see **JEW OF MALTA**

BARBARA (or **BARBARY**) **ALLEN** (or **ALLAN**) (*traditional*) see **ALLEN**

THE BARON in *Meet the Baron* (1937) etc. by 'Anthony Morton' aka John Creasey

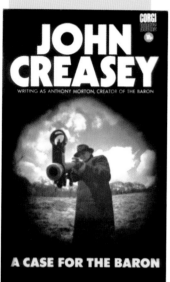

John Mannering is the Baron, a lithe, lean, elegant man-about-Mayfair and a legend in his time. Surrounded by an aura of glamour and romance, the ex-jewel-thief is, the author assures us, the most brilliant dare-devil cracksman in the annals of crime. Despite which, he is consulted by New Scotland Yard for help with crimes they cannot solve on their own, and their gratitude goes to his head: he becomes a crime-buster (though he remains not averse to a little thieving on the side). He was renamed Blue Mask in America to avoid confusion with another character.

The Baron's adventures, largely in the 1940s, began with *Meet the Baron*, immediately followed by *The Baron Returns* (also 1937). Later adventures include *The Baron at Bay* (1938), *Alias the Baron* (1939), A *Branch for the Baron*, *Blame the Baron*, *Shadow the Baron*, *A Case for the Baron*, *The Baron Returns* et cetera until *The Baron, King-Maker* in 1975.

In the mid-60s ATV screened a series loosely based on Creasey's character in which an American 'antiques expert' helped the British Secret Service recover stolen jewellery and art. **Steve Forrest** was *The Baron*, young **Sue Lloyd** was the love interest (Cordelia Winfield), and Mannering's magnificent motor, a Jensen, registration BAR 1, was even more charismatic than the stars.

SAWNEY BEANE in *The Man-Eater of Scotland* (1825) by Edward Lloyd

A particularly horrible real-life villain whose ghastly exploits were recounted in the 'penny magazine' *The Terrific Register* and which ran to over a hundred episodes. Back in the late fourteenth century Beane and his girlfriend, reduced to eking out a miserable existence in a cave, had begun to kill and rob passing travellers. They destroyed the evidence by eating their victims – often after pickling, salting and preserving their carcasses. Various relations – some of whom enjoyed incestuous relationships – joined the pair until, it was said, the gang reached nearly fifty people. Their crimes went undiscovered for twenty years until, after a botched attack on a married couple, the husband escaped to raise the alarm. King James IV led an army of 400 men to take the family – still resident in their caves – and to discover the horrendous remains of their victims. Retribution was salutary. The men's penises were cut off and burned, and their hands and legs were hacked from their bodies. Their women were made to watch their men bleed to death before they too were trussed up and thrown into the same fire.

DOCTOR BICKLEIGH in *Malice Aforethought* (1931)
by Francis Iles
An ordinary little man who turns to murder and becomes too confident. The opening lines in the classic crime novel *Malice Aforethought* have become two of the most often quoted in crime fiction: 'It was not until several weeks after he had decided to murder his wife that Dr Bickleigh took any active steps in the matter. Murder is a serious business.' Bickleigh's crime (gradual murder of a spouse by repeated small doses of arsenic) was inspired by the real-life case of the alleged murderess Florence Maybrick in 1889.

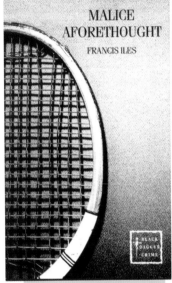

Malice Aforethought came out in 1931 and has been in print ever since. The BBC screened the story as a four-part serial in 1979 with **Hywell Bennett** as Dr Bickleigh.

BIG BROTHER in *Nineteen Eighty-Four* (1949)
by George Orwell
There are people (not you, gentle reader) who don't realise that *Big Brother* did not start out as a TV reality show. He began in one of the most famous books of the twentieth century, where he was the supposedly benevolent dictator whose face was everywhere and who could see everything – due mainly to the placing of two-way television sets in every living room. (Big Brother was the regime, rather than a specific individual, though he would come to be personified as the cold bureaucrat O'Brien.) Big Brother appeared omnipotent but actually ruled only one third of the world, Oceania, a state kept in a perpetual state of cold war with the world's other two empires (since war unites people against outsiders and justifies a permanent 'state of emergency'). Big Brother stifled thought ultimately by violence but mainly by 'dumbing down' his people with inane but compelling

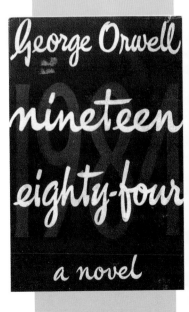

television shows, pop music, an increasingly simplified (thus restricted) language and the rewriting of history (copied from the Stalinist Soviet Union) in which entire episodes, when undesirable, were written out. Language and thought were corrupted with 'double-think' to subvert the meaning of words and thus make all expression meaningless, for example: 'War is Peace; Freedom is Slavery; Ignorance is Strength.' In place of real news the state-run information channels presented banal 'human interest' tales, propaganda and repetitive slogans such as 'Big Brother is Watching You.' Big Brother's opponent in the book was Winston Smith, but he had no chance against the power of an all-pervasive state. Smith wasn't killed. Instead, Big Brother had him subjected to violent mind control and brain washing until, in the ironic ending to the book, Winston betrayed everything he once believed in and learnt instead to 'love' Big Brother. (This scene, incidentally, took place in *Room 101*, a location which, like the reality show Big Brother, has since taken on a life of its own.)

Orwell hastily wrote *Nineteen Eighty-Four* in the last year of his life (he knew he was dying of TB) and it was published in 1949. It has never been out of print.

The first film version of *1984* came in 1956. It was directed by Michael Anderson, strayed pointlessly from the book, and starred (confusingly) **Edmund O'Brien** as Winston Smith and **Michael Redgrave** as a treacherous General O'Connor. **Donald Pleasance** and **Patrick Allen** were among the functionary villains. Fittingly, it was in 1984 that an improved version came out, directed by Michael Radford, and starring **John Hurt** as Smith and **Richard Burton** as O'Brien. A fine but grey and depressing film, it was lightened a little by music from **The Eurythmics**.

In 1954, when it first appeared on TV *1984* caused shock and even outrage, mainly among politicians. **Peter Cushing** played the hero Winston Smith, while **Andre Morell** landed the villain's part of O'Brien. The play was adapted from the book by Nigel Kneale, of *Quatermass* fame, and he also wrote the 1965 version in which O'Brien was played by **Joseph O'Connor**. The Reality Show *Big Brother*, based on an idea developed on Dutch TV, began on Britain's Channel 4 in 2000 and was for many critics as great a villain and corrupter of society as was O'Brien. Where O'Brien's subjugated citizens were forced to keep a two-way TV in their apartments to let the State monitor their behaviour, so the hapless participants in this game cum 'psychological experiment' volunteered to imprison themselves with a cynically selected band of fellow flatmates in a *Huit Clos* of a set where they were monitored by 24/7 television cameras, and had every detail of what they did there captured and broadcast to the watching world. George Orwell came close, but not even he foresaw this.

BLACKADDER. Title character in the TV series, 1983 to 89

A lying, cheating, cowardly, and utterly reprehensible rogue with no redeeming characteristics who nevertheless became a hugely popular TV villain. Played and initially part-written by **Rowan Atkinson**, the series (initially called *The Black Adder*) began with Atkinson as Edmund, Duke of Edinburgh (no relation or similarity to Atkinson's contemporary Duke) who, in the days of the Wars of the Roses, supposed himself to be a possible heir to the throne. **Tony Robinson** established himself as the Black Adder's cretinous servant Baldrick. The series wasn't a great success but, by retaining some of its cast while changing the writers from Atkinson and Richard Curtis to Curtis and Ben Elton, it was given a second chance three years later. This far better series time-warped into the reign of Elizabeth I (**Miranda Richardson**) and added **Stephen Fry** as Lord Melchett (an even more supercilious aristo than Blackadder, whose original nickname had now been melded into one word). The third series, a year later, jumped again, into the Georgian age (**Hugh Laurie** was the clueless George, Prince of Wales), and the fourth and final series sprang into the First World War. The other stalwart of the series, **Tim McInnerny**, should be added to the four men listed above. Apart from the four main series, the show produced several one-offs – a Christmas special, a Comic Relief skit and an oddity intended for screening in the Millennium Dome.

THE BLACK KNIGHT in *A Game of Chess* (1624)

by Thomas Middleton

The allegorical villain in Middleton's satirical comedy. The Black Knight stood for the real-life Spanish Ambassador (the Marquis de Gondomar) who was loathed by the English populace but at the time courted by King James. The real-life Ambassador was trying to ally Protestant England to Catholic Spain by arranging a marriage between the Prince of Wales and a Spanish princess. This was parodied in the play in the form of a game of diplomatic chess – virtually meaningless to a present-day audience but splendidly clear to the audience then, who were strongly against the proposed marriage and any compromise with Spain. The play was political dynamite and was banned after nine performances. Thomas Middleton was arrested and jailed.

THE BLACK MONK in *The Black Monk* (1844)
by James M Rymer
Morgatani, the Black Monk, plots to kill Richard Coeur de Lion and to rule England via Richard's brother King John. His scheme is complicated but untroubled by historical accuracy. (For example, he plots with Jesuits, though they didn't appear for another three centuries.) Morgatani kills Sir Rupert Brandon's wife Alicia and tries to have Sir Rupert convicted for the crime. He seduces a wizard's sister, drives the wizard to insanity, poisons and imprisons another knight and attempts to poison a few more. Eventually he meets his doom buried alive in a secret passage beneath his blazing stronghold. This Gothic thriller appeared in 'penny parts' in *Lloyd's Penny Weekly Miscellany* which the prolific Rymer edited.

BLACKSHIRT in *Blackshirt* (1925)
by 'Bruce Graeme' aka Graham Montague Jeffries
Working name of the gentleman thief **Richard Verrell** whose first appearance in 1925 seemed little more than a variant on the *Raffles* stories, but whose books went on (via different authors) into the 1960s, revealing the public's curious soft spot for villains with posh manners. The first Blackshirt book sold over a million copies before the Second World War. Thus it is no surprise that the knave returned to action again and again, first with *The Return of Blackshirt* (1927) then *Blackshirt Again* (1929) and in seven more books until 1940, at which point the ageing Blackshirt's fictional son Anthony took over in the inevitably named *Son of Blackshirt* (1941). He was rapidly promoted in *Lord Blackshirt: The Son of Blackshirt Carries On* in 1942 and brought back again in *Calling Lord Blackshirt* in 1943. Confusingly, some time after the war, the original Blackshirt came back to life, in a new series written by the author's son (thus the fictional father was brought back by the real-life author's son) calling himself Roderic Graeme (thus re-using his father's nom de plume). That series began in 1952 with *Concerning Blackshirt* and jogged along for a total of nineteen titles ending with *Blackshirt Stirs Things Up* in 1968.

BLIFIL in *Tom Jones* (published in 1749) by Henry Fielding
The nephew of Squire Allworthy who brought him up, but

unlike him in every way. He is mean and nasty, especially to the foundling looked after by the same goodly squire. That foundling is Tom Jones. Blifil eventually manages to have Tom banished from the house (setting him off on the adventures that form the main part of the book) and with Tom gone he tries his luck with Tom's sweetheart Sophia Western (more for her fortune than for her female charms). Blifil's amorous approaches are repulsed but he persuades the squire and Sophia's father to promote the marriage. Sophia flees to London where, after many more action-packed pages, she marries a hopefully reformed Tom Jones. Almost inevitably for this kind of novel, Tom is revealed to be the rightful heir and Blifil's schemes come to naught.

In the hugely successful 1963 film *Tom Jones*, directed by Tony Richardson, Blifil was played by the wonderfully creepy and gangling **David Warner**.

BLOFELD in sundry **James Bond** books starting with *Thunderball*, by Ian Fleming.

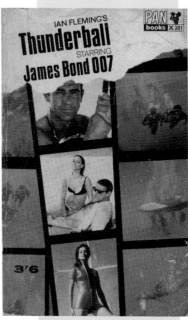

Master spy and agent working for Bond's principal adversary, the international conglomerate SPECTRE (Special Executive for Counterintelligence, Terrorism, Revenge and Extortion) which Blofeld founded. Among the various super-powered villains that frequent the books, Ernst Stavro Blofeld is the most efficient and tenacious. He is highly intelligent and has degrees in engineering and radionics.

Blofeld's film appearances include:
From Russia With Love: played by **Anthony Dawson**
You Only Live Twice: played by **Donald Pleasance**
On Her Majesty's Secret Service: played by **Telly Savalas**
Diamonds Are Forever: played by **Charles Gray**
Never Say Never Again: played by **Max von Sydow**

BLUESKIN. *Various authors, mainly anonymous*
Supposed companion and fellow burglar of **Jack Sheppard**. Blueskin was the nickname of Joseph Blake who gained it from his dark unshaven chin. Both men were captured by the duplicitous thief-taker **Jonathan Wild**. A Penny Dreadful called *Blueskin* appeared in 1867.

BOBADILL in *Every Man In His Humour* by Ben Jonson (first performed 1598, first published 1601, but extensively revised and reissued 1616)

A cowardly but boastful captain. The comic character stands out in the play and is also known for his having been acted several times by the unstoppable Charles Dickens at amateur theatricals in the 1840s.

BOSOLA in *The Duchess of Malfi* (written around 1613) by John Webster

Principal villain in this villain-stuffed Jacobean tragedy. Bosola is a cynical ex galley slave who is placed as servant to the widowed Duchess by his brothers so he can spy on her and prevent her from taking her steward, Antonio, as her second husband – which of course she does. Bosola discovers she is pregnant by Antonio and betrays her to the brothers, who place the Duchess in his charge. Bosola and the brothers, one of whom is a Cardinal, subject her to various mental tortures before strangling her, her children and her faithful waiting woman. Now come the switches in character common to many Jacobean tragedies. One brother goes mad, imagining himself to be a wolf, and Bosola is so struck by the Duchess's tenderness and dignity that he repents his crime, goes over to Antonio's side and kills the other brother – only to discover that it is not the Cardinal he has killed but Antonio. Though Bosola does now kill the Cardinal he is himself killed by the Cardinal's insane wolf-man brother – who in turn, is killed by Antonio's friends. The play, though admired, is notorious for the blood baths of its final scenes.

Bosola:
> *O, I am gone!*
> *We are only like dead walls or vaulted graves*
> *That, ruined, yield no echo. Fare you well.*
> *It may be pain, but no harm for me to die*
> *In so good a quarrel. O, this gloomy world!*
> *In what a shadow, or deep pit of darkness*
> *Doth, womanish and fearful, mankind live!*
> *Let worthy minds ne'er stagger in distrust*
> *To suffer death or shame for what is just:*
> *Mine is another voyage.* (Dies)

Epitaph to a violent end in *The Duchess of Malfi*

MR BOUNDERBY in *Hard Times* (1854) by Charles Dickens

He was a rich man: banker, merchant, manufacturer, and

*what not. A big, loud man, with a stare and a metallic
laugh. A man made out of coarse material, which
seemed to have been stretched to make so much of him.
A man with a great puffed head and forehead, swelled
veins in his temples, and such a strained skin to his
face that it seemed to hold his eyes open and lift his
eyebrows up. A man with a pervading appearance on
him of being inflated like a balloon, and ready to start.
A man who could never sufficiently vaunt himself a
self-made man. A man who was always proclaiming,
through that brassy speaking-trumpet of a voice of his,
his old ignorance and his old poverty. A man who was
the Bully of humility.*

Bounderby described in *Hard Times*

The Josiah Bounderby character created by Dickens was a
rare thing in literature, a new kind of villain, a businessman
whose wrongdoing comes not so much from deliberate villainy
as from his single-minded, unsympathetic application of
business rules. He and his associate **Gradgrind** typify the type
of hard-hearted businessmen who squeeze every ounce and
more, both from their workers and from their profit margins.
Bounderby is a self-made man of whom his mother is
understandably proud, but he pays her to stay away from him.
The only sign that Bounderby is in any way human lies in his
fixed desire for Gradgrind's teenage daughter Louisa – a desire
which, because it will be sanctified by marriage and made
respectable, seems reasonable to both men. Since the
publication of *Hard Times* both men have been much quoted
and parodied, Gradgrind for his insistence on facts ('Facts alone
are wanted in life.') and Bounderby for the way he liked to
exaggerate the hardships of his upbringing.

*'I hadn't a shoe to my foot. As to a stocking, I didn't know
such a thing by name. I passed the day in a ditch, and the
night in a pigsty. That's the way I spent my tenth birthday.
Not that a ditch was new to me, for I was born in a ditch.'
… Mrs Gradgrind hoped it was a dry ditch?
'No! As wet as a sop. A foot of water in it,' said Mr
Bounderby.
'Enough to give a baby cold,' Mrs Gradgrind considered.
'Cold? I was born with inflammation of the lungs, and of
everything else, I believe, that was capable of inflammation,'
returned Mr Bounderby. 'For years, ma'am, I was one of
the most miserable little wretches ever seen. I was so*

sickly, that I was always moaning and groaning. I was so ragged and dirty, that you wouldn't have touched me with a pair of tongs.'

… Mrs Gradgrind meekly and weakly hoped that his mother –

'My mother? Bolted, ma'am,' said Bounderby.

Mrs Gradgrind, stunned as usual, collapsed and gave it up.

'My mother left me to my grandmother,' said Bounderby; 'and, according to the best of my remembrance, my grandmother was the wickedest and the worst old woman that ever lived. If I got a little pair of shoes by any chance, she would take 'em off and sell 'em for drink. Why, I have known that grandmother of mine lie in her bed and drink her fourteen glasses of liquor before breakfast!'

Recollections of childhood from *Hard Times*

SIR DANIEL BRACKLEY in *The Black Arrow*
by Robert Louis Stevenson (serialised in *Young Folks* in 1883 and published in book form five years later)
Villainous uncle-cum-guardian to Joanna Sedley, the heroine of this Victorian children's adventure, set in the late fifteenth century. After Joanna has been freed from his clutches by brave young Richard Shelton, Sir Daniel is embroiled intermittently in Stevenson's gung-ho plot which climaxes in the Battle of Shoreby, after which Richard is knighted. Brackley's fate is to be slain by 'John Amend-All', leader of the Brotherhood of the Black Arrow. In the 1948 film directed by Gordon Douglas (aka *The Black Arrow Strikes*) Sir Daniel was played by **George Macready.**

THE BREWSTERS in *Arsenic and Old Lace* (1939)
originally by Joseph Kesselring
The homicidal family at the heart of Frank Capra's classic film farce, made in 1941-1942 but not released till 1944. Two well-meaning but dangerously dotty old ladies, Abby and Martha Brewster (played on screen by **Josephine Hull** and **Jean Adair**), help ease life's pain for a series of lonely old men by treating them to delicious but poison-laced elderberry wine. Their even more dangerous mad brother Jonathan (**Raymond Massey**) then buries the bodies in the cellar, while the one upright sibling, Mortimer Brewster (**Cary Grant**), scampers around trying to cover things up. With lines like Martha's wistful 'One of our gentlemen found time to say "How delicious" before

he died' it is no surprise that the film was adapted from a Broadway stage hit by Kesselring. The play ran there for four years and remained a favourite with repertory and amateur companies everywhere for decades. British companies usually ignore that fact that the play is actually set in Brooklyn.

PENITENT BROTHEL in *A Mad World, My Masters*
by Thomas Middleton (first printed in 1608)
Licentious and wonderfully-named rogue in the comedy who, while intriguing with the foolish **Follywit** (see his own entry) and the courtesan Gullman, tries to seduce the fair wife of the crusty and suspicious Hairbrain.

SIR JOHN BRUTE in *The Provok'd Wife* by Sir John Vanbrugh (first produced 1697)
No prizes for guessing the psychological makeup of this character. The debauched and heavy-drinking aristocrat is unhappily married to Lady Brute who married him for his money and, although technically faithful, is now dallying with the beau Constant (less aptly named). Sir John comes home unexpectedly (after having been arrested for drunkenness and riotous behaviour) to find his wife and niece playing cards with Constant and his friend Heartfree, who has his eye on the niece. Despite much huffing and puffing, including a threatened duel and some hiding in closets, the whole fracas quietens down, and at the end of the play the Brutes are left locked in antagonistic matrimony.

BIG GER CAFFERTY in the *Inspector Rebus* books by Ian Rankin
Recurring crime boss in the Inspector Rebus books, often at the root of the trouble but never brought to book by the dogged investigator. Big Ger pulled himself up from the gutter in classic Scottish tradition and now uses his ill-gotten wealth and power to live life on the hog. Unlike Rebus.
Cafferty shook his head slowly, then grasped the arms of the chair and started to rise to his feet. 'But now it's time for bed. Next time you come, bring that nice DS Clarke with you, and tell her to pack her bikini. In fact, if you're sending her, you can stay at home.' Cafferty laughed longer and louder than was merited as he led Rebus towards the front door.
from Fleshmarket Close by Ian Rankin

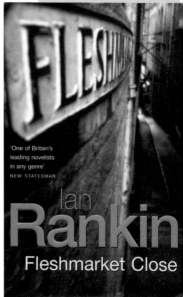

'One of Britain's leading novelists in any genre'
NEW STATESMAN

Ian Rankin
Fleshmarket Close

C

THE CALIPH in *Hassan* by James Elroy Flecker (published 1922 but written eight years earlier)

The ruler in old Baghdad in what must now be judged a politically incorrect play. The cruel and corrupt Caliph orders the execution of Rafi, King of the Beggars, for attempting to save his innocent sweetheart Pervaneh from the Caliph's harem. (Pervaneh is executed with Rafi.) Hassan, a middle-aged sweetshop owner, loves another of the Caliph's courtesans, Yasmin, and is forced to flee the kingdom along the Golden Road to Samarkand. The poetic drama caused a fuss in its day – for its eroticism and sadism, rather than its anti-Islamic leanings – and barely managed to gain a licence from the Lord Chamberlain. After a debut in German (in the city of Darmstadt) it was first performed in English at His Majesty's Theatre in 1923 (where it followed *Chu-Chin-Chow*) and included music specially composed by Delius and ballet numbers by Fokine. Flecker's Caliph contrasts strongly with the romantic hero of another great stage success, *Kismet*.

WALTER CALVERLEY in *A Yorkshire Tragedy* (a short play first performed in 1606 at the Globe Theatre). Anonymous, but probably by Thomas Middleton

A real-life murderer dramatised. When the play was published in 1608 its title-page claimed Shakespeare as its author, but nothing in the text supports that claim. The real-life Calverley was executed in 1605 for the murder of his two children and attempted murder of his wife, who survived the stabbing. Before his fit of frenzy Calverley had starved his children and frequently beat his wife, but finally he repented and confessed his crimes.

CAPTAIN MIDNIGHT

Romanticised highwayman who featured in some nineteenth century Penny Dreadfuls.

THE CARDINAL in *The Cardinal* by James Shirley (first performed in 1641)

Main character in this late Jacobean-style tragedy. The Cardinal is an evil, scheming figure who plots to have his nephew Columbo married to Rosaura, who actually loves and marries Alvarez. As part of a masque the disguised Columbo slays Alvarez on his wedding night, but the spunky Rosaura persuades a disgruntled friend, Hernando, to kill Columbo in a duel. The Cardinal, in full vengeance mode, storms back intending to rape Rosaura but is prevented by Hernando. The spectacular climax (to an otherwise dull play) has Hernando stabbing the Cardinal and killing himself – at which point the injured Cardinal announces that he has poisoned Rosaura but can offer an antidote, some of which he will drink himself to prove that is not a poison. She drinks, only to have the evil one announce that it was indeed a poison, but he drank it since he was dying anyway. His malicious joy is short-lived as a doctor tells him the stab wound had not been mortal and had he not drunk the poison, he would have lived. Thus the audience is sent home happy.

JAMES CARKER in *Dombey and Son* by Charles Dickens (published in 1848)
Manager of the firm in the book of that name. Carker has the entire confidence of its owner, Mr Paul Dombey, and uses his position of trust to wield a great influence over him. Dombey enlists Carker's help in persecuting his (Dombey's) second wife for failing to provide a male heir but she, a spirited lady, elopes with Carker to punish her husband – and then quickly leaves him. Carker is now revealed as a failed lover as well as an incompetent and near-crooked business manager. He meets his end in a spectacular train crash (one of Dickens's most colourful pieces of writing, and generally assumed to have been affected by his own near-death on and consequent loathing of the railway).

CARLOS in *The Fatal Marriage* by Thomas Southerne (first performed 1694)
Wicked manipulator in this post-Jacobean tragedy, and brother to the rightful but doomed husband Biron, whose marriage to Isabella was against his father's wishes. For this offence the father sends Biron to fight at the siege of Candy, where he is reported killed. From here, one might think one could write the script oneself, but no: Carlos does not want the fair Isabella for his own bed but wants her married to a man called Villeroy. In fact, any man would suffice, since with Biron supposedly dead the marriage would remove Isabella and, crucially, her son from the line of inheritance, leaving all for Carlos. Biron, of course, returns, but Carlos kills him. Isabella then kills herself, and the sins of Carlos are revealed. A successful and oft-revived play in its day, it was based on *The Nun*, or *The Perjur'd Beauty*, a novel by Mrs Aphra Behn – identified by Virginia Woolf as the first English woman to earn her living by writing.

C

CARMILLA of *In A Glass Darkly* (1872) by J. S. Le Fanu
Arguably **the first female vampire**, Carmilla is the subject of a short story of that name in this Le Fanu collection. Each of the stories purports to come from the casebook of a supernatural investigator, Dr Hesselius, and the book is an early classic of occult literature. Carl Theodor Dreyer based his 1932 film *Vampyr* on the story. Other films have been (usually loosely) based on *Carmilla*, of which perhaps Roy Ward Baker's *The Vampire Lovers* (1970) was the best.

SIMON CARNE in *The Prince of Swindlers* (1897)
by Guy Boothby
Perhaps **the first Gentleman Thief** (in fiction at any rate) who predated **Raffles, Colonel Clay** etc.

CASSIUS in *Julius Caesar* by William Shakespeare
(around 1599)

Roman villain with 'a lean and hungry look' who notes that 'There is a tide in the affairs of men, which taken at the flood, leads on to fortune'. He and his fellow conspirators must, as he continues, 'take the current when it serves, or lose our ventures.' The conspiracy is against Caesar, despite Caesar's having pardoned Cassius after the civil war with Pompey when he made Cassius praetor. Cassius nevertheless conceives and persuades Brutus to join the plot against Caesar. In the ensuing unrest after the assassination the two men lead armies against the avenging Octavius and Marc Anthony. But Cassius loses the first engagement and rather than face ignominy he falls on his sword and dies. Caesar said of him: 'He thinks too much: such men are dangerous'.

In the memorable film (for various reasons) *Julius Caesar* of 1953, directed by John Houseman, Cassius was played in classical style by **John Gielgud** against an extraordinarily modern **Marlon Brando** as Marc Anthony. There have been other less memorable versions.

CATHERINE in *Catherine* by William Makepeace Thackeray
(published in *Fraser's Magazine* in 1839 and 40)
Eponymous anti-hero of this short novel. The story is unlike almost anything else Thackeray wrote, being as sordid as he could make it, although his characteristic lightness and love of irony let him down and made the text softer than the 'Newgate Novel' satire he intended. The story is taken from the *Newgate*

Calendar and is based on that of a real-life murderess Catherine Hayes who was executed in 1726 for the murder of her husband. Her death was as gruesome as anything a novelist could invent for once she had been sentenced to death by burning at the stake, her executioner should, by custom, have 'mercifully' strangled her as the fire was lit – but he held back too long, and the fierce flames drove him back. Catherine was left to scream, writhe and kick at the flames as they consumed her. (The details were reported in a swiftly-produced Penny Dreadful, *Catherine Hayes, or Crime and Punishment*.) In his more sober version, Thakeray partly justified her crime by having her seduced by an invented lover, Galgenstein.

THE CHILD CATCHER in *Chitty-Chitty Bang Bang* (1964) by Ian Fleming

Villainous parent-reliever at the heart of this magnificent children's adventure. He ruins a jaunt in the magical motor car for the goody-goody kids Jeremy and Jemima. His motives are homicidal, rather than paedophilian, though he uses such trusted child-luring snares as shouting 'Lollipops! Ice-cream! Chocolate! All three today.' That an author more famous as the creator of James Bond should have written a genuine classic is perhaps less of a surprise than that the film version (despite frequent reshowings on TV) was a turkey or, more correctly, an emu, since it didn't fly. **Robert Helpmann** did what he could with the part. Most people will never find out that the book is far better than the film.

CHILDE WATERS *Anonymous*

Cold young aristocrat who impregnates his page, the fair Ellen, and then goes on to treat her shamefully, leaving her to bear his child in the stable where one of the pregnant girl's tasks is to tend his horse. Only when he overhears Ellen singing her sad lullaby does he relent and, too late, agree to marry her. The story is told in many a folk song. It is one of the most beautiful and can be found in the *Reliques of Ancient English Poetry* collated by Thomas Percy in 1765.

JONAS CHUZZLEWIT in *Martin Chuzzlewit* by Charles Dickens (published in 1844)

Cousin to Martin Chuzzlewit but quite unlike him. The mean, violent and unscrupulous Jonas attempts to poison his own father to gain his inheritance. When blackmailed over this by

Montague Tigg, Jonas kills him too. He marries Mercy Pecksniff and makes her life a misery. The only person who can stop this vicious man is the overlooked, decrepit and apparently senile Old Chuffey, his father's clerk, who knows and eventually reveals the truth. Jonas' final collapse, and later suicide, make an unlikely end for such a powerful character. The story hasn't been filmed but was splendidly adapted by BBC TV in 1994, when **Keith Allen** made as nasty and frightening a Jonas as one could wish for.

ANGEL CLARE (Thomas Hardy) see Alec **d'Urberville**

CLAUDIUS in *Hamlet* (c.1601) by William Shakespeare
Uncle to Hamlet, he poisoned Hamlet's father, married his widow Gertrude, and thus ascended to the throne of Denmark. These dark deeds are related in the first scene of the play by the Ghost of Hamlet's Father in an attempt to spur his son to revenge. Claudius is far from a one-dimensional villain; he is a competent ruler, and genuinely fond of Gertrude, and she of him (one feels there is an unwritten story there). As the play progresses he is troubled by an uneasy conscience, especially when Hamlet instructs a band of touring players to enact a scene uncomfortably similar to that of the real murder. ('The play's the thing wherein we'll catch the conscience of the king.') Claudius banishes Hamlet to England in company with Rosencrantz and Guildenstern and asks the King of England to have Hamlet killed. But Hamlet escapes and returns to **Elsinore**. Claudius arranges a duel for him with Laertes (Ophelia's brother) thinking Laertes will win – though in case he doesn't, Claudius has ready a chalice of poisoned wine. In the final bloody scene the poison dispenses with Hamlet, Laertes, Gertrude and Claudius himself. As the dying Hamlet remarks: 'The rest is silence.'

This was not the most obviously cinematic Shakespeare play, but of various versions, **Laurence Olivier**'s 1948 film (he directed and played the title role) is the most remarkable. **Basil Sydney** was his Claudius. Tony Richardson's low-budget 1969 film sticks honourably to the text: **Nicol Williamson** played Hamlet and **Anthony Hopkins** was Claudius (22 years before his most villainous appearance in *Silence of the Lambs*). **Mel Gibson** predictably made an Action Man *Hamlet* for Franco Zeffirelli in 1990, when **Alan Bates** appeared as Claudius.

COLONEL CLAY in *An African Millionaire* by Grant Allen (first serialised in *Strand* magazine from June 1896)
A bald, bespectacled but wiry gentleman crook (one of the first)

who features in Grant Allen's 1897 book of the serial. His name comes from his amazing ability to disguise and reshape his face as if it were made of modeller's clay.

BY GRANT ALLEN.

I.—THE EPISODE OF THE MEXICAN SEER.

'He is a Colonel, because he occasionally gives himself a commission; he is called Colonel Clay, because he appears to possess an indiarubber face, and he can mould it like clay in the hands of the potter. Real name, unknown. Nationality, equally French and English. Address, usually Europe. Profession, former maker of wax figures to the Musée Grévin. Age, what he chooses. Employs his knowledge to mould his own nose and cheeks, with wax additions, to the character he desires to personate.'

Clay described by Sir Charles in *An African Millionaire*

"Well, I shall catch him yet," Sir Charles answered, and relapsed into silence. This was at the end of episode one, and was to prove easier said than done.

MRS CLENHAM in *Little Dorrit* (1857) by Charles Dickens
Dickens's take on the wicked step-mother – although we don't realise she is not the real mother of Arthur Clenham until late in the story (she is his father's second wife). Mrs Clenham seems at first no more than a stony-hearted businesswoman, her heart as shrivelled as her crippled body, but we come to learn that in the past she suppressed a will by which Little Dorrit (and thus her entire family) would have gained. Mrs Clenham lives in an uncared-for ruin of a house with her business partner Jeremiah **Flintwinch** and it is through carelessness on the part of the Flintwinches that she becomes vulnerable to the villain **Rigaud** and that everything is dragged into light.

On a black bier-like sofa in this hollow, propped up behind with one great angular black bolster, like the block at a state execution in the good old times, sat his mother in a widow's dress. She and his father had been at variance from his earliest remembrance. To sit speechless himself in the midst of rigid silence, glancing in dread from one averted face to the other, had been the peacefullest occupation of his childhood. She gave him one glassy kiss, and four stiff fingers muffled in worsted... With her cold grey eyes and her cold grey hair, and her immovable face, as stiff as the folds of her stony headdress – her being beyond the reach of the seasons seemed but a fit sequence to her being beyond the reach of all changing emotions

Arthur is re-introduced to Mrs Clenham in *Little Dorrit*

In a superb piece of casting against type, Mrs Clenham was played by **Joan Greenwood** in the masterly screen adaptation (two films with a combined length approaching six hours) directed by Christine Edzard in 1988. Then in 2008 **Judy Parfitt** seized the role with even greater venom.

THE COLLECTOR in *The Collector* (1963) by John Fowles
Deceptively bland narrator to the novel. He is a featureless clerk and amateur butterfly collector whose life has been transformed by a win on the football pools. Instead of using the money to transform his life in a meaningful way he uses it to indulge a secret fantasy: he kidnaps an attractive art student, Miranda, and keeps her locked away as he would keep a butterfly for study. He tries to explain this, quite reasonably, he thinks, to his prisoner (and hence to the reader). But after going through the inevitable reactions to her capture and imprisonment, Miranda assumes his motives must be sexual, and offers sexual gratification – only to find that his sexual disturbance is more bizarre.

The 1965 film starred **Terence Stamp** as the collector, with **Samantha Eggar** as Miranda, but it was less effective than the book. William Wyler directed.

COMUS in *Comus* (1634) by John Milton
A wicked pagan god invented by Milton for this 'pastoral entertainment' presented as a masque at Ludlow Castle. The son of the gods Circe and Bacchus, Comus is presented as a sorcerer who lures travellers to his lair, where he plies them with potions that transform their faces to those of animals. In the masque, he traps a lady in a magic chair and tries to force her to drink the potion or give up her virginity. Her brothers burst in to free her, but though Comus escapes, they are unable to free her from the magic chair. Fortunately, the goddess Sabrina is on hand, summoned by the song 'Sabrina Fair', and she releases the lady by means of magic drops of water from the River Severn. Comus is thus one of the few stage villains allowed the luxury of escape.

WILLIAM CORDER based on a *real-life character*

Corder's name is less immediately recognisable than that of his victim, **Maria Marten**, murdered – or in some versions, merely buried – in the Red Barn in Suffolk in May 1827. The original murder was a sordid business: Corder got rid of his illegitimate child and, subsequently, its mother. The story proved irresistible for melodrama because the missing Maria's body was found as a direct result of her mother having a repeated dream telling her that her daughter had been buried in the barn. The mother was so adamant with her story that, if only to pacify her, the floor of the barn was dug up, and Maria's body was exposed. Most stage versions heighten the language and drama beyond what must have actually occurred.

William: *You can never be my wife. Even now there is a wealthy heiress of my parents' choice awaiting me to conduct her to the Holy Altar, but this cannot be while you live.*

Maria: *William, you mean –*

William: *That I have lured you here with the one intent, and that is of ridding myself of you for ever.*

Maria: *Rid of me; how?*

William: *There is only one way open to me and that is – death!*

Maria: *Surely you would not murder me? You only say this to frighten me. You are jesting with me. 'Tis a cruel jest, William.*

William: *Let your eyes rest upon mine and read the jest upon them. Should that not convince you, gaze there:*

C

(points to trap). *Let them rest upon the grave ready for the coming of its victim.*

from an anonymous Victorian stage script in the possession of Cambridge University

The trial took place in May 1828 and when Corder was hanged the following August, in Norwich, the spectacle attracted a crowd of ten thousand people. Maria's skeleton was exhibited to the public, and a transcript of the trial was bound in William Corder's skin.

VITTORIA COROMBONA in *The White Devil* (originally spelt *White Divil*) by John Webster. First performed in 1612

Female lead in Webster's Jacobean shocker. Wife of the amiable, boring and near-impotent Camillo, she prefers the lusty Duke of Brachiano who is unfortunately also married, to Isabella, sister of Francisco, Duke of Florence. In telling Brachiano of a 'dream' she hints that the best solution would be for both their spouses to be killed. Brachiano, spurred on by Vittoria's villainous brother **Flamineo**, poisons his wife while Flamineo, meanwhile, dispenses with Camillo, breaking his neck and making it look like a riding accident. So far, so Jacobean. In the celebrated central trial scene Vittoria defends herself against charges of adultery and murder. The fact that Brachiano lusted after her, she says, is no proof she killed her husband:

Condemn you me for that the duke did love me?
So may you blame some fair and crystal river
For that some melancholic distracted man
Hath drown'd himself in it.
…
Sum up my faults, I pray, and you shall find
That beauty and gay clothes, a merry heart,
And a good stomach to feast, are all,
All the poor crimes that you can charge me with

The White Devil, Act III, scene II

In a court rigged against her, this powerful defence is not enough to save her, and her punishment (bizarre, to our modern eyes) is that she be condemned to imprisonment in 'a house of penitent whores'. (Our modern eyes might also see the similarities between her case and the celebrated trial in 1922 of Edith

Thompson, condemned to death for the murder of her husband, despite there being no dispute that the killing was, in fact, carried out by her lover Percy Bywaters. Thompson encouraged him, but could not be shown to have taken any part in the actual crime.) A modern audience – and perhaps any women in the audience of 1612 – might question whether Vittoria is a real villain at all. Her 'lust' might have been deemed a virtue in a man, and her only crime in the play is that, by telling of her symbol-ridden dream, she suggests and perhaps abets the murders.

But in Jacobean theatre such distinctions mattered little: in a typically gory ending Vittoria, Brachiano and Flamineo are killed by Francisco helped, oddly, by Lodovico (odd because Lodovico was previously in love with Brachiano's wife). As he prepares to kill Vittoria, Lodovico righteously proclaims: 'O, thou glorious strumpet! Could I divide thy breath from this pure air when it leaves thy body, I would suck it up and breathe it on some dunghill.' But she mocks him with 'Methinks thou dost not look horrid enough.' He delays his knife to argue, but she defeats his every taunt. 'I shall welcome death,' she says. 'I'll meet thy weapon half way.' When he sneers that she trembles, she retorts that in death she'll not shed a single tear and that if she looks pale then it will be only from loss of blood, not fear. He stabs her, but she scoffs, 'That was a manly blow; the next thou giv'st, murder some sucking infant: then thou wilt be famous.' But despite her spirit, the wound is mortal.

Vittoria: *Oh, my greatest sin lay in my blood.*
   Now my blood pays for it.

It might have been some comfort to Vittoria if she'd known that within a minute of her death, Lodovico himself is slain.

RICHARD 'DIXIE' COSTELLO recurring villain in the *Harry Martineau* series by Maurice Proctor

Costello was the town's top organised crime figure in Proctor's series, set in the 'great northern metropolis' of Granchester (a fictionalized version of Manchester in the 1950s and '60s), spending most of the series eluding Martineau's ever-tightening grip. Sometimes Costello was at the heart of whatever criminal enterprise fuelled the novel, while at other times he was on the sidelines. He made his first appearance in the second Martineau novel, *The Midnight Plumber* (1957), and was finally caught in the penultimate book in the series, *Exercise Hoodwink* (1967). But a series villain is no use behind bars, so he was soon out again, seeking revenge, in the last of the Martineau series, *Hideaway* (1968).

NOW FILMED AS THE GOLDEN COMPASS MOTION PICTURE

Northern Lights

"One of the supreme literary dreamers and magicians of our time" Guardian

Mrs COULTER

in the *His Dark Materials* trilogy by Philip Pullman

Marisa Coulter heads a faction of the Church known as the General Oblation Board (or 'The Gobblers' as it is known to street urchins). She and Lord Asriel are parents to the heroine Lyra (though Lyra has yet to discover this) and although Mrs Coulter may seem charming she has a sinister side. Under her guidance, the Board has been secretly kidnapping children from Lyra's world and using them as 'lab rats' in experiments at their Bolvangar laboratory. By cutting away a child's daemon, the Board thinks a child can grow up not knowing sin. (Mrs Coulter's own daemon, never named, is a golden furred and black-faced cruel monkey who seldom speaks.) Late in the series, Mrs Coulter had a chance to redeem her earlier villainy: when she discovers that the church means to kill Lyra she kidnaps her and hides her in a cave. But by now her daughter has come to hate and mistrust her.

In the BBC TV version of *His Dark Materials* **Emma Fielding** played Mrs Coulter. In the film verison, **Nicole Kidman** took the role.

CUTPURSE (Middleton and Dekker) see **MOLL CUTPURSE**

THE DALEKS

(*Doctor Who*, conceived by scriptwriter Terry Nation in 1963)

With their metallic bodies a cross between a hot-air ventilator and the Michelin Tyre Man, the Daleks are perennial opponents for the Doctor. Trundling on castors around innumerable TV sets and croaking '*Exterminate!*', these tireless beasties have no emotion and seek only to destroy any creature standing between them and their determination to be lords of every universe. They were, in fact, programmed that way by the power-crazed scientist Davros when he recreated them from the dying race of Kaleds. (He failed to realise that, hate-filled as he'd made them, they would show him no gratitude.) Despite being cold, ruthless and implacable, their squat and homemade carcases let them seem, on screen, little more than recalcitrant toys. Until the 2006 TV series they were hampered further by being unable to fly, and although finding found a cure for that, they still had one fatal flaw: within their glittering shells they concealed a slowly pulsing corporeal being. In 2006, the life-form inside what appeared to be the last Dalek appeared to break all the rules of what had gone before when it displayed an emerging conscience. For a few minutes the audience was asked to feel sympathy for the old and dying enemy. But it couldn't last. Daleks have no conscience, no compassion, and remain the Doctor's eternal foe.

TV series of *Doctor Who* have come and gone since 1963 attracting one of the largest cult followings of anything on television. Although the Doctor has changed (he can regenerate and become another actor) the Daleks have remained imperishable – and essential to the success of the show.

The film *Dr Who and the Daleks* (1965) had none of the fun and enjoyable tackiness, let alone the cult-inspiring mystery, of the television series. Daleks appear also in many of the *Doctor Who* story books.

D'AMVILLE in *The Atheist's Tragedy* (or *The Honest Man's Fortune*) published in 1611 (ascribed to Cyril Tourneur)
No villain got his desserts more justly than the villain D'Amville (no first name, but 'The Atheist' of the title). He is determined to marry off his sickly son Rousard to the wealthy Castabella, and so sends her fiancée Charlemont off to war. With the aid of Belforest, Castabella's father, and of Belforest's lecherous wife Levidulcia, d'Amville achieves his end – only to have his hopes dashed when his son proves to be impotent. D'Amville murders Charlemont's father and attempts to seize Castabella for himself. Charlemont (alerted by his father's ghost: where have you heard that one before?) returns in the nick of time, only to find himself accused of murder (actually carried out, of course, by d'Amville). The wicked d'Amville offers to execute him himself, but as he raises the axe to strike he accidentally dashes out his own brains. Fortunately, he has just enough time to confess before he dies. The innocuous and compliant Charlemont (Castabella seems to have no luck with husbands) is left to moralise feebly that 'Patience is the honest man's revenge.'

DANBY CROKER in *The Exploits of Danby Croker* (1916) by R Austin Freeman
Master forger and anti-hero of a series of tales set before the First World War.

JAMES DALTON in *Ticket of Leave Man* by Tom Taylor (staged in 1863)
James 'The Tiger' Dalton was a City financier and cunning

passer of forged banknotes in Taylor's important early crime drama. (It was at a performance of Taylor's *Our American Cousin*, incidentally, that Abraham Lincoln was assassinated in Washington DC.) Dalton's scheme ensnares the play's hero, Bob Brierly, who is sent to prison. When Bob is released – as a 'Ticket of Leave Man' – Dalton, a master of disguise, continues to frustrate his attempts to lead an honest life. Dalton is confounded by the detective hero, **Hawkshaw**.

MRS DANVERS see **De WINTER**

NAN DARRELL
Romanticised highwaywoman who featured in one or two Nineteenth Century Penny Bloods.

MADAME DEFARGE in *The Tale of Two Cities* (1859)
by Charles Dickens
A minor but chilling character, and a supreme example of a **tricoteuse**, a woman who sits and knits placidly beside the guillotine as the condemned are executed. She and her husband keep a wine shop in St Antoine. Defarge is a revolution fanatic, harsh and implacable, and instrumental in having Charles Darnay sentenced to death, simply because he is related to the marquis. To her, all aristocrats must die. Her list of 'enemies of the revolution' is stitched into her knitting. Cross-stitch is too mild for her.

The best film version must be Jack Conway's 1935 film starring **Ronald Colman** as Sydney Carlton, in which **Blanche Yurka** was a memorably creepy Madame Defarge.

DE FLORES in *The Changeling* by Thomas Middleton & William Rowley (first performed 1622 but not printed till 1653)
A scheming and ugly servant who reveals himself as a sexual predator in the violent and steamy seventeenth century play. In the first scene of the play De Flores finds a glove belonging to Beatrice Joanna, who he knows despises him. Lecherously stroking her fine glove he chuckles, 'She had rather wear my pelt tanned in a pair of dancing pumps than I should thrust my fingers into her sockets here.' Beatrice Joanna is a beautiful young noblewoman engaged to Alonzo but in love with Alsemero. Desperate to marry the man she loves she makes the disastrous mistake of enlisting her despised servant De Flores (variously spelt as one or two words) to murder Alonzo – which he does readily, deciding to bring Alonzo's ring as proof that the

man is dead: evidence Beatrice Joanna did not expect.

De Flores: *I've a token for you.*
Beatrice: *For me?*
De Flores: *But it was sent somewhat unwillingly;*
I could not get the ring without the finger.
Beatrice: *Bless me! What hast thou done?*
De Flores: *Why, is that more than killing the whole man?*
The Changeling, Act III, scene IV

Beatrice has promised any reward but is horrified when De Flores claims her body as his prize. She has no choice but to submit to him. Having sacrificed her virginity she avoids discovery on her wedding night by substituting her maid Diaphanta, who is a virgin, into her darkened bed chamber. The results are worse than you would predict. Beatrice is both jealous of Diaphanta and in sexual thrall to De Flores. When Alsemero finds his bride closeted with her mocking servant the scene is set for a violently Jacobean ending.

Swarthy-skinned De Flores is both charismatic and utterly unscrupulous, taking both Alonzo's life and Beatrice Joanna's virginity with black humour and glee. He was an outrageous villain portrayed memorably by **Bob Hoskins** in a stand-alone TV play and the story was reset in modern times in Russell James's novel *The Annex* (2002). In both these versions, as in a number of stage revivals, the ludicrous subplot to which the title *The Changeling* actually refers was dropped.

ROBERT DEMPSTER in *Scenes of Clerical Life* (1858) by George Eliot
One of the more dreadful of the many drunken brute husbands to be depicted in Victorian 'improving' fiction, Dempster appears in the third and final tale of Eliot's early work. He is a swaggering lawyer in the grim industrial town of Milby, where he beats and berates his unfortunate wife Janet till she, like him, turns to drink. His worsening ill-treatment finally forces her to flee her home and seek refuge with the evangelical Reverend Tryan, who helps her forswear the demon drink. Dempster, though, remains too fond of the bottle, and eventually suffers a fatal fall from his gig.

CRUELLA DE VIL in *One Hundred and One Dalmatians* (1956) by Dodie Smith
This haughty 'dognapper' remains outstanding among many notable villains of children's fiction. Aristocratic, rich and at times hysterical, Cruella's fiendish scheme is to kidnap

Dalmatian puppies and turn their spotted coats into furs for humans.

Disney's 1961 film of the book was a deserved success and stood out at a time when many feared the studio had lost its way. Its advertising told the story without mentioning the terrifying Cruella, 'When the puppies were dognapped, Scotland Yard was baffled … the city helpless … THEN the dogs took over to solve the mystery!'. As the film remained a favourite, a non-animated version eventually followed in 1996, starring **Glenn Close** as Cruella. Though not as good as the cartoon version, *101 Dalmatians* was well worth watching, but its sequel *102 Dalmatians* (2000), again with Close, was a disappointment.

DIMITRIOS in *The Mask of Dimitrios* (1939) by Eric Ambler
In the troubled Balkans after the Second World War the gun-running Dimitrios provoked a border incident to increase the sales of his arms trading company Eurasian Credit Trust (a typical Ambler irony). It was typical of his activities. But Ambler's tale begins when the death of Dimitrious is announced by Turkish harbour police who have found a corpse floating in the Bosphorus. His death and colourful career is investigated by Charles Latimer, an over-confident university professor cum crime writer (another Ambler irony, coldly satirising the Golden Age) who decides that, despite his involvement in gun-running, drugs, white slave trafficking, prostitution and terrorism, Dimitrios had been no more than a businessman.

The Mask of Dimitrios was published in 1939 (U.S. title *A Coffin for Dimitrios*) and made into a so-so film of 1944, when it was directed by Jean Negulesco and starred **Zachary Scott**, **Sidney Greenstreet** and **Peter Lorre**.

CONSTANTINE DIX in *The Memoirs of Constantine Dix* (1905) by Barry Paine
An early, but by no means the earliest, Gentleman Thief.

DOL COMMON (Ben Jonson) see **FACE**

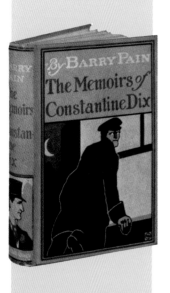

DON JOHN in *Much Ado About Nothing* (written 1598 to 9) by William Shakespeare
One of Shakespeare's vindictive bastards, Don John is the illegitimate brother of Don Pedro, Prince of Arragon. In a classic 'dressing up the maid' scene he fools Don Pedro's friend Claudio (who Don John hates) into questioning his fiancée's

virtue and then later rejecting her at the altar. As the play is a comedy, all comes right in the end, with Don John's plot unravelled by 'shallow fools' – the comic policemen Dogberry and Verges.

DOONE FAMILY in *Lorna Doone* (1869) by R D Blackmore

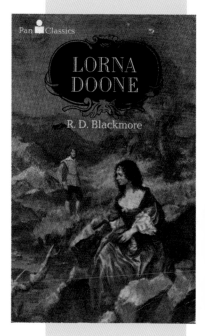

The Doones are the villains of a story in which Lorna is the heroine. Published in 1869 and an enormous success for at least a century, it tells of a vicious criminal family, the Doones, who wreak terror across Exmoor. In a violent early episode they murder the father of twelve-year-old **John Ridd,** but the boy is saved by Lorna, the apparent daughter of the clan. John grows up to hate the Doones but cannot help loving Lorna. His adventures (encompassing the Monmouth rebellion) bring him up against the Doones again and again, until he finally rescues Lorna from the evil **Carver Doone** (his rival for Lorna) during a storm. Ridd is instrumental in ending the Doones' despotic reign of terror, and celebrates by marrying Lorna – only to have Carver Doone appear in church and shoot her. She does recover, and Ridd has his revenge. It then transpires that Lorna is not actually a Doone after all, but is the kidnapped daughter of a noble Scottish family.

The best film version (though it trundles now) was Basil Dean's in 1935, starring **John Loder**, **Victoria Hopper**, **Margaret Lockwood**, **Roy Emerson** and **Roger Livesey**. A lesser version came in 1951, and a TV film in 1990.

FIDELITY DOVE in *The Exploits of Fidelity Dove* (1927) by 'David Durham', aka Roy Vickers

A female thief in a lesser series from an author more famed for his 'inverted' mysteries.

DRACULA in *Dracula* (1897) by Bram Stoker

Stoker's *Dracula* is one of the most famous villains of all time. His origins go back to the real life 'Vlad the Impaler' or Dracole Waida, who ruled Wallachia from 1456 to 1464 and was feared throughout the Middle East and Europe for his ferocity. His nickname came from his having captors impaled alive on stakes thrust through their torsos. Vlad invoked such terror that in peasant and primitive communities it was rumoured he never died: he was so diabolical he could never die. Unexplained deaths and disappearances were laid at his door. He was the

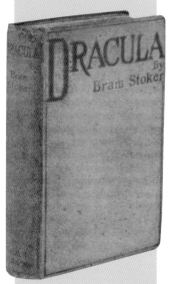

bogeyman (*nosferatu* in Romanian). His lust for blood caused him to be linked with stories of both the vampire bat and the incubus which, according to legend, feasted like parasites on sleeping humans, sucking first their blood and then their very soul.

Among various retellings and exaggerations of Dracole's already lurid life story were *Nosferatu* (originally from Romanian legend), *Varney the Vampire or The Feast of Blood* (by James Malcolm Rymer) and Sheridan Le Fanu's *Carmilla*, but of course the greatest came from the pen of the nineteenth century pulp-writer and theatrical impresario Bram Stoker. In Stoker's story can be found all the trappings associated with the Count in horror films: his ancient and apparently empty castle; the frightened peasantry; his bevy of female vampires; his vital need for blood. Among other fundamentals established in the book are the facts that Dracula casts no reflection in a mirror, can transform himself into a bat, can be killed by no ordinary weapon, and fears instead only daylight and the holy signs of Christianity.

The story is so well known as to have become a modern myth. When solicitor's clerk Jonathan Harker goes to Transylvania to convey a property he arrives at an apparently empty castle far from anywhere 'from whose tall black windows came no ray of light, and whose broken battlements showed a jagged line against the moonlit sky.' But the castle is not unoccupied…

'I heard a heavy step approaching behind the great door, and saw through the chinks the gleam of a coming light. Then there was the sound of rattling chains and the clanking of massive bolts drawn back. A key was turned with the loud grating noise of long disuse, and the great door swung back.

Within stood a tall old man, clean shaven save for a long white moustache, and clad in black from head to foot, without a single speck of colour about him anywhere. He held in his hand an antique silver lamp, in which the flame burned without chimney or globe of any kind, throwing long quivering shadows as it flickered in the draught of the open door. The old man motioned me in with his right hand with a courtly gesture, saying in excellent English, but with a strange intonation: 'Welcome to my house. Enter freely and of your own free will!'

He made no motion of stepping to meet me, but stood like a statue, as though his gesture of welcome had fixed him into stone. The instant, however, that I had stepped over the threshold, he moved impulsively forward and, holding out his

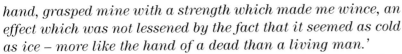

*hand, grasped mine with a strength which made me wince, an
effect which was not lessened by the fact that it seemed as cold
as ice – more like the hand of a dead than a living man.'*

from *Dracula* by Bram Stoker

How true that last remark was Harker did not realise. Clearly,
this is not the Dracula we know from the movies, but he is just
as sinister. Stoker's magnificent description is worth continuing:

*'His eyebrows were very massive, almost meeting over the
nose, and with bushy hair that seemed to curl in its own
profusion. The mouth, so far as I could see it under the heavy
moustache, was fixed and rather cruel-looking, with
peculiarly sharp white teeth; these protruded over the lips,
whose remarkable ruddiness showed astonishing vitality in a
man of his years. For the rest, his ears were pale and at the
tops extremely pointed; the chin was broad and strong; and the
cheeks firm though thin. The general effect was one of
extraordinary pallor.*

*Hitherto I had noticed the backs of his hands as they lay on
his knees in the firelight, and they had seemed rather white
and fine; but seeing them now close to me, I could not but
notice that they were rather coarse – broad, with squat fingers.
Strange to say, there were hairs in the centre of his palm. The
nails were long and fine, and cut to a sharp point. As the
Count leaned over me and his hands touched me, I could not
repress a shudder. It may have been that his breath was rank,
but a horrible feeling of nausea came over me, which, do what
I would, I could not conceal. The Count, evidently noticing it,
drew back; and with a grim sort of smile, which showed more
than he had yet done his protuberant teeth, sat himself down
again on his own side of the fireplace. We were both silent for
a while; and as I looked towards the window I saw the first
dim streak of the coming dawn. There seemed a strange
stillness over everything; but as I listened I heard as if from
down below in the valley the howling of many wolves. The
Count's eyes gleamed, and he said:*

*'Listen to them – the children of the night. What music they
make!'*

from *Dracula* by Bram Stoker

That last line is perhaps the most famous ever uttered by the
actor **Bela Lugosi** – but its appearance here only demonstrates
how many of the cinematic traits of Dracula can be found in
Stoker's book. Here, in one paragraph, come three more:

'I had hung my shaving glass by the window, and was just beginning to shave. Suddenly I felt a hand on my shoulder, and heard the Count's voice saying to me, 'Good morning.' I started, for it amazed me that I had not seen him, since the reflection of the glass covered the whole room behind me. In starting I had cut myself slightly, but did not notice it at the moment. Having answered the Count's salutation, I turned again to the glass to see how I had been mistaken. This time there could be no error, for the man was close to me, and I could see him over my shoulder. But there was no reflection of him in the mirror! The whole room behind me was displayed; but there was no sign of a man in it, except myself. This was startling, and, coming on the top of so many strange things, was beginning to increase that vague feeling of uneasiness which I always have when the Count is near; but at the instant I saw that the cut had bled a little, and the blood was trickling over my chin. I laid down the razor, turning as I did so half round to look for some sticking plaster. When the Count saw my face, his eyes blazed with a sort of demoniac fury, and he suddenly made a grab at my throat. I drew away, and his hand touched the string of beads which held the crucifix. It made an instant change in him, for the fury passed so quickly that I could hardly believe that it was ever there.

'Take care,' he said, 'take care how you cut yourself. It is more dangerous than you think in this country.'

from *Dracula* by Bram Stoker

Here we have Dracula's lack of a reflection, his craze for blood, and his inability to get past a crucifix. Soon after this, Stoker exposes and exploits the rampant sexuality of Dracula and his undead acolytes. Harker is warned by Dracula to keep to his room at night. Had he done so and not, as in every fairy story, disobeyed his host's command, he might have survived unharmed. But like Eve in Eden's garden his curiosity was to be his tasty doom. (See **The Undead**.)

The scene now shifts to Whitby, on the north Yorkshire coast. Dracula comes to England to claim the property he has bought, landing at Whitby via a deserted ship and soon himself known to Harker's pining girlfriend Mina Murray and her luscious friend Lucy Westenra. She, like Eve or, perhaps, like the foolish sister in Christina Rossetti's *Goblin Market*, responds to a mysteriously sensuous call of the wild. She invites Count Dracula in, and the scene is set for bats, bloodletting and nocturnal visitations. As in many cinematic variations, Lucy's fate is subsequently explained by the cabbalistic Dr Abraham

Van Helsing, a man who knows the only way to trap and defeat the monster. It will require the aid of cloves of garlic and a sharpened wooden stake.

So attractive is Dracula and the vampire myth that innumerable books have followed Stoker's masterpiece. Some simply retell the story and can be ignored, while many spin off into variations, sequels and pastiche, and are usually recognisable by their having *Dracula* in their titles. Among these variations came one year, 1978, in which the Count twice met the Great Detective, in the books *The Holmes-Dracula File* (Fred Saberhagen) and *Sherlock Holmes versus Dracula* (Loren D Esteman). Like Holmes, he is universal enough to have appeared in a number of 'non-fiction' biographical accounts. Raymond Rudorff's case-file *The Dracula Archives* (1971) was the result of several years' research and out-does most of these quasi documentaries.

The vampire king has appeared in innumerable films (one can't say countless films) among which the most memorable portrayals have been by **Max Schreck** as Count Orlock in *Nosferatu, Eine Symphonie des Grauens* (directed by F W Murnau in 1922) and **Bela Lugosi** as *Dracula* in Tod Browning's impressive 1931 film. The fine 1936 sequel *Dracula's Daughter* was made without Lugosi, though he had made the part his own: he had dark eyes and pale skin, an odd accent (he was Hungarian and learnt the part phonetically), a haunting screen presence (risible to us now but not to audiences then), and great dialogue, from 'I bid you welcome' to 'Children of the night.' But he would have rivals.

Christopher Lee (surely the greatest) starred in a series of classic Hammer films directed by Terence Fisher. The first, *Dracula*, (*Horror of Dracula* in America), was in 1958, when the tall mesmeric count (reborn and revitalised from Stoker's old man with white hair) had a mere thirteen lines in the entire movie – which was shot in just 25 days. Most later versions, even when better made, have not had the same kitsch appeal. But in a 1979 German-language film of *Nosferatu*, when Werner Herzog remade Murnau's 1922 one, **Klaus Kinski** gave us probably the most authentic (if slowest) vampire one will ever see on screen. Perhaps the best of many variations was Francis Ford Coppola's pretentiously titled 1992 opus, *Bram Stoker's Dracula* (though of course that's just what it was not), starring **Gary Oldman** as the Count. Other bizarre titles include:

Dracula: Dead and Loving It in 1995
Dracula: Pages from a Virgin's Diary in 2002
The Batman versus Dracula in 2005

Dracula versus Frankenstein (or, oddly, *Teenage Dracula*) in 1971
Billy the Kid versus Dracula in 1966
The Spanish epic, *Killer Barbys versus Dracula* in 2002
Dracula 2000 made in 2000 by Patrick Lussier, not to be confused with:
Wes Craven presents Dracula 2000 in 2000, followed by
Wes Craven Presents Dracula II: Ascension in 2003 and his
Dracula III: Legac in 2005
Die Hard Dracula in 1998
Dracula's Dog in 1978
The Erotic Rites of Countess Dracula (2001) didn't make it beyond video, although surprisingly, *Emmanuelle versus Dracula* found a TV home in 2004.

The 1974 TV movie *Dracula* starring **Jack Palance** in the title-role is worth a mention (though it may never reappear on screen). TV's most recent crack at the story, more soberly titled *Dracula*, came during the Christmas holiday week of 2006, in a thorough work-over from writer Stewart Harcourt. It was directed by Bill Eagles and starred one of TV's perennial men of menace, **Marc Warren**, as the Count.

JOHN JASPER DROOD in *The Mystery of Edwin Drood* (1870) by Charles Dickens
Opinions vary as to whether Drood was a villain at all, for the book he appears in was never finished. (Dickens died before reaching the end and left only a few tantalising clues to how the story might end.) Certainly Drood *looks* guilty: a cathedral organist who is also a secret opium taker; guardian to nephew Edwin but in love with Edwin's fiancée Rosa Budd; and reputedly a hypnotist. On the eve of Edwin's disappearance Jasper incites his ward to quarrel with a friend, then spreads news of their disagreement. When Edwin disappears it is his friend, Neville Landless, who falls under suspicion. But surely, Jasper has the motive? We will never know. There have been a number of 'solutions' to this last unfinished book, including a famous mock trial in 1914 with G K Chesterton as judge, George Bernard Shaw as Foreman of the Jury, and well-known writers acting as characters from the book. Some lawyers played themselves. That court found Jasper guilty, but as others have pointed out, we can't even be sure that young Edwin is dead. Might he not be that strange man Dick Datchery, an amateur detective who is almost certainly in disguise? Isn't John Jasper too obvious a villain? It seems likely that Dickens had a last-minute twist up his sleeve but he died before he could show it.

DUESSA in *Faerie Queen* (1590 to 1596) by Edmund Spenser
In Spenser's revered but nowadays seldom read verse drama, Duessa is an evil enchantress and daughter of Shame, Deceit and Falsehood. In Book I she helps the magician Archimago (who represents Hypocrisy) to trick and imprison the knight Redcross, guardian to Una, representing Truth. Elsewhere, she transforms Fradubio (Doubt) into a tree, and uses her magic against Redcross to make him lose a fight against a Saracen knight. Later she persuades him to drink from an enchanted pool which robs him of his strength. Duessa is initially seen as an aggressive allegory for the Roman Catholic church, while at other points in the very long poem she can be considered a slanderous parody of Mary, Queen of Scots, of Mary Tudor and of Roman Catholics in general. In Book V Duessa, standing for Mary, Queen of Scots, is executed by Queen Mercilla, standing for Queen Elizabeth.

ALEC D'URBERVILLE in *Tess of the d'Urbervilles* (1891)
by Thomas Hardy
A parson's son, and later an itinerant preacher, Alec capitalises on his father's false claim to be nobly descended, and seduces the eponymous Tess in Hardy's bleak (and at the time, notorious) novel. The resultant child dies at its impromptu midnight baptism and Tess quits the area, later to marry another Parson's son, **Angel Clare**, the far-too-holy and, in the eyes of many, greater villain (through his sanctimonious hypocrisy) than the rakish, vulgar Alec. After Angel has thrown up his hands in horror at her history, the abandoned Tess finds work on a farm until she takes up with Alec a second time. Alec has by now become an unlikely and hypocritical itinerant preacher. At this stage he could have been presented as a man making up for past misdeeds, but Hardy shows him instead as being unpleasantly superior and falsely pious, an unworthy match for Tess. Then the repentant Angel reappears – only to recoil again at her living with Alec. Tess, afraid she will lose her beloved Angel again, stabs Alec to death and flees with Angel Clare to the New Forest. In the eyes of the law, she is the only villain. She is pursued, caught, and hanged at 'Wintoncester' jail.

Roman Polanski's 1979 film was a perhaps inevitably long drawn-out affair, beautiful to look at, with the sultry **Natassja Kinski** in the title role, **Leigh Lawson** as Alec and **Peter Firth** as Angel Clare. ITV screened the drama as a two-parter in 1998, with **Justine Waddell** as Tess, **Jason Flemyng** as Alec and **Oliver Milburn** as Angel Clare.

JAMES DURIE in *The Master of Ballantrae* (1889) by Robert Louis Stevenson
James is the eponymous Master of the estate from Stevenson's novel, though not the hero. He is the moody, violent and impetuous brother to the dull but virtuous Henry who became Master when James was reported killed at Culloden, fighting for the Young Pretender. Worse, Henry has married James's apparently bereaved sweetheart. When James returns he is understandably disturbed, but carries his disgruntlement too far. He is rude, violent and unscrupulous in his demands for money from the estate. The two brothers fight a duel, and once again James appears to have been killed. His reappearance – virtually a resurrection, it seems to Henry and his wife – causes them to flee to America. James pursues them, only to have Henry, emboldened by his success in the first duel, confront and attempt to kill him again. James escapes death and humiliation by the extraordinary means of having his servant bury him alive. When he then reappears from the grave a third time the shock is too much for Henry and, in a melodramatic, half supernatural conclusion, both brothers are interred in the same grave.

William Keighley's 1953 film concentrates more on the earlier part of the story, in particular the rivalry between the brothers over who will fight for Bonnie Prince Charlie. **Errol Flynn** played James, and **Anthony Steel** played Henry. It's not a film to seek out.

CLAUDE DUVAL in *Claude Duval, The Dashing Highwayman* serialised in the 1850s by the publisher Edward Lloyd
As the title suggest, Duval was a gentleman highwayman, quite a dandy, and a supposed friend of **Dick Turpin**.

EDMUND in *King Lear* (1604/5) by William Shakespeare
'Now, Gods, stand up for bastards!' Edmund cries. Instigator of much of the trouble in King

Lear (other than that instigated by Lear himself), Edmund is the bastard son of Gloucester and therefore half brother to Gloucester's real son and heir Edgar. But why, Edmund asks, should being a bastard deprive him of his legacy?

Why bastard? Wherefore base?
When my dimensions are as well compact,
My mind as generous, and my shape as true,
As honest madam's issue? Why brand they us
With base? With baseness? Bastardy? Base, base
– Who, in the lusty stealth of nature, take
More composition and fierce quality
Than doth, within a dull, stale, tired bed
Go to the creating of a whole tribe of fops
Got between sleep and wake?
Edmund's revealing soliloquy from Act I, scene II of *King Lear*

Superficially charming (especially at first) Edmund is a classic Shakespearian schemer who forges a letter to cause Gloucester to disinherit Edgar, seduces both of Lear's spiteful daughters, and encourages **Goneril** to poison her husband. His one attempt at a good deed (at the end of the play when he himself is mortally wounded) comes too late to achieve its aim.

ARTHUR ENGLISH

Arthur English was both the comedian's stage name and the name of his most famous character, an impudent wide-boy spiv who flourished in the impoverished, rationed and put-upon years after the Second World War. He became popular on radio and guested in various shows as well as having his own strip in the magazine *Radio Fun*. The character had been honed in music hall, and the actor went on to portray other characters on TV including Slugger in *Follyfoot*, Mr Harman in *Are You being Served* and Arthur in *In Sickness and in Health*. When 'cast away' on *Desert Island Discs* he chose as his luxury 'a weekend in Paris'. He got away with it too.

LIZZIE EUSTACE in *The Eustace Diamonds* (1873) by Anthony Trollope

Trollope could be relied upon to create realistic villains such as might be found in everyday society. In the third book of the *Palliser* series the beautiful but shallow gold-digger Lizzie marries Sir Florian Eustace who obligingly dies a few months later, leaving her the family estates

WORLD'S CLASSICS

ANTHONY TROLLOPE
THE EUSTACE DIAMONDS

and, she claims, the titular diamonds which she spirits away. Lawyers demand the diamonds back. Lizzie swiftly flutters her eyes at lawyer cousin Frank but, although he's tempted, he has found true love elsewhere in the form of a governess, so Lizzie turns for help instead to the languid Lord Fawn. He proposes, but insists that the diamonds be given back, thus prompting Lizzie to put off their marriage indefinitely. She moves into Portray on the family estate (legitimately hers), has a gay old time and plays two more suitors off against each other. During her later travels Lizzie stops overnight in a Carlisle hotel, only to have her jewel casket stolen from her bedroom. She reports the theft to the police but neglects to add that she had removed the diamonds beforehand and still has them. Secretly triumphant, she returns to her London home but is robbed again, and this time really does lose the diamonds. What can she tell the police? Exposed as a cheat, she whips round each of her former suitors, each of whom now turns her down – each, that is, except a dubious preacher, Mr Emilius, who she marries. Then, in a Trollopian irony, Mr Emilius turns out to be as untrustworthy as she.

'She had never been made love to after this fashion before. She knew, or half knew, that the man was a scheming hypocrite, craving her money, and following her in the hour of her troubles, because he might then have the best chance of success. She had no belief whatever in his love. And yet she liked it, and approved his proceedings. She liked lies, thinking them to be more beautiful than truth. To lie readily and cleverly, recklessly and yet successfully, was, according to the lessons which she had learned, a necessity in woman, and an added grace in man.

from *The Eustace Diamonds*

FACE in *The Alchemist* (1610) by Ben Jonson

In Jonson's Jacobean comedy, Face is the crafty servant who, when his master is absent, uses their Blackfriars house as a base for various scams. He proves himself a credible conman by introducing a succession of 'gulls' to his partners **Subtle** (the so-called alchemist) and **Dol Common** (Subtle's consort). They promise each victim that their 'philosopher's stone' will, in some way, make their dreams come true. For Sir Epicure Mammon, and for the Puritan fanatics Tribulation and Ananias Wholesome, the stone will turn base metal into gold (which the men hope will bring very different rewards, as their names

suggest). It will make Abel Drugger's apothecary shop succeed, gambler Dapper start to win, and Kastril, the nouveau riche bumpkin, learn sophisticated ways and find a husband for his sister, Dame Pliant. Or so they all hope. Eventually the master returns and discovers what has been going on, but Face marries him off to Dame Pliant and all is well. **Leo McKern** and **Esmond Knight** starred in a particularly effective revival of the play directed by Tyrone Guthrie at the *Old Vic* in 1963.

FAGIN in *Oliver Twist*
(first serialised in monthly parts in 1838) by Charles Dickens
One of Dickens's most famous and effective villains, Fagin is a master fence running a small army of boy pick-pockets who scour London in search of easy pickings. Typical plunder is a silk handkerchief (far more valuable than it would be today) which a boy would 'lift' from an unsuspecting man's back pocket. Oliver sees the takings when he first meets Fagin, 'whose villainous-looking and repulsive face was obscured by a quantity of matted red hair. He was dressed in a greasy flannel gown, with his throat bare; and seemed to be dividing his attention between the frying pan and a clothes-horse, over which a great number of silk handkerchiefs were hanging.' Fagin's lair is a superbly described warren of interconnecting rooms in a terrace of derelict houses in East London, and among his gang are the **Artful Dodger** and **Bill Sikes**. In the far from politically correct Victorian era it seemed no sin to emphasise

Fagin's Jewishness although, as with all the best villains, he is delineated broadly enough to become appealing to the reader, mainly through his wheedling, manipulative but ultimately threatening patterns of speech. He trains Oliver as a pickpocket in the same way he trained all his boys:

'... *placing a snuff-box in one pocket of his trousers, a note-case in the other, and a watch in his waistcoat pocket, with a guard chain round his neck, and sticking a mock diamond pin in his shirt, buttoned his coat tight round him, and putting his spectacle-case and handkerchief in his pockets, trotted up and down the room with a stick, in imitation of the manner in which old gentlemen walk about the streets any hour of the day. Sometimes he stopped at the fireplace, and sometimes at the door, making believe that he was staring with all his might into shop windows. At such times he would look constantly round him, for fear of thieves, and keep slapping all his pockets in turn, to see that he hadn't lost anything, in such a very funny and natural manner that Oliver laughed till the tears ran down his face*

from *Oliver Twist* by Charles Dickens

However he may have been portrayed on nineteenth century stages, Fagin has usually been softened by actors since, although when **Alec Guinness** emphasised his pantomimic Jewish features in the archetypal David Lean film of 1948, he caused unexpected offence and protest. There had been earlier versions: a silent film directed by Frank Lloyd in 1922, and a forgettable 1933 movie directed by William Cowen. Fagin became almost lovable when portrayed by **Ron Moody** in the 1968 Carol Reed film of the 1960 Lionel Bart musical *Oliver*. In 1982 *Oliver Twist* was needlessly remade in a film directed by

Clive Donner starring **George C Scott** as a typically gutsy Fagin. There was also a Disney cartoon version, *Oliver and Company*, in 1988 in which Oliver was a cat and the Dodger a winsome dog. Disney, one felt, had lost the plot. Then along came Roman Polanski in 2005 to direct yet another version of *Oliver Twist*, this time with **Ben Kingsley** in the role of Fagin.

Alan Bleasdale cleverly adapted the tale for ITV in 1999, straightening out and improving the storyline, and clarifying the role of Oliver's half brother **Monks** (played by **Marc Warren** in his customary sinister fashion). Fagin was played in that version by **Robert Lindsay.** In BBC's 2007 five-part Christmas series, Fagin was played by a rather less villainous **Timothy Spall**.

COUNT FATHOM (Tobias Smollett) see **FERDINAND**

GUY FAWKES *Real-life character* (1570 – 1606)
Guy Fawkes is Britain's most famous fall-guy and one of the few historical characters to have a day named after him, being ceremoniously burned in effigy throughout the land every November 5th. He was born a Protestant in York but converted at an early age to Catholicism, and throughout his twenties was sufficiently ardent to serve in the Spanish army in the Netherlands. Inveigled by Catesby into the Gunpowder Plot he returned to England in 1605. At the Opening of Parliament on the 5 November the plotters intended to blow up both the Commons and Lords, together with King James I (son of Mary, Queen of Scots). They secreted 36 barrels of gunpowder into the

cellars below the House of Lords, and all might have gone to plan had one of the conspirators, Tresham, not betrayed them. Fawkes was the man caught red-handed with the explosives. Several other conspirators, Catesby among them, fled but were later captured. Catesby was shot. Guy Fawkes was tried and hanged on the 31st January 1606. As the one caught with the gunpowder, Fawkes remains the most famous of the plotters, and is often thought of as the man who single-handedly tried to bring down Parliament. It is curious that he is remembered (albeit often inaccurately) while the leader Catesby fades into history and the traitor Tresham is hardly remembered at all. Guy Fawkes is so much a part of British (or certainly English) custom and folklore that he has become almost mythical – our greatest villain, though one for whom many have a sneaking sympathy.

BASIL FAWLTY TV legend

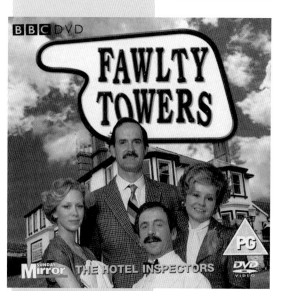

An irascible, permanently angry hotelier who has high hopes for his modest hotel in the equally modest Torquay, Fawlty anticipates attracting a better class of guest who will appreciate his wit and ability to create a refined environment – both of which he is the last person in the world who could provide. He hates his life, his wife, his staff, his guests, and anything mechanical which misbehaves. Guests and staff live in fear of him, though his unflappable wife treats him with disdain. To most people Basil is sarcastic and patronising, while to those he imagines might be the sort of guests he craves, he fawns and cringes even more than **Uriah Heep**. The two TV series (written by Cleese and his then-wife Connie Booth) were short, hilarious and immensely popular. They included many unforgettable scenes such as those in the episodes The Hotel Inspector, the Gourmet Evening, Chasing the Rat, the Blonde Tourist, Fixing the Stag's Head, Don't Mention The War, and Beating the Car That Wouldn't Start.

FERDINAND, COUNT FATHOM in *The Adventures of Ferdinand Count Fathom* (1753) by Tobias Smollett
The anti-hero of Smollett's mock-heroic novel, Ferdinand is the bastard son of a camp-follower to Marlborough's army who,

while robbing the dead on the battlefield, saves the life of Count de Melvil, causing the noble Count to unofficially adopt the boy and bring him up alongside his own son – for which good deed Ferdinand seduces the Count's daughter and skips off to Vienna. He continues his dark deeds there in the company of the wicked **Ratchcali**, seducing and ruining women and dealing in fake antiques. When he returns to England, he is caught cheating at cards and is thrown into a debtor's prison, only to be released by the Count's honourable son. Ferdinand repays this favour by trying to rape the young man's girlfriend. His life of scandal and debauchery continues with deceit, quackery and marriage to a wealthy widow, all leading to another spell of imprisonment. At this point in the rambling tale Smollett rather loses interest in 'Count Fathom' and concentrates instead on the 'decent' characters. This twist spoils the book. (Eighteen years later, Smollett gave Ferdinand a cameo reappearance in his finest novel *The Expedition of Humphry Clinker*.)

SIR AUSTIN FEVEREL in *The Ordeal of Richard Feverel* (1859) by George Meredith
A villain with the highest of motives, Sir Austin was abandoned by his wife for the more romantic attractions of a poet. To him, the lessons of that unfortunate episode seem clear: no more airy-fairy romantic nonsense but duty and hard work instead. In the aptly-titled 'Ordeal', Sir Austin subjects his son Richard to a 'System' of education of his own devising (one that would find lingering support in some quarters today). Richard is educated at home, away from distracting and pernicious outside influences (especially female and thus romantic ones). Despite having his nose kept to the grindstone, Richard manages to glance up long enough to spot fair Lucy Desborough and to fall instantly in love. Lucy is only a farmer's daughter but is irresistible to a young man who has seen nothing but textbooks. Despite her relatively low station they marry in secret, and when Sir Austin realises what's going on he rips the couple apart, carries Richard to London and browbeats the young man into putting filial duty first. But London is not the best place in which to keep a young man from temptation. One of Sir Austin's friends, **Lord Mountfalcon**, has eyes and itchy fingers for Lucy and persuades the susceptible Richard that part of his 'duty' is to assist fallen women and teach them the error of their ways. This, of course, can only end one way, and before long the startled young man has become entangled with the gloriously-named Bella Mount.

Richard's guilt about Bella prompts him to take himself abroad until he realises that his true duty is to return to Lucy and to take up his proper duties as a father. Meanwhile, Mountfalcon has courted Lucy. Richard fights a duel with him and is wounded, while Lucy, overcome with the turbulence around her, falls ill to 'brain fever' and dies. The somewhat melodramatic plot is designed to demonstrate the perils of parental autocracy and over-restraint. Sir Austin Feverel embodies its inevitable failure.

FLAMBEAU in *Father Brown* short stories by G K Chesterton
A master criminal, introduced initially as an adversary to Chesterton's whimsical detective Father Brown, but soon converted to become the chubby priest's advisor and confidante. His appearances are scattered throughout the Brown books in *The Innocence of Father Brown* (1911), *The Wisdom of Father Brown* (1914), *The Incredulity of Father Brown* (1926), *The Secret of Father Brown* (1927), *The Scandal of Father Brown* (1935).

The bumbling cleric was portrayed in the 1974 ITV series by *Doctor in the House* and *Genevieve* star **Kenneth More** and Flambeau (here the Father's friend and moved far from villainy) was played by **Dennis Burgess**.

The Detective was the American title for a splendid British film, *Father Brown*, made in 1954, starring **Alec Guiness** as Brown and **Peter Finch** as Flambeau. There had been earlier efforts, of which the only notable version, *Father Brown, Detective* came out in 1934 with **Walter Connolly** as Brown and **Paul Lukas** as Flambeau. Flambeau was seen as the master jewel thief in these films.

FLAMINEO in *The White Devil* by John Webster (first performed in 1612)

Flamineo: 'O men,
That lie upon your death-beds, and are haunted
With howling wives! Ne'er trust them; they'll re-marry
Ere the worm pierce your winding-sheet, ere the spider
Make a thin curtain for your epitaphs'
The White Devil, Act V, scene VI

Flamineo is the villainous brother to **Vittoria Corombona** in Webster's confused, uneven play. Vittoria is unsatisfactorily married and Flamineo first encourages her adulterous affair with Brachiano, then later plays a major part in helping kill both Brachiano's wife and Vittoria's husband – arranging the death of the latter so it appears to have been from a riding accident. Flamineo, who appears to care for nobody except, perhaps, his sister, berates his own mother when she asks, 'What? Because we are poor, shall we be vicious?' by demanding, 'What means have you to keep me from the galleys – or the gallows?' Later he falls out with their virtuous brother Marcello and kills him before their mother's eyes. Marcello, dying, warns, 'There are some sins which heaven doth duly punish in a whole family.' Despite all his strength and violent ambition Flaimineo meets the traditional fate of Jacobean villains: a blade of steel in the final act.

> *'My life was a black charnel. I have caught*
> *An everlasting cold; I have lost my voice*
> *Most irrevocably. Farewell, glorious villains.*
> *This busy trade of life appears most vain,*
> *Since rest breeds rest, where all seek pain by pain.*
> *Let no harsh flattering bells resound my knell;*
> *Strike, thunder, and strike loud, to my farewell!*
> (Dies)
>
> *The White Devil*, Act V, scene VI

SIR PETRONEL FLASH in *Eastward Hoe* (1605)
by George Chapman, Ben Jonson & John Marston
An apparently flush but actually penniless adventurer in a comedy contemporary with Shakespeare's later plays who is sought out and married by the brash Gertrude Touchstone because she believes that marrying him will enable her to travel in her own coach. Of such is ambition made. Sir Petronel packs her off (in said coach) to an imaginary castle, snaffles her dowry, and hightails for Virginia in the company of a dodgy apprentice, Quicksilver. They don't get far. They are wrecked on the Isle of Dogs, brought to trial and made to spend a mere few days in prison. The play's authors were similarly incarcerated for a short spell, because an incautious scene in Act III lambasting the Scots offended King James I (also known as James VI of Scotland).

FLASHMAN in *Tom Brown's Schooldays* (1857)
by Thomas Hughes, and later by George MacDonald Fraser
Memorably vicious and self-assured bully in Hughes's novel, he was 'about seventeen years old, and big and strong for his age. He played well at all games where pluck wasn't much wanted,' and is furious when some of the younger boys see through him:

> *While he was in the act of thrashing them, they would*

roar out instances of his funking at football, or shirking some encounter with a lout of half his own size. These things were all well enough known in the house, but to have his disgrace shouted out by small boys, to feel that they despised him, to be unable to silence them by any amount of torture, and to see the open laugh and sneer of his own associates (who were looking on, and took no trouble to hide their scorn from him, though they neither interfered with his bullying or lived a bit the less intimately with him,) made him beside himself. Come what might, he would make those boys' lives miserable.

An insight into Flashman, from *Tom Brown's School Days*

His torments of the young and virtuous Tom include roasting him in front of a roaring open fire like a piece of human toast. (Could this be where the phrase 'You're toast' comes from? Probably not.) In the book, Flashman is eventually foiled by Tom and his equally upright friend East and is eventually expelled (from Rugby School, where the game of rugby is said to have originated) for the lesser crime of drunkenness.

That would have been the end of the matter if, more than a century later, MacDonald Fraser had not recognised that Flashman was by far the most interesting character in the book (some would say the only interesting character) and was worth reviving for a pastiche sequel. That book was *Flashman: From the Flashman Papers 1839-1842* and was, as the title suggests, a supposed memoir reconstructed from Flashman's diaries. Told therefore in the first person, and recounting his exploits from Flashman's point of view (sometimes crossly contradicted by his fictional editor in footnotes), it reintroduces the adult Harry Flashman in what was to become the first of a brilliant series – funny, sexy, at times exciting and always historically accurate. Flashman has the knack of turning up (often against his will) in the thick of some of the nineteenth century's most famous and dangerous episodes. As an adult, he has lost none of the caddishness given him by Thomas Hughes, but in the Fraser books his trickery, cowardice and knavery with women make him endearing. He fights at Balaclava with the Light Brigade, becomes embroiled in the slave trade, gets lost in the Khyber Pass, the Far East, the American Civil War and elsewhere, and in every scrape he feints and squirms his way out of trouble, desperate to save his hide. Each time, he succeeds through some comic misunderstanding to be thought a hero once again. The ladies think him dashing (and he beds some famous ladies, including royalty), most men are taken in by him, but through his confessional diaries we know the truth. In his riotous diaries Flashman is refreshingly frank about himself:

'As you know, in spite of the published catalogue of my career – Victoria Cross, general rank, eleven campaigns, and all that mummery – I've always been an arrant coward and a peaceable soul. Bullying underlings and whipping trollops always excepted, I'm a gentle fellow – which means I'll never do harm to anyone if there's a chance he may harm me in return. The trouble is, no one would believe it to look at me; I've always been big and hearty and looked the kind of chap who'd go three rounds with the town tough if he so much as stepped on my shadow, and from what Tom Hughes has written of me you might imagine I was always ready for devilment. Aye, but as I've grown older I've learned that devilment usually has to be paid for.

from Flash For Freedom

Harry Flashman certainly pays for all his devilment but he gets – and delivers – good value in return. He is one of the most lovable rogues in modern fiction. The original Thomas Hughes classic was first published in 1857 and has been in print ever since, largely because its moral rightfulness made it a natural choice as a school prize. (For over a century good results at school were rewarded, on Prize Day, with the presentation of a suitable book, inside which was an impressively printed label inscribed with the winner's name and subject.) Hughes's worthy story was filmed first by Hollywood in 1940 under director Robert Stevenson and then in Britain in 1951 with director Gordon Parry. Although more lively than the book, neither film has stood the test of time, though in the second, **John Forrest** was a chilling Flashman.

Of the second, far more enjoyable George MacDonald Fraser book series, *Flashman: From the Flashman Papers 1839-1842* (1969) came first and was an immediate best-seller. It was followed by *Royal Flash* (1970), *Flash for Freedom* (1971), *Flashman at the Charge* (1973), *Flashman in the Great Game* (1975), *Flashman's Lady* (1977), *Flashman and the Redskins* (1982), *Flashman and the Dragon* (1985), *Flashman and the Mountain of Light* (1990). *Flashman and the Angel of the Lord* (1994) should have been the last but in response to constant demands from hungry fans Fraser brought out another, *Flashman on the March* in 2005.

The 1975 film *Royal Flash*, directed by Richard Lester and starring **Malcolm McDowell** atop a splendid cast, fired some spirited broadsides but managed to miss with practically every shot.

FLEDGEBY in *Our Mutual Friend* (1864-5) by Charles Dickens
Villainous money-lender who conducts his trade under the name 'Pubsey & Co'.

FLINTWINCH FAMILY in *Little Dorrit* (1857) by Charles Dickens
Three members of the family creep through the labyrinthine plot (and Dickens doesn't use a name like Flintwinch for nothing). Before the book begins, **Ephraim Flintwinch** was master of a lunatic asylum compelled by his sins to leave the country, at which time his brother entrusted him with a box of incriminating documents belonging to **Mrs Clenham**. Ephraim loses them to **Rigaud**, a Belgian crook. Back in London, **Mrs Affery Flintwinch**, 'a tall, hard-favoured sinewy old woman who in her youth might have enlisted in the Foot Guards without much fear of discovery' has become a frightened, half-mad old lady, terrified both by the crumbling old house that she lives in and by her malevolent husband **Jeremiah Flintwinch**, who eventually defrauds his business partner **Mrs Clenham**.

> '*He was a short, bald old man, in a high-shouldered black coat and waistcoat, drab breeches and long drab gaiters. He might, from his dress, have been either clerk or servant, and in fact had long been both. There was nothing about him in the way of decoration but a watch, which was lowered into the depths of its proper pocket by an old black ribbon, and had a tarnished copper key moored above it, to show where it was sunk. His head was awry, and he had a one-sided, crab-like way with him, as if his foundations had yielded at about the same time as those of the house, and he ought to have been propped up in a similar manner*
Jeremiah described in *Little Dorrit*

Little Dorrit was superbly adapted for the screen by Christine Edzard in 1988 and the resultant two-part film lasted nearly six hours (the two parts were shown separately). Flintwinch was wonderfully brought to life by the old Variety entertainer and comedian **Max Wall**. For BBC TV in 2008 Jeremiah (and his twin brother Ephraim) were played by **Alvn Armstrong**.

FOLLYWIT in *A Mad World, My Masters* by Thomas Middleton (printed 1608)

A comic scallywag, chronically short of money, who, rather than wait for his inheritance, chooses instead to rob his grandfather, Sir Bounteous Progress. Many of the characters in this play are wonderfully identifiable by their names (see **Brothel**). Follywit, never the brightest, belatedly marries the courtesan Gullman under the extraordinary misapprehension that she's a virgin. Not only is she far from that, she is in fact his grandfather's long-term mistress. Follywit, therefore, has been 'gulled'.

SOAMES FORSYTE in the *Forsyte* series by John Galsworthy. Mistakenly thought by many to be have been the villain of *The Forsyte Saga* (a series of initially three but, eventually, nine books beginning with *The Man of Property* in 1906 and continuing into the 1930s) Soames is the eponymous man of property who, though he loves his first wife Irene in his upright and sober fashion, nevertheless treats her (in her opinion) as his 'property'. She becomes increasingly frigid in her relations with him, eventually refusing him 'his marital rights' altogether until, maddened with frustration, he forces himself upon her. It was this scene – and the question of whether the rape of a wife by her husband was actually a crime – that excited both readers and, later, television viewers, and which branded Soames as a villain. In fact, he was a scrupulously honest, almost too respectable man of irreproachable behaviour for whom behaving correctly was more important than behaving as a human being (a distinction he would have impatiently dismissed). When his wife leaves him he remarries, has a daughter Fleur, and in turning all his affection to her he becomes as blind in his devotion as he had previously been in his lack of it.

Galsworthy applied the word 'saga' to only the first three of the Forsyte novels: *The Man of Property* (1906, which originally stood alone), *In Chancery* (1920) and *To Let* (1921), although he would write a further six full-length novels and some short stories about the family. In the landmark BBC TV series of *The Forsyte Saga* in 1967 the portrayal of Soames by **Eric Porter** was so electric that it made his screen career.

COUNT FOSCO in *The Woman in White* (1860)
by Wilkie Collins

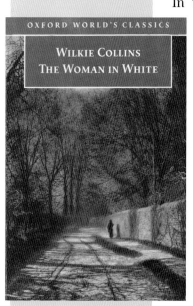

In the second half of his finest book, Collins introduced a splendid and beguiling villain, a man who, unlike many nineteenth century villains, was neither an evident scoundrel nor a rogue masquerading unconvincingly as virtuous. Count Isidor Ottavio Fosco is a fat but charming Italian nobleman of dubious lineage and with a knack for turning up at inconvenient times. He makes few threats, is far from dastardly, but has the fatal charm of a snake – and like a snake he dotes on small animals: his fondness for pet canaries and white mice, far from weakening him, makes him all the more sinister. (He also likes brightly coloured waistcoats, and makes a half-hearted attempt to woo the investigating heroine Marian Halcombe.) His dastardly plan is hatched in partnership with the equally unscrupulous **Sir Percival Glyde** and begins with the unjust incarceration of an heiress, **Laura Fairlie**, in an asylum so the wicked knight can get her money.

The Woman in White, published in 1860, is Collins's finest book and has never been out of print. It was staged as a Victorian melodrama, was a silent film four times and was remade in 1948 (*The Woman in White* directed by Peter Godfrey) as a heavy slow-moving version which even **Sidney Greenstreet** as a memorable Fosco could not save.

Television versions appeared in 1957, 1966 and 1982 (when **Alan Badel** played Fosco) before a fast-moving (if necessarily abbreviated) version in 1997 with **Simon Callow** a deceptively charming Fosco.

THE FOUR JUST MEN in *The Four Just Men* (1905)
by Edgar Wallace

The Just Men of the title are four rich vigilantes prepared to right wrongs by whatever means are necessary, including those that the law itself will not countenance – such as murder. Their ideal targets are men so powerful they think themselves above the law, and the techniques used by the team are almost impossible to crack. Or so Wallace thought. As famous as the actual book is the fact that Edgar Wallace decided to promote it with a thousand pounds of advertising (a huge sum then) and to include in every copy a tear-out competition form offering a further five hundred pounds in prizes to readers who could guess how the four men would get rid of the true villain (a wicked Foreign Secretary with a scheme to revise the law to restrict civil liberties). Not content with this, Wallace booked a poster campaign and some cinema advertising. The upshot was that he found himself two thousand pounds in debt. To settle it he had to borrow heavily and sell the rights to the book to George Newnes for seventy-five pounds. It is hardly necessary to say that after he had sold the rights for this paltry sum, the book sold very well.

The Four Just Men came out in 1905, with the results summarised above, but its sales success led Wallace to produce some increasingly far-fetched sequels: *The Council of Justice* (1908), *The Just Men of Cordova* (1917), *The Law of the Four Just Men* (1921), *The Three Just Men* (1925 – giving a clue to the plot surprise in the previous), and *Again the Three Just Men* (1928).

The Four Just Men was a 1939 film directed by Walter Forde starring **Hugh Sinclair**, **Francis L Sullivan**, **Frank Lawton** and **Griffith Jones** as the Four. BBC Television made a series based on their adventures in 1959 and 1960 which starred **Jack Hawkins**, **Richard Conte**, **Dan Dailey** and **Vittorio de Sica** in the roles. These four were more 'just' than their predecessors.

FRANCESCHINI in *The Ring and the Book*
by Robert Browning (originally issued in four parts, November 1868 to February 1869)
Count Guido Franceschini is the cruel villain at the heart of Browning's book-length story-poem (his most ambitious and perhaps greatest work). An impoverished nobleman of Arezzo, Franceschini contracts what he thinks will be a profitable marriage to Pompilia, only daughter of the Comparinis. When they realise he has no money they try to annul the marriage and have their dowry

returned. Franceschini treats his bride shamefully, his brother lusts after her, and in desperation she persuades a young priest to help her escape back to her parents. Here she learns that she is not their natural daughter but was in fact abandoned by a prostitute. The furious Franceschini storms the house and murders the parents, leaving Pompilia to die later of her wounds. Browning's story is based on a real-life seventeenth century Roman scandal and gains in power by being told not only as a poetic drama but one presented as monologues from the different points of view of twelve narrators.

FRANCISCO in *Sforza, The Duke of Milan*
by Philip Massinger (published in 1623)

Francisco is the evil favourite of the Duke of Milan. When his master loses a battle with the Emperor Charles and is in fear of his life, he writes to Francisco (memo to self: never write to a villain; it will be used against you) telling Francisco to gently end the life of his beloved wife Marcelia, should he (the Duke) be killed. Duke Sforza seems to have forgotten that he has previously raped Francisco's sister Eugenia, and it is no surprise to the audience when Francisco, not averse to tasting the Duke's wife for himself, shows her the letter without fully explaining its context. It's not enough to persuade Marcelia to give herself to him in the Duke's stead (always a vain hope, one suspects) but she does, not unreasonably, turn against her husband and upbraid him on his return. He, Sforza, has meanwhile become persuaded that she has indeed slept with Francisco – a suspicion reinforced by Francisco's telling him, untruthfully, that Marcelia tried to seduce him, but that he manfully resisted. This causes Sforza, never the easiest of husbands, to kill his wife. As she dies she reveals the truth and Francisco has to make a quick exit. Unaccountably, other than for dramatic effect, Francisco then returns to court disguised as a Jewish doctor capable of bringing Marcelia back to life. In a typical lethal climax Francisco poisons Sforza and is himself put to torture. They don't write plays like that today.

FRANKENSTEIN in *Frankenstein* (1818) by Mary Shelley
Often wrongly thought to be the name of the monster, Frankenstein is actually the name of the doctor who creates him. Doctor Victor Frankenstein – a medical student rather than

a real doctor – practised around the turn of the eighteenth and nineteenth centuries. For reasons of scientific research and, to an extent, to help make his name, he conducts secret experiments with galvanism in an attempt to reanimate a dead body made from parts assembled from stolen corpses.

'I do not remember to have trembled at a tale of superstition, or to have feared the apparition of a spirit. Darkness had no effect upon my fancy; and a churchyard was to me merely the receptacle of bodies deprived of life, which, from being the seat of beauty and strength, had become food for the worm. Now I was led to examine the cause and progress of this decay, and forced to spend days and nights in vaults and charnel houses. My attention was fixed upon every object the most insupportable to the delicacy of the human feelings. I saw how the fine form of man was degraded and wasted; I beheld the corruption of death succeed to the blooming cheek of life; I saw how the worm inherited the wonders of the eye and brain. I paused, examining and analysing all the minutiae of causation, as exemplified in the change from life to death, and death to life, until from the midst of this darkness a sudden light broke in upon me – a light so brilliant and wondrous, yet so simple, that while I became

dizzy with the immensity of the prospect which it illustrated, I was surprised that among so many men of genius, who had directed their inquiries towards the same science, that I alone should be reserved to discover so astonishing a secret.

Frankenstein explains what drove him (from *Frankenstein*)

Frankenstein succeeds in bringing life to his creation by using electricity harnessed during a thunder storm (we assume: this is his unvarying methodology on screen but his techniques are withheld from us in the book – lest the secrets get out!) Only then does he begin to question what he has done:

'I beheld the wretch – the miserable monster whom I had created. He held up the curtain of the bed; and his eyes, if eyes they may be called, were fixed on me. His jaws opened, and he muttered some inarticulate sounds, while a grin wrinkled his cheeks. He might have spoken, but I did not hear; one hand was stretched out, seemingly to detain me, but I escaped, and rushed down stairs. I took refuge in the court-yard belonging to the house which I inhabited; where I remained during the rest of the night, walking up and down in the greatest agitation, listening attentively, catching and fearing each sound as it were to announce the approach of the demoniacal corpse to which I had so miserably given life.

from *Frankenstein*

But he cannot abandon his creation; the deed is done. And the unthinking Frankenstein is unprepared for the not unreasonable demands from 'the creature' to be treated sympathetically as a human. Frankenstein had intended only to create life (hardly a modest ambition), to achieve a major breakthrough in science and to gain personal acclaim. He had given no thought to the consequences of his experiment or to his responsibilities to the living being he would create. Hence the quotation from *Paradise Lost* chosen by Mary Shelley for the title-page of the first edition:

'Did I request thee, Maker, from my clay
To mould me man? Did I solicit thee
From darkness to promote me?

PENGUIN CLASSICS

MARY SHELLEY

Frankenstein

The living being does not start out as a monster, if indeed he ever becomes one. Instead, he is pathetic, lonely and wretchedly aware of his ugliness and ill-formed state. It is the doctor's disregard for him and his needs that leads the creature to run away and to seek, disastrously, to make a life for himself in the wild. The creature (Mary Shelley deliberately does not humanise him with a name) cannot survive alone; he is awkward, ungainly and unable to control his body or to rein in his strength. Despite himself, he kills, and is duly condemned as a monster. Frankenstein himself, if he does not fully see the error of his ways and the dangers of over-reaching ambition, loses everything he hoped for and once held dear. He, the doctor, is the archetypal 'mad scientist', blinkered and ambitious, discarding common sense and good practice in his determination to achieve a result, putting science first, before humanity.

Frankenstein, or the Modern Prometheus was written as a Gothic Novel by Mary Shelley in 1818 when she was just nineteen. Legend has it that the story was conceived and first told by her during a late-night story-telling session with the poets Byron and Shelley, their own contributions being eclipsed by hers. From time to time it has been alleged that one of the men must have written it and attributed the tale to her, as if it were impossible for an intelligent and imaginative teenager to make up a horror story. But the evidence is against this: though the full text was drafted later, and although her husband, Shelley, made suggestions, those amendments (as can be seen

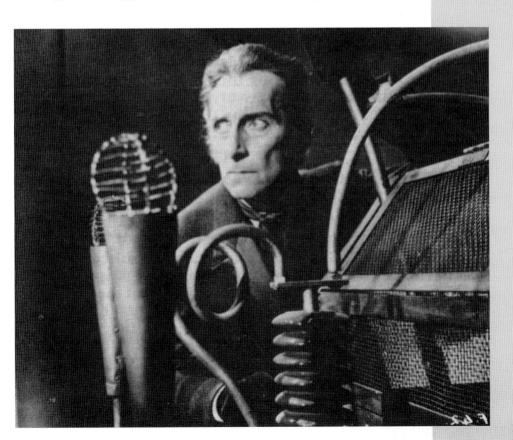

F

by an annotated edition which still exists) are little more than editorial. Mary Shelley herself later wrote three other full-length romances.

After two (lost) silent versions, the first talking film of Frankenstein is still thought of as the classic – often perhaps by people who have not actually seen it. James Whale's beautifully shot, but errant, 1931 film starred **Colin Clive** as Frankenstein and, memorably, **Boris Karloff** as his shambling creature. Karloff's stitched and bolted together, lugubrious and pathetic form set the pattern of how the monster should look, a pattern which has been repeated in practically every filmed or graphic version since. The film itself, though, strayed widely – and for the most part, mistakenly – from Mary Shelley's far better plot. Whale went on to direct *The Bride of Frankenstein* in 1935 when Clive and Karloff repeated their performances as doctor and monster but were joined by the wonderfully weird **Elsa Lanchester** as the constructed 'bride'. (She also played Mary Shelley in a prologue to the film.) Numerous other films have followed, the better of which include *Son of Frankenstein* (1935, Karloff again) and *Frankenstein Meets the Wolf Man* (1943, better than it sounds, with **Bela Lugosi** miscast as the creature and **Lon Chaney Jr** much better as the Wolf Man).

Britain joined the fray in 1957 with Hammer's *The Curse of Frankenstein* starring (inevitably) **Peter Cushing** as Frankenstein and **Christopher Lee** as what was by now a less

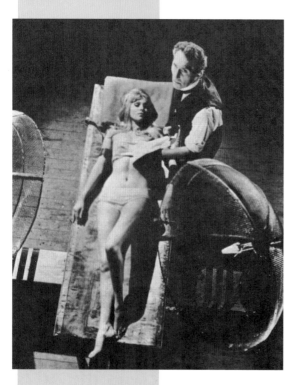

subtle monster. Lee dropped out for the following year's *Revenge of Frankenstein*, although the script improved. Seen today, it is clear that the Hammer series has dated, although 1969's *Frankenstein Must Be Destroyed* is just about worthwhile.

Back in 1973 a TV movie – *Frankenstein: The True Story* (well, hardly) – played intelligently with the plot, having a script by Christopher Isherwood and a quite different (more handsome) monster played by **Michael Sarrazin**. Britain hit back again in 1984 with an ITV film in which **Robert Powell** played Frankenstein and **David Warner** tugged the heartstrings as the monster. The 1993 TV movie, *Frankenstein*, with **Randy Quaid** as the creature, is not a complete waste of a wet evening if there's nothing else on, but the following year's *Mary Shelley's Frankenstein* reinforces the lesson Never Trust A Movie That Quotes The Author's Name. One of many 'improvements' to the original story came late in 2007 when ITV showed Jed Mercurio's modern-day version, with Frankenstein recast as a woman (**Helen McCrory**) working on stem-cell research who creates a monster in her laboratory. It was an interesting, if insufficiently developed scenario, in which the best thing was the entirely rethought make-up and prosthetics for the abject monster, played by **Julian Bleach**.

FU-MANCHU in The *Fu-Manchu* series by Sax Rohmer, aka Arthur Sarsfield Ward

> *'Imagine a person, tall, lean and feline, high shouldered, with a brow like Shakespeare and a face like Satan, a close-shaven skull, and long, magnetic eyes of the true cat-green. Invest him with all the cruel cunning of an entire eastern race, accumulated in one giant intellect, with all the resources of science past and present, with all the resources, if you will, of a wealthy government – which, however, already has denied all knowledge of his existence. Imagine that awful being, and you have a mental picture of Dr Fu Manchu, the yellow peril incarnate in one man.*
>
> From *The Mystery of Dr Fu Manchu*

The most famous wily oriental of them all – evil, virtually indestructible and bent on world domination – who is heroically opposed by the Burmese Commissioner, Nayland Smith. Among Fu-Manchu's allies and accomplices at one time or another are the inevitable cat (this one having its claws coated with deadly poison), various spiders, a snake, a giant centipede, sundry strange but deadly insects, an Abyssinian sacred baboon, a Cantonese rat and an army of zombies He also has a beautiful slave girl, Kâramanèh, who not only rescues him from tight corners but exerts her erotic influences on the stiff-upper-lipped narrator of the books, Doctor Petrie. ('The body of Kâramanèh was exquisite: her beauty of a kind that was a key to the most extravagant rhapsodies of Eastern poets. Her eyes held a challenge wholly Oriental in its appeal; her lips, even in repose, were a taunt.' – from *The Mystery of Dr Fu Manchu*.)

The books are, as Julian Symons says in *Bloody Murder*, 'absolute rubbish, penny dreadfuls in hard covers, interesting chiefly in the way they reflect popular feeling about the 'Yellow Peril' which in these books, as a character remarks, are "incarnate in one man".' They are, needless to say, politically incorrect, but for several decades before they were written it had been commonplace for Orientals – usually Lascar or Chinese – to be portrayed automatically as villains. The books were a huge success, and ran from the first, *The Mysterious Dr. Fu-Manchu* in 1913 to *Emperor Fu-Manchu* in 1959. Long after Rohmer's death that year a collection of previously unpublished short stories was issued under the characteristic title *The Wrath of Fu-Manchu* (1979). In 1984 an oddity appeared out of the blue: *Ten Years Beyond Baker Street*, by Cay Van Ash (Rohmer's biographer) pitted Fu Manchu against Sherlock Holmes.

Most Fu-Manchu films are dreadful and unlikely to be shown again. After some short silent shockers came an early talkie in 1929, *The Mysterious Dr Fu Manchu* (**Warner Oland** played the Doctor), but the best (of a pretty poor bunch) came in 1932 when **Boris Karloff** stepped in to breathe life into the role, assisted by a deliciously evil **Myrna Loy** as his daughter, in *The Mask of Dr Fu Manchu* directed by Charles Brabin and Charles Vidor. A kind word should be given also to a 1960s series starring **Christopher Lee** as Fu Manchu and which began with *The Face of Fu Manchu* in 1965, directed by Don Sharp. **Peter Sellars** attempted to send up the role in *The Fiendish Plot of Dr Fu Manchu* (1980) but it didn't work.

It should be noted that 'Sax Rohmer' was born in Birmingham to Irish parents (in 1886), never went to China, knew nothing about the Chinese, and for Fu Manchu's final incarnation during the Second World War Rohmer converted his villain to an ally of the West. *O tempora, O mores*!

ALF GARNETT in *Till Death Us Do Part*
One of television's most popular villains, but a villain nevertheless, given to mouthing off at the slightest opportunity with what, even in the let-it-all-hang-out 1970s, were outrageously non-PC sentiments. Garnett, created by left-wing scriptwriter Johnny Speight, was a racist, right wing, homophobic, chauvinistic, narrow-minded, foul-mouthed and stunningly ignorant bully, as well as being belligerent and intolerant to his long-suffering wife, daughter, son-in-law and almost anyone else who crossed his path. Only to those bigger and stronger than himself or to his social

superiors did Garnett's manor change: then he became servile and nauseously subservient. This foul creature was created by Speight as a salutary example of an extreme East End bigot, deliberately made comic but to be laughed *at* rather than with. But the hilariously appalling lines given him by Speight, and the warmth of Warren Mitchell's portrayal, made Garnett one of the nation's most loved TV creations, thus subverting the very point this extreme caricature was supposed to raise. It was as if Hitler had been reincarnated and deified as the Pope.

SIR JOHN GLUTTON see **TURPIN**

GOLDFINGER in *Goldfinger* (1959) by Ian Fleming
The villain after whom this Bond novel is named. His golden touch is exhibited early in both the film and the book when he has a troublesome ex-mistress painted all over in gold leaf – a fabulous luxury, she thinks, unaware that having had every pore of her skin clogged by gold she will slowly expire. Goldfinger's main aim in life is to explode a small atomic bomb inside Fort Knox, thus contaminating much of the world's gold supply and making it unusable. (He, of course, has his own supply.) Only one man can stop a villain as ruthless and devious as this. *Goldfinger* was the seventh Bond book.

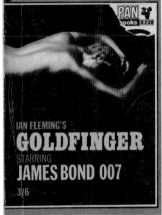

   Albert R Broccoli's classic 1964 film (third in the **Connery** series) had **Gert Frobe** as a splendid Goldfinger. The film is repeated on TV almost as often as radio repeats the fantastic version of the title-song thumped out by the magnificent **Shirley Bassey**.

GONERIL in King Lear (written around 1605)
by William Shakespeare
One of the King's three daughters. Lear foolishly abdicates his crown and disinherits his good daughter Cordelia in favour of her ambitious and malicious sisters, Goneril and Regan. Goneril soon shows her colours. First she becomes impatient with her father when he comes to stay. 'Idle old man,' she rants behind his back. 'that still would manage those authorities that he hath given away.' She instructs her servants to treat him badly, so he will leave her house for Regan's, then she moves on through increasing highhandedness to a dramatic climax where in a doomed attempt to secure the undivided love of the villain Edmund, she scorns her husband ('Milk-livered man!' she

mocks him to his face), seduces Edmund ('Decline your head: this kiss, if it dare speak, would stretch your spirits up into the air') and, finally, she poisons her sister Regan. (When the unsuspecting Regan clutches her stomach and cries, 'Sick, O, sick,' Goneril turns aside to quip, 'If not, I'll never trust medicine!')

THOMAS GRADGRIND in *Hard Times* (1854)
by Charles Dickens

> *'Thomas Gradgrind, sir. A man of realities. A man of fact and calculations. A man who proceeds upon the principle that two and two are four, and nothing over, and who is not to be talked into allowing for anything over.'*
> From *Hard Times*: Gradgrind is introduced to the reader

A villain (though ultimately reformed) and the strongest character in one of Dickens's shorter and some say weaker novels, Gradgrind thinks of himself as a plain-speaking, no-nonsense businessman, a model for any man who believes in a stronger, healthier England run by practical men.

> *'With a rule and a pair of scales, and the multiplication table always in his pocket, sir, ready to weigh and measure any parcel of human nature, and tell you exactly what it comes to. It is a mere question of figures, a case of simple arithmetic.'*
> Gradgrind's methodology explained in *Hard Times*

He is in fact cold, heartless and without sympathy for his fellow beings, a harsh Dickensian caricature of those initially persuasive utilitarian philosophers, Jeremy Bentham and Samuel

PENGUIN CLASSICS
CHARLES DICKENS
HARD TIMES

Smiles. Facts are facts with Gradgrind, and workers are to be ground down. Even his daughter, the typically sweet Louisa, must be denied romance and married advantageously to the oleaginous old lecher **Bounderby**, a fellow businessman in grimy Coketown. Gradgrind's son Tom is put to work in Bounderby's bank but, free at last from his repressed upbringing, he cuts loose and robs his employer. Before Gradgrind is forced to face the true realities of life (that there is more to existence than mere Fact) Dickens gives him memorable opportunities to expound his chilling catechism. Here he declares in 'a plain, bare, monotonous vault of a schoolroom':

> *'Now, what I want is, Facts. Teach these boys and girls nothing but Facts. Facts alone are wanted in life. Plant*

nothing else, and root out everything else. You can only form the minds of reasoning animals upon Facts: nothing else will ever be of any service to them. This is the principle on which I bring up my own children, and this is the principle on which I bring up these children. Stick to Facts, sir!'

The opening paragraph in *Hard Times* sets the mood

Hard Times was serialised on television in 1977, with **Patrick Allen** as Gradgrind.

DORIAN GRAY in *The Picture of Dorian Gray* (1890) by Oscar Wilde

In the novella, Dorian Gray is a Wildean young man about town, debonair and dangerously handsome, whose life of hedonism and sin leaves him enviously unmarked. How can such constant dissipation leave him untouched? Loved and desired by men and women alike, they long to learn his secret which is, as we discover, that he has sold his soul to remain eternally young. While he remains young and beautiful he conceals in his attic a devilish portrait which ages on his behalf, showing in its lined and pock-marked face all the ravages he has escaped. There is a moral to the story, in that when the portrait is destroyed – as in fiction it has to be – the effect is reversed: the broken picture reverts to its painted state and the roué dies with all his scars. But along the way Wilde gives Dorian and his worldly friends clever and seductively witty speeches with which they flaunt the decadent philosophy of the *fin de siècle*.

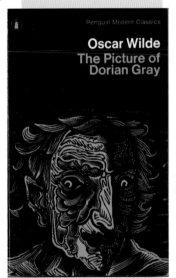

The Picture of Dorian Gray was published in 1890. It was decently filmed in 1945 with **Hurd Hatfield** in the title role (the film directed by Albert Lewin) and remade (a mistake, as usual) as plain *Dorian Gray* in 1970 with **Helmut Berge** in the role. The story was also shown on BBC television in 1976 with **Peter Firth** as Dorian.

GRENDEL & HIS MOTHER in *Beowulf* (anonymous)

Grendel was a pitiless monster which lay waste to terrified Danish villagers until fought by Beowulf in the famous epic of some 3,200 lines. Written in Old English, it would originally have been an oral tale, and is believed to date from the eight century. Rising from the mire and coming out at night, Grendel was an underwater giant in roughly human shape, said to be a son of Cain, who lived beneath the depths with his/its mother and from time to time came up on land to devour human quarry. The

monster seemed invincible until it met Beowulf – who first fought and destroyed Grendel, cutting off his arm, then the following day tackled Grendel's vengeful mother and cut off her head. The simple tale has tremendous power, and remains a vital part of the literature tradition both as an early English text and as an exciting tale in its own right. The text has been updated and retold several times (there is a fine version from Seamus Heaney), and in 2007 inspired a major film (with impressive use of animatronics) starring **Ray Winstone** as Beowulf. It is perhaps most effective when told live by **Hugh Lupton**, Britain's finest exponent of oral storytelling.

GRIPE AND MONEYTRAP in *The Confederacy* (1705)
by John Vanbrugh
Rich but skinflint moneylenders at the heart of Vanbrugh's comedy who fall in love with each other's wives. The comedy revolves around Mrs Gripe's having pawned a necklace to a Mrs Amlet, whose ne'er-do-well son Dick steals it and gives it to his servant Brass to sell on his behalf. Brass, of course, takes it to Gripe, who recognises it. But when Gripe confronts his wife she and Mrs Moneytrap lambast their husbands for their tightfistedness. Throughout all this, Dick Amlet is trying to win the heart of Gripe's daughter Corinna. All ends happily.

JACK HAVOC in *Tiger in the Smoke* (1952)
by Margery Allingham
Havoc is the Tiger of Allingham's tautest thriller. He is a vicious criminal determined on his release from jail to wreak revenge and re-establish himself as king of London's underworld – or at least king of the motley crew of misfits who wait in dread for his return. Off-stage for much of the book, his presence hangs menacingly over every page, so much so that when he finally confronts his enemies (including a barely noticeable Albert Campion) there is an inevitable sense of anticlimax. Until then – and even, to an extent, during the climax itself – the book is a masterpiece of atmospheric, faintly surreal melodrama.
'He was a man who must have been a pretty boy, yet his face could never have been pleasant to look at. Its

ruin lay in something quite peculiar, not in an expression only but something integral to the very structure. The man looked like a design for tragedy. Grief and torture and the furies were all there naked,, and the eye was repelled even while it was violently attracted. He looked exactly what he was, unsafe.'

Havoc appears – more than 100 pages into *The Tiger In The Smoke*

CATHERINE HAYES (William Makepeace Thackeray) see **CATHERINE**

HEATHCLIFF in *Wuthering Heights* (1847)
by Emily Bronte
Many a romantic female heart will protest at Heathcliff's name being listed in this register. He is a romantic villain, but a villain nevertheless, whose villainy is of a kind that men condemn, though women excuse. Emily Bronte's only novel – and perhaps the best of all the Bronte novels – follows a complex timeline and is revealed from different points of view, each of which tells of an obstinate, angry boy, plucked as an orphan from the Liverpool streets and adopted into the family of Mr Earnshaw, to live in a house on the Yorkshire moors called Wuthering Heights. (Wuthering is a dialect word for turbulent weather.) The ungrateful Heathcliff has some cause for resentment in that he is bullied by Hindley, one of the Earnshaw children, but over the years he falls passionately in love with Hindley's sister Catherine. (He does everything passionately.) Heathcliffe, who hasn't learnt not to eavesdrop, thinks he hears Catherine say it would be degrading for her to marry him, so he quits the house. Had he listened a little longer he would have heard her say that she loved him nevertheless.

Time passes and Catherine makes an easy but unfortunate marriage. Then Heathcliff returns. The truculent boy is now an unpleasant young man. He harries and nags at Catherine to such an extent that she dies in childbirth (her husband's child, not Heathcliff's) and, for no apparent motive other than spite, he marries her sister-in-law Isabella. On his rampage of self-centred cruelty Heathcliff makes his wife's life unbearable, plagues the now dissolute Hindley and mistreats Hindley's son until, by an excess of Alpha Male behaviour, he gains control of Wuthering Heights. It all takes time. He pushes the young Catherine, born to his beloved Cathie when she died in childbirth, into marrying the sickly Linton, his own son by Isabella – and again his

WORDSWORTH CLASSICS

EMILY BRONTE

Wuthering
Heights

COMPLETE AND UNABRIDGED

motives are disgraceful: the marriage will give him unfettered control over Wuthering Heights. But Linton dies and the more spunky Catherine Mark Two sets her sights on Hareton, Hindley's son brought up so cruelly by Heathcliff. Heathliffe does what he can to thwart this union, but by now he has become a half mad, quasi-mystic slavering and raving old man who finally dies to clear the way for a belatedly happy ending.

How this mean self-centred bully won the hearts of countless female readers – and decades later, won them again in darkened cinemas – is inexplicable to men of normal sensibility. In 1939 Sam Goldwyn realised that in a film he could make the story more credible by casting an actor with genuine romantic appeal, **Laurence Olivier**, as Heathcliff. In his *Wuthering Heights* (a thoroughly American version but successful) Goldwyn set Olivier against an equally strong **Merle Oberon** as Catherine. That film was a triumph, but its successors have been predictable disappointments. Luis Buñuel made a stylish but unsuccessful attempt in 1953 in which **Jorge Mistral** played Heathcliff; Robert Fuest made a good-looking but over-hasty version in 1970, starring **Timothy Dalton** against **Anna Calder-Marshal**; Peter Kosminsky's 1992 attempt, with **Ralph Fiennes** in the part, is mentioned here only to warn you not to waste your time in watching it. BBC TV can't leave the story alone, with adaptations in 1948 (**Kieron Moore** as Heathcliff), 1953 (**Richard Todd** as Heathcliff), 1962 (**Keith Michell**'s turn), 1967 (**Ian McShane** and his beautiful black hair), 1978 (**Ken Hutchison**) and 1998 saw **Terry Clynes** play Heathcliff when young and **Robert Cavanah** play him as an older man.

URIAH HEEP in *David Copperfield* (1850) by Charles Dickens Where some Dickensian villains burst full-blooded onto the page, Uriah Heep creeps into the story, seeming at first little more than an oily, mealy-mouthed and over-servile clerk. Heep pretends to be both a loyal book-keeper to his kindly employer Wickfield and a friend to Copperfield but is in fact steadily cooking the books to defraud and eventually blackmail his master. At the same time he is spreading slander to discredit the innocent Copperfield. Heep masks his devious practices and 'detestable cant of false humility' with an irritating air of ingratiating servility, frequently rubbing his hands together and describing himself and his low-born family as being 'ever so

'umble' But on one occasion, in a rare moment of candidness, he opens himself to David more than usually:

> *'Father and me was brought up at a foundation school for boys; and mother, she was likewise brought up at a public, sort of charitable, establishment. They taught us all a deal of umbleness – not much else that I know of, from morning to night. We was to be umble to this person, and umble to that; and to pull off our caps here, and to make bows there; and always to know our place, and abase ourselves before our betters. And we had such a lot of betters! Father got the monitor-medal by being umble. So did I. Father got made a sexton by being umble. He had the character, among the gentlefolks, of being such a well-behaved man, that they were determined to bring him in. "Be umble, Uriah," says father to me, "and you'll get on. It was what was always being dinned into you and me at school: it's what goes down best. Be umble," says father, "and you'll do!" And really it ain't done bad!'*
>
> Uriah Heep's training, from *David Copperfield*

Heep was played by **Roland Young** in the superb 1935 film directed by George Cukor and by **Ron Moody** in the 1970 TV movie. The story is in fact a TV perennial, having been made five times, in 1956, 1966, 1974, 1986 and 1999. **Martin Jarvis** was the surprising choice for Heep in the 1974 version, **Paul Brightwell** in 1986 and **Nicholas Lyndhurst** a perspiring triumph in 1999.

MICHAEL HENCHARD in *The Mayor of Casterbridge* (1886) by Thomas Hardy

The title character is a drunken farmhand who sells his wife and baby daughter to a stranger at a country fair before giving up the drink and remodelling himself to become a wealthy man and mayor of the town. Inevitably, the wife returns – eighteen years later – to bring him down again. He is left with only drink for consolation.

In the 1978 BBC2 adaptation by Dennis Potter, Henchard was played by **Alan Bates**.

CAPTAIN HOOK in *Peter Pan* stories (various 1902 to 1911) by J M Barrie

A loud and vigorous pirate captain who seeks to skewer the eternally young **Peter Pan**. He will stop at nothing to entrap him, even kidnapping children to lure him close. Hook met his nemesis in the jaws of the crocodile which snapped off part of his right arm years before and has pursued him patiently ever since.

Though Peter Pan first appeared in Barrie's *The Little White Bird* (1902) Captain Hook had to wait for the stage version, *Peter Pan, or The Boy Who Wouldn't Grow Up*, in 1904, which was, in turn, made into a novel by Barrie in 1911 (actually called *Peter and Wendy*). The story has been retold by others often.

Film versions of *Peter Pan* would not be complete without Captain Hook, and the first such (very much a film of the play) came out in 1924. Disney's extended version in 1953 still stands far above several limper TV versions. **Hans Conreid** provided the voice of both Hook and Mr Darling (a common doubling of the roles). PJ Hogan's 2003 Australian film included a stand-out performance from **Jason Isaacs** in the same doubling of Hook and Mr Darling.

HORNER in *The Country Wife* (1675) by William Wycherley
In Restoration Comedy, the name reveals the character. Horner is the horny libertine who manages to bed an enviable number of women as well as the title character, Margery, Mr Pinchwife's younger spouse, brought to London to celebrate the marriage of Pinchwife's sister Alithea to a Mr Sparkish (who is marrying her mainly for her dowry).

Among those they meet in town is the naughty Horner, who has spread the rumour that he is impotent. It's a claim few men would make about themselves but it makes Horner seem a harmless companion for other men's wives, a ruse he exploits before and throughout the play until, at its climax, various ladies realise they have been sharing Horner's favours. But they can hardly expose the man, so they agree to maintain the fiction of his impotence, thus leaving him free to continue his deceits. (Alithea has meanwhile dropped the inattentive Sparkish for a Mr Harcourt.) The play was attacked at the time for its supposed obscenity, and was revised by David Garrick in 1766 in a ludicrously 'clean' version (*The Country Girl*) from which Horner was excised.

GEORGE HOTSPUR in *Sir Harry Hotspur of Humblethwaite* by Anthony Trollope (serialised 1870)
There are few out-and-out villains in Trollope, but Sir Harry's nephew George comes close (Augustus **Melmotte** and Lizzie **Eustace** are about the only other worthwhile contenders). George is charming but unreliable, a gambler, a cheat, and a man not averse to female company. Sir Harry has made it clear that

his fortune will be left to his daughter Emily (though a man –
even George – would have been the natural inheritor) and Emily,
inevitably, falls for George. She believes she can reform him but
won't marry him without Sir Harry's consent. Before long she is
appraised of George's true character: He has been caught
cheating at cards, is in debt, and has lied to her. George agrees
to abandon his hopes for Emily if Sir Harry will pay off his debts.
The poor girl dies broken-hearted after learning that not only
has he deserted her but he has married his long-term mistress.

ARTHUR HUNTINGDON in *The Tenant of Wildfell Hall* (1848)
by Anne Brontë
Huntingdon is a pathetic drunk more than a true villain. His
interest lies less in his role as the heroine's secret husband than
in it being widely assumed that Anne Brontë based his character
on that of her own dissolute brother **Branwell**. In the book,
Huntingdon's wife has fled from him with her young son to
Wildfell Hall. There her dubious status (she hasn't revealed her
marriage) causes tongues to wag. She falls for the honest
farmer, Gilbert Markham, to whom she eventually has to
confess the truth. Huntingdon finally dies of drink, leaving the
way clear for a happy ending.

BBC television screened the story first in 1968 with **Corin
Redgrave** as Huntingdon, and again in 1996 when he was played
by **Robert Graves**.

MR HYDE in *The Strange Case of Dr Jekyll and Mr Hyde*
(1886) by Robert L Stevenson
Hyde is the *alter ego* of Doctor Jekyll in Stevenson's famous

Sketches for Mr Hyde by E. J. Sullivan

novella. At its simplest level Mr Hyde is a separate
being, a malevolent beast the good doctor turns
into when he partakes of his strange elixir, but as
Stevenson himself makes clear, the Hyde character
is the beast within the doctor, the suppressed self
which is released when all repressions are released
by his mind-altering drug. The mysterious liquid
reveals to Jekyll what he *wants* to do but is too
inhibited to acknowledge. Jekyll is a nineteenth
century doctor, moralistic and censorious, but
once he takes the drug, and while its influence
lasts, all his repressed urges are allowed to surface
and be fulfilled in the guise of a conveniently
separate self, Mr Hyde. *The Strange Case of Dr
Jekyll and Mr Hyde* remains an enjoyable novella

today, a work which has encouraged various sequels, reworkings and dramatisations, as well as numerous analyses and dissertations (usually Freudian) often longer than the original book.

The story appeals to film-makers and, among several silent versions, John S Robertson's 1920 version with **John Barrymore** in the role stands out. Rouben Mamoulian reprised the story with sound in 1932 using the excellent **Frederic March** to play the dual title role, and in 1941 came the version you are more likely to see off-peak today (though it's not as good as Mamoulian's) starring **Spencer Tracy** and directed by Victor Fleming. We will ignore a comic version made in 1995. Back in 1981 **David Hemmings** took on the role in a British TV movie directed by Alastair Reid. A more extensive six-part updating of the story (called simply *Jekyll*) appeared on British TV in 2007 with **James Nesbitt** in the title role.

IACHIMO in *Cymbeline* (written around 1609/10) by William Shakespeare

In a play that is only partly successful, Iachimo is a cynical Roman who accepts a wager from Posthumus (banished to Rome) on the virtue of Posthumus's new wife Imogen (restrained in England). Iachimo travels to England and attempts to seduce Imogen. She resists.

Undeterred, he tricks his way into her bedchamber, hides in a trunk and while she sleeps he discovers a mole in a secret place on her breast. Back in Rome, this information is enough to convince Posthumus that Iachimo has slept with Imogen, and Iachimo wins the wager. The confusion that follows is stoked by disguises, lies, mistaken identities and the apparent death of Imogen (upon whose body is spoken the famous dirge 'Fear no more the heat of the sun') until Iachimo is finally made to reveal how he came by his intimate knowledge. The name Iachimo is said to be a diminutive of **Iago**.

IAGO in *Othello* by William Shakespeare (written 1602, performed 1604, amended till 1623)

Probably the blackest-hearted villain in Shakespeare's canon and motivated by little more than scorn for mankind and a special hatred for his master Othello, the Moor of Venice. Othello, a black man highly respected and promoted to high authority because of his military prowess, is unwise enough to trust Iago, his former right-hand man, even when Iago accuses Othello's blameless young wife Desdemona of infideltity. The seeds of the tragedy are sown in the first scene of the play, when Iago complains to his friend Roderigo that while Othello is feted for his valiant service to the Venetian state he, Iago, his ensign on the field, has been overlooked: Othello has appointed a civilian, Cassio, as his lieutenant. Iago tells Roderigo that though he now hates Othello he will continue to serve him. He warns, 'We cannot all be masters, nor all masters cannot be truly followed. In following him I follow but myself; Heaven is my judge – not I for love and duty, but seeming so, for my peculiar end.' In that same opening scene the two men taunt Desdemona's father in undisguised racist terms. 'Even now, now, very now, an old black ram is topping your white ewe,' Iago tells him, deliberately provoking an immediate confrontation between the senator and the new people's champion. Desdemona placates her father, but Iago assures Roderigo that the marriage cannot succeed; 'It is merely a lust of the blood. It cannot be that Desdemona should long continue her love to the Moor.' For two reasons: 'These Moors are changeable in their wills,' and 'when she is sated with his body she will find the error of her choice.'

Iago continues to inflame the foolish Roderigo by insinuating that Desdemona already has eyes for Cassio: 'The knave is handsome, young, and hath all those requisites in him that folly and green minds look after; a pestilent, complete knave, and the woman hath found him already.' 'I cannot believe that in her,' Roderigo replies, fooled by Iago, as Othello will be fooled, into believing the wildest accusation against the woman he desires. Iago incites him against his own enemy, the hated Cassio, and sets up a drunken fight in which Cassio wounds a senator. Iago reports partially to his master: 'I had rather had this tongue cut from my mouth than it should do offence to Michael Cassio,' he declares piously – but the damage is done, and Cassio is dismissed. Again, such is the power of Iago's oily tongue that Cassio too turns to him for assistance. Iago advises Cassio to have Desdemona plead his cause, and meanwhile Iago slips the first suggestion to Othello that between Cassio and Desdemona lies more than friendship.

Iago: *Did Michael Cassio, when you wooed my lady, know of your love?*

Othello: *He did, from first to last. Why do you ask?*

Iago: *But for a satisfaction of my thought; no further harm.*

Othello: *Why of thy thought, Iago?*

Iago: *I did not think he had been acquainted with her.*

Othello: *Oh, yes, and went between us very oft.*

Iago: *Indeed!*

Othello: *Indeed – ay, indeed. Discern'st thou aught in that? Is he not honest?*

Iago: *Honest, my lord?*

Othello: *Honest, ay, honest.*

Iago: *My lord, for aught I know.*

The first seeds of suspicion. Act III, scene III of *Othello*

Everything is now in place. All Iago needs is some tiny piece of 'evidence' to cement the suspicions against Michael Cassio, and he finds it in the form of Desdemona's handkerchief, dropped by Othello and swept up swiftly by Iago. Othello has two fatal weaknesses: he cannot see evil in Iago, and he cannot see virtue in his wife. Iago finds him brooding on her constancy. He takes his chance:

Iago: *She may be honest yet. Tell me but this.*
    Have you not sometimes seen a handkerchief
    Spotted with strawberries in your wife's hand?
Othello: *Oh, I gave her such a one; 'twas my first gift.*
Iago: *I know not that. But such a handkerchief –*
    I am sure it was your wife's – did I today
    See Cassio wipe his beard with.
        He needs say no more. Act III, scene III of *Othello*

Though Othello's foolish jealousy brings about the inevitable tragedy of the play, it is Iago's unblinking villainy which ensures that the tragedy is inescapable. He engineers a fight between Roderigo and Cassio, and when he sees Cassio easily win the bout he wounds Cassio himself. Othello meanwhile wakes his sleeping bride, confronts her with the handkerchief, and will not accept her innocence. He stifles Desdemona before he learns – from Iago's wife – how he has been fooled. It is too late. Desdemona is dead, Othello kills himself in grief, and Cassio survives. Iago's final words are as defiant as were his deeds:

'Demand me nothing. What you know, you know.

From this time forth I never will speak word.'

The accompanying illustration shows Sir Henry Irving playing Othello at the Lyceum in 1881 when he and the American tragedian Booth alternated the parts of Iago and Othello. Said Harry Furniss who drew the sketch, 'A happy idea that doubled their audience, for if one saw Booth as Othello, one would go a second time to see him as Iago. Irving never did anything finer than Iago.....nor perhaps anything as badly as Othello.'

Irving as Othello.

ITV screened *Othello* as a two-hour Andrew Davies modernisation in 2001 (set in London!) when **Christopher Eccleston** sneered his way effectively through the part – here named 'Ben Jago', against **Eamonn Walker**'s 'John Othello'. The two were Metropolitan policemen competing for the same top job.

Cinema has placed more faith in Shakespeare's original. **Orson Welles** directed a fine 1952 production with himself as Othello and (in an astonishing but successful piece of casting) **Michael MacLiammoir** as Iago. With Welles facing his usual financing difficulties, the film took three years to make, was technically patchy, but was reissued in improved form in 1992. Perhaps the best version was Stuart Burge's 1965 superbly cast film starring **Laurence Olivier** as Othello and a deceptively good-humoured **Frank Finlay** as Iago. But Oliver Parker's 1995 film ran it close (indeed, modern audiences would probably prefer it). In this, the relatively unknown **Laurence Fishburne** played Othello and **Kenneth Branagh** was at his best as Iago. Mention should also be made of Zeffirelli's lovely 1986 film of Verdi's opera (sung in Italian) in which **Placido Domingo** sung Othello and **Justino Diaz** matched him as Iago.

JACK THE RIPPER. *Real-life character*

Though the Ripper was far from fictional, so little is really known about him and so much has been written, that he exists more as a legend than as real. What *do* we know? In less than three months during 1888 several prostitutes were murdered in London's Whitechapel and their mutilated bodies were left with organs crudely removed – not so crudely as to scotch the theory that only a man with medical knowledge could have carried out the crime. His first victim, Annie Chapman, had her uterus cut out. Each of those that followed was similarly treated, with his final victim, Mary Kelly, left lying on a bed with her throat cut, her body slashed with a knife all over, her nose and breast cut off and her entrails pulled out. These were hideous crimes indeed. The Ripper, whoever he was, wrote mocking letters to the Press – thus ensuring that, if the ghastliness of his crimes were not enough to do so – his *nom de plume* was seldom off the news pages. Whether the Ripper himself wrote the letters will never be known (his identity will not either, despite the theories) and it is at least possible that they were the creation of an enterprising journalist. Written in suspiciously literate bad grammar (e.g 'I was goin' to hopperate again close to your ospitle') and addressed to 'the Old Boss' the letters read as if drafted by a melodramatist rather than a criminal. (The 'Old Boss' sounds like a slang term for the police but is a term not listed in Partridge's massive *Dictionary of the Underworld* nor in Ware's *Passing English of the Victorian Era*. It seems more likely to be either a theatrical invention or a sly dig at the author's editor.)

Newspaper accounts at the time revelled in the horror of the crimes, playing down the fact that the murdered women were all, or nearly all, prostitutes, and playing up the genuine gruesomeness of the killings. Here was a ghastly fate that could befall any woman in your family! For some months the newspapers dwelled on and revisited the crimes, hounded the police and waited for the denouement. Once it began to become clear that the murders might never be solved, *and that the killer was still out there,* journalistic imaginations ran riot. Many have suggested their own solution and culprit. Some of the more notable include:

- He was a prominent London surgeon
- He was a butcher by trade
- He was a deranged aristocrat
- He was the Prince of Wales
- He was the artist, Walter Sickert (Patricia D Cornwell's hypothesis)
- He was a Polish Jew (as claimed by the Assistant Metropolitan Police Commissioner at the time)
- He was a body snatcher, or supplier of body parts to the medical trade
- He was an escaped lunatic from Broadmoor (claimed the *Sun* in February 1894)
- He was, beyond doubt, James Maybrick, Mr J K Stephen, Montague Druitt, William Gull, the Duke of Clarence, or a Russian doctor named Konovalov. Or someone else.

Jack the Ripper has featured – often starred – in many books, both fiction and non-fiction, beginning a few months after his short reign of terror with J F Brewer's *The Curse Upon Mitre Square* (1899) and frightening post-Edwardian readers in Mrs Belloc Lowndes's *The Lodger* (1913). Colin Wilson declared him a homosexual sadist in *Ritual in the Dark*, 1960. Peter Ackroyd and Nicholas Meyer have fictionalised him (see films below), as has Iain Sinclair (*White Chapell, Scarlet Tracings*, 1987). Among foreign authors attracted to the story are the American, Robert Bloch and the German, Frank Wedekind. The Ripper lurked behind Alban Berg's opera *Lulu* and Pabst's brilliant silent film of the same name. Serious non-fiction accounts include Don Rumbelow's level-headed *The Complete Jack The Ripper* (1975), Stephen Knight's *Jack the Ripper: The Final Solution* (1976), Shirley Harrison's *The Diary of Jack the Ripper* (1993), Stewart Evans and Paul Gainey's *The Lodger: the Arrest and Escape of Jack the Ripper* (1995) and P D Cornwell's fantastical *Portrait of a Killer* in 2001.

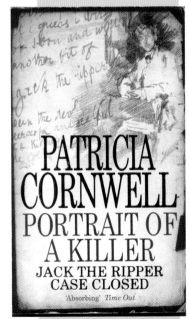

Film versions of the story have linked him with Sherlock Holmes (in the 1976 film *The Seven Per Cent Solution*, directed by Herbert Ross and adapted by Nicholas Meyer from his own novel) and Batman (in *Gotham By Gaslight*). More straightforward accounts have appeared in Robert

Baker's *Jack The Ripper* (1958) and the 1988 TV movie of the same name, written and directed by David Wickes and starring **Michael Caine** as the real-life original investigating officer, Detective Inspector Frederick Abberline of Scotland Yard.

THE JACKAL in *The Day of the Jackal* (1971)
by Frederick Forsyth

So famous did this book and film become that it is easy to forget the main character is a villain, a professional assassin hired by the OAS to kill the French President General de Gaulle. Forsyth

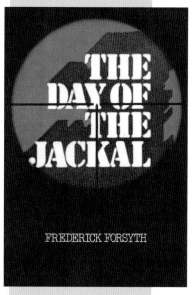

gave himself the seemingly impossible task of maintaining the reader's interest in a story that could have only one ending (since, at the time of publication, de Gaulle was indisputably alive and the Jackal's mission must end in failure). We learn little about the character and background of the Jackal. Instead, we live through every moment as he conducts his meticulous planning and preparation for the deed itself. This concentration on detail, mixed into recognisable contemporary events, thoroughly researched, set the blueprint for Forsyth's later works.

Forsyth claimed to have written *The Day of the Jackal* in a mere thirty-five days – a claim which flabbergasted most fellow authors (and was probably intended to do just that). Said Forsyth, 'I thought I'd write a novel. It turned out to be *The Day of the Jackal*. I didn't realise as I wrote it that it was going to be this big blockbuster which would change my life.' It became a massive best-seller.

The book was filmed in 1973 by Fred Zinnemann, starring **Edward Fox** as the polite but coldly professional Jackal, and was a deserved success. A film 'based on' the screenplay (rather than on the book, which was an odd decision) and called simply *The Jackal* was made in 1997 with **Richard Gere** in the title role. Stay with the original.

SID JAMES

Comic actor who more often than not used his own name (or a pun on it) for his roles – an allowable conceit since he usually played the same lovable cockney rogue. (James was in fact South African.) He made his mark as the nation's favourite villain on radio as 'Sid' in *Hancock's Half Hour* and in the many *Carry On* films. He kept his name for his title role in *Citizen James* (BBC TV 1960) though he dropped the surname for some of his other TV comedy roles. But he never lost his dirty chuckle.

SIR JASPER *Anonymous*
A lascivious (and, one assumes, moustache-twirling) old knight who is the subject of one of the best-known and simplest rugby songs. Each verse consists of just two lines. The first is repeated three times but in each successive verse one word is dropped from the end of the three lines. Hence the affected line begins as 'Oh, Sir Jasper, do not touch me,' becomes 'Oh, Sir Jasper, do not touch … ', and moves from 'Oh, Sir Jasper, do not … ' until its final and deeply expressive 'Oh … '. Throughout the ditty the fourth line remains 'And they rolled between the sheets with nothing on at all'.

DOCTOR JEKYLL (see **HYDE**)

THE JEW OF MALTA in *The Jew of Malta*
(written around 1590) by Christopher Marlowe
Anti-hero of a play rarely performed today, due to its anti-Semitism. The play itself is an exercise in excess. Barabas, a Jewish merchant, counts his 'infinite riches in a little room' and might have stayed in it counting jewels and dreaming romantically had he not, first, been persecuted by local Christians and, second, had all his money confiscated to appease the demands of Turkish invaders. His house is requisitioned and used as a nunnery. It is also where his gold is hidden.
> '*My gold, my gold, and all my wealth is gone!*
> *You partial heavens, have I deserved this plague?*
> *What, will you thus oppose me, luckless stars,*
> *To make me desperate in my poverty?*'
> *The Jew of Malta*, Act I

To retrieve the gold he sends his daughter, Abigail – 'a fair young maid, scarce fourteen years of age' – into their old house to become a nun. After she has retrieved the gold – 'O girl! O gold! O beauty! O my bliss!' – she recoils from her father's growing avarice and returns to the nunnery to become a nun for real. In his fury Barabas becomes the blackest villain and forfeits sympathy. He kills every occupant of the nunnery, including his daughter, with a bowl of poisoned porridge (an unusual murder weapon, seldom used). Knowing that she is dying, Abigail makes confession to a Friar – a confession he cannot reveal.
Abigail: *Pray, therefore, keep it close*
> *Death seizeth on my heart: ah, gentle friar,*
> *Convert my father that he may be saved,*
> *And witness that I die a Christian.* (Dies)

Friar: *Ay, and a virgin too: that grieves me most.*

The Jew of Malta, Act III

Now Barabas rages. He poisons wells. He betrays the Maltese to the Turks, then attempts to assassinate the Turkish commander during a banquet by doctoring the floor so it will collapse under the diners' weight. Playwright Marlowe, for some reason, spares the Turks this dramatic fate but creates a ghastly death for Barabas by having him topple into a cauldron beneath that unstable floor. (It is usually assumed that the cauldron contains more of his poisoned porridge, though the text doesn't make this completely clear. What Marlowe had against porridge remains unknown.)

MRS JEWKES (Samuel Richardson) see **MR B**

DON JOHN (Shakespeare) see **DON**

ELISABETH KANE in *The Franchise Affair* (1948) by Josephine Tey

A plausible villainess, fifteen years old, who claims to have been kidnapped, held captive for several weeks and starved and beaten by two apparently respectable women (mother and daughter) in a somewhat isolated house on the outskirts of a small town. Extraordinary as her story is, it is supported by her physical state – and in any case, why should she lie? She has made no attempt to blackmail the women, and has no history with them that might have led her to seek revenge. Unlikely as her charge is, the police have heard worse, and once the story breaks, the press have a field day. They and the people living nearby hound the accused women who, throughout the book, can find no convincing refutation of the girl's accusation. This simple premise becomes a nightmare for them, one with which many readers can identify – and it is that simplicity which makes both the plot and the ordinary-seeming Elisabeth so chilling. (Tey's story is loosely based on an 18th Century case about a girl named Elizabeth Canning.)

KARLA in *Smiley* books by John Le Carre
A cool and professionally remorseless Russian master-spy who counters and confounds British intelligence agent **George Smiley**. Though he is present in *Tinker, Tailor, Soldier, Spy*

(1965) he has an even greater role in *Smiley's People* (1980). Karla was played by **Patrick Stewart** (Smiley by **Alec Guinness**) in BBC TV's *Tinker, Tailor, Soldier, Spy* (1979). They reprised their roles in *Smiley's People* in 1982.

TOM KING in *Tom King, The Bold Highwayman* by Edward Lloyd (serialised in the 1850s)
The publisher Lloyd ran the King stories in Penny Dreadfuls in the hope of repeating the success found with highwaymen such as **Dick Turpin**. It is unlikely King actually existed, though there was a real-life highwayman called Matthew King. Popular myth had it that Tom King was accidentally shot by his friend Turpin at the Red Lion Inn in Whitechapel. This could have grown from the story in the real-life newspaper *The Evening Post* in May 1737 that *Matthew* King had been shot at the Green Man Inn, near Whitechapel. The paper stressed that King was shot *not* by Turpin (so the rumour had already started) but by the thief-taker known as Bayes.

HOWARD KIRK in *The History Man* (1975)
by Malcolm Bradbury
Anti-hero of Bradbury's most popular work, Kirk is an archetype of liberal but self-indulgent 1970s university education. A radical sociologist who taught at the University of Watermouth (assumed by many to be the University of East Anglia), he is more concerned to advance his career and bed his students than to further their education. Kirk stands for many who reached adulthood in the 1960s but in the following decade allowed their idealism to sour. He is amoral, manipulative, unfaithful – and exasperatingly successful. Bradbury's book was a satire that pinned its subject to the wall like a sheet of flipchart paper.

The book was already a critical success before the 1981 BBC2 TV series made it a popular one also. Christopher Hampton adapted it to bring out its sex, cynicism and humour and the strong cast had **Antony Sher** playing Howard Kirk, **Geraldine James** his wife, and **Isla Blair** the sumptuously sexual social psychologist.

MR KURTZ in *Heart of Darkness* (1899) by Joseph Conrad
The enigmatic Kurtz is a shipping agent sent out to the 'heart of Africa' by his employers years before the book begins and sought now by the story's narrator, Marlow, a somewhat colourless narrator who tells several of Conrad's tales. In this, the best of those stories, Marlow must undertake a hazardous

river journey, deep into unknown and apparently hostile territory, to find his man. Kurtz, whose gainful employment had been to ship ivory to his employers, has, Marlow feels, 'gone native'. In fact he has gone further, beyond assimilation itself: Kurtz has become a despotic, half-crazed ruler of his dark, oppressive, amorphous, ill-defined domain. His rule is barbaric and he enforces it by methods which include human sacrifice. When Marlow finds him he is dying, lost and unrepentant, although his much-quoted final words suggest that at the very end he briefly sees the world – or the world he has created – clearly. 'The horror! The horror!' Kurtz exclaims.

Conrad's novel was the unlikely inspiration for Francis Ford Coppola's epic 1979 Vietnam war movie *Apocalypse Now* starring **Robert Duvall** and **Martin Sheen**, but featuring **Marlon Brando** as a wrecked and mumbling Colonel Kurtz.

LA BELLE DAME SANS MERCI in *La Belle Dame Sans Merci* by John Keats (written in 1819 and published in 1820)
> *'I met a lady in the meads*
> *Full beautiful – a faery's child.*
> *Her hair was long, her foot was light,*
> *And her eyes were wild.'*
> From *La Belle Dame Sans Merci* by John Keats

La Belle Dame is one of poetry's most famous wicked women, the haunting subject of a poem thought of little importance by its author but which became a major inspiration to the Pre-Raphaelites – which perhaps says much about their attitude to femininity. She is a mysterious elfin lady who has bewitched the narrator of the poem, a doomed knight, 'alone and palely loitering'. The poem's morbid but romantic symbolism – and easily remembered lines – have assured it a permanent place among the nation's favourite poems.

LADY AUDLEY see **AUDLEY**

JOE LAMPTON in *Room at the Top* by John Braine (1957)
The anti-hero, rather than out-and-out villain, in Braine's ground-breaking novel, set in a straight-laced and impoverished Britain shortly after the Second World War. Joe, determined to better himself, moves to a northern town in which he works as a book-keeper for the council. In this apparently modest position Joe finds he can use his contacts and ability to influence council contracts and decisions and ingratiate himself

with local businessmen, one of whom has a quiet and unmarried daughter. Joe ditches his recently acquired older mistress, seduces the daughter and makes her pregnant, thus giving her father little alternative other than to accept him as his son-in-law. (Such were the mores of the 1940s.) Joe's success in *Room at the Top* is re-examined in *Life at the Top* (1962) where after thirteen years the marriage of Joe and his wife Susan has grown worse than stale.

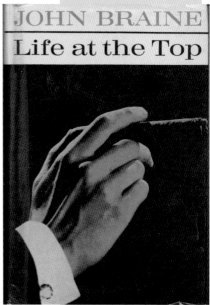

Room at the Top was filmed in 1958 by director Jack Clayton and won great acclaim. Joe Lampton was played with deliberate lack of charm by the icily handsome **Laurence Harvey**. **Heather Sears** played Susan, and **Simone Signoret** contrasted magnificently as Joe's betrayed mistress. Somehow this trio managed to suppress the barnstorming **Donald Wolfit** as Susan's father. *Life at the Top* (1965, directed by Ted Kotcheff) also starred Harvey but with **Jean Simmons** as Susan. It failed to capture the flavour of the first film, as perhaps its makers were aware, since they included flashbacks from *Room at the Top* (the Harvey/Signoret scenes) and these flashbacks were probably the best part of the movie. The film *Man at the Top* (1975, directed by Mike Vardy) starred **Kenneth Haigh** and was a spin-off from the TV series, also called *Man at the Top*, based on *Life at the Top* and screened on ITV in 1970-1972, starring **Kenneth Haigh** as Joe Lampton and **Zena Walker** as Susan.

LICKCHEESE (Bernard Shaw) see **MR SARTORIOUS**

HARRY LIME in *The Third Man* (1950) by Graham Greene
Although Harry Lime makes only fleeting, late appearances in both the film and Greene's novella, he dominates them both. (The book was published in 1950, a year after the film was released in 1949). Lime is a black marketeer who thrived in the Second World War and survives immediately after in the ruins of war-torn Vienna. His racket has been the supply of adulterated medicines, and it is of no concern to him if the let-down drugs he supplies will often fail to serve their purpose and if, in some cases, the patient will die. This callous philosophy is explained in one of the high spots of the film, when Lime (**Orson Welles**) takes his pre-war friend Holly (**Joseph Cotton**) to the top of a fairground Ferris wheel to look down on the crowd below:

'Look down there. Would you really feel any pity if one of those ... dots stopped moving for ever? If I offered you twenty thousand pounds for every dot that stopped, would you really, old man, tell me to keep my money – or would you calculate how many dots you could afford to spare? Free of income tax, old man, free of income tax.

From Greene's script – or Welles's improvisation? – in Carol Reed's film *The Third Man*

But for all his bravado, the post-war Lime is finished. He has nowhere to go. His life is spent flitting between shadows among tumbledown bombed buildings, and by the end of the story he is reduced to scurrying like a trapped rat in the sewers of the city, hunted and outnumbered, unable to escape.

A television series (1959 to 1962) entitled *The Third Man* and starring **Michael Rennie** was entertaining enough but had nothing to do with Greene's creation.

LIVIA in *Women Beware Women* (c.1625) by Thomas Middleton
A useful but dangerous woman to know, if you lived in seventeenth century Tuscany. In the play, Livia first helps her brother Hippolito bed his niece Isabella, then helps the Duke of Florence (Francesco de Medici) bed the wife of a merchant, young Leantio. Leantio's wife, Bianca Capello, should have been chaperoned by her mother, whom Livia has distracted from her duty by playing chess with her. Later, Livia completes the circle by bedding Leantio. Hippolito takes exception to this and kills Leantio, spurring an enraged Livia to reveal his incestuous relationship with Isabella, thus setting up a lethal end to the tragedy.

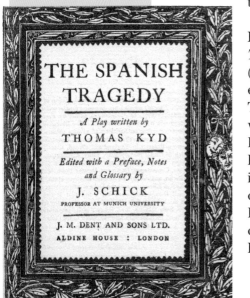

THE SPANISH
TRAGEDY

A Play written by
THOMAS KYD

Edited with a Preface, Notes and Glossary by
J. SCHICK
PROFESSOR AT MUNICH UNIVERSITY

J. M. DENT AND SONS LTD.
ALDINE HOUSE : LONDON

LORENZO & BALTHAZAR in *The Spanish Tragedy* by Thomas Kyd
(written around 1587 and much amended in the ensuing half-century)
The son of Don Cyprian, Duke of Castille, Lorenzo wants their prisoner of war Balthazar (son of the Portugese viceroy, and treated with respect by Lorenzo's family) to be accepted by his sister Bel-imperia as her husband. (This would soothe and cement the relationship between Spain and Portugal following the 1580 war between those countries.) Unfortunately, Bel-imperia loves Horatio, son of Hieronimo, Marshall of Spain. When

Lorenzo and Balthazar discover Bel-imperia and Horatio together at night in Hieronomo's garden they kill Horatio and hang his body from a tree. Hieronomo discovers his son's body (naturally, for dramatic effect) and, in a famous scene, runs mad with grief. Determined to avenge his son, he and Bel-imperia have the murderers revealed by another dramatic convention, the staging of a play within a play. During this play, *Solyman and Persde*, both villains are killed and the mortified Bel-imperia stabs herself and dies. Hieronomo goes mad again, bites out his tongue, then kills himself. Melodramatic as the plot appears, *The Spanish Tragedy* is considered to be **the prototype of English 'revenge tragedy'**, containing what were to become its hallmark ingredients of vengeance, ghosts, a play within a play and lots of gore.

LORD LOVEL in *The Old English Baron* (1777)
by Clara Reeve
It is the medieval 1430s and Sir Walter Lovel has sold the castle he came by illegitimately and has thus disinherited the true heir, the worthy (rather too worthy for some) Edmund Twyford who, on his return to his rightful domicile, finds that every door opens of its own accord to receive him. 'I accept the omen,' he says unsurprisingly. He had in fact made a rather less propitious visit earlier, when the castle was occupied by the man who had bought it from Sir Walter, and on that occasion he spent the night in a haunted chamber, in which 'the furniture, by long neglect, was decayed and dropping to pieces; the bed was devoured by the moths, and occupied by the rats, who had built their nests there without impunity for many generations.' Edmund noticed that the gloomy room had two doors:

> 'He recollected the other door, and resolved to see where it led to; the key was rusted into the lock, and resisted his attempts; he set the lamp on the ground and, exerting all his strength, opened the door, and at the same instant the wind of it blew out the lamp, and left him in utter darkness. At the same moment he heard a hollow rustling noise like that of a person coming through a narrow passage. Till this moment not one idea of fear had approached the mind of Edmund; but just then, all the concurrent circumstances of his situation struck upon his heart, and gave him a new and disagreeable sensation. He paused a while and, recollecting himself, cried out aloud – What should I fear'
> from *The Old English Baron* by Clara Reeve

Unlike most villains in this directory, Sir Walter is almost a minor character in the tale, a villain certainly, and in the latter pages, after his trial by combat, Miss Reeve spends an extraordinary amount of time detailing how his property fraud is put right. Partly because of this, Sir Walter Scott, in his role of critic, complained of her 'grave and minute accounting', but modern critics tend to agree that the book is an important early example of Gothic fiction.

ROBERT LOVELACE in *Clarissa* (serialised in 1748 and 49) by Samuel Richardson

One of the founding rakes of literature, Lovelace lusts after, and eventually rapes, the beautiful heroine in this, **the longest novel in English** – over a million words in all – presented in the form of letters. Some modern readers might say that Lovelace is hardly a villain at all. He certainly has a case. After being rejected as a suitor for her sister he falls in love with Clarissa but is considered unsuitable by her family, who want her to marry a Mr Solmes. Confused Clarissa refuses to marry Mr Solmes and keeps up an impassioned correspondence with Lovelace. After he has helped her escape (or, as he might have thought, elope) he tries to press home his advantage but she, exceptionally virtuous, both refuses him and fails to realise that he has housed her in an upmarket London brothel. He presses harder (but fairly, it must be said) but Clarissa is as determined to keep her virginity as Lovelace is to breach it. Mutual frustration builds (it's a very long novel) until in trend-setting bodice-ripping style he eventually drugs and rapes her. He then repents and offers marriage again. But Clarissa Harlowe will not succumb. She later wilts and dies.

Lovelace is a handsome aristocratic libertine, rich and charming, even if he doesn't have what Clarissa desires (whatever that was), and, to accord with moral sensibilities he eventually meets his doom (in a duel). The book was a huge success, and the modern reader may feel that Lovelace could have had his way with almost any other woman in Europe. Three questions remain. Was Lovelace the villain he was painted to be? Did Clarissa's virtue or her pride prevail? And isn't this pretty much the same story as Richardson's earlier success, *Pamela*? (see **Mr B**.)

LUCIFER. *Traditional*. Another name for Satan, or the devil.

BARRY LYNDON in *Barry Lyndon* (1844)
by William Thackeray
Wicked Irish narrator of the novel variously called *The Luck of Barry Lyndon, Memoirs of Barry Lyndon* or simply *Barry Lyndon*, first serialised in *Fraser's Magazine* four years before the author's *Vanity Fair*. Lyndon is an extremely unreliable narrator, deliberately so, from an author well-known but out of fashion now, who enjoyed displaying himself in the guise of entirely different first-person narrators (a soldier, a snobbish servant, an amiable buffer, the Fat Contributor, et cetera).

Born Redmond Barry, with an unerring instinct for the wrong, Lyndon involves himself in a succession of 'many cruel persecutions, conspiracies and slanders', as he puts it – amusing for the reader but not for his victims. En route from his birthplace, Brady's Town (which he flees after a duel), via Dublin (where he changes his name to Barry Redmond), the army (where he fights ingloriously in the Seven Years War, on both sides, naturally) and a reconnection with his family (in the form of a reprehensible cardsharp uncle) Barry continues an entirely unmerited rise to fortune. His final change of name occurs when he woos and wins the widowed Countess Lyndon. Inevitably, he spends all her money, ruins both her and himself, and ends his days in the Fleet Prison.

Stanley Kubrick's 1975 British film starring **Ryan O'Neal** received mixed notices. No one disputed that it was beautifully shot and obsessive in its detail – but was anything happening in the pretty pictures? Said critic Michael Billington at the time, 'Far from recreating another century, it more accurately embalms it.' Other reviews were kinder – some especially so – but any film about an unscrupulous rogue needs more charisma than O'Neal showed here.

MACBETH & LADY MACBETH in *Macbeth*
by William Shakespeare (written around 1606)
Most villains have started on their path before the story starts, but not this famous pair. The play (Shakespeare's shortest) opens after a battle, with the meritorious generals Macbeth and Banquo meeting three witches on a blasted heath. The trouble begins immediately, when the witches prophesy (in dangerously enigmatic terms) that while Macbeth will become King of Scotland, Banquo's sons will take the throne. When his passionate wife (in every sense) hears of this she urges her hesitant husband (whose nature, she feels, 'is too full of the milk of human kindness') to speed things along by killing off the

present king. This they do, but only after Macbeth has overcome a fit of conscience: 'Is this a dagger which I see before me, the handle toward my hand?' He recognises it as 'a dagger of the mind, a false creation, proceeding from the heat-oppressed brain,' but he knows what he must do. Lady Macbeth drugs the king's servants and lays their weapons beside them as evidence that *they* killed their master. Had the king not resembled her father, she declares, *she* would have killed him. Macbeth kills the king offstage and emerges from the chamber ashen-faced and weak-kneed.

Macbeth: *'I had most need of blessing, and 'Amen' stuck in my throat.'*

Lady M (abruptly): *These deeds must not be thought after these ways. So, it will make us mad*

Macbeth rambles on: *Methought I heard a voice cry, 'Sleep no more! Macbeth does murder sleep.' – the innocent sleep, sleep that knits up the ravelled sleeve of care; the death of each day's life, sore labour's bath, balm of hurt minds, great nature's second course, chief nourisher in life's feast –*

Lady M will have none of this: *What do you mean? You do unbend your noble strength to think so brainsickly of things. Go, get some water and wash this filthy witness from your hand.* She realises what he has in his hand. *Why did you bring these daggers from the place? They must lie there. Go, carry*

them, and smear the sleepy grooms with blood.
    Lady Macbeth is stronger than he, from *Act II, scene II*

    For good measure, they engage murderers to kill Banquo and his son, but the son escapes and, at a banquet of Scottish nobles, Banquo's ghost comes back to haunt Macbeth. For a moment he suspects a trick: 'Which of you has done this?' but when he addresses the ghost, Lady Macbeth leaps in to calm things down: 'Sit, worthy friends: my lord is often thus, and has been from his youth……The fit is momentary; upon a thought he will again be well.' She lies. And in a quick aside she turns on her husband to ask: 'Are you a man?' But Macbeth can't shake the ghost and Lady Macbeth dismisses their guests: 'Stand not upon the order of your going, but go at once.' Left alone together, Macbeth tells her, 'It will have blood; they say, blood will have blood.' Prophetic words. He consults the witches again:

Witches: *Double, double toil and trouble;*
 Fire burn and cauldron bubble.
 Cool it with a baboon's blood,
 Then the charm is fair and good.
Hecate: *O, well done! I commend your pains;*
 And every one shall share in the gains.
 And now about the cauldron sing
 Like elves and fairies in a ring,
 Enchanting all that you put in.
Witch: *By the pricking of my thumbs,*
 Something wicked this way comes.
 Open, locks, whoever knocks.
Enter Macbeth, who cries:
 How now, you secret, black and midnight hags!
 What is it you do?
Witches: *A deed without a name.*
    The witches placate him, from Act IV, scene I

MACBETH

    Macbeth, the victorious general, regains his strength of purpose. When Scottish clan leaders ('Thanes') arise against him he has the wife of their leader, Macduff, and their children killed (leaving the poor actor who plays Macduff to utter one of the worst lines in Shakespeare: 'What? All my pretty chickens and their dam at one fell swoop?'). By now, neither Macbeth nor his flinty wife are strong enough to control a rapidly disintegrating situation. Lady Macbeth has an unexpected attack of conscience and after a famous scene in which she walks and talks in her sleep, wiping her hands to

Irving as Macbeth.

remove imaginary blood and crying, 'Out, damn'd spot, out I say,' she commits suicide, leaving her increasingly fatalistic husband to see the witches' cruel prophesies come true. He would not be defeated, they said, until Birnam Wood arose and came to Dunsinane – but the wily English soldiers ripped branches from the trees and used them as camouflage as they advanced. He could not be killed by man born of woman, they said. But the leader of the invading army, Duncan's son Malcolm, reveals that he was born prematurely, 'untimely ripped' from his mother's womb. Malcolm kills Macbeth and takes the throne.

When Macbeth was written, James the First of England (Fourth of Scotland) had recently come to the throne. He was said to be descended from the real-life Banquo. Thus had Shakespeare made the last of the witches' prophesies come true.

Both Macbeths are parts hungered for by actors. Irving, seen here in Harry Furniss's illustration was, says Furniss, 'a failure in the part from the moment he entered. His reading was wrong: no doubt from a student's point of view it was right to make Macbeth a weak coward, but from a theatrical point of view it was wrong.' That's an assertion about which actors and directors have argued since – was Macbeth a weak man led on by his wife, or was he confounded by his own ambition? Perhaps the Fates themselves were set against him. On stage, many actors have triumphed in the title-role. The famous **Sarah Siddons** (1755 to 1831) was a notable Lady Macbeth as, closer to our own time, was **Helen Mirren**. **Orson Welles** and **Jeanette Nolan** took the parts on screen in an arty 1948 movie which was generally successful, provided you could bear to hear the actors speaking Shakespeare's lines in Bardic Scottish. Roman Polanski's 1971 version was equally bold; both sexy and violent, the film benefited from more than creditable performances from **Jon Finch** and **Francesca Annis**.

MACHEATH in *The Beggar's Opera* (1728) by John Gay
Most famous as **'Mack the Knife'** he was originally the anti-hero of Gay's musical drama and of its less well-known sequel *Polly* (1729). Captain MacHeath was a highwayman who secretly married Polly Peachum and was betrayed by her

criminal father and sent to Newgate prison. MacHeath featured in a number of broadsides and 'Penny Bloods', but the idea of entertaining a conventional theatre audience with a musical drama set among criminals and the lower orders was a novelty in its day. Since then, *The Beggar's Opera* has directly and indirectly inspired many musicals, the most successful of which is Bertholt Brecht's *Threepenny Opera*, written in 1928 in collaboration with the composer Kurt Weill, in which the famous song *Mack the Knife* appears. A film of *The Threepenny Opera* was directed by Pabst in 1931 (remade much later by Wolfgang Staudte in 1965) and was later novelised by Brecht as *The Threepenny Novel*. John Gay's original drama remains far from forgotten: *The Beggar's Opera* continues to be staged and was filmed in 1952 by Peter Brook with **Laurence Olivier** as MacHeath. One of its revivals, Richard Eyre's National Theatre production in 1983 with **Paul Jones** as MacHeath, was shown on Channel 4.

MAD CAREW in *The Green Eye of the Little Yellow God* by J Milton Hayes
 In this famous Victorian stage recitation, Carew is an unwitting villain, committing his crime through sacrilege and disrespect for others' religions.
He was known as mad Carew by the subs of Katmandu,
He was hotter than they felt inclined to tell.
But for all his foolish pranks he was worshipped in the ranks,
And the colonel's daughter smiled on him as well.

To show his love for the colonel's daughter he left the ball at night and crept out to steal the sacred stone for her – but when he offered it:
She upbraided poor Carew in the way that women do,
Though both her eyes were strangely hot and wet.
But she wouldn't take the stone, and Carew was left alone
With the jewel that he'd chanced his life to get.
*

When the ball was at its height, on that still and topic night,
She thought of him and hastened to his room.
As she crossed the barrack square she could hear the dreamy air
Of a waltz-tune softly stealing through the gloom.
*

His door was open wide with silver moonlight shining through;

M

The place was wet and slippery where she trod.
For an ugly knife lay buried in the heart of mad Carew -
'Twas the vengeance of the little yellow god.

It could have been the back-story to *The Moonstone* by Wilkie
Collins.

MADAME DEFARGE (Charles Dickens) see **DEFARGE**

MANFRED in *The Castle of Otranto* by Horace Walpole
(written in 1765)

Villain-hero of the first Gothic tale of terror, a mercifully
short one for which the word melodramatic is an
understatement. (Walpole's embarrassment at having
written it caused him to hide behind the pseudonym
Onuphrio Muralto, which sounds like but appears not to
be an anagram for something more sinister.) Manfred,
the medieval Prince of the eponymous castle – illegally
gained through murder – hopes to marry his son to a
wealthy marquis's daughter. But when he loses the lad to
a supernatural accident he decides to divorce his wife
and marry the girl himself to acquire both her wealth and
another heir. The terrified girl escapes with the help of a
lusty young peasant (who naturally turns out to be
nothing of the sort) and when Manfred confronts the
transformed peasant and stabs the girl he finds that in
his haste he has, in fact, killed his own daughter. In
fulfilment of a prophecy a ghost tears down the castle
and the peasant inherits all.

The book was an enormous and long-lasting success, and
appears never to have been out of print.

MARKHEIM in *Markheim*
(a short story) by Robert L Stevenson
Anti-hero of the tale who murders a shopkeeper on Christmas
Day only to be confronted by a mysterious being who turns out
to be the manifestation of his own conscience. The story is one
of a number illustrating an interest of the day in dual
personalities and the second self.

MASKWELL in *The Double Dealer* by William Congreve
(written and first staged in 1693)
One of the delights of Restoration Comedy is that while puns
can be subtle the names seldom are. Maskwell is the duplicitous

Double Dealer and one-time lover of the flighty Lady Touchwood who now has the hots for the unresponsive Mellefont, her husband's nephew and heir who, to add insult to injury, is about to marry the much younger and more tasty Miss Cynthia Plyant. Lady Touchwood persuades the easily persuadable Maskwell to prevent the marriage. Maskwell fancies Cynthia for himself and goes about his task by suggesting to her father that Mellefont is, in fact, bedding Lady Plyant. For good measure he hints to Lord Touchwood that Mellefont is bedding his lady too, adding strength to his suggestion by the time-honoured ruse of having Lord Touchwood find Mellefont in his wife's bedchamber. The duped Touchwood disinherits Mellefont, Maskwell comforts Cynthia, and all goes to plan until Lady Touchwood realises that her old flame Maskwell intends to marry the younger lass. She gives him a verbal what-for, is overheard by Lord Touchwood, and all the naughtiness comes to naught.

MASTER OF BALLANTRAE (Stevenson) see **DURIE**

MATILDA in *The Monk* (1796) by Matthew G Lewis
Matilda is the wickedly seductive Devil's emissary in this notorious pre-Victorian shocker. She enters a monastery dressed as a boy, poses as a model for the Virgin Mary, and then seduces and thoroughly depraves the young Spanish monk **AMBROSIO**. Having inflamed but not slaked his lust, Matilda urges him to ravish and ruin a young girl and her mother living nearby. (They turn out to be his mother and sister.) Thus the devil's work is well and truly done. After the huge success of this book (never out of print) the author became known as 'Monk' Lewis.

MATILDA in *Matilda* (1907) by Hillaire Belloc
Not to be confused with the entry above. Belloc's *Matilda, Who Told Lies, and was Burned to Death* is from his first set of *Cautionary Tales For Children* (1907). The title tells it all.

LOUIS MAZZINI in the book and (more familiar) film *Kind Hearts and Coronets*
The name is usually forgotten but the character is not. In the perennial film success (directed by Robert Hamer in 1949 and based on a novel by Roy Horniman) Mazzini is the smoothly villainous heir to a dukedom whose inheritance is inconveniently blocked by eight family members with a better claim. What else can a gentleman do but murder them? Mazzini,

impeccably portrayed by **Dennis Price**, works his way through the disposal of them all – with all eight played on screen by **Alec Guiness** – until at last, it seems, the dukedom must be his. *En route* he has an adulterous affair with **Joan Greenwood** and marries **Valerie Hobson**. All is made acceptable, though, by a final twist in which…….well, if you're one of the few people not to have seen the film, go out and find yourself a copy.

MR McGREGOR in *The Tale of Peter Rabbit* (1902) by Beatrix Potter
The scourge of all vermin, especially rabbits, and husband to the equally fearsome (to rabbits) Mrs McGregor ('Father had an accident there; he was put in a pie by Mrs McGregor.'). Peter nearly comes to the same sad end, but escapes without his shoes and blue jacket. McGregor, of course, is the gardener – but to all rabbits, and therefore to many children, is a veritable villain.

THE MEKON in *Eagle* comics (from 1950) conceived, drawn and written by Frank Hampson
Green, dome-headed intergalactic enemy of **Dan Dare** (who was the cover-boy of *Eagle* comic from its inception in 1950 to its demise in 1967, though there have been revivals). The Mekon comes from Earth's neighbour Venus and is a **'Treen'**, an evil race whose main aim seems to be to subordinate or destroy the human race. Having an enormous brain-filled head and tiny body, the Mekon's weak and ugly physique causes him to rely instead on his mighty intellect, which always loses out to Dan Dare's brawn and pluck and refreshingly human resourcefulness.

MELGANIK Radio and TV series
Recurring villain and adversary to the crime-busting heroes in *Dick Barton – Special Agent*. In the short-lived ITV series of 1979 Melganik was played by **John G Heller**.

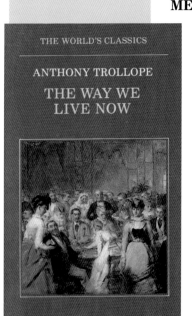

AUGUSTUS MELMOTTE in *The Way We Live Now* (1875) by Anthony Trollope
Melmotte himself was a large man, with bushy whiskers and rough thick hair, with heavy eyebrows, and a wonderful look of power about his mouth and chin. This was so strong as to redeem his face from vulgarity; but the countenance and appearance of the man were on the whole unpleasant, and, I may say, untrustworthy. He looked as though he were purse-proud and a bully.
from *The Way We Live Now*

Melmotte is an enviably rich financier who has only to mention a favoured stock for a stampede of eager speculators to send its price up through the ceiling. When a man of his reputation promotes shares in a Central American railway the public's frenzy knows no bounds. Aristocrats gamble heavily and ordinary folk invest their life savings. Melmotte becomes a Tory MP and mixes with the highest in the land, most of whom respect and fear him. But they do not like him: he is rich but he is commerce, and has something vulgar about him. We readers, of course, can see where this is heading. The rail company is a fraud, and its exposure comes just as his other ventures lose their lustre. It transpires that to

shore up the share price he dipped into his daughter's trust fund. (She, meanwhile, has been thrown around between suitors in the marriage market.) Melmotte's eventual disgrace comes swiftly. Unable to face the shame and repercussions, he comes home drunk from the House of Commons and commits suicide. Thousands of investors are ruined, his daughter Marie who fought gamely to protect her future is cheated by her prospective husband, while the few who spoke out against widespread greed and profligacy gain no reward.

> *'But of course, my dear,' continued Melmotte, 'I had no idea of putting the money beyond my own reach. Such a transaction is very common; and in such cases a man naturally uses the name of some one who is very near and dear to him, and in whom he is sure that he can put full confidence. And it is customary to chose a young person, as there will be less danger of the accident of death. It was for these reasons, which I am sure that you will understand, that I chose you. Of course the property remained exclusively my own.'*
>
> from *The Way We Live Now*

The BBC screened *The Way We Live Now* in a superb production adapted inevitably by Andrew Davies in 2001. **David Suchet** was a magnificent Melmotte, portraying him, correctly, as an over-ambitious businessman rather than a conventional Victorian villain, and **Shirley Henderson** was riveting as Marie.

MENDOZA in *The Malcontent* (1604) by John Marston
A two-timing villain at the heart of Marston's drama, Mendoza is Chief Minister to Genoa's Duke Pietro, and supposed helper to the deposed Duke Altofronto who, as an avenging hero, has disguised himself as the malcontented jester Malvole. Mendoza deposes Pietro, seduces his wife, and tries for the same end with Altofronto's wife Maria. It's all far too complicated to succeed, and in an equally complicated ending the two deposed Dukes combine against Mendoza and unmask him at a ball.

MEPHISTOPHELES or **MEPHISTOPHILIS** in *Dr Faustus* by Christopher Marlowe (published 1604, and revised 1616)

The devil's agent in one of the greatest Jacobean dramas, which is itself based on a medieval legend of the man who sold his soul. The name Faustus is that of an apparently real-life German necromancer Dr Georg Faust in the century before. His story was related in the *Faustbuch* (1587), translated by Marlowe himself as *The Historie of the Damnable Life and Deserved Death of Doctor John Faustus*. In the play, Faustus summons up the devil, who sends his agent Mephistopheles to contract with Faustus to sell his soul to him in exchange for 24 years on earth in which he will be granted anything he desires. Faustus plays the game by asking for everything he can get, including a reincarnation of Helen of Troy (greeted with the line 'Was this the face that launched a thousand ships?') and an interview with Lucifer himself, who displays to Faustus the pleasures associated with each of the Seven Deadly Sins. But as his time on earth runs out, Faustus realises the awfulness of his mistake and tries to broke another deal. Some chance. Marlowe presents Mephistopheles as a highly intelligent villain, differing greatly from those in other Jacobean dramas and, in truth, a more worthy character than the all-too-human Dr Faustus.

MR MERDLE in *Little Dorrit* (1857)
by Charles Dickens
The financier who, people imagine, can do no wrong. He was a familiar enough figure in real life in the nineteenth century, causing thousands to lose their savings, and a type that appears in a number of other Victorian works of fiction (**Melmotte** in *The Way We Live Now* is the most obvious). Merdle arrives in the final quarter of the book, when Dorrit's gullible father

William, released from the Marshalsea debtor's prison by an unexpected legacy, is one of many who believes what the great man recommends. Dorrit loses his money again.

Mr Merdle's right hand was filled with the evening paper, and the evening paper was full of Mr Merdle. His wonderful enterprise, his wonderful wealth, his wonderful Bank, were the fattening food of the evening paper that night. The wonderful Bank, of which he was the chief projector, establisher, and manager, was the latest of the many Merdle wonders. So modest was Mr Merdle withal in the midst of these splendid achievements that he looked far more like a man in possession of his house under a distraint than a commercial Colossus bestriding his own hearthrug, while the little ships were sailing in to dinner.

Behold the vessels coming into port!

… Nobody had the smallest reason for supposing the clay of which this object of worship was made to be other than the commonest clay, with as clogged a wick smouldering inside of it as ever kept an image of humanity from tumbling to pieces. All people knew (or thought they knew) that he had made himself immensely rich; and, for that reason alone, prostrated themselves before him, more degradedly and less excusably than the darkest savage creeps out of his hole in the ground to propitiate, in some log or reptile, the Deity of his benighted soul.

… Three or four ladies of distinction and liveliness used to say to one another, "Let us dine at our dear Merdle's next Thursday. Whom shall we have?" Our dear Merdle would then receive his instructions; and would sit heavily among the company at table and wander lumpishly about his drawing-room afterwards, only remarkable for appearing to have nothing to do with the entertainment beyond being in its way.

Meet Mr Merdle, from *Little Dorrit*

In 1988 Christine Edzard made the definitive film of *Little Dorritt* – two films, in fact, telling the story from two points of view, running to close on six hours in all, and superb throughout. Merdle was **Michael Elphick**. BBC TV produced it as a serial in 2008, with **Anton Lesser** an exhausted Merdle.

TOBY MERES in the TV series created by James Mitchell

When ITV ran *Callan* between 1967 and 1972 the series was in shocking contrast to more conventional portrayals of British Intelligence, with Callan (played by **Edward Woodward**) a tired and errant agent who, as he had become a nuisance to his

RED FILE FOR CALLAN

ORIGINALLY PUBLISHED AS **A MAGNUM FOR SCHNEIDER**
JAMES MITCHELL

employers, was now 'dispensable'. Callan's only friend, it seemed, was the unwashed and odoriferous petty crook 'Lonely' (played superbly by **Russell Hunter**) and among his many enemies the unscrupulous and self-serving fellow agent Toby Meres stood out. Unlike Callan, Meres had been educated in a private school (from which, of course, he had been expelled) and now used his (possibly false) upper class mannerisms and accent both to ingratiate himself with his employers and to irritate and put down Callan. (Lonely was too far beneath his contempt for Meres to bother with.) **Anthony Valentine's** portrayal was so strong that his role grew from conventional upper class rival to almost dual billing with the equally excellent Woodward.

RONALD MERRICK in the *Raj Quartet*
by Paul Scott (four novels published from 1966 to 1975)
Malicious army police officer who runs through Scott's series set in the last days of Britain's Indian Empire (1942 to 1947). Merrick is an uncomfortable man, uncomfortable in his class (he is lower class while the Brits about him are, or appear to be, upper or upper-middle class) in his sexuality (he is a closet homosexual), and in his Britishness (he lives in what he regards as an alien country). As Indian Independence comes ever closer, Merrick's uncompromising attitude and vicious behaviour becomes more pronounced, but in the final book, *A Division of the Spoils*, Merrick himself is murdered – in appropriately unclear circumstances.

The highly-regarded books were serialised on TV in 1984 as *The Jewel in the Crown*, in which Merrick was superbly played by **Tim Pigott-Smith**.

MILLWOOD in *The London Merchant*, or *The History of George Barnwell* by George Lillo (first performed at Drury Lane in 1731)

Millwood: *How do I look today, Lucy?*
Lucy: *Oh, killingly, madam! A little more red and you'll be irresistible. But why this more than ordinary care of your dress and complexion? What new conquest are you aiming at?*
Millwood: *A conquest would be new indeed.*
Lucy: *Not to you, who make 'em everyday.*

Act I, scene II of *George Barnwell*

That the author should identify his heroine by her surname only is an indication of what he thought of her. Millwood (we never learn her first name) is a bold and heartless courtesan who ensnares the naïve eighteen year old George Barnwell in the play of that name and leads him into a life of crime. Millwood, well versed in the ways of men, asks why, when they believe women who've lost their virtue are guilty of the vilest behaviour, men stop at nothing to seduce them of their innocence. As a consequence, 'guilt makes them suspicious and keeps them on their guard; therefore we can take advantage only of the young and innocent part of the sex, who never having injured women, apprehend no danger from them.' This dubious justification does not excuse her corruption of the goody-goody George, who she persuades to rob his employer and kill his uncle. Popular as the play was in its day, young George is unbelievably self-righteous. He exclaims in a soliloquy, 'A thief! Can I know myself that wretched thing, and look my honest friend and injured master in the face? Though hypocrisy may awhile conceal my guilt, at length it will be known, and public shame and ruin must ensue.' Millwood is by far the sparkier of the pair. When they are arrested and she faces execution she makes her final defiant speech:

> Men of all degrees and all professions I have known, yet found no difference but in their several capacities; all were alike, wicked to the utmost of their power.
>
> What are your laws of which you make your boast but the fool's wisdom and the coward's valour, the instrument and screen of all your villainies? By them you punish in others what you act yourselves, or would have acted had you been in their circumstances. The judge who condemns a poor man for being a thief had been a thief himself had he been poor.
>
> Thus have you gone on deceiving and deceived; harassing, plaguing and destroying one another. But women are your universal prey.
>
> Act IV, scene II of George Barnwell

JASPER MILVAIN in *New Grub Street* (1891)
by George Gissing
Milvain is the only successful writer in the group described in this cautionary tale for writers. He is cynical, superficial and sharply aware of what sells and what does not. Marian Yule loves him but he ignores her until she succeeds to an inheritance. He then proposes, but when the legacy fails he

breaks from her and marries the widow of an author whose worthy works never sold. Milvain's philosophy (more in tune with modern publishing, perhaps) is that 'to please the vulgar you must, one way or another, incarnate the genius of vulgarity.' Literature is a trade, and the successful man of letters should be a skilled tradesman: 'He thinks first and foremost of the *markets* ... We people of brains are justified in supplying the mob with the food it likes. If only I had the skill, I would produce novels out-trashing the trashiest that ever sold fifty thousand copies.' But he plumps for the easier option – and becomes a critic. Nothing changes, writers would say.

MISOGONUS in *Misogonus* (written and performed at Trinity College, Cambridge, around 1570).
Author uncertain, but possibly Anthony Rudd
Vice-ridden main character in the play of the same name, which took the story of the Prodigal Son but inverted it to have the Prodigal stay at home and the Good Brother go away. Thus, rather than have the Prodigal's debauchery and misbehaviour occur off-stage, that behaviour formed a large part of the play – and helped earn it a bad name for coarseness and amorality. In an ending more unlikely than that in the bible parable, the return of the good brother, Eugonus, causes Misogonus to repent and presumably to reform.

MISTER MIST in *Sexton Blake* adventures by various authors (Edwardian to 1930s)
Mister Mist, the Invisible Man, was barely a criminal at all. Though nominally a villain he was a decent and sporting opponent (and confusingly, sometimes an ally) to Sexton Blake. He could be a particular nuisance to the government and on one occasion stole the Mace from the House of Commons; on another he revealed that the Chancellor's wife was being blackmailed.

THE MIXER in *The Mixer* (1927) by Edgar Wallace
In his book of the same name Edgar Wallace introduced one of his lesser villains, the thief **Anthony Smith**, known to his underworld companions as The Mixer.

MOLL CUTPURSE in *The Roaring Girl* (1610)
by Middleton and Dekker
In this comedy Moll is a vibrant, sword-wielding thief and forger

who agrees to help the play's hero Sebastian marry his beloved Mary against the wishes of his mean and grasping father. Their plan is to stage a marriage, apparently between Sebastian and Moll, but actually between Sebastian and Mary. His father finds the idea of his son's marriage to the dubious Moll as disagreeable as one to Mary (unsurprisingly) and sends his unpleasant servant Trapdoor to deceive Moll and disrupt their plans. But she is too much for him and the faked marriage goes ahead. Moll is therefore a villain in law but not in practice. In real life Moll Cutpurse was the assumed name of one **Mary Frith** (not the Mary that Sebastian marries!) who, curiously, was not apprehended until two years after the play was staged.

MONEYTRAP (see **GRIPE AND MONEYTRAP**)

THE MONK (see **AMBROSIO**)

MONKS in *Oliver Twist* (1838) by Charles Dickens
Monks is the man behind the mystery in *Oliver Twist*. At first he is introduced into the story in small doses, appearing from the shadows in which he lives. 'The man who was seated there was tall and dark, and wore a large cloak. He had the air of a stranger, and seemed, by a certain haggardness in his look, as well as by the dusty soils on his dress, to have travelled some distance.' The 'haggardness' in his look is a reference to his facial scars, presumably from syphilis, although in a story for family reading Dickens only hints at this indelicate topic. (Mr Brownlow confronts him: '... you, who from your cradle were gall and bitterness to your own father's heart, and in whom all evil passions, vice, and profligacy festered, till they found a vent in a hideous disease which has made your face an index even to your mind.') The confrontation (and revelation) comes late in the book, until when Monk's place in the story has been kept unclear. Only then do we learn Monk's real name, Edward Leeford – and his motive.

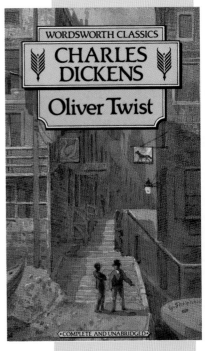

In the great David Lean *Oliver Twist* of 1948 Monks was played by **Ralph Truman**. He was played with brio by **Marc Warren** in ITV's fine 1999 four-part adaptation, and by the up-and-coming villain **Julian Rhind-Tutt** in BBC's fast-moving serial of Christmas 2007.

PHILLIPE de MONTALT in *The Romance of the Forest* (1791) by Mrs Radcliffe (her third novel)

A licentious Marquis who goes to extraordinary lengths to have his way with the spiky Adeline La Motte when a chance accident to her coach compels her to seek refuge in his abbey tower. (Straightforward violence, one feels, would have been simpler.) Adeline has already been cruelly treated by her family but with her response to Montalt she shows herself, arguably, as Gothic fiction's first independent-minded heroine.

MONTONI in *The Mysteries of Udolpho* by Mrs Radcliffe (1794, but set much earlier, at the end of the Sixteenth Century)

Montonoi is one of the great Gothic Novel villains, and towers above the other characters as he tries to have his wicked way with the romantically-named orphan heroine Emily de St Aubert (now his niece, lucky fellow, as he has married her tyrannical but foolish aunt, Madame Cheron). Montoni captures Emily, imprisons her in the gloomy castle of Udolpho somewhere in the Italian Apennines, and afflicts her with a sequence of apparently supernatural trials before she, plucky girl, escapes to the welcoming arms of her true lover, the noble but cash-stretched Chevalier de Valencourt. Her escape is in part due to Montoni's not having his mind fully on the job, as he has spent much of his time pillaging the countryside and harrying poor Auntie to death. In fact, Montoni's supernatural powers turn out to be something of a fraud, since the weird events have all been either set up by him or have earthly explanations. Thus could Mrs Radcliffe's readers enjoy the shivers of the supernatural – because in the end the story had not been hokum. Despite Mrs Radcliffe's status as the First Queen of Gothic, this story is indebted, in part, to Horace Walpole's *The Castle of Otranto* (see **Manfred**). *Udolpho* was one of the main sources for Jane Austen's satire *Northanger Abbey*.

MOONLIGHT JACK Romanticised highwayman who featured in some nineteenth century Penny Dreadfuls.

COLONEL SEBASTIAN MORAN in *The Empty House* (1905) by Sir Arthur Conan Doyle

Second in command to Sherlock Holmes's greatest adversary Moriarty, and, according to Holmes, 'the second most dangerous man in London'. Once it was revealed that Holmes had survived mortal combat at the Reichenbach Falls it was impossible that Moriarty should have survived also, so in the later short story *The*

Empty House Doyle brought Moran to the fore. Moran, as his rank suggests, had been a fine soldier before he turned to crime.

MORDRED *Legendary*
The principal male villain of Arthurian legend, a treacherous knight of the Round Table, who plays a vital role in each variation of the story. In the earliest accounts (Geoffrey of Monmouth's *History of the Kings of Britain*, written in 1137, and Malory's *Morte d'Arthur*, written around 1470) he is the bastard son of King Arthur and Queen Margause (sometimes spelt Margawse or Morgawse or even Morcades) and brother to several other knights: Gawain, Gareth, Gaheris and Aggravaine. Geoffrey of Monmouth complicates the plot further by making Mordred's mother be Arthur's sister. (Further confusion comes from Arthur's sister, in some versions of the tale, being **Morgan Le Fay**.) Mordred (a knight himself) usurps the throne while Arthur is in France, attempts to seduce Arthur's wife (and thus his own stepmother) Guinevere, and fights Arthur for the kingdom on his return, a fight in which each man delivers a fatal blow. Tennyson's version, which must be even further from any truth, sees Mordred (spelt Modred here) expose an adulterous affair between Queen Guinevere and Launcelot. (Other spelling variations include Medrawd, his name in the Welsh *Mabinogion*, and Medraut in the tenth century *Annales Cambiae*, a Latin history which places the fatal battle as occurring in the year 537.)

Cinema has struggled with Arthurian legend. The 1953 version, *Knights of the Round Table*, was dull, and the 1967 film of the stage musical *Camelot* was a disaster. John Boorman's 1981 *Excalibur* was a rather wonderful extravaganza, full of sex, mud and gore, in which the director's son **Charley Boorman** played young Mordred and **Robert Addie** played him fully-grown. Then, of course, there was Cherie Lunghi ...

MORGAN LE FAY *Legendary*
As well as the early versions of the Arthurian legend given in **Mordred** above there are two notable twentieth century book trilogies: first by T H White and later by Mary Stewart. The bewitching Morgan Le Fay plays a larger part in both of these. In every tale, if she appears at all, Morgan is an enchantress or witch, and sister (sometimes half-sister) to King Arthur. Often she is Queen of Avalon, the 'island of apples' to which Arthur's body is carried to rest. In some versions Morgan competes for his love (or at least his bed) with Guinevere. In all versions she plots against him, and in Mallory's *Morte d'Arthur* she steals

Excalibur. She appears in a more benign role in the 1370 alliterative poem *Sir Gawain and the Green Knight*, and in some Celtic legends Morgan is the Lady of the Lake. Most story-tellers now like to make Morgan a beautiful witch, more 'enticing' than Queen Guinevere.

Helen Mirren played a sexy Morgan (named Morgana there) in John Boorman's 1981 *Excalibur*

DOCTOR MOREAU in *The Island of Dr Moreau* (1896) by H G Wells
Evil scientist who conducts experiments to turn animals into humans – a worrying idea from an author who was to develop an interest in eugenics and to maintain that interest even as the Nazis were talking of breeding a master race in the 1930s. Wells was, as ever, before his time, and the various concepts of this story – the mad scientist, the secret island, the mutated animals – would be re-used and adapted by countless other writers.

Irresistible for cinema, *The Island of Lost Souls* was Wells's story in a 1932 film directed by Erle C Kenton in which **Charles Laughton** played Dr Moreau, and *The Island of Dr Moreau* was the 1977 version directed by Don Taylor and starring **Burt Lancaster**.

MORGATANI see The **BLACK MONK**

PROFESSOR JAMES MORIARTY
in several *Sherlock Holmes* stories by Sir Arthur Conan Doyle
The world's greatest detective required a master villain to match him, and Moriarty was that man – 'the Napoleon of crime,' as he is described by Sherlock Holmes in *The Final Problem* (1893). Much of his villainy happens off stage. Indeed, we know of his evil only through Holmes's grim prognostication: 'He is the organiser of half that is evil and of nearly all that is undetected in this great city. He is a genius, a philosopher, an abstract thinker. He has a brain of the first order. He sits motionless, like a spider in the centre of its web, but that web has a thousand radiations, and he knows well each quiver of each of them.' Thus we see Doyle break one of the cardinal rules of fiction writing: show, not tell. Doyle tells us Moriarty is a great villain; he shows us little evidence – except, of course, for that famous showdown at the Reichenbach Falls when both men fall to their apparent deaths. That fall would settle little: Holmes lived, and so did the man who was not with them that fatal day, Moriarty's second in command, Colonel Sebastian **Moran**. (Moriarty

would appear in some later Holmes stories but Doyle set them *before* Moriarty's death in *The Final Problem*.). The two John Gardner books, *Moriarty* (1974) and *The Revenge of Moriarty* (1975), stand out among the various sequels by other authors. Moriarty also appears in *The Infernal Device* by Michael Kurland in 1978.

On stage and screen Moriarty has been too useful to ignore. He returned first in 1899 in a stage play, *Sherlock Holmes*, written by the American actor **William Gillette** (who played Holmes), and he appeared on screen (silently) in 1916 when played by **Ernest Maupin** in *Sherlock Holmes* (against William Gillette as Holmes) and by **Booth Conway** in *The Valley of Fear* (against **H A Saintsbury** as Holmes).

Gustav von Seyfferitz played Moriarty in 1922 (again the film was called *Sherlock Holmes*; John Barrymore was in the title role) and in 1929 **Harry T Morey** played him in *The Return of Sherlock Holmes* (Clive Brook playing Holmes for the first time). Moriarty was heard on screen first when **Ernest Torrence** took over in 1932 (the title *Sherlock Holmes* yet again; the detective, Clive Brook), to be quickly followed by **Lyn Harding** (in *The Triumph of Sherlock Holmes*, 1935, and *Silver Blaze*, 1937, both with Arthur Wontner as Holmes). **George Zucco** was Moriarty in 1939 (*The Adventures of Sherlock Holmes* where he faced **Basil Rathbone as Holmes**). **Lionel Atwill** played him in 1942 in the wartime *Sherlock Holmes and the Secret Weapon* (again against Rathbone), **Henry Daniell** in 1945 (*The Woman in Green*, with Rathbone), **Hans Söhnker** in 1962 (*Sherlock Holmes and the Deadly Necklace*, a German co-production, with **Christopher Lee** as Holmes), **Leo McKern** in 1975 (*The Adventures of Sherlock Holmes' Smarter Brother*, with **Douglas Wilmer** as Sherlock and **Gene Wilder** as Sigerson Holmes) and **Laurence Olivier** in 1976 (*The Seven Per Cent Solution*, in which **Nichol Williamson** played Holmes). Older readers will remember a smooth-voiced Moriarty becoming a mainstay of *The Goon Show* on radio from 1952 to 1960 – programmes which, thankfully, have been repeated somewhere ever since. **Spike Milligan** played Moriarty.

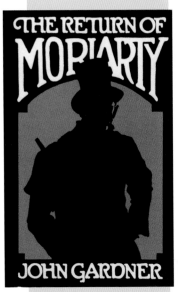

MOSCA see **VOLPONE**

MR MURDSTONE & HIS SISTER JANE
in *David Copperfield* (1849/50) by Charles Dickens
The first and coldest villain in a generally amiable book, Mr Murdstone – a gentleman with beautiful black hair and whiskers

– courted and married the fatherless David's timid young mother.

His hair and whiskers were blacker and thicker, looked at so near, than even I had given them credit for being. A squareness about the lower part of his face, and the dotted indication of the strong black beard he shaved close every day, reminded me of the wax-work that had travelled into our neighbourhood some half-a-year before. This, his regular eyebrows, and the rich white, and black, and brown, of his complexion – confound his complexion, and his memory! – made me think him, in spite of my misgivings, a very handsome man. I have no doubt that my poor dear mother thought him so too.

A child's eye view, from *David Copperfield*

David heard Murdstone laughing with his friends about 'the pretty little widow' while walking with him to a hotel. Murdstone saw David listening and hushed his friends: 'Take care if you please. Somebody's sharp.' David is suspicious, we fear the worst, but there is nothing he can do to stop his mother marrying the handsome stranger. Once married, Murdstone's cruel nature is soon revealed.

'David,' he said, making his lips thin, by pressing them together, 'if I have an obstinate horse or dog to deal with, what do you think I do?'

'I don't know.'

'I beat him.'

I had answered in a kind of breathless whisper, but I felt, in my silence, that my breath was shorter now.

'I make him wince, and smart. I say to myself, "I'll conquer that fellow"; and if it were to cost him all the blood he had, I should do it. What is that upon your face?'

'Dirt,' I said.

Mr Murdstone establishes himself, in *David Copperfield*

Dickens's masterstroke in *David Copperfield* is to give his conventionally dark and hirsute villain a terrifying *sister*, a woman as implacable as her brother.

A gloomy-looking lady she was; dark, like her brother, whom she greatly resembled in face and voice; and with very heavy eyebrows, nearly meeting over her large nose, as if, being disabled by the wrongs of her sex from wearing whiskers, she had carried them to that account. She brought with her two

uncompromising hard black boxes, with her initials on the lids in hard brass nails. When she paid the coachman she took her money out of a hard steel purse, and she kept the purse in a very jail of a bag which hung upon her arm by a heavy chain, and shut up like a bite. I had never, at that time, seen such a metallic lady altogether as Miss Murdstone was.

Enter Miss Murdstone, in *David Copperfield*

Back in 1935 George Cukor made the definitive film, in which the Murdstones had only tiny parts (**Basil Rathbone** was a chilling Murdstone).

Ever popular on TV, *David Copperfield* has been screened in 1956, 1966, 1974 and 1986, all on BBC television. These, and the limp non-BBC 1970 TV film directed by Delbert Mann, were supplanted by BBC's 1999 two-part drama in which the nasty **Trevor Eve** found his metier as Murdstone, supported by the cranky **Zoë Wannamaker** as his sister. A young **Daniel Radcliffe** (before his emergence as Harry Potter) was one of two actors playing Copperfield as a boy.

NAPOLEON in *Animal Farm* (1945) by George Orwell
Prime porker in this political allegory, Napoleon is the leader of the pigs who take over the farm and run it on communal lines under which, although the pigs' original intentions are politically sound, they become increasingly corrupted as they abuse their power. In the allegory, Napoleon clearly represents Stalin, whose corruption of communism is echoed in the book. Napoleon's most famous revolutionary slogan – plastered on the farm walls – is 'All animals are equal, but some animals are more equal than others.' The more noble animals who attempt to stand against their new leaders (notably Snowball and Boxer) are exiled, and the bloated pigs finally make a cynical arrangement of convenience with the farmer they originally deposed (Mr Jones).

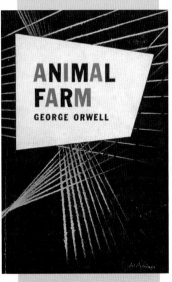

The 1955 cartoon film of the book was a travesty (in that its ending was changed due, reputedly, to the CIA's insistence that the film show the plucky non-communist animals standing up to the reds and being rescued by democracy-inclined outsiders). The film was directed by John Halas, narrated by Gordon Heath, and all the voices were by **Maurice Denham**.

OLD NICK *Traditional*
Another name for Satan, or the devil.

RALPH NICKLEBY in *Nicholas Nickleby* (1839)
by Charles Dickens
Scheming uncle to Nicholas, a money-lender and therefore in Dickens's eyes a miser, Nickleby is in total contrast to his light-hearted and good-natured nephew whose future he attempts to spoil, initially by placing the boy with the ghastly schoolmaster **Wackford Squeers**. He had also placed a lame orphan boy, Smike at the school – but with Dickens and many other nineteenth century authors one watches out for orphans: Smike turns out to be the son of Ralph Nickleby, who only realises his error when the boy has died.

Mr Ralph Nickleby was not, strictly speaking, what you would call a merchant: neither was he a banker, nor an attorney, nor a special pleader, nor a notary. He was certainly not a tradesman, and still less could he lay any claim to the title of a professional gentleman; for it would have been impossible to mention any recognised profession to which he belonged .. He wore a sprinkling of powder upon his head, as if to make himself look benevolent; but if that were his purpose, he would perhaps have done better to powder his countenance also, for there was something in its very wrinkles, and in his cold restless eye, that seemed to tell of cunning that would announce itself in spite of him.

from *Nicholas Nickleby* by Charles Dickens

BBC screened the drama in 2001, with **Charles Dance** playing the villainous uncle. In the 1947 Michael Balcon film directed by Alberto Cavalcanti **Cedric Hardwicke** played Ralph.

DOCTOR NIKOLA in five *Doctor Nikola* books (1895-1902) by Guy Boothby
In a bizarre take on the villain of melodrama, Doctor Nikola is enigmatic, unscrupulous and almost superhuman. His origins are obscure, though in part oriental; where he lives and why he does what he does is not explained; he is a master of disguise and a superb mesmerist; he can charm men and women to obey his will. Nikola also has the essential accoutrement: a vicious and diabolical **black cat**. He appeared first in *A Bid For Fortune* (also known as *Doctor Nikola's Vendetta*) in 1895, quickly followed by *Doctor Nikola*, serialised in *Windsor* magazine in 1896. This story became as lurid and complicated as the three which

followed, with Nikola meeting the narrator on an ocean cruise and luring him into a feverish oriental adventure during which our hero was imprisoned, tortured, hypnotised and chased by maddened Chinamen armed with knives. *Farewell Nikola* closed the series in 1902. Different artists illustrated these hugely successful stories and showed entirely different ideas of how Nikola – or his cat – should look. Their inability to pin him down is, of course, how the Doctor would have wanted it.

DOCTOR NO in *Doctor No* (1958) by Ian Fleming
The villain after whom this James Bond adventure is named. His modest ambition (typical for a Bond novel) is to take over the world. *Doctor No* is the sixth Bond book but became the **first Bond film** (directed by Terence Young way back in 1962). **Sean Connery**, of course, was Bond, James Bond. **Joseph Wiseman** was Doctor No.

O'BRIEN eponymises **BIG BROTHER**

ODDJOB in *Goldfinger* (1959) by Ian Fleming
Vicious hitman assistant to the master criminal **Goldfinger**. Oddjob's preferred method of assassination is to hurl a razor-brimmed bowler hat as others would hurl a frisbee. In the 1964 Bond film Oddjob was played by **Harold Sakata**.

SIR GILES OVERREACH in *A New Way To Pay Old Debts* by Philip Massinger (first performed 1622)
Monstrously avaricious and extortionate, Sir Giles has gained possession of his foolish nephew Frank Wellborn and is in the process of ruining him completely when Lady Allworth (who has her reasons) steps in with a plan to save him. She pretends she wants to marry Frank herself and persuades Sir Giles (his eye ever on the main chance, for she is rich) to advance him money. Her stepson Tom, meanwhile, loves Overreach's daughter but cannot marry her as Sir Giles is determined she will marry the more highly-placed Lord Lovell. Everyone unites in a complex plot to trick Sir Giles, and a happy ending ensues for all – except, of course, for Overreach, who goes mad and is incarcerated. In Massinger's play, Overreach was based on the real-life extortioner Sir Giles Mompesson. The part became a favourite with barn-storming thespians.

SIR WILLOUGHBY PATTERNE in *The Egoist* (1879)
by George Meredith

Despite having a name which makes one think of blue and white china, Willoughby Patterne is *The Egoist* in Meredith's novel. Rich and handsome but at the same time arrogant and egotistical, he spurns the intelligent but fading Laetitia Dale for the more spritely (if misnamed) Constantia Durham who, once she realises the kind of man her fiancée is, elopes with an officer of the Hussars. Patterne then courts Clara Middleton, daughter of a drunken scholar, but no sooner does she accept his troth than she too comes to her senses and tries to escape marrying him. Patterne's pride won't let him be jilted a second time, so their tussle takes up a large part of this long book – long enough for Clara, too, to find another suitor (a poor but honest scholar) – and long enough for the despairing Willoughby to ask sad Laetitia to marry him instead. With dignity she refuses. Curiously, Meredith doesn't end the book with this triple turndown, but has Laetitia finally relent and marry him after all.

PECKSNITH in *Martin Chuzzlewit*
by Charles Dickens (serialised 1843 and 4)

'Mr Pecksniff was a moral man: a grave man, a man of noble sentiments and speech.' Thus does Dickens introduce him ironically in the story. In truth, Seth Pecksmith is not so much a villain as a five-star hypocrite. He earns his living as an architect, schmoozing his clients and exploiting his underlings (passing their work off as his own) and voicing his high moral take on everything beneath his nose. It is typical of the man that he names his two long-suffering daughters Charity and Mercy.

   Martin Chuzzlewit is Dickens's most unpopular book in America and has not been filmed, though it has twice been aired in Britain for BBC TV, first in 1964 and again (a fine production) in 1994 when **Tom Wilkinson** was a splendidly nasty Pecksmith.

PEEPING TOM *Traditional*

Coventry's most famous villain. When the medieval Leofric imposed an unjust tax on the inhabitants of that city, his wife, Lady Godiva, begged him not to do it. He laughingly agreed – but only if she would ride through the streets of the city naked at noon. She took him at his word, and asked the citizens to remain indoors with their windows shuttered as she passed by. Everyone gratefully agreed – except for the all-too-human Peeping Tom. He was struck blind for this sin. Though originally a traditional tale it has been retold frequently, the more famous versions being by Leigh Hunt, Tennyson, and the earlier poet Michael Drayton. The story has inevitably appealed to graphic artists also.

Peeping Tom has become a byword for spying on one's neighbours, and in 1960 inspired a notorious film of that name, directed by Michael Powell and starring **Karl Boehm** as a voyeuristic amateur photographer whose hobby leads him on to sadistic murder. Powell's *Peeping Tom* was so vilified by the press that his career never recovered. The film gained recognition as a minor masterpiece only after Powell's death (though not from all critics).

PETER QUINT in *The Turn of the Screw* (1898) by Henry James
Not to be confused with **Quilp**. Here, in one of James's most accessible stories – one that actually *has* a story – two children in a lonely house catch glimpses of what appears to be the ghost of Peter Quint, an evil if charismatic man who turns out to have once been the lover of their decidedly flaky governess. Quint leads them astray – or is everything that happens imagined by the sexually frustrated, unstable governess?

A cinch for dramatisation, *the Turn of the Screw* was re-titled *The Innocents* in a 1950 William Archibald adaptation made into a seminal 1961 film directed by Jack Clayton in which **Peter Wyngarde** played Quint and **Deborah Kerr** was a magnificent governess. Michael Winner didn't like the original title either, and called his dreadful 1972 extended version *The Nightcomers*; with **Marlon Brando** in the role. The correct title was used by director Rusty Lemorande for his wooden 1992 film and by Benjamin Britten for his 1954 opera which is still performed.

CARL PETERSON in *Bull-dog Drummond* books by 'Sapper'
Bull-dog Drummond's main adversary in a series of four early Drummond novels (probably the best of them; the Drummond series went astray after Carl died). Peterson is an international

criminal, an inventor, a pursuer of women, and is sufficiently unscrupulous to match the far from squeamish all-British hero. Carl is aided, abetted and generally well looked after by his spunky mistress **Irma**. (Drummond himself is variously spelt Bull-dog, Bulldog and even Bull Dog at different times.)

Peterson is his opponent for the first four books in the series, starting with *Bull-Dog Drummond* (1920) and continuing with *The Black Gang* (1922) and *The Third Round* (1924) until Carl meets his doom at the end of the fourth story *The Final Count* (1926). Their confrontations are collected in an omnibus *Bull-dog Drummond: His Four Rounds With Carl Peterson*.

PINCH in *The Comedy of Errors* by William Shakespeare (first performed 1594)
Pinch is described in the play as:
    '... *a hungry, lean-faced villain,*
    A mere anatomy, a mountebank,
    A threadbare juggler, and a fortune-teller,
    A needy, hollow-eyed, sharp-looking wretch,
    A living-dead man.
Which pretty well says all that needs be said.

PINKIE in *Brighton Rock* (1938) by Graham Greene
The teenage gang leader in Greene's novella set in a run-down Brighton. Pinkie is both impulsively violent – to those he thinks that he can master – yet, though he tries to hide it, is terrified of a world he does not understand. He uses his violence and unpredictable recklessness to dominate the rather puny members of his little gang and to impress the girl he hastily marries so she cannot be used as a witness against him. But he is not man enough for her, though she doesn't realise it, and neither is he man enough to face the thugs who are out to get him. Both the book and the film are memorable, though they achieve their impact in different ways. In the book Greene uses a surging, impressionistic prose style which suggests unpredictable swollen tides beating against the Brighton piers and pebbled shore. The film, *Brighton Rock* (1947), was directed by John Boulting and starred **Richard Attenborough**. Shot in dramatic black and white and reeking biliously of its period, it revolves around the magnetic presence of the callow and vulnerable Attenborough. A climactic sequence in which Pinkie, knowing he will be caught and possibly killed, records a cruel farewell message for his trusting bride, is one of cinema's most powerful trick endings.

SIR HARGRAVE POLLEXFEN in *The History of Sir Charles Grandison* (1753-4) by Samuel Richardson

In this book Richardson tried to present a virtuous man (Grandison) to stand beside the virtuous heroines of his earlier books, *Pamela* and *Clarissa* (see Mr **B** and **Lovelace**) and his plot begins with much the same set-up as in those earlier novels. Once again a virtuous young lady (Harriet Byron) is pursued and courted by a licentious would-be lover (Pollexfen) and once again, when she doesn't succumb, he abducts her and carries her off to be locked up in his country manor. Here the story veers off disappointingly from Richardson's earlier successes with Harriet screaming lustily and being overheard and rescued by Sir Charles (gallant, virtuous and rich). Goodness prevails eventually, for Sir Charles is affianced elsewhere, but that second part of the story gets very tedious so I won't bore you with it here.

PRINCE JOHN *Much-maligned real-life character*

In many of the Robin Hood stories Prince John is doubly evil, firstly as the villainous employer of the unscrupulous Sheriff of Nottingham and secondly as temporary overlord of the kingdom during the absence of his saintly brother Richard the Lionheart, away fighting Muslims in the Crusades (*plus ça change*).

Perhaps his earliest appearance on TV was in the popular ITV series *The Adventures of Robin Hood* (1955-9) starring **Richard Greene** as Robin, **Alan Wheatley** as the Sheriff of Nottingham and (perhaps because of other commitments during the long run of the series) three actors as Prince John: **Hubert Gregg**, **Brian Haines**, and finally that arch screen villain **Donald Pleasance**.

ROMNEY PRINGLE in *The Adventures of Romney Pringle* (1902) by Clifford Ashdown

Ashdown never seemed sure whether his Romney Pringle was a villain or hero. Conceived at a time when shady heroes were rather in vogue (roughly concurrent with the more famous **Raffles**) the slippery and insouciant Pringle is loosely engaged as a literary agent cum occasional detective, but is more of a chancer, using the difficulties other people get into – which they sometimes ask him to help solve – as a means of lining his own pockets. Pringle lives as rakish a life about town as his funds will stretch to, but he dresses well, shaves cleanly, and presents an undeservedly respectable air. We will never know for sure whether Ashdown was having a dig at a particular literary agent he knew, or at agents in general, or was simply responding to that readiness of some of the reading public to identify themselves with romantic villains, but he had no trouble in having his Pringle adventures published in the respectable *Cassell's* magazine through 1902 and 1903. Ashdown soon tired of Pringle and reverted to his own name of R Austin Freeman to write a renowned series about the scientific detective, Doctor Thorndyke.

The Adventures of Romney Pringle were collected into a single volume in 1902 (Ward Lock) and remains one of the rarest volumes of crime short stories for collectors. It stood alone until a selection of the later stories was collated as *The Further Adventures of Romney Pringle* in a limited American edition of 1970 (published by Oswald Train of Philadelphia).

QUILP in *The Old Curiosity Shop* (1841) by Charles Dickens
An elderly man of remarkably hard features and forbidding aspect, and so low in stature as to be quite a dwarf, though his head and face were large enough for the body of a giant. His black eyes were restless, sly, and cunning; his mouth and chin bristly with the stubble of a coarse hard beard; and his complexion was one of that kind which never looks clean or wholesome. But what added most to the grotesque expression of his face was a ghastly smile which, appearing to be the mere result of habit and to have no connection with any mirthful or complacent feeling, constantly revealed the few discoloured

fangs that were not yet scattered in his mouth, and gave him the aspect of a panting dog. His dress consisted of a large high-crowned hat, a worn dark suit, a pair of capacious shoes, and a dirty white neckerchief sufficiently limp and crumpled to disclose the greater portion of his wiry throat. Such hair as he had was of a grizzled black, cut short and straight upon his temples, and hanging in a frowzy fringe about his ears. His hands, which were of a rough coarse grain, were very dirty; his finger-nails were crooked, long, and yellow.

From *The Old Curiosity Shop* by Charles Dickens

One of Dickens's most frightening villains, though an utterly non-PC creation today, as two of his menacing characteristics are his small size (he is dismissed by Dickens as a dwarf) and his deformities (he doesn't walk, he scuttles; and he is unable to speak properly). Daniel Quilp is malevolent and odious in every way, and his physical shape personifies his warped nature. He makes his money by lending it and by renting property to desperate souls. Early in *The Old Curiosity Shop* he evicts the saintly Little Nell and her doddering grandfather from their home, and once they are on the road he pursues them – or pursues Nell. We all know why, though it's never stated. Or is it? When her grandfather wants a private word with Quilp to whom he owes money he sends Nell from the room with a kiss on the cheek:

'Ah!' said the dwarf, smacking his lips, 'what a nice kiss that was – just upon the rosy part. What a capital kiss!' Nell was none the slower in going away for this remark. Quilp looked after her with an admiring leer, and when she had closed the door, fell to complimenting the old man upon her charms.
'Such a fresh, blooming, modest little bud, neighbour,' said Quilp, nursing his short leg and making his eyes twinkle very much; 'such a chubby, rosy, cosy, little Nell!' The old man answered by a forced smile, and was plainly struggling with a feeling of the keenest and most exquisite impatience. It was not lost upon Quilp, who delighted in torturing him, or indeed anybody else when he could.

*'She's so,' said Quilp, speaking very slowly, and feigning
to be quite absorbed in his subject, 'so small, so compact,
so beautifully modelled, so fair, with such blue veins and
such a transparent skin, and such little feet, and such
winning ways – but bless me, you're nervous. Why
neighbour, what's the matter? I swear to you,' continued
the dwarf, dismounting from the chair and sitting down
in it with a careful slowness of gesture very different
from the rapidity with which he had sprung up unheard,
'I swear to you that I had no idea old blood ran so fast or
kept so warm.'*

From *The Old Curiosity Shop* by Charles Dickens

In the 1934 film of *The Old Curiosity Shop* Quilp was played by
Hay Petrie, and in Disney's 1995 version he was played by **Tom
Courtenay** (surely too tall?). There was also a bizarre but not
too dreadful musical film, *Mr Quilp*, made in 1975 with (the less
tall) **Anthony Newley** as Daniel Quilp.

ITV served him better for Christmas 2007 when **Toby Jones**
put real menace into the part.

QUINT see **PETER QUINT**

MAJOR QUIVER-SMITH in *Rogue Male* (1939)
by Geoffrey Household
Pseudonym of the enemy agent sent to hunt down and kill the
anonymous hero of Household's best and best-known thriller.
Off-stage for much of the book, but deadly and efficient enough
to send the resourceful hero to extraordinary lengths to escape
him – culminating in his entombing himself in a covered pit
beneath the ground in a spot of moorland where no one can find
him – no one, that is, except the Major. Their confrontation is
inevitable, and wonderfully bizarre.

The book was first filmed as *Man Hunt* directed by Fritz Lang
in 1941 with **George Sanders** as Quiver-Smith, but the 1976
remake, for once, was arguably as good: Robert Florey's *Rogue
Male* starred **Peter O'Toole**, with **John Standing** as Quiver-
Smith.

THE RACKRENT FAMILY in *Castle Rackrent* (1800)
by Maria Edgeworth
In Edgeworth's very readable comic tale, successive generations
of an alternately vicious and dissolute family maintain a
disastrously incompetent and uncaring rule over their Irish land,

tenants and property throughout the sprawling eighteenth Century. The story is briskly told by **one of the first unreliable narrators**, Thady Quirk, the obsequious old retainer for whom the dreadful Rackrents can do no wrong.

A J RAFFLES in various *Raffles* books and stories by E W Hornung

Raffles was the ultimate gentleman thief; a debonair 'character' of the Gay Nineties, good enough at cricket to have played at Lord's, a lady's man and sought-after house-guest, he was, though few others knew it, a brilliant thief. He entered bedrooms, cracked safes and stole priceless jewellery less for its value than for the 'thrill of the game'. The stories are narrated by his friend and occasional (if somewhat reluctant) accomplice Bunny Manders who acts as a kind of authorial conscience by frequently urging Raffles to mend his sinful ways. Manders had joined Raffles reluctantly:

WORDSWORTH CLASSICS
E.W. HORNUNG
Raffles: The Amateur Cracksman
·COMPLETE AND UNABRIDGED·

In his handsome unmoved face I read my fate and death-warrant; and with every breath I cursed my folly and my cowardice in coming to him at all. Because he had been kind to me at school, when he was captain of the eleven, and I his fag, I had dared to look for kindness from him now; because I was ruined, and he rich enough to play cricket all the summer, and do nothing for the rest of the year, I had fatuously counted on his mercy, his sympathy, his help! Yes, I had relied on him in my heart, and I was rightly served.

from *Raffles: The Amateur Cracksman*

There is, to modern eyes, something slightly suspect in Bunny's being so much in thrall to the boy he had fagged for at their boarding school.

Again I see him, leaning back in one of the luxurious chairs with which his room was furnished. I see his indolent, athletic figure; his pale, sharp, clean-shaven features; his curly black hair; his strong unscrupulous mouth. And again I feel the clear beam of his wonderful eye, cold and luminous as a star, shining into my brain – sifting the very secrets of my heart.

from *Raffles: The Amateur Cracksman*

After successful appearances in *Strand* magazine and elsewhere, the first collection, *The Amateur Cracksman* (later re-titled *Raffles: The Amateur Cracksman*) was published in 1899, *Raffles* in 1901, *A Thief in the Night* in 1905 and *Mr*

Justice Raffles in 1909. Hornung also collaborated on two Raffles plays: *Raffles: The Amateur Cracksman* in 1903 and *A Visit from Raffles* in 1909.

Between these, Hornung produced *Stingaree, A Thief in the Night* in which the eponymous Stingaree, working in Australia, tried for the same success as had his English forbear. (Hornung had lived for two years in Australia in the 1880s.) He wrote a number of other books, some poetry, a detective novel *The Crime Doctor* (1914) and in 1919 produced his final book *Notes of a Camp-Follower*. Ernest William Hornung was born in Middlesborough on 7 June 1866, lived at Partridge Green in Sussex and died on 22 March 1921. Other authors have continued the Raffles franchise, most notably Barry Perowne (a pseudonym for Philip Atkey) who contributed numerous Raffles stories to magazines in the Thirties, many of which continued to be collected in book form right through to the 1970s.

Raffles first appeared on screen, bizarrely, in two Sherlock Holmes films made in Denmark in 1908 by the Nordisk Film Company, when he was played by **Holger Madsen**. **John Barrymore** was the first American Raffles, in 1917; **Ronald Colman** the first talking Raffles (in George Fitzmaurice's 1930 *Raffles*); **David Niven** the first English Raffles (in Sam Wood's not quite so good 1940 *Raffles*).

Nastily debonair **Anthony Valentine** starred in a decent 1977 TV series following a 1975 pilot, and **Nigel Havers** had a crack in a TV stand-alone, *Gentleman Thief*, in 2001.

JACK RANN
Rann was a highwayman friend of **Dick Turpin**, and was nicknamed 'Sixteen-String Jack' because he wore eight differently coloured ribbons on each knee.

RASHLEIGH in *Rob Roy* (1817) by Sir Walter Scott
Rashleigh is the wicked cousin and unwanted wooer of Diana Vernon who is in turn loved by Francis Osbaldistone, the awkwardly named hero. When Francis discovers Rashleigh's plans to ruin both him and his father he turns for help to the outlaw highlander **Rob Roy**. Diana and Rob Roy (an astonishingly noble outlaw, far too decent to be entered as a villain here) each do more than the book's hero to defeat Rashleigh's plans. When they expose his villainy and reveal that he embezzled money from Francis's father, Rashleigh turns to the law and betrays Rob Roy. His thanks is to be slain by the outlaw.

One might have expected *Rob Roy* to make cast-iron cinema, but neither the 1953 nor the slightly better 1995 remake have tempered well.

RATCHCALI see **FERDINAND**

RAZUMOV in *Under Western Eyes* (1911) by Joseph Conrad
Guilt-ridden but still a villain, Razumov learns the consequences of one evil deed. He is a student in St Petersburg who betrays a friend, Victor Haldin, an idealist who seeks shelter with him after he has assassinated a minister of state. Sent to Geneva as a secret agent, Razumov is welcomed by the very people he is there to spy upon. Though he has no sympathy with their cause, his guilt increases and eventually he is foolish enough to confess. The revolutionaries don't share his qualms: they attack him and burst his eardrums. He wanders out, now deafened, and doesn't hear the tram that runs him down.

REBECCA see **DE WINTER**

REGAN in *King Lear* by William Shakespeare (written around 1605)
Second of the king's three daughters and one of the play's two evil sisters. After her father has abdicated his power Regan shows neither respect nor gratitude. 'Oh, sir, you are old,' she sneers when he comes to her as guest. 'Nature in you stands on the very edge of her confine. You should be ruled and led by some discretion, that discerns your state better than you do yourself.' Typically for a Shakespearian villain, she has a case – for her aged father has become irrational. Today we might say he has Alzheimer's or an angry senility. But Regan has no sympathy. Far from honouring Lear she orders him about and puts his servant in the stocks. She becomes increasingly imperious, and eventually collaborates with her husband Cornwall in plucking out Gloucester's eyes (Gloucester has sheltered Lear). She conducts an adulterous affair with **Edmund** but falls victim, in the end, to her equally grasping sister **Goneril**, who wants Edmund too.

RICHARD III in *Richard III* by William Shakespeare (first published 1597, though performed c. 1591)

Whatever the historic rights and wrongs (and biographers still argue) Shakespeare's king is evil through and through. But who can resist a villain who stamps on stage to deliver one of the most famous puns in Shakespeare in the play's very first line? ('Now is the winter of our discontent made glorious summer by this *son* of York.') At the opening of the play, Richard Crookback has yet to become king. As Duke of Gloucester and younger brother to the ailing King Edward IV, he will need to remove his older brother George, Duke of Clarence, if he is to inherit the throne. No problem. Richard has Clarence drowned in a butt of Malmsey and, after imprisoning Edward's two young sons in the Tower, he has them murdered also. Three adult rivals – Hastings, Rivers and Grey – are next eliminated. To solidify his claim he 'encourages' the death of his wife – thus leaving him free to marry Edward's daughter Elizabeth (though she at least escapes his clutches). In case Richard's behaviour did not seem bad enough Shakespeare took advantage of dubious historic evidence to portray him as a repulsive limping hunchback. Yet, largely because Shakespeare gave him a series of gloriously sardonic wisecracks and had him share his fears and ambitions in soliloquies that scintillate with black humour and self-awareness, Richard has become one of the Bard's most popular villains. Keeping (roughly) with historic reality, Shakespeare had Richard meet his end at the battle of Bosworth Field when he confronted the Earl of Richmond, head of the rival house of Lancaster and subsequent installer of the Tudors to the English throne. It was in this battle that the defeated Richard was reduced to stalking the battlefield on foot crying, 'A horse! A horse! My kingdom for a horse!'

Of all the barnstorming performances since, the most memorable of modern times was **Laurence Olivier**'s on film. Made in 1955 (directed by Olivier) it remains the archetypal interpretation – so much so that people who never saw the film still imagine Richard as Olivier portrayed him. Stage actors try to play him differently, but whenever they do, no matter how successfully and to what critical laudation, audiences still leave the theatre feeling that somehow this one was not quite how it should be played.

ROGUE RIDERHOOD in *Our Mutual Friend* (1865) by Charles Dickens
A rough and ready, truculent riverside workman who blackmails Bradley Headstone, only to have his generally ineffectual victim drag him to death in the water when he (Headstone) commits suicide. **David Bradley** was memorable in the part in BBC's 1998 four-part adaptation.

MONSIEUR RIGAUD in *Little Dorrit* (1857) by Charles Dickens
A Belgian scoundrel (he may have murdered his wife) who comes into possession of a box of incriminating papers entrusted to **Ephraim Flintwinch** and uses them to squeeze money from the equally flinty **Mrs Clenham**. But no good comes of it, and in a climax of near supernatural retribution he meets his doom in the ruins of her house when it collapses on him. His minor part in the book was expanded for the BBC TV serial of 2008, when **Andy Serkiss** was a sinister Riguad.

TOM RILEY in *The Blue Lamp* (1949)
The man who shot George Dixon. In the climax to the not-at-all-bad film directed by Basil Dearden, honest PC Dixon (played, of course, by Jack Warner, yet to become established as TV's **Dixon of Dock Green**) was shockingly killed by a cheap little punk (Tom Riley) played against type by one of British cinema's greatest heartthrobs, **Dirk Bogarde** (then very young and relatively unknown).
Riley: 'Get back! This thing works. Get back! Get back, I say!'
PC Dixon does not respond.
Riley shoots – twice: bang, bang. Dixon falls to the ground.
from *The Blue Lamp*

The film is famous both for Bogarde's selfless and convincing performance and for its having apparently killed off one of TV's longest running characters before his series had begun.

THE RINGER Almost simultaneous book and play
The Ringer (1929) by Edgar Wallace:
Who had not heard of The Ringer? His exploits had terrified

R

London. He had killed ruthlessly, purposelessly, if his motive were one of personal vengeance. Men who had good reason to hate and fear him had gone to bed, hale and hearty, snapping their fingers at the menace, safe in the consciousness that their houses were surrounded by watchful policemen. In the morning they had been found stark and dead. The Ringer, like the dark angel of death, had passed and withered them in their prime.

From *The Ringer* by Edgar Wallace

One of Edgar Wallace's greatest successes, *The Ringer* began as a play, *The Gaunt Stranger*, written by Wallace in 1925, then adapted by him with the help of Gerald du Maurier, and re-titled. *The Ringer* is a melodrama, no less enjoyable for that, and the description of its eponymous anti-hero above is from the novelisation written by Wallace in 1929 to follow the play's success in 1926. Ever prolific, Wallace followed this book immediately with *The Ringer Returns* (aka *Again the Ringer*) also published in 1929. The Ringer (real name **Henry Arthur Milton**) is a master criminal who, in a neat twist to the conventional crime plot, chases the lawman, a dubious lawyer involved in his sister's death. The Ringer has such confidence in his own skills that he announces in advance that he will kill the lawyer at a specific time. The police determine to thwart him but … he is the Ringer!

The Ringer was staged at Wyndham's Theatre on 1 May 1926, the week of the General Strike, and for the company to succeed with a play under those conditions was a coup indeed. Frank Curzon, who financed it, made £30,000 from the original production but Wallace received only £7,000 in royalties, half of which he insisted in making over to du Maurier. Wallace learnt from this and in the following six years earned more than £100,000 from his later, usually less effective, plays. In its cunning denouement the play shares a trick with London's longest-running play of any kind, *The Mousetrap*. That trick, and the general story, was Wallace's own but he never hid his debt to du Maurier. His dedication printed in the novelisation reads: "My dear Gerald: This book is 'The Gaunt Stranger' practically in the form that you and I shaped it for the stage. Herein you will find all the improvements you suggested for 'The Ringer' – which means that this is a better story than 'The Gaunt Stranger'. Yours, Edgar Wallace."

The first film version was *The Ringer* in 1931 starring **Patrick Curwen**, and the best version was *The Gaunt Stranger* (1938) starring **Sonnie Hale**. **Donald Wolfit** reprised the part in *The Ringer* in 1952.

ROLLO in *The Bloody Brother, or Rollo, Duke of Normandy*
by Fletcher, Jonson, Chapman & Massinger (first performed
around 1616 but not published till 1639)
Evil son of the Duke of Normandy. To ensure or enlarge his
legacy, Rollo kills his brother Otto and threatens death to
anyone who stands between him and his intended ends. When
he adds the benevolent tutor Baldwin to his done-to-death list,
Baldwin's daughter Edith plans to kill him in revenge, but
feminine scruples cause her to hesitate at the crucial moment.
Fortunately the brother of another of Rollo's victims
arrives in time to do the deed himself.

Barnaby Rudge
*with an introduction
by Peter Ackroyd*

Dickens

MR RUDGE in *Barnaby Rudge* (1841)
by Charles Dickens
Initially a mysterious stranger but eventually revealed to
be the innocent but slow-witted Barnaby's father. Unlike
his son, Mr Rudge is a murderer (he killed his employer,
Reuben Harewood, and a gardener, whose disfigured
corpse is assumed to be Rudge's) and he is a tormenter of
his wife. *Barnaby Rudge*, one of Dickens's least popular
stories, was published in 1841, immediately after *The Old
Curiosity Shop*. Both stories ran in serial form in *Master
Humphrey's Clock*, a multi-tale magazine format started
by Dickens but which he eventually abandoned.

RUPERT OF HENTZAU in *The Prisoner of Zenda*
(1894) by Anthony Hope
*Then a young man jumped out from behind the trunk of
a tree and stood beside us. As I looked on him, I uttered an
astonished cry; and he, seeing me, drew back in sudden
wonder. Saving the hair on my face and a manner of
conscious dignity which his position gave him, saving also
that he lacked perhaps half-an-inch – nay, less than that, but
still something – of my height, the King of Ruritania might
have been Rudolf Rassendyll, and I, Rudolf, the King.*
from *The Prisoner of Zenda*

This enjoyable tale of Ruritanian swashbuckling sets Rudolf
Rassendyll, a witty and courageous Englishman, against Rupert,
his amusing but dastardly doppelganger, in a bid for the Ruritanian
throne. Rassendyll's involvement comes from their strong physical
resemblance, so much so that the beautiful Princess Flavia falls
for him. Rupert was too likeable a rogue to be killed off quickly, so
he survived into a sequel, *Rupert of Hentzau* (1898).

Douglas Fairbanks was a magnificent Rupert in David O Selznick's excellent 1937 film, against **Ronald Colman** as Rudolf. Richard Thorpe's 1952 remake with **James Mason** as Rupert and **Stewart Granger** as Rudolf was great fun, but the 1979 remake was entirely unnecessary. One can have too much of a good thing.

Rupert Hentzau was in his trousers and shirt; the white linen was stained with blood, but his easy, buoyant pose told me that he was himself either not touched at all or merely scratched. There he stood, holding his bridge against them, and daring them to come on; or, rather, bidding them send Black Michael to him; and they, having no firearms, cowered before the desperate man and dared not attack him.

from *The Prisoner of Zenda*

SILAS RUTHYN (see UNCLE SILAS)

LORD RUTHVEN in *The Vampyre, A Tale* (1816)
by John William Polidori

Claimed by some to be the first literary manifestation of a vampire. Lord Ruthven is the 'vampyre' at the beating heart of Polidori's short story written at the Villa Diodati on Lake Geneva for that famous story-writing contest in 1816 when Mary Shelley wrote *Frankenstein*. (Polidori was Lord Byron's secretary.) There were only three entries to the contest: Polidori's *The Vampyre, A Tale*, Byron's unfinished and therefore ineligible *A Fragment*, and Mary Shelley's superb *Frankenstein*.

Lord Ruthven is a vampire in a pre Bram Stoker mould, though he shares some characteristics. Why, when he appeared in society, did he create a sense of awe? 'Some attributed it to the dead grey eye, which, fixing upon the object's face, did not seem to penetrate, and at one glance to pierce through to the inward workings of the heart; but fell upon the cheek with a leaden ray that weighed upon the skin it could not pass.' Ruthven's motives are somewhat different to those of the later Dracula. He seeks out the fair and innocent, that he might tempt, corrupt and then abandon them. The sinful he rewards, 'when the profligate came to ask something, not to relieve his wants, but to allow him to wallow in his lust, or to sink him still deeper in his iniquity, he was sent away with rich charity.' The fair and innocent he ruins: *... he had required, to enhance his gratification, that his victim, the partner of his guilt, should be hurled from the pinnacle of unsullied virtue, down to the lowest abyss of infamy and* *degradation: in fine, that all those females whom he had sought, apparently on account of their virtue, had, since his departure, thrown even the mask aside, and had not scrupled to expose the whole deformity of their vices to the public gaze.*

From *The Vampyre, A Tale* by Polidori

FEDERICO ANDAHAZI
The
Merciful Women
Translated by Alberto Manguel

Though Polidori's tale is sometimes credited as the first vampire story, it is clear from the text that Polidori assumes his reader has already heard of vampires and will know what a vampire does. Vampires had, after all, haunted central European mythology for centuries. But Polidori extends the usual simple premise of an undead creature sucking blood purely in order to preserve its own existence to one where the 'evil one', while it does indeed suck and depend on blood, is equally determined to root out goodness and to corrupt whatever it can.

A particularly imaginative (and outrageous) re-imagining of that famous contest at the Villa Diodati can be found in Federico Andahazi's book *The Merciful Women*, translated from the Spanish and published by Doubleday in 2000.

MR SARTORIOUS in *Widowers' Houses* (1892)
by Bernard Shaw
Winner by a short head as the most villainous character in the play. Introduced to us as a wealthy self-made businessman, Sartorious has a daughter, Blanche, who the respectable Harry Trench would like to wed. Sartorious will consent only if his daughter is accepted as an equal by Trench's aristocratic family. Sartorious is then shown to be a usurious slum landlord, but when Trench spurns him Sartorious reveals that a substantial part of Trench's own income comes from the same source. In fact, Sartorious and his rent collector **Lickcheese** collect some of his rents for him. Trench had never concerned himself as to the sources of his income. After a degree of dramatic coming and going, Trench and Blanche (no saint herself) do marry, and everyone accepts the commercial realities – which require, according to Shaw, 'fattening on the poverty of the slum as flies fatten on filth.'

SAURON in *The Lord of the Rings*
by J R R Tolkien (published in 1954 & 5)
Sauron is the Dark Lord and potential master of Middle-Earth

and his stronghold is the fearsome Mordor. He was the owner and hence *Lord* of the Rings, whose Ring of Power fell into the hands of Bilbo Baggins in *The Hobbit* (1937) and is passed on to Frodo Baggins (Bilbo's son) in the ensuing trilogy, which took 12 years to write. The trilogy concerns Sauron's attempts to wrest the ring from Frodo as the plucky young hobbit and his companions undertake their quest to thwart him by disposing of the ring in the Crack of Doom – inconveniently located inside Mordor. Sauron's wicked helpers include **Saruman** the magician, the **Orcs**, the **Lord of the Nazgûl**, and **Shelob** the giant spider.

SCHEDONI in *The Italian, or the Confessional of the Black Penitents* (1797) by Ann Radcliffe
From the author of *The Mysteries of Udolpho* (see **Montoni**) comes this archetypal evil monk (monks are a favourite villain in Gothic novels). Schedoni is easily the most interesting character in this Gothic pot-boiler. Being both a monk and a bandit helps. He gets up to the usual Gothic mischief, capturing

fair Ellena and whisking her off to his nunnery where, never satisfied, he is about to kill her when he realises (or thinks he realises) that she's his daughter. But there are more twists to come ...

SCROOGE in *A Christmas Carol* (1843)
by Charles Dickens
Fiction's most famous reformed villain. A grasping old miser and tyrannical employer of Bob Cratchit, a clerk who is only grudgingly allowed a holiday on Christmas Day, Scrooge is 'visited' on Christmas Eve by three Ghosts of Christmas: Past, Present and Yet To Come. The ghosts take him on dreamlike journeys in which, invisible, he can look upon his life and judge the effects of his behaviour on other people. In these sentimental journeys Scrooge comes to realise the error of his ways. He sees how heartless and despicable he has become – whether his victims say so or not – and when the ghosts have gone (or when he wakes) he finds it is the morning of Christmas Day. He still has time to make amends.

A Christmas Carol was the author's annual 'Christmas Book' for 1843 and by far the most successful. The story has been staged, televised, parodied and filmed. A classic BBC radio version starred **Sir Ralph Richardson** as Scrooge, and their TV version in 1999 starred **Patrick Stewart**.

Film versions include *Scrooge* (1935) directed by Henry Edwards with late-Victorian thespian **Sir Seymour Hicks** in the title role; *A Christmas Carol* (1938) directed by Edwin L Marin with the forgotten **Reginald Owen** making a decent stab at the part; *A Christmas Carol* (1951) directed by Brian Desmond-Hurst with **Alastair Sim** as the definitive Scrooge in undoubtedly the best film version; *Scrooge* (1970) directed by Ronald Neame as a musical, with **Albert Finney** over the top and not at his best; *A Christmas Carol* (1984) directed by Clive Donner with **George C Scott** heading a largely British cast in a well-made TV movie; and *Scrooged* (1988) directed by Richard Donner as a modern-day satire on big business with **Bill Murray** unable to save a leaden Christmas pudding of a movie. There will be more.

BASIL SEAL in *Black Mischief* (1932)
and *Put Out More Flags* (1942) by Evelyn Waugh
An at times engaging, at times too cynical, well brought up young man who, in the first book, helps an ex-Oxonian school friend, Seth, in his role as self-appointed Emperor of Azania, where he enforces ludicrous reforms. In the course of these escapades Basil cheats, seduces and eventually dines upon the flesh of Prudence, the ambassador's inaptly named daughter. Having lived by the law of the jungle and survived all that West Africa can throw at him, Basil returns to a disinterested London at the end of the 1930s to continue his adventures in *Put Out More Flags*. In the first year of World War Two (the phoney war) Basil announces himself as a billeting officer, a role which allows him to accept bribes from well-off families who have no wish to accommodate **the Connollys**, a family of appalling evacuees. During the war, says Basil, the last thing he wants to do is fight for his country. Rather, he will be 'one of those people one heard about in 1919; the hard-faced men who did well out of the war.' In both comic novels Basil Seal is amoral, callous, selfish and a generally nasty piece of work. But Waugh clearly loved him and, despite yourself, you can't help liking the fellow too. Blast his eyes.

ARTHUR SEATON in *Saturday Night and Sunday Morning* (1958) by Alan Sillitoe
It may seem a little harsh to call Arthur a villain but he does sleep with his friend's wife while the friend works a night shift,

and his attitude to work would seem villainously anarchic to his employer. Seaton is perhaps the best-drawn working class hero or anti-hero in the post-war raft of Angry Young Men novels and plays. Working in a Nottingham bicycle factory with few prospects beyond it and little to look forward to other than Saturday night drunkenness and snatched casual sex, he has more to be angry about than have the heroes of other novels of the time. His pugilism and cheerful bloody-mindedness remains authentic on the page today.

Saturday Night and Sunday Morning was splendidly filmed in 1960, directed by Karel Reisz and it provided a break-through for **Albert Finney**, who was memorable as Arthur. The film, like the book, was an archetypal social drama, probably the best of its kind. It must have helped that Sillitoe wrote the script.

JOHN SELF in *Money* (1984) by Martin Amis
A monstrous, self-loathing director of successful but hideous films and (mainly) TV commercials who floats like a bloated carcass on a scummy sea of money and 1980s excess. He lives in a world that many yuppies might have thought they'd envy – trans-Atlantic business flights, top hotels, film studios, complacent starlets and models, self-styled film stars, media tycoons and, ultimately, plush but lonely hotel bedrooms. The novel itself (in which Martin Amis himself is a character) is a deliberately overblown satire of that money-mad decade.

BECKY SHARP in *Vanity Fair* (1847/8)
by William Makepeace Thackeray
The full title is *Vanity Fair : A Novel Without A Hero*. Becky is an enormously engaging villain (to many readers the heroine) of Thackeray's finest novel (and to many readers again, his only good one) which was written as a serial in 1847 and 1848 and was illustrated throughout by the author. Becky is first encountered when she is released from an academy for young ladies, an establishment at which she has not been allowed to forget she is almost penniless (an artist's daughter). As she rides away she determines to succeed in the world – which she does, on a roller coaster ride which cocks a snoot at Victorian values. She succeeds by her wits and feminine guiles. Pert and pretty, she encourages men to fall in love with her, whether she is married at the time or not. She marries twice, first netting her employer's son (a better choice than the old man himself who lusted after her) and then the honest soldier Dobbin, who is unable to reform her. The good Dobbin, and Becky's good (in both senses) friend Amelia Sedley

are an obvious contrast with pert Becky but, good as they are, they lack all her colour and appeal. Most Victorians preferred Becky. Thackeray clearly did, but he knew his duty, and by the end of the tale his perky heroine cum villainess had come down in the world – but only after lots of adventures and lots of fun.

After a lack-lustre attempt in 1932 to film the story (*Vanity Fair* directed by Chester M Franklin, with **Myrna Loy** as Becky) Hollywood changed the title for their 1935 Rouben Mamoulian film, calling it *Becky Sharp* instead (with the title role performed by **Miriam Hopkins**). This was a better effort, but remains in the record books mainly as the first full Technicolor feature. Producers then avoided the book for years, until Julian Slade made it into a stage musical in 1962. Mira Nair directed a not-bad version in 2004 with the emphasis on comedy, in which **Reese Witherspoon** made a far better job of Becky than anyone had expected.

BBC TV first cast **Joyce Redman** as Becky in 1956, then scored a big success with **Susan Hampshire** as a delicious Becky in a 1969 serial, which they followed in 1998 with another tip-top six-part production (written inevitably by Andrew Davies) starring **Natasha Little** in the role.

JACK SHEPPARD. Real-life villain, subsequently fictionalised Sheppard was a thief and petty criminal whose real fame came from his uncanny ability to break out of custody – to such an extent that it was said that 'no jail could hold him'. Born in Stepney in 1702, orphaned at the age of one and brought up in a workhouse, he robbed his first employer and came under the influence of '**Edgeworth Bess**' (the prostitute Elizabeth Lyon) who gave him a real thief's education. Cunning as he was, Sheppard couldn't avoid being captured several times. He was sent to St Giles's Roundhouse, to the New Prison and eventually to the condemned cell of Newgate Prison. He escaped from them all, and his escape from Newgate required him to climb a blocked chimney, break through several doors, scale the roof and lower himself to the ground outside by means of a blanket rope. On another occasion he escaped via the governor's house:

Jack visits his mother in Bedlam. (Cruikshank, 1839)

He passed silently down the first flight of stairs, but in turning the banisters his chains clanked – he heard the voice of a young woman exclaim, 'Lord! What's that?' A man in a tender voice replied, 'Nothing my love but a dog or cat.' Jack thought he heard a kiss follow the speech, but he stayed not to hear farther; but he turned back, and waited for a couple of hours. All was quiet, he again descended. Just as he reached the same spot as before, the drawing-room door opened, he heard a gentleman take leave and go downstairs followed by the maid-servant with a light: he followed swiftly down and hid himself behind an abutment at the bottom of the stairs. He hard a whispering in the passage; he heard a struggle and a kiss. 'Happy people,' thought he. 'You little think what an unhappy wretch you have near you.' The street-door opened and shut, the maid-servant passed by him, smiling and setting her cap to rights as she ascended the stairs. He got into the passage when he heard her in the room above, he unfastened the door, and was once more in the streets of London: thus accomplishing one of the most hazardous and extraordinary escapes upon record.

from *The Life and Adventures of Jack Sheppard*,
anonymous 1845

Over-confidence did for him. He eventually drove in an open coach past Newgate Prison wearing gorgeous stolen clothes, after which he drank too much and was recaptured. His subsequent execution, when he was a mere twenty-two, drew a crowd of two hundred thousand people. In riots after his hanging, troops had to quell the crowd. The Dictionary of National Biography later said that sermons for some time afterwards urged the faithful to emulate him spiritually by 'ascending the chimney of hope to the leads of divine mediation'.

The anonymous story quoted above competed with a fanciful *History of Jack Sheppard* by John Williams in 1839 and *The Life of Jack Sheppard* in 1840. (In the former, Bess is an innocent lass cheated out of her inheritance.) Another early book about Sheppard was by Daniel Defoe, and a significant biography written by Harrison Ainsworth appeared in *Bentley's Magazine* in 1839. These accounts competed with more lurid ones, including the version which had Jack married to Edgeworth Bess and sharing a room with her in the New Prison. (His escape was made using a rope fashioned from her underclothes.) In an 1837 tale he associated with the youthful **Blueskin**. The more time passed from Sheppard's death the more fantastical became the stories. By 1911, in an Aldine Boy's Library version, Jack had become a captain in the army, was engaged for a hundred guineas by a dubious baronet, and consorted with confederates such as **Sixteen-String Jack** and **Half-Hanged Smith**. By 1947 he had become the subject of a rather flat radio drama on the Home Programme (*The Bowl of St Giles*).

SHERIFF OF NOTTINGHAM *Traditional*
Principal villain in the many stories of **Robin Hood**. Hood's main adversary, the Sheriff, who as a lawman is only doing his job, is normally portrayed as cruel and scheming, sometimes downright dishonest. Whether Hood actually existed remains conjectural. If he did exist he seems as likely to have haunted the England's North East as Nottinghamshire, but whatever the facts of the matter (which by now we will never know) the stories place Hood and the Sheriff firmly in Nottinghamshire's **Sherwood Forest**. The tales date from the fourteenth century, from when a medieval legend survives in the form of five poems and part of a play. (A Yorkshire Pipe Roll mentions a 'Robertus Hood fugitivus' as early as 1230.)

In the several film versions of the story **Alan Rickman** (in the 1991 *Robin Hood: Prince of Thieves*) has a good claim to the best Sheriff of Nottingham and **Roger Rees** the funniest (in the 1993 *Robin Hood: Men in Tights*). **Robert Shaw** was wasted as the Sheriff in Richard Lester's *Robin and Marian* (1976) – a good idea that didn't come off – with the scene set twenty years later and ancient rivalries still being fought out by somewhat ancient protagonists. **Sean Connery** played Robin.

For many television viewers ITV's long-running *The Adventures of Robin Hood* (1955-9) was the classic Robin Hood series. It starred **Richard Greene** as Robin and **Alan Wheatley** as the Sheriff – whose boss, the evil **Prince John**, was played by three actors over the run of the series: **Hubert Gregg**, **Brian Haines**, and finally that arch screen villain **Donald Pleasance**. **Nickolas Grace** played the Sheriff in HTV's *Robin of Sherwood* between 1984 and 1986. The BBC made a comedy series for children, *Maid Marian and her Merry Men* in 1989 and again in 1993 in which **Tony Robinson** played the sherriff. A different kind of comic nastiness was added by **Keith Allen** in the BBC's anachronistic 2007 version, in which **Jonas Armstrong** played Robin Hood.

SHYLOCK in *The Merchant of Venice* by William Shakespeare (written 1596-8)

Was he a villain? Until the twentieth century it was a question seldom asked. Shylock, like Fagin, was an evil Jew, an obvious villain, the character to hiss throughout the play. But Shakespeare's villains were rarely wicked through and through (any more than his heroes were wholly decent) and any intelligent examination of the text reveals that Shylock was a much put-upon man, used but derided by fellow citizens, betrayed by his daughter and at no time treated like a human being. Even the trial scene at the end is weighted against him, with the fair Portia allowed to win the case by a barely legal and clearly unreasonable stratagem.

At the start of the play Shylock (much in demand by merchants at this point) is persuaded by the cash-struck Antonio to lend money against the supposed certainty of his ship coming in. Shylock, who knows the vagaries and risks of shipping, wants firm collateral and strikes a bond whereby if the money is not repaid within three months he can slice a pound of flesh from Antonio's body. Antonio is unwise enough not to realise that, no matter how unlikely an eventuality, one should never pledge one's life on it. Despite his confidence, his ships founder and the debt falls due. He cannot pay and Shylock refers him to his bond. Antonio won't – or cannot – negotiate, and it is left to Portia, the wife of his best friend, to argue his case for him in court. (She appears dressed as a man.) Her stratagem is to insist that Shylock takes exactly a pound of flesh, and only flesh, and without shedding a drop of

blood (since blood was not in their agreement). This dubious argument wins (how could it fail, in a court arranged against him?) and Shylock loses half his property to Antonio and half to the state, on the (equally dubious) grounds that he had sought the life of a

Venetian citizen. The play is a comedy, so all ends happily, with Antonio's share of the money being transferred to Shylock's eloping daughter (Jewish she may be, but she eloped with a gentile) after which comes the sudden announcement that, after all, Antonio's ships are safe.

The first sympathetic portrayal of Shylock was as long ago as 1741, when **Charles Macklin** astonished audiences – and, no doubt, some fellow actors – by showing Shylock's dignity under disparagement and revealing the justice of Shylock's case.

> *Hath not a Jew eyes? Hath not a Jew hands, organs, dimensions, senses, affections, passions? … If you prick us, do we not bleed? If you tickle us, do we not laugh? If you poison us, do we not die?*
>
> Shylock the man: from *The Merchant of Venice*

BILL SIKES in *Oliver Twist* (1838) by Charles Dickens
A stoutly-built fellow of about five-and-thirty, in a black velveteen coat, very soiled drab breeches, lace-up half-boots, and grey cotton stockings, which enclosed a very bulky pair of legs, with large swelling calves – the kind of legs that, in such costume, always look in an unfinished and incomplete state without a set of fetters to garnish them. He had a brown hat on his head, and a dirty belcher handkerchief round his neck, with the long frayed ends of which he smeared the beer from his face as he spoke. He disclosed, when he had done so, a broad heavy countenance with a beard of three day's growth, and two scowling eyes, one of which displayed various parti-coloured symptoms of having been recently damaged by a blow.

from *Oliver Twist* by Charles Dickens

Sikes is quite possibly Dickens's nastiest villain. He stamps out of the shadows in *Oliver Twist* and would have dominated the book had **Fagin** not been there too. Sikes is utterly violent, with no redeeming features – despite which he is loved by his dog and the luckless Nancy. The scene near the end of the book when he murders her is genuinely shocking, and became one of the author's most celebrated public readings.

In the 1948 David Lean film Sikes was played by a melodramatic but scary **Robert Newton**. Earlier versions include a silent film

directed by Frank Lloyd in 1922 and a forgettable 1933 movie directed by William Cowen. Sikes softened a little when he was portrayed by **Oliver Reed** in *Oliver*, the 1968 Carol Reed film of the 1960 Lionel Bart musical. The non-musical *Oliver Twist* was remade in 1982, a film directed by Clive Donner, and there was a Disney cartoon version, *Oliver and Company*, in 1988 in which Oliver became a cat and the Dodger a dog.

Andy Serkis played Sikes in the 1999 Alan Bleasdale adaptation for ITV and Nancy was played by **Emily Woof**. BBC's 2007 soap opera serial version cast **Tom Hardy** in the part.

LONG JOHN SILVER in *Treasure Island* (1883) by Robert Louis Stevenson

Along with Barrie's **Captain Hook**, Long John Silver is not only a pirate but has become one of Britain's most loved villains, perhaps because he features in a book remembered nostalgically from childhood, or perhaps simply because he is a pirate, for whom the nautical British have always had an unjustified affection. Hook lost a hand; Long John lost a leg. In Stevenson's story, Long John (in the guise of a cook) and his pet parrot **Captain Flint** trick their way onto the good ship *Hispaniola*, where he befriends the innocent young hero of the tale, **Jim Hawkins** who – coincidentally or is it? – has set out on a quest to find the lost treasure of a certain Captain Flint. (The parrot Flint is given to screeching 'Pieces of eight! Pieces of eight!' at intervals, to which Silver replies with authentic-seeming but bowdlerised salty seaman's slang.) Jim overhears Long John and his confederates planning to mutiny and seize the treasure and, in a stirring if bloody fight, he helps the rest of the crew defeat the pirates. The treasure is located on the island with the aid of another colourful character, the marooned Ben Gunn.

In Victor Fleming's vigorous *Treasure Island* of 1934 the flamboyant Silver was played by the almost as brilliantly named **Wallace Beery**. In the 1972 John Hough version he was played by **Orson Welles**, and in a decent 1990 TV movie, directed by Fraser Heston, Long John was credibly presented by the director's father **Charlton Heston**. Incredibly, all three big names were upstaged by an even bigger ham, **Robert Newton**, in the classic Byron Haskin 1950 film and its follow-up *Long John Silver*, in 1953.

Television versions have included *The Adventures of Long John Silver*, a 1957 ITV serial made in Australia, in which **Robert Newton** reprised his role and young **Kit Taylor** played Jim Hawkins. The BBC screened a serial version of *Treasure Island* in 1978 with **Alfred Burke** in the role, and followed it with a 1986 variant set ten years later, *John Silver's Return to Treasure Island*, with the rumbustious **Brian Blessed** in the part.

SIXTEEN-STRING JACK (a pseudonym for **Jack Rann**)

HAROLD SKIMPOLE in *Bleak House* (1852-3)
by Charles Dickens
Skimpole scrapes through life, scrounging on his friends and repaying them with malicious gossip and minor dishonesties, but survives through a combination of feckless good humour and appeals to his benefactors' good nature. A slight character, who hides his selfishness behind a veil of childish simplicity, he is perfectly content to hover in the background as long as he is in the warm and within sight of his next meal. As such, he barely scrapes into this collection of more dastardly villains, although at one point his mischief-making turns the plot. He brought real-life trouble to his creator, when Dickens was accused of basing the character too closely on people he knew – specifically, his writer friend Leigh Hunt and the outspoken artist and critic Benjamin Robert Haydon. Later editions of *Bleak House* bore a preface from Dickens denying that Skimpole was a portrait of Leigh Hunt. (He didn't apologise to Haydon who, by that time, was dead.)
   BBC TV has screened *Bleak House* three times – in 1959, 1985 and 2005. **T P McKenna** played Skimpole in 1985 and **Nathaniel Parker** was a surprising hit (given Skimpole's unsympathetic nature) in the sensational 'soap opera' version of 2005.

DANIEL SKIPTON in *The Unspeakable Skipton* (1959) by Pamela Hansford Johnson
An author's revenge, perhaps, upon who knows whom among her rivals. (Rumour has it that the target was the flamboyant 'Baron Corvo' aka Frederick Rolfe.) Skipton, as the title suggests, is unscrupulous and craven, an incompetent pimp, rogue and conman – and a would-be writer. He is immersed in the production of what he – and only he – is convinced will be a masterpiece. Chronically short of funds, he wastes a good deal of writing time in attempts to con money from a party of tourists

in Bruges, a bookseller (who, naturally, is sharper than he), and a likely-looking Count. The bookseller uses the Count to trick and sink the unspeakable Skipton.

JOSHUA SMALLWEED in *Bleak House* (1853)
by Charles Dickens

Smallweed is a grotesque minor character, the head of a dreadful family of mean-minded graspers. He is a money-lender and, when the opportunity arises, black-mailer – 'a leech in his disposition, he's a screw and a vice in his actions, a snake in his twistings, and a lobster in his claws'. Though part crippled and confined to a makeshift wheel-chair, Smallweed's cunning and ferocity make him all the more dangerous, and his attempt to blackmail Sir Leicester Dedlock is foiled only by the assiduous Inspector Bucket. Smallweed's wife is a drowsy drudge, perpetually falling asleep by the fire; his son Bartholomew a grubby young clerk; and his daughter Judy is as tight-faced as her father – she is described as having never owned a doll, and having never played at any game.

The character is a gift to an actor. When Bleak House was televised in 1985 Smallweed was played by **Charlie Drake**. In the nation-gripping 2005 'soap opera' version scripted by Andrew Davies the actor **Phil Davis** stole every scene he entered, pushed along on his rickshaw by the fearsome Judy (played by the wonderfully sneering **Loo Brealey**) to whom he would irritably bark 'Shake me up, Judy' – a line from the book that TV developed into a catch-phrase.

ANTHONY SMITH (see The **MIXER**)

NATHAN SPIKER (see **TURPIN**)

SPRING-HEELED JACK by several authors
A cross between the highwayman Dick Turpin and the thief and jail-breaker Jack Sheppard who, like a bogeyman, could spring up almost anywhere, making him the nineteenth century

equivalent of one of the indestructible opponents of Batman, Superman or any of the American graphic comic anti-heroes. Spring-Heeled Jack originated in a real-life scare of 1837, when stories sprang up of London being plagued by a satanic fire-breathing character with horns, a tail, bat-like wings and massive body. Penny Dreadfuls leapt at the story and to the coat of hair running down his back they added a pair of devil's horns sprouting from his forehead. Their supernatural Spring-Heeled Jack manifested himself in thunderstorms and flew on bat-like wings. His nickname came originally from his supposedly having springs inserted into the heels of his boots, allowing him to both outrun and outleap any normally shod pursuer. Meanwhile, in real-life London, enough women complained of his having scared them (he was never reported to have actually assaulted them) that the Lord Mayor ordered special constables to look out for him. Before long, appearances were reported throughout the south and Midlands.

The story became more fabulous with each telling until inevitably it faded, apart from one or two revivals some fifty years later. He was a nineteenth century figure, too fantastical to survive long into the twentieth century, and after a number of highly varied appearances in Victorian tales such as the anonymous *Spring-Heeled Jack, the Terror of London* and a four-act drama of 1863 entitled *Spring-Heeled Jack, or The Felon's Wrongs* he faded to a close in an ill-fated *Spring-Heeled Jack Library* from the Aldine Publishing Company in 1904. Jack's sworn adversary by then was the supposed Thief-Taker **Jonathan Wild**.

WACKFORD SQUEERS in *Nicholas Nickleby* (1839)
by Charles Dickens
Typically appalling school headmaster of the aptly named Dotheboys Hall who, as his name suggests, believes in robust punishment of young boys.
Mr Squeers's appearance was not prepossessing. He had but one eye, and the popular prejudice runs in favour of two. The eye he had was unquestionably useful, but decidedly not ornamental, being of a greenish grey, and in shape resembling

the fanlight of a street door. The blank side of his face was much wrinkled and puckered up, which gave him a very sinister appearance, especially when he smiled, at which times his expression bordered closely on the villainous. His hair was very flat and shiny, save at the ends, where it was brushed stiffly up from a low protruding forehead, which assorted well with his harsh voice and coarse manner. He was about two or three and fifty, and a trifle below the middle size; he wore a white neckerchief with long ends, and a suit of scholastic black, but his coat sleeves were a great deal too long, and his trousers a great deal too short; he appeared ill at ease in his clothes, and as if he were in a perpetual state of astonishment at finding himself so respectable.

from *Nicholas Nickleby* by Charles Dickens

In Michael Balcon's production of 1947, directed by Alberto Cavalcanti **Alfred Drayton** was Squeers to **Derek Bond's** Nicholas.

STARLIGHT NELL
Romanticised highwaywoman who featured in one or two nineteenth century Penny Bloods.

STEERPIKE in *The Gormenghast Trilogy* (1946, 1950, 1959) by Mervyn Peake
In the three books that make up this epic comic fantasy, *Titus Groan*, *Gormenghast* and *Titus Alone*, Steerpike rises from kitchen servant boy to dubious regency. He plots with two of Titus's sisters to acquire their brother's inheritance, burns a library (there is no greater crime), lies, manipulates, plots a rape and carries out gruesome murder. *Titus Alone* is primarily about the life of Titus, heir to the kingdom.

BBC2 screened *Gormenghast* in 2002 as a fine four-part drama. **Jonathan Rhys Meyers** played the unstoppable Steerpike in a star-studded cast of principally comic actors.

SUBTLE (Ben Jonson) see **FACE**

SVENGALI in *Trilby* (1894) by George du Maurier
Svengali's name is known to millions, and those who have never read Du Maurier's short novel assume he is little more than a manipulative hypnotist. In the book he is a sinister musician (a

Jew, all too often used cast as villain in stories of the time) who takes the young and impressionable singer Trilby O'Ferral and trains her via hypnosis to sing more beautifully than she has ever sung before. At the peak of her short and brilliant career Svengali dies. His dark influence dies with him and Trilby finds herself unable to sing. Indeed, she loses her voice altogether. The book became an enormous success and remained so till the First World War.

In the year following publication **Herbert Beerbohm Tree** played Svengali on stage. Film versions began in the silent era, with **John Barrymore** on top form as the first talking Svengali in a film directed by Archie Mayo in 1931. *Svengali* was remade in 1954 (directed respectfully but turgidly by Noel Langley) with the ultra-theatrical **Donald Wolfit** in the role. A TV movie *Svengali* was made in 1983 by Anthony Harvey with **Peter O'Toole** in the part.

FRANK THORNEY in *The Witch of Edmonton* (c.1621)
by Rowley, Dekker & Ford
One half of the plot of this tragi-comedy (the non-witch half) concerns the bigamous Thorney who, having married Winifred, then marries Susan Carter. (His father insists that Frank's inheritance depends upon it.) Having thus done his duty, Frank murders Susan and tries to throw blame on two of her previous suitors. He fails and is duly executed.

SQUIRE THORNHILL in *The Vicar of Wakefield* (1766)
by Oliver Goldsmith
Archetypal villainous squire in a complex but enjoyable tale of misfortune and deception. Thornhill pretends to help the impoverished vicar, Dr Primrose, but seduces the vicar's daughter and pretends to marry her. He has a serious crack at the brother's ex-fiancée too, while trying to pack the brother himself off into the army. The ruined sister runs away but, after much tribulation, is brought back by her father, at which point Thornhill calls in the vicar's debts and has him thrown into jail. When the vicar's son challenges him to a duel, Thornhill has him imprisoned too. He then abducts the second daughter. Nevertheless, by the intercession of a fairy-tale good uncle, all the victims come to happiness and Squire Thornhill loses everything.

CECIL THOROLD in *The Loot of Cities* (1905)
by Arnold Bennett
A less stylish gentleman thief than **Raffles** but with acceptably

Robin Hood principles, who makes his appearance in Bennett's 1905 short story collection.

GENERAL TILNEY in *Northanger Abbey* (1818)
by Jane Austen
The assumed villain (assumed by the credulous heroine, Catherine Morland) in Austen's pastiche Gothic novel, Tilney's place in this volume is due to his villainy being almost entirely in her imagination. Catherine, swept away by the romantic thrills induced by Gothic novels such as *Mysteries of Udolpho*, misinterprets Tilney's crumbling family home as a Gothic castle of imprisonment or worse, and Tilney himself as an English **Montoni**. Tilney is an irascible old grump. Believing – erroneously – that despite what he first imagined, Catherine is without money and therefore no fit match for his son, he treats her rudely and orders her from his house. By the time she leaves, Catherine is convinced he is a monster, but his son Henry rushes after her to make a suitably romantic declaration. When General Tilney discovers that Catherine does have money after all, his attitude changes. Hardly commendable, but far from villainly.

The BBC screened *Northanger Abbey* in 1986 with **Robert Hardy** as General Tilney, while in Granada's 2007 version **Liam Cunningham** had the part.

SWEENEY TODD by Thomas Peckett Prest and others
The inspiration for the Demon Barber of Fleet Street can be traced back to a fourteenth century murderous Scottish barber, **Sawney Bean**, and to at least two barber cum pie-maker enterprises from France (one in the fourteenth, one in the eighteenth century). In the second, better documented, real-life case (recorded in Monsieur Fouché's *Archives of the Police* and subsequently in newspapers either side of the Channel) a barber in the Rue de la Harpe in Paris was found to have a basement beneath his shop linked to a popular pie-maker's next door, in which were found some three hundred human skulls and a string of pearls belonging to one of the missing customers. Some decades later the story was rediscovered, probably from a mention in the **Newgate Calendar**, but debate continues as to by whom. Perhaps someone translated it (freely) from the French – and George Augustus Sala has been suggested. But most authorities credit a prolific hack writer, Thomas Peckett Prest, who was one of those who helped construct the mountain of **Penny Dreadfuls** published by Edward Lloyd in the 1840s. Some authorities put the authorship with James Malcolm Rymer

rather than Prest, but this seems unlikely; Prest almost certainly originated the series, while Rymer jumped on the band wagon – though Prest was also an acknowledged plagiariser of Charles Dickens (probably contributing to Lloyd's quickly produced *Penny Pickwick*, *Oliver Twist* and *Martin Guzzlewit*) and he also claimed, unlikely as it seems, to have been related to the Dean of Durham.

The story came out as a Lloyd shocker, *The String of Pearls (A Romance)*, in the 1840s published in a staggering ninety-two parts (it was originally billed as a mere 18). In 1847 one of the most famous Victorian melodramas, initially called *A String of Pearls, or The Fiend of Fleet Street* and later *Sweeney Todd, the Demon Barber of Fleet Street*, by George Dibdin Pitt, was staged at Hoxton's Britannia Saloon.[1] The story was too good to be left alone, and from 1846 a succession of reworkings began in Lloyd's innocently entitled weekly magazine *People's Periodical and Family Library*. Little changed in the basic essentials of the story: Sweeney Todd would slit the throat of his victim, before working a monstrous lever to tilt his barber's chair and expel the occupant to the cellar below. He had a young assistant (**Tobias Ragg**) who had no idea what was going on; and became romantically involved with the attractive widow (**Mrs Lovett**) who owned the pie-shop; and there was always a dog belonging to a victim, which sat outside the shop and howled. Todd developed a repertoire of darkly comic lines, 'You're in hurry, sir? Don't worry. There's not a shop in London can polish off a chap as quickly as I can here.' 'You, boy! Pop around the corner and watch the clock strike while I polish off this gentleman.' The widow's pies, of course, were 'the tastiest bits in London.' They were so tender, good sir, and the gravy defied description. In real life at this time there was a pie shop in Fleet Shop close to where Thomas Prest set his story. It did a roaring trade.

'Now, Tobias, listen to me, and treasure up every word I say.'
'Yes, sir.'
'I'll cut your throat from ear to ear if you repeat one word

---

[1] It has been claimed that Pitt's play was staged earlier, in 1842, *before* Prest's serial, but no one has ever found definite evidence (such as a playbill) to support this.

of what passes in this shop, or dare to make any supposition, or draw any conclusion from anything you may see, or hear, or fancy you see or hear. Now, you understand me – I'll cut your throat from ear to ear. Do you understand me?'

'Yes, sir, I won't say nothing. I wish, sir, as I may be made into veal pies at Lovett's in Bell Yard if I as much as says a vord.'

From *The String of Pearls* by Thomas Prest, 1848

In rhyming slang, Sweeney Todd was a natural for the Flying Squad – hence the Squad's common nickname, The Sweeney.

Sweeney Todd was a successful musical (1979, with music by Stephen Sondheim and lyrics by Hugh Wheeler). The story was a gift for the silent cinema and found perhaps its most famous incarnation in George King's 1936 talkie when the appropriately named **Tod Slaughter** took the mantle. (He was more fun than was the rest of the film.) In 2007, director Tim Burton filmed Sondheim's musical – now called *Sweeney Todd: The Demon Barber of Fleet Street* , with **Johnny Depp** as Todd and **Helena Bonham Carter** as Mrs Lovett. **Ray Winstone** was a thoughtful Todd on TV in 2006.

HARRY TRENCH (Bernard Shaw) see **MR SARTORIOUS**

THE TRIFFIDS in *The Day of the Triffids* (1951)
by John Wyndham

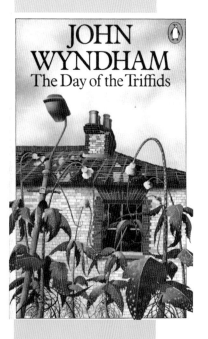

Memorably described by David Pringle as 'the most celebrated vegetables in fiction' these rapid-growing, deadly 'plants' are in fact colonisers from outer space who descend to earth after a spectacular meteor show which has blinded most of the world's population. Against the Triffids' lethal tendrils we blind humans have little chance. But, as in many later survivor sagas, a small group of untouched humans join forces to fight back. *The Day of the Triffids* is a landmark of what was then called science fiction.

Steve Sekely made a moderately successful film of the book in 1963. It starred **Howard Keel**. A British TV six-part series was shown in 1981, directed by Ken Hannam and starring **John Duttine** and **Emma Relph**. A TV movie, confined to cable, came out in 1997. Despite the actors starred above, it should be remembered that the villains were all vegetables.

'Del Boy' TROTTER in *Only Fools and Horses*
(written by John Sullivan for BBC TV from 1981)

The nation's favourite, least threatening, and least competent villain. The elder brother and nominal guardian to his even dimmer younger brother (Rodney) and to (originally) Granddad Trotter and (when Granddad died) to Uncle Albert, Del Boy imagines himself to be fly, sharp and sophisticated. But he will never be more than a part-time, unsuccessful market trader. His flash but awful clothes (a decade out of date), his vulgar jewellery, his appalling council flat (permanent repository to cardboard boxes of unsellable tat) and, memorably, his pitiful once-yellow Robin Reliant three-wheeler car, all demonstrate how far he is from his self-image. His unregistered company is 'Trotter's Independent Trading Company' (TITCO) and his three-wheeler car bears the unimpressive strapline 'New York, Paris, Peckham', though the car is unlikely to manage a journey further than the Peckham border. Sophisticated repartee from Del Boy comprises catch phrases such as 'Lovely jubberly', 'Apres moi the deluge' and 'You plonker, Rodney.' Episode after episode of this superb series saw Del Boy breeze into the flat (368 Nelson Mandella House) full of his latest can't-fail scam, guaranteed to fall to pieces in the next half hour. Much of the family's life outside the flat is spent (typically for TV soaps) in the local pub (The Nag's Head) where they meet and tussle with a fine supporting cast of regulars including, notably, Trigger, Denzil, Mickey Pearce, Boycie and Marlene. Rodney's eventual on-off romance with Cassandra, and Del Boy's with Raquel, were among the factors which lifted the series from mere comedy to classic, and when Del Boy finally became a father the episode touched the nation. By then it had long been obvious that beneath the banter the Potters were warm-hearted, rounded and, caricatures as they might be, believable and real.

SERGEANT TROY in *Far From The Madding Crowd* (1874) by Thomas Hardy.

PENGUIN CLASSICS

THOMAS HARDY

Far From the Madding Crowd

A villain in most men's eyes, though not necessarily in women's, Troy is dashing, handsome, handy with a sword, and generally irresistible to females, even if they half guess he will abandon them. He makes Fanny Robin pregnant but refuses to marry her because she has made the minor fault of turning up for their wedding at the wrong church. Instead he marries the book's heroine Bathsheba Everdene. He treats her wrong, squanders her money, then takes off to sea. (You begin to see why male readers lose patience with him.) After he is assumed to have been lost at sea Bathsheba is set to marry again only to have Troy, the perennial bad penny, reappear at the engagement party and claim her for his own. The hopeful fiancée shoots him.

One could see, in the epic film of the book made by John Schlesinger in 1967, when Troy was played by the impossibly handsome **Terrence Stamp**, that no matter how much men may fulminate, women prefer a blue-eyed rascal. (Which explains some of the men that women fall for.)

MR TULKINGHORN in *Bleak House* by Charles Dickens (serialised 1852 and 53)

Family lawyer to Sir Leicester Dedlock, he takes pains to unpick the mystery of Lady Dedlock's past. When he threatens to reveal her secret to her husband she flees the house and, perhaps on purpose, perhaps from grief, dies in the snow. Tulkinghorn is a bleak and pitiless drudge who persecutes Lady Dedlock firstly because Sir Leicester is his client and she has deceived him (albeit for his own good) and secondly because she has transgressed the strict letter of the law. Tulkinghorn believes that law comes before justice, and his behaviour demonstrates Dickens's low opinion of lawyers and the legal system. (The whole book is an attack on the legal profession.)

In the sensational BBC TV serial version screened in 2005 **Charles Dance** added a suffocating layer of sadism to the forces driving this menacing lawyer. **(Peter Vaughan** had played him in the 1985 version.) Dance's memorable portrayal made Tulkinghorn a larger and more chilling character than Dickens created, and his pernickety lack of feeling as he persecuted the fair lady was fuelled by palpably sexual cruelty. Dance was a tall, lean and unyielding man dressed in dull clerical black while Dickens's Tulkinghorn was older and more dessicated, 'rusty to look at' and wearing 'knee-breeches tied with ribbons, and gaiters or stockings'. Dickens's Tulkinghorn was deliberately detestable; Dance's unforgettable.

DICK TURPIN *Real-life character*

A real-life highwayman (born in 1706) whose fame rests mainly on fictionalised accounts of his supposed exploits, initially in pamphlets and 'Penny Bloods' but then extended onto the stage and into marginally better books. Turpin's appeal to the British public lay partly in his romanticised image as a 'chivalrous' outlaw (robbing from the rich, being courteous to women, etc.) and perhaps even more in his having a beautiful horse, **Black Bess**. Most famous of all their escapades was the ride from London to York (no mean feat on horseback) to escape capture. His life, inevitably, was short: he ended on the gallows.

Not many days before his execution he purchased a new fustian frock and a pair of pumps, in order to wear them at the time of his death: and, on the day before, he hired five poor men, at ten shillings each, to follow the cart as mourners; and he gave hatbands and gloves to several other persons; and he also left a ring, and some other articles, to a married woman in Lincolnshire, with whom he had been acquainted.

On the morning of his death he was put into a cart, and being followed by his mourners, as above-mentioned, he was drawn to the place of execution, in his way to which he bowed to the spectators with an air of the most astonishing indifference and intrepidity.

When he came to the fatal tree, he ascended the ladder; when his right leg trembling, he stamped it down with an air of assumed courage, as if he was ashamed to be observed to discover any signs of fear. Having conversed with the executioner about half an hour, he threw himself off the ladder and expired in a few minutes.

He suffered at York, on the tenth of April, 1739.

From *The Newgate Calendar*

The tale was repeated – and embellished – in various chapbooks and broadsides, but the first Turpin story of any note was

Rookwood written nearly a century later in 1834 by W Harrison Ainsworth, and in this tale can be found an account of Turpin's ride to York on his horse Black Bess. (Harrison claimed that he turned out a hundred pages of this adventure in twenty-four hours.) Later but longer than Ainsworth's epic was *Black Bess, or The Knight of the Road* by Edward Viles, a serial in 254 weekly parts, running to 2,028 pages (and reputed to be the longest Penny Dreadful ever) subsequently bound into one vast tome in 1868. (So long was this story that it has been suggested that Viles was a pseudonym for several authors combined.) Later, Edwardian children read from the *Dick Turpin Library* (published by the Aldine Company). Stories of the gallant highwayman continued till long after the Second World War and Turpin retained his grip on public imagination until the last quarter of the twentieth century when, perhaps facing too many more sophisticated rivals, he finally lost his hold. (See also **Tom King**.)

A late flicker of life came in 1979 when ITV screened a set of adventures (called *Dick Turpin*) in which an altruistic Turpin (**Richard O'Sullivan**) battled with the evil Sir John Glutton (**Christopher Benjamin**) and his steward Nathan Spiker (**David Daker**).

MAY TURPIN

Fictitious sister to Dick, herself a highway robber who featured in a few nineteenth century Penny Bloods.

TOM TURPIN

Fictitious brother to Dick, less popular than May, who also featured in one or two Penny Bloods. Readers presumably recognised the tales as a rip-off.

THE UGLY SISTERS Numerous authors

Pantomime's favourite villains, though they pre-date pantomime.Coming from one of the earliest fairy stories (probably originating in the Far East but known in Germany in the sixteenth century and set down by Perrault in 1697) the story we know as *Cinderella* has retained its basic form, telling of a little cinder girl bullied by her elder or step sisters (versions vary) and left behind while they whisk away to balls. Whatever may have been the original story, for several centuries Cinderella has been transformed by a Fairy Godmother and transported to the ball where she wins the heart of the prince. He loses her at midnight and sets off later throughout his kingdom looking for the one girl whose foot will fit the delicate slipper she left behind. Pantomime has fun with scenes of the grotesque Ugly Sisters trying to cram their feet into the tiny glass slipper, though in some of the earlier fairy tales that scene is considerably more bloody. In pantomime the sisters are by convention played by men, and are far meatier parts than the often anaemic Cinderella and her prince.

Walt Disney made a charming animated film *Cinderella* in 1950, but sounds-like titles such as *Cinderella Jones* (1946), *Cinderfella* (1960) and *Cinderella Liberty* (1973) should be avoided. Rossini turned the tale into a delightful opera *La Cenerentola* in 1817.

UNCLE OSWALD in *Uncle Oswald* (1979) by Roald Dahl
Oswald Hendryks Cornelius deceased, the connoisseur, the bon vivant, the collector of spiders, scorpions and walking-sticks, the lover of opera, the expert on Chinese porcelain, the seducer of women, and without much doubt the greatest fornicator of all time.

From *Uncle Oswald* by Roald Dahl

This is how Oswald is introduced to us by his nephew in his introduction to the great man's scandalous memoirs. Oswald, at what would for most men be the tender age of seventeen, learns of an almost magical powder, formed from the crushed carcasses of the Sudanese Blister Beetle, compared to which Spanish Fly seems a mere tyro aphrodisiac. Oswald acquires and exploits the said powder, makes a large fortune and, by dint of sampling his own product, makes thousands of sexual conquests. He is not a man to be trammelled by irksome rules but he does have one: to sleep with no woman, no matter how splendid, more than once. Nothing, in his opinion, lives up to that first, and therefore unrepeatable performance. Women are attracted to Oswald not because of his prowess (how could they know, until they've slept with him?) but because of his physical attractions. He is good-looking, of course, but – being a Dahl creation – he indulges in hobbies which, in any other man, might seem nerdy but which in

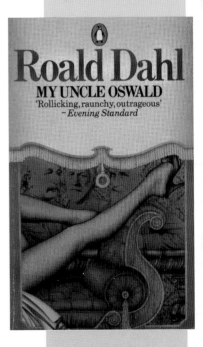

him are shiveringly irresistible to women: particularly his passion for scorpions and spiders. Even his walking-sticks turn them on. It's a hilarious tale, and sadly, the only one in the series. The book is like Uncle Oswald himself: you only get it once.

UNCLE SILAS in *Uncle Silas* (1864) by Sheridan Le Fanu

From the Victorian master of horror came a grand tale of a wicked uncle, *Uncle Silas*, to whose lonely home is sent his orphaned niece seeking protection. The story is narrated by her: 'A girl, of a little more than seventeen, looking, I believe, younger still; slight and rather tall, with a great deal of golden hair, dark grey-eyed, and with a countenance rather sensitive and melancholy, was sitting at the tea-table, in a reverie. I was that girl.'

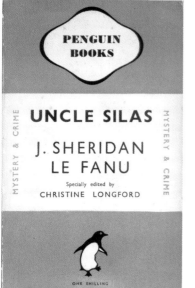

Maud is rich, attractive, young and vulnerable – but, unlike the reader, cannot see into the dark heart of Silas. Unusually for an unscrupulous Gothic villain, he has no vigour. Fond of religious quotations (like Maud's dead father he is a follower of the mystic sectarian Swedenborg) Silas spends much of his time on his sick bed but, again as she is slow to realise, his frequent illnesses are no more than the after-effects of opium. None of this apparent weakness lessens his wickedness. His main plan is to lay his hands on fair Maud's treasures at second hand by marrying her off to his boorish wastrel son. Maud, not unnaturally, refuses. In desperate need of Maud's money Silas then decides to have her killed. Helping him in his endeavours is an untrustworthy French governess (another stock Victorian villain but superbly painted) named **Madame de la Rougierre**. Can there be any escape for Maud?

Here is the moment she meets him for the first time:

The next moment I was in the presence of Uncle Silas. At the far end of a handsome wainscoted room, near the hearth in which a low fire was burning, beside a small table on which stood four waxlights in tall silver candlesticks, sat a singular-looking old man. The dark wainscoting behind him, and the vastness of the room, in the remoter parts of which the light expended itself with hardly any effect, exhibited him with the forcible and strange relief of a finely painted Dutch portrait. For some time I saw nothing but him. A face like marble, with a fearful monumental look, and, for an old man, singularly vivid, strange eyes. His eyebrows were still black, though his hair descended from his temples in long locks of the purest silver and fine as silk, nearly to his shoulders.

He rose, tall and slight, a little stooped, all in black, with an ample black velvet tunic, rather a gown than a coat, with loose sleeves, showing his snowy shirt some way up the arm, and a pair of wrist buttons, then quite out of fashion, which glimmered aristocratically with diamonds. His wild eyes were fixed upon me; an habitual contraction, which in certain lights took the character of a scowl, did not relax as he advanced towards me with his thin-lipped smile.

From *Uncle Silas*

The story is one of growing suspense building to a tense and thrilling climax (especially if read in the sensitively abridged Penguin version) yet has attracted little attention from film-makers. *Uncle Silas* (aka *The Inheritance*) was a well-made if slightly ponderous 1947 thriller directed by Charles Frank, with **Derrick DeMarney** as the uncle and **Jean Simmons** as poor young Maud.

FRANCIS URQUHART in *House of Cards* (1989)
by Michael Dobbs

For many who work in politics, as Michael Dobbs did, every Chief Whip is a villain *ipso facto*, and it must have seemed an amusing idea to Dobbs, the Tory's ex Chief of Staff, to cast one as the anti-hero to his novel. But a Chief Whip answers to no one, and Dobbs' character would be no exception. Strong as he was in the book, Francis Urquhart was to become immortal on TV. Urquhart exists in a parallel reality. When we first meet him Margaret Thatcher has just fallen from power, and will be replaced as leader by a less effective male. Urquhart sees his chance and plots to become Prime Minister himself.

He moves on from slander and scheming to murder – bringing the viewer into his confidence through a series of witty amoral asides. A favourite trick (one of his milder) was to drop a hint to someone he wanted to influence but then refuse to confirm it by saying, 'You might think that, but I couldn't possibly comment.' It became his catchphrase. The sly asides, his outrageous actions, and the magnificent performance of **Ian Richardson** in the role made him TV's number one villain of the year, with his catchphrase repeated ad nauseam up and down the land.

House of Cards was a four-part mini-series in 1990, a huge success, and BBC's best-selling TV drama of the early Nineties. There had to be a follow-up – and there the troubles began, for the TV adaptation by Andrew Davies had more than adapted Dobbs' text, going so far as to kill off a character who continued in the books. Dobbs could either alter his books to match the adaptation or continue in yet another parallel reality. He wasn't helped by the fact that, as is often the case, far more people knew the story from TV than had read or would ever read his books. Dobbs stuck to his guns and eventually withdrew his name from the TV credits.

The first four-parter was followed by *To Play the King*, again from a Dobbs novel, in which Prime Minister Urquhart struggled with a newly installed king who had a liberal green agenda, and this series was followed in turn by another adapted from Dobbs by Andrew Davies: *The Final Cut*. Here Urquhart's past came from further back to haunt him. And here Michael Dobbs said, 'That's enough.'

VARNEY THE VAMPIRE in *Varney The Vampire*
(serialised in the 1840s) by James Malcolm Rymer
A tall figure is standing on the ledge immediately outside the long window. It is its fingernails upon the glass that produces the sound so like the hail, now that the hail has ceased. Intense fear paralysed the limbs of that beautiful girl. That one shriek is all she can utter – with hands clasped, a face of marble, a heart beating so wildly in her bosom, that each moment it seems as if it would break its confines, eyes distended and fixed upon the window, froze with horror. The pattering and clattering of the nails continue. No word is spoken, and now she fancies she can trace the darker form of that figure against the window, and she can see the long arms moving to and fro, feeling for some mode of entrance.

From *Varney the Vampire* by James Malcolm Rymer

Varney is the eponymous anti-hero of an 1840s 900-page serial shocker, also known as *The Feast of Blood*, which pre-dates Bram Stoker's *Dracula* by nearly fifty years but whose main character shares Dracula's penchant for toothsome young ladies, preferably asleep in bed, with their necks, if nothing else, exposed. He had once been Sir Francis Varney but in his later, undead existence he sports fang-like teeth and even longer fingernails, comes out only at night, and although he has been 'killed'

several times, he always awakens to a further stretch of eternal darkness. Rymer's Penny Blood serial ran for 220 chapters but was finally closed emphatically by the author when in a postscript he had Varney ('to prevent the possibility of a reanimation of his remains') take his own life by leaping into the smouldering crater at Vesuvius. Presumably he didn't hear his publisher curse him for ending such a potentially rich franchise.

VATHEK in *Vathek* (1786) by William Beckford
The archetypal cruel Caliph, the ninth, Beckford tells us, of the Abassides, and the grandson of Haroun Al Raschid. In this relatively short, bizarre comic fantasy, Vathek, a monstrously self-indulgent Caliph, becomes obsessed (or perhaps bewitched) by an itinerant magician who promises him untold pleasures. But the magician's price includes such trifles as 'the blood of fifty of the most beautiful sons of thy visors and great men'.Their lives are of little consequence to Vathek:
When he was angry one of his eyes became so terrible that no person could bear to behold it, and the wretch upon whom it was fixed instantly fell backward, and sometimes expired. For fear, however, of depopulating his dominions and making his palace desolate, he but rarely gave way to his anger.
from *Vathek* by William Beckford

Vathek, with his vast wealth and his palaces 'frequented by troops of young females beautiful as the houris and not less seducing' was already rich enough, one might have thought, to resist temptation. But he was not content with one superb palace. He added five more. In the first one, 'The Eternal or Unsatiating Banquet', food and wine never ran out. In 'The Temple of Melody, or the Nectar of the Soul', music and poetry were unceasing. 'The Delight of the Eyes, or the Support of Memory' was one entire enchantment. 'The Incentive to Pleasure' was a Palace of Perfumes, and 'The Retreat of Joy, or the Dangerous' housed young women who, uncharacteristically for the Caliph, were encouraged to 'receive with caresses all whom the Caliph allowed to approach them'. (His own harem, of course, was housed elsewhere.) Readers might regret that most of Vathek's adventures take place outside these fascinating palaces. Unsurprisingly, in the end, 'the Caliph Vathek who, for the sake of empty pomp and forbidden power had sullied himself with a thousand crimes, became a prey to grief without end and remorse without mitigation'. Quite right too.

V

VERLOC in *The Secret Agent* (1907) by Joseph Conrad

As a two-timing bomb-laying anarchist Verloc ought to lie high on the list of British villains but his hesitant over-intellectualised ineptness makes him a hard character to categorise. Leading man in the tale, he is a double agent between the London police, the Russian embassy and various anarchist groups. For cover he runs a small back-street shop in Soho. When his Russian contact Vladimir tells him to blow up the Greenwich Observatory, Verloc briefs his retarded stepson Stevie to carry the bomb. Stevie manages to blow himself up in Greenwich Park, and in the ensuing investigation Verloc crumbles. He confesses to his wife (Stevie's mother) and she stabs him with a carving knife. Another anarchist, with whom she had hoped to flee the country, steals her money and abandons her. In her general grief she leaps to her death from a Channel ferry. The sordid, cramped setting to the story reflects the shallow motives and puny idealism of the anarchists.

Alfred Hitchcock's *The Secret Agent* (1936) is a different story. It is set in Switzerland and is about a plot to kill an enemy spy. Christopher Hampton's 1996 *The Secret Agent* is an uncharacteristically dull version of Conrad's tale in which **Bob Hoskins** and a powerful cast do what they can but fail (rather like Verloc himself when you come to think about it).

VICAR OF BRAY *Anonymous*

Subject of a long-popular eighteenth century song and a character who has given his name to a form of self-serving lack of loyalty. In the song the vicar cheerfully admits to having adapted his behaviour and apparent beliefs to whichever king or queen sat on the throne. He has survived through the reigns of Charles, James, William, Anne and George – but whatsoever king may reign, he will still remain 'the vicar of Bray, sir'.

VINDICE or sometimes VENDICE

in *The Revenger's Tragedy* published 1607)

ascribed variously to Cyril Tourneur and/or Thomas Middleton (even occasionally to John Webster)

Vindice (Latin for Vengeance) is an example of a villain created within a play – or of a good man made to behave villainously by his chosen course of action. The play opens with Vindice mourning the murder of his mistress, poisoned by the Duke. In classic Jacobean noir fashion Vindice addresses his opening monologue to her skull:

THE
REVENGERS
TRAGÆDIE.

As it hath beene sundry times Acted,
by the Kings Maiesties
Seruants.

AT LONDON
Printed by G. E l d, and are to be fold at his
houfe in Fleete-lane at the figne of the
Printers-Preffe.
1608.

Thou sallow picture of my poisoned love,
My study's ornament, thou shell of death,
Once the bright face of my betrothéd lady,
When life and beauty naturally filled out
These ragged imperfections ...

Revenger's Tragedy Act I, scene I

Vindice's plan is to insinuate himself into the Duke's court by pretending to be as base a villain as he is – but an amusing and useful villain, well suited to a notably corrupt court: the Duke's own stepson has been accused of rape; the Duke's wife, the stepson's mother, has fallen for the Duke's own bastard son; and her other two sons are scheming to disinherit the Duke's eldest son by his first marriage. Vindice assures the Duke that such behaviour is nothing new to him:

I have been witness to the surrenders of a thousand
virgins ...
Some father dreads not, gone to bed in wine, to slide
from the mother
And cling the daughter-in-law;
Some uncles are adulterous with their nieces,
Brothers with brothers' wives. O, hour of incest!
Any kin now, next to the rim o' the sister
Is man's meat in these days; and in the morning
When they are up and dressed and their mask on,
Who can perceive this?

Revenger's Tragedy, Act I, scene III

To be a worse villain than any in this nest of vipers is a tall order but Vindice rises to the challenge. Too well: when he tells the Duke he'll try to persuade his own mother to pimp his sister to the Duke's eldest son he pleads the merits of the case to her so cynically that it never occurs to him his mother might agree.

Vindice: *Live wealthy, rightly understand the world*
And chide away that foolish country girl
Keeps company with your daughter: Chastity.
Mother: *Oh fie, fie. The riches of the world cannot hire*
A mother to such a most unnatural task.
Vindice: *No, but a thousand angels[1] can.*

Revenger's Tragedy Act I, scene I

The sight of gold persuades his foolish mother (but not his sister), and it leaves Vindice to reflect, 'Were it not for gold and

The Revenger's Tragedy
CYRIL TOURNEUR
Edited by BRIAN GIBBONS

The New Mermaids
General Editors PHILIP BROCKBANK and BRIAN MORRIS

[1] An Angel was a gold coin first minted in the reign of Edward IV.

women, there would be no damnation.' Vindice continues to play the villain with brutal expertise and this will be his – the Revenger's – tragedy. In his wicked guise he reveals to the Duke the adultery of his wife and son, he devises a trick to have the rapist son executed, and he finally murders the Duke and all key members of his family. With the court purged of this evil family and the noble Antonio come to replace the Duke, it is time for Vindice – his conscience clean – to cheerfully admit that it has all been his and his brother's doing. 'Lay hands upon those villains!' Antonio cries. 'How on us?' demands Vindice. 'Was it not for your good, my lord?' But Antonio is far from grateful: 'You that would murder him would murder me.' Vindice will be executed. He is left with one consolation: his enemies are dead, and revenge is surely his. 'It is time to die when we are ourselves our foes.'

VITTORIA COROMBONA see COROMBONA

VOLDEMORT
in the *Harry Potter* series by J K Rowling
Lord Voldemort is a half-blood wizard and ex-student of Harry's college, Hogwarts, who surrounds himself with Death Eaters, nasty wizards who do his bidding, while he tries to gain ultimate power. His real name, according to the books, is Tom Marvolo Riddle – an anagram of 'I am Lord Voldemort'. In the back-story before the series began Voldemort, believing a prophecy that the infant Harry would grow up to destroy him, set out to kill the child but succeeded only in killing his parents. The attempt to kill Harry left the boy with a lightning bolt scar on his forehead. Harry's struggles with Voldemort run through all the books until their final showdown in *Harry Potter and the Deathly Hallows*. First in the book series was *Harry Potter and the Philospher's Stone* (1997) but it wasn't until the fourth (*Goblet of Fire*) that Rowling described her villain. He was 'tall and skeletally thin,' she said, with a face 'whiter than a skull, with wide, livid scarlet eyes and a nose that was a flat as a snake's, with slits for nostrils'. She expanded the description by adding that his 'hands were like large, pale spiders; his long white fingers caressed his own chest, his arms, his face; the red eyes, whose pupils were slits, like a cat's, gleamed still more brightly through the darkness'.
In the films *Harry Potter and the Goblet of Fire* (2005) and *Harry Potter and the Order of the Phoenix* (2007), Voldemort was played by **Ralph Fiennes**

VOLPONE in *Volpone*
(written and performed between 1605 to 1607)
Volpone: *What should I do*
But cocker up my genius, and live free
To all delights my fortune calls me to?
I have no wife, parent, child, ally,
To give my substance to; but whom I make
Must be my heir: and this makes men observe me:
This draws new clients daily to my house,
Women and men of every sex and age,
That bring me presents, send me plate, coin, jewels,
With hope that when I die (which they expect
Each greedy minute) it shall then return
Tenfold upon them.

Volpone Act I, scene I

Volpone is one of the great comic rogues of Jacobean theatre and hero of Jonson's play of the same name. The characters' names, translated from the Latin, symbolise their nature. Volpone (the Fox) is an avaricious and cunning old merchant who devises a ruse to screw money from those around him; he pretends to be dying and lets it be known that he will leave his fortune to whoever seems to be his best friend. His 'friends' rush in to prove their worth. Corbaccio (the carrion crow) offers to disinherit his own son in favour of Volpone; the lawyer Voltore (the vulture) says he will break any law to please him; Corvino (the raven) promises to let Volpone sleep with his virtuous wife. Volpone carries out these deceptions with the aid of his servant **Mosca** (the fly), whose view of the world is summed up in his remark that 'almost all the wise world is little else, in nature, but parasites and sub-parasites.' To add to the fun and to watch the others discomfited, Volpone and Mosca pretend Volpone is dead and that he has in fact willed all his property to Mosca. But Mosca, sensing a prize, turns on his master and tries to blackmail him. The whole scheme comes crashing down. Everyone is punished except Corvino's wife and Corbaccio's son.

Volpone: *Who's that there, now? A third!*
Mosca: *Close! To your couch again. I hear his voice:*
It is Corvino, our spruce merchant.
Volpone: (lies down as before) *Dead.*
Mosca: *Another bout, sir, with your eyes.* (Anointing them)
Who's there? (Corvino enters)
Signor Corvino! Come most wished for. O,
How happy were you, if you knew it, now!

Corvino: *Why? What? Wherein?*
Mosca: *The tardy hour is come, sir.*
Corvino: *He is not dead?*
Mosca: *Not dead, sir, but as good. He knows no man.*
Corvino: *How shall I do, then?*
Mosca: *Why, sir?*
Corvino: *I have brought him here a pearl.*
Mosca: *Perhaps he has so much remembrance left*
  As to know you, sir.
  He still calls on you; nothing but your name
  Is in his mouth ... (To Volpone) He's here, sir.
  And he has brought you a rich pearl.
  ... Sir, he cannot understand, his hearing's gone,
  And yet it comforts him to see you –
Corvino: *Say, I have a diamond for him, too.*
Mosca: *Best show it, sir;*
  Put it into his hand; 'tis only there
  He apprehends: he has his feeling yet.
  See how he grasps it!

       Volpone *Act I, scene V*

George Antheil wrote an opera *Volpone* in 1953.

CHARLEY WAG

A serial character created in the 1860s, probably by George Augustus Sala (though he, as a 'respectable' journalist, indignantly denied it)

Conceived as 'the new Jack Sheppard' or 'the Boy Burglar', this cheeky felon had a series of spirited adventures in **Penny Dreadfuls**. The stories were as impudent as their hero, casting scurrilous aspersions at aristocrats, preachers and magistrates, and generating a small flood of complaints from their readers (more likely from their readers' parents) – all of which was cheerfully thrown into the story, 'Since I had the misfortune in a luckless moment to introduce these clerical parties into my story,' the author interposed on one occasion, 'a terrific volley of letters from unknown correspondents has been fired at my offended head. It seems, if I am to believe these ladies and gentlemen, that there really are no naughty parsons in existence, and even if there were, it is not the proper thing to represent them in their natural colours. There are a great number of people in the world who do not like to hear the truth, and a great many who do not like truth to be told.'

Charley Wagg was not to be taken seriously. His story began

with him, as an unwanted baby, being thrown into the Thames by his wretched mother, and when rescued, sent to a workhouse called Saint-Starver-cum-Bag-o'-Bones. He later fought urchins in Slogger's Alley and in his early teens was 'a regular rascal where a pretty girl is concerned.' His career as a fantasy thief climaxed with his breaking into the Bank of England before he was briefly reunited with his mother, who turned out to have been a duchess all the while. But the story was still selling, so a grisly coda was added in which his unfortunate mother met her death at the hands of her mad husband, while young Charley set off to wreak more havoc in foreign parts.

SILAS WEGG in *Our Mutual Friend* (1865)
by Charles Dickens
Wegg is an illiterate stall-holder, inordinately proud of his wooden leg, who gets an undeserved position reading to the good-hearted illiterate former servant Nicodemus Boffin after Boffin has inherited a fortune. Wegg discovers a later will that negates the legacy and tries to use the knowledge to blackmail Boffin – all in vain, as it happens, since there turns out to have been an even later will.

    Wegg was played by **Kenneth Cranham** in BBC TV's four-part 1998 skilful adaptation. Earlier TV versions came in 1958 and 1976.

SIR WALTER WHOREHOUND
in *A Chaste Maid in Cheapside* by Thomas Middleton
(written 1613, published 1630)
Dissolute old rake at the heart of this bawdy comedy who, short of money as usual, plots to marry pretty young Moll Yellowhammer (a goldsmith's daughter) while at the same time passing off his mistress as his niece and marrying her to the goldsmith's son. Young Moll skips through her trials and tribulations only to marry her young lover Touchwood in the end. Whorehound meanwhile has hopes of an inheritance from the childless Lady Kix – till she is made pregnant by Touchwood's father. So Whorehound loses his money, his hopes, and finally his mistress (who goes on to open a bordello in the Strand) and he ends the play imprisoned for debt.

WIDMERPOOL in *A Dance to the Music of Time*
a 12-book series (1951 to 1975) by Anthony Powell
    The same characters develop and run through this English *roman fleuve*, with the astonishing Widmerpool the most

cunningly drawn. Met first in *A Question of Upbringing* as an awkward, ugly, unpopular child, he is easily overlooked and underestimated. What appears at first as little more than his understandable petulance and aggrieved envy turns out to be an insatiable lust for worldly success. As he rises and clings to power he destroys the careers, romances and sometimes the very lives of those about him. (His activities lead directly to the deaths of two of his schoolmates.) In the early novels the reader has the advantage over Widmerpool's contemporaries because the series is narrated by Nicholas Jenkins (a writer) looking back and commenting on what he describes. Without such a device Widmerpool would be ignored in the large cast of apparently more interesting characters. We watch him rise through murky finance, flirtations with 1930s fascism, comfortable army service, a career in politics, until he ends up as a Lord.

In 1997 Channel 4 condensed the series into a four-part TV drama whose cast list included John Gielgud, Alan Bennett, Zoe Wannamaker, Michael Williams, Miranda Richardson and Eileen Atkins – but **Simon Russell Beale** landed the plum part of Widmerpool.

JONATHAN WILD Real-life character, but fictionalised by various authors

If hypocrisy makes a villain doubly villainous, then Jonathan Wild (1682 to 1725) was one of the most heinous of them all. Presenting himself as a Thief-Taker and recoverer of stolen goods, his real income came from his other career as a robber, fence, pimp and murderer – for which, eventually, he was hung at Tyburn (on the lesser charge of housebreaking). He was reputed to have had six wives and (as was probably true) a gang of followers. Daniel Defoe romanticised Wild in *Jonathan Wild* (1725, the year of Wild's execution) and Henry Fielding did later in *The Life of Mr Jonathan Wild the Great* (1743). Fielding's work is the greater (even if it is one of his shorter novels). It is a satire, comparing Wild's career with that of rich society, and it introduces a host of colourful characters, including Laetitia Snap, his bright but hypocritical wife (and daughter of another thief-taker); Tishy and Doshy, their daughters; Fireblood, Blueskin and Count la Ruse, his confederates; and Heartfree the unfortunate jeweller (who, along with his wife,

Jonathan Wild's house (contemporary print).

suffers endless unjustified torments and punishments, caused by Wild). A non-fiction biography of Wild, *Thief-Taker General* by G Howson, was published in 1970.

REBECCA DE WINTER in *Rebecca* (1938)
by Daphne du Maurier
A spoiler alert is surely unnecessary, since you'll remember that the previous mistress of **Manderley**, the dead and apparently saintly Rebecca, first wife of Maxim de Winter (as cold a name as you could wish for) was in fact spiteful, adulterous and generally detestable. The story spins on the fact that Maxim – who his second wife believes still dotes on his first wife – found out her sins and hated her. Rebecca never appears, yet dominates the book – to such an extent that the second wife, who narrates the tale, is nameless throughout. The presence of the first wife seems to saturate the house:

It came to me that I was not the first one to lounge there in possession of the chair; someone had been before me, had surely left an imprint of her person on the cushions, and on the arm where her hand had rested. Another one had poured the coffee from that same silver coffee pot, had placed the cup to her lips, had bent down to the dog, even as I was doing.

from *Rebecca,* by Daphne du Maurier

A second villain within the story, Rebecca's companion (perhaps in more ways than one) **Mrs Danvers**, who has been kept on by Maxim as housekeeper, is eaten up with jealousy and loathing for Maxim and his new bride, and ultimately sets fire to Manderley and burns it to the ground. Mrs Danvers is a memorable, satisfying villain in her own right, but can't compare with the hellish Rebecca. Nobody can.

An exception to the rule that it takes a bad book to make a good film came with Hitchcock's wonderful 1940 *Rebecca* starring **Joan Fontaine** as the heroine and **Laurence Olivier** as Maxim de Winter. The film, like the book, gripped from its opening line, 'Last night I dreamt I went to Manderley again.'

Television has tried to match Hitchcock's version, starting as early as 1947 when **Dorothy Black** played Mrs Danvers for BBC. **Anna Massey** played her in 1979 (BBC again) and **Diana Rigg** in 1997 (for ITV). Rebecca herself, of course, is a role of little interest.

THE WITCH OF EDMONTON in *The Witch of Edmonton* (c. 1621) by Dekker, Ford and Rowley

In the seventeenth century tragi-comedy of this name the witch is the assumed villain – assumed to be a witch by her neighbours because she is poor and uneducated – who, driven finally to seek some form of revenge for their unfair cruelty, sells her soul to the devil. She says, 'Some call me witch. And being ignorant of my self they go about to teach me to become one.' Her story is contrasted in the play with that of a true villain, a bigamist, **Frank Thorney**, who murders one of his two wives to save himself from disinheritance. *The Witch of Edmonton* was written around 1621 (inspired by the case of Elizabeth Sawyer, hanged as a witch in April of that year) by the three playwrights writing for the Henslowe acting company.

YAHOO in *Gulliver's Travels* (1726) by Jonathan Swift
Not to be confused with the internet search engine, the first Yahoo will be encountered in the fourth voyage of *Gulliver's Travels* in the country of the Houyhnhnms, a race of centaur-like creatures who keep the filthy Yahoos as slaves. Yahoos are more human in appearance than are the Houyhnhnms, and both races exhibit extreme aspects of human behaviour: Houyhnhnms look like horses but are cold and rational, while Yahoos look human (albeit unkempt specimens) and are in every way more vice-ridden and obscene.

Gulliver's Travels was an ambitious and successful joint venture between Channel 4, NBC and RHI back in 1996, when it was made as a four-part series and remained faithful to the book.

ZELUCO in *Zeluco* (1786) by John Moore
Thoroughly wicked subject of Moore's admonitory novel of the same name, a Sicilian nobleman who begins as a nasty child and continues into bestial adulthood. Few sins escape him: he is lustful, lying and treacherous; his violence extends to murder – even of his own child; and he drives his wife insane. In the novel his reprehensible activities are set against some curious comic interludes with a pair of Scotsmen, Buchanan and Targe.

ZENITH THE ALBINO serial character
(early twentieth century) by various authors
One of the many adversaries of Sexton Blake, longer-lasting than most. His infra-red binoculars allowed him to locate the hidden treasures of London's wealthy whose only recourse was: to send for Sexton Blake. But, as Tracy Chapman once sang: *It won't do no good to call; the police always come too late, if they come at all.*

FURTHER EVIDENCE

These Corrupt, Rotten Books

Are we entitled to enjoy reading about villains? Do such stories corrupt us? Are we leading ourselves astray? These are not new questions. For as long as stories have been written, critics, parents and lawmakers have worried that the world is going to pot, that things are not as they used to be, and that the Golden Age is lost.

> *'Get thee gone then, thou cursed book, which hath seduced so many precious soules; get thee gone, thou corrupt, rotten book, earth to earth, and dust to dust; get thee gone into the place of rottenness, that thou mayest rot with thy author, and see corruption.'*
>
> from *A Short Oration at the Burial of his Heretical Book*, by Francis Cheynell, in 1644

Back in the Nineteenth Century the Penny Dreadful was routinely castigated for leading innocent young bloods astray, as if wicked thoughts would never have penetrated their louse-ridden craniums had it not been for the poisonous infusions dripped in by thriller writers. Much the same point is made today of X-rated videos and violent computer games. Such a view, said G.K. Chesterton a hundred years ago, 'rests upon the theory that the tone of the mass of boys' novelettes [sic] is criminal and degraded, appealing to low cupidity and low cruelty. This is the magisterial theory, and this is rubbish.'

Stanley l Wood '96

Chesterton was a writer much concerned with morality – and he was a strong defender of intellectual freedom. He was a moralist, poet, polemicist and off-and-on Catholic propagandist, and is better known today as the creator of over sixty Father Brown detective stories.

To Chesterton, readers of Penny Dreadfuls were less corrupted by their books than were those detached intellectuals who read, or at least displayed on their drawing room tables, 'books recommending profligacy and pessimism'. He pointed out that although low fiction might set its scenes in sink estates and pathology labs (or in country house libraries or a flat in Baker Street) and although its readers might rinse their hands and dirty their feet in squalid putrescence, they nevertheless remained perversely untainted. In contrast, said Chesterton, literary intellectuals, those desiccated souls who don't read low fiction, were the 'morbid exceptions'; they were the criminal class, in that they intellectualised and therefore supported criminal values, while 'the vast mass of humanity, with their vast mass of idle books and idle words, have never doubted and never will doubt that courage is splendid, that fidelity is noble, that distressed ladies should be rescued, and vanquished enemies spared.'

It was a strongly argued point, delivered in Chesterton's characteristically passionate style. One wonders if he ever read what was reputed to be the longest Penny Dreadful ever written: *Black Bess, or The Knight of the Road* by Edward Viles. Viles added this Chestertonian foreword to its bound edition (published in 1868):

'*The author of* Black Bess, or The Knight of the Road, *has one request to make:*

> *It is that those who have, unread, condemned the present work will take the trouble to peruse it. And an entire change of opinion will be the result, because in no place will vice be commended or virtue sneered at; nor will any pandering to sensuality, suggestion of impure thoughts or direct encouragement of crime be discovered; neither are there details of seduction, bigamy, adultery and domestic poisoning, such as indispensable ingredients of our popular three-volume novels. On the contrary, the work will be found full of exciting personal adventures such as can never be re-enacted until the railways are swept away and the stage coaches replaced on our highways – until, in fine, the present state of things is changed to what it was a century and a half ago. If anyone is weak-minded enough to be carried away by the idea that a highwayman's career as depicted in these pages can be equalled in reality at the present day he must be imbecile indeed. Let not the 'Life of Robin Hood' fall into the hands of such a one or, sure as fate, Sherwood Forest would be his destination, with bows and arrows for his stock in trade.*

from *Black Bess, or The Knight of the Road* by Edward Viles

Viles's spirited defence might have been fair for his *Black Bess* but the same defence could not be extended to other stories found in the Penny Dreadfuls of his day. They had more than their fair share of the 'seduction, bigamy, adultery and domestic poisoning' he mentioned, and the 'exciting personal adventures' within them were not all set 'a century and a half ago'. But his point (which was Chesterton's point also) remains fair: crime stories, melodramas, tales of villainy (the meat and drink of Shakespeare) do not corrupt; they provide a safe place to which a reader can escape and indulge in fantasies. Violent they may be, even perverse, but the stories provide for adults what fairy stories provide for children. No matter how charismatic the author makes the villain, the reader knows that crime does not pay and that virtue, hopefully, will triumph over all. We know it, though while reading we may prefer to pretend we don't know it, when we sympathise with the Big Bad Wolf as opposed to the foolish and disobedient Red Riding Hood – and we callously switch loyalties at the end of the tale, when the woodman comes to the rescue. In the world of fiction, or at least in the healthy groves of crime fiction and other tales of terror, villainy is exciting but courage is splendid. In these tales of villainy we find a truly moral world in which, as G K Chesterton wrote, 'fidelity is noble, distressed ladies will be rescued, and vanquished enemies will be nobly spared.'

Censorship

Print is dangerous. It can challenge Authority, and Authority – be it the authority of state or religion – has from its inception fought to suppress and control the dissemination of ideas through print. Religious authorities have been the sternest censors – they still are – but censorship remains the dictator's tool. The most rigid censorship is applied against ideas which deny or contest the rulings of an authority, ideas which might remove power from the powerful, though in this book we are more concerned with censorship on the grounds of unacceptable morality. It is one thing for a religious or a state authority to forbid the active promotion of crime or anarchy, but when an authority seeks to forbid discussion on moral grounds its argument grows weaker. One can understand – but not condone – a dictator's wish to prevent challenge to his rule, or a church's wish to stop the promotion of another religion or denial of God. But censorship is insidious. With incremental steps the dictator or church clamps down on behaviour or the promotion of behaviour which, although it does not directly challenge their authority, does not accord with how those in power think others should behave. From forbidding the active promotion of such behaviour, the authority moves on to forbid any discussion of it at all. Religious authority is worse than State in this respect. Religions, more often than governments, ban books. And for as long as authority has sought to ban books, writers and thinking people generally have sought to overturn those bans. Should any book be banned?

Should any work of art be banned? Given the impossibility of reaching agreement on what is and what is not a work of art, should any book, pamphlet, picture, play or performance be banned? Who is to decide what to ban and what not? What is morality, anyway?

A little over a hundred years ago, in his essay *A Defence of Detective Stories* G. K. Chesterton remarked that 'morality is the most dark and daring of conspiracies' and that 'civilization itself is the most sensational of departures and the most romantic of rebellions.' Morality, to this devout Catholic, was not a fixed absolute but was, like civilisation, whatever we defined it to be. So, he suggested, we should encourage free discussion – even if, during the course of that discussion, topics were raised which made us uneasy or with which we disagreed. Chesterton expanded this idea in another of his essays, *A Defence of Penny Dreadfuls*: '*One of the strangest examples of the degree to which ordinary life is undervalued is the example of popular literature, the vast mass of which we contentedly describe as vulgar..*

There is no class of vulgar publications about which there is, to my mind, more utterly ridiculous exaggeration and misconception than the current boys' literature of the lowest stratum. This class of composition has presumably always existed, and must exist. It has no more claim to be good literature than the daily conversation of its readers to be fine oratory, or the lodging-houses and tenements they inhabit to be sublime architecture. But people must have conversation, they must have houses, and they must have stories. The simple need for some kind of ideal world in which fictitious persons play an unhampered part is infinitely deeper and older than the rules of good art, and much more important.'

He could have been talking of our own age when he added:
'*It is the custom, particularly among magistrates, to attribute half the crimes of the Metropolis to cheap novelettes. If some grimy urchin runs away with an apple, the magistrate shrewdly points out that the child's knowledge that apples appease hunger is traceable to some curious literary researches. The boys themselves, when penitent, frequently accuse the novelettes with great bitterness, which is only to be expected from young people possessed of no little native humour.*'

Apart from intellectual snobbery, he suggested, there was a propensity for magistrates and journalists – if not the miscreants themselves – to seek someone outside themselves on whom to lay the blame for misbehaviour. Even today in our own age we are tempted to blame twenty-first century crime and horror stories for corrupting young innocents. But despite the anxious interference of politicians, we should remember that stories of blood and gore have always underpinned literary culture – think *Beowulf* or Shakespeare or those bloodthirsty Greek tragedies.

To Chesterton it was of no importance whether the story was well written or not, 'Bad story writing is not a crime.' Magistrates were wrong to blame popular fiction for poor behaviour, he said.

> '*Among these stories there are a certain number which deal sympathetically with the adventures of robbers, outlaws and pirates, which present in a dignified and romantic light thieves and murderers like Dick Turpin and Claude Duval. That is to say, they do precisely the same thing as Scott's* Ivanhoe, *Scott's* Rob Roy, *Scott's* Lady of the Lake, *Byron's* Corsair, *Wordsworth's* Rob Roy's Grave, *Stevenson's* Macaire, *Mr. Max Pemberton's* Iron Pirate, *and a thousand more works distributed systematically as prizes and Christmas presents. Nobody imagines that an admiration of Locksley in* Ivanhoe *will lead a boy to shoot Japanese arrows at the deer in Richmond Park; no one thinks that the incautious opening of Wordsworth at the poem on* Rob Roy *will set him up for life as a blackmailer. In the case of our own class, we recognise that this wild life is contemplated with pleasure by the young, not because it is like their own life, but because it is different from it. It might at least cross our minds that, for whatever other reason the errand-boy reads* The Red Revenge, *it really is not because he is dripping with the gore of his own friends and relatives.*'

When we speak of 'the lower classes', Chesterton warned, 'we mean humanity minus ourselves. This trivial romantic literature is not especially plebeian: it is simply human.' And far from concerning ourselves with the tastes of 'the lower classes', Chesterton felt, we should query those of the 'educated classes'. Here is his genuinely challenging conclusion:

> '*It is the modern literature of the educated, not of the undereducated, which is avowedly and aggressively criminal. Books recommending profligacy and pessimism, at which the high-souled errand boy would shudder, lie upon all our drawing room tables.*' (A pleasingly archaic touch there.)

> '*If the dirtiest old owner of the dirtiest old bookstall in Whitechapel*' dared to display such works (in other words, if everyday crime books were as soaked in depravity as was fine literature) '*his stock would be seized by the police.*' An archaic touch again because, in today's world,

anything goes and good authors too, who once knew better words, now only use four-letter words – but we take GK's point. Literature, from its earliest days when ancient Greeks wrote of incest, bestiality, paedophilia and patricide, has seldom hesitated to wade nipple-deep in the salty seas of sex and violence. Literature has been tried in courts for obscenity more often than has crime fiction.

On the theme of low fiction,

'These things are our luxuries,' said GK. *'And with a hypocrisy so ludicrous as to be almost unparalleled in history, we rate the gutter-boys for their immorality at the same time we are discussing (with equivocal German professors) whether morality is valid at all. At the very instant we accuse it (quite unjustly) of lubricity and indecency we are cheerfully reading philosophies which glory in lubricity and indecency. At the very instant that we charge it with encouraging the young to destroy life, we are placidly discussing whether life is worth preserving.'*

His words again seem archaic, perfumed as they are with the musty odour of pages written more than a century ago, but in truth his phrases would need little adjustment to make them relevant in the pages of today's Sunday papers, let alone in the *Literary Review*, the *Spectator* or the *London Review of Books:* low fiction corrupts, while highbrow meanderings do not. Thus it is all right for Shakespearian characters to pluck out a rival's eyes, to practise black magic, incest and regicide; it is all right to teach these scenes in junior schools; but it is not all right for innocent schoolchildren to read of them in the books they finger for pleasure in their innocent bedrooms at dead of night. (Though modern gutter-boys don't read. They don't even watch videos. Instead they prefer to manipulate reality with their thumbs.)

Back with Chesterton and the 'educated' class:

'It is we who are the morbid exceptions; it is we who are the criminal class. This should be our great comfort. The vast mass of humanity, with their vast mass of idle books and idle words, have never doubted and never will doubt that courage is splendid, that fidelity is noble, that distressed ladies should be rescued, and vanquished enemies spared .. So long as the coarse and thin texture of mere current popular romance is not touched by a paltry culture it will never be vitally immoral. It is always on the side of life. The poor – the slaves who really stoop under the burden of life – have often been mad, scatter-brained and cruel, but never hopeless. That is a class privilege, like cigars. Their drivelling literature will always be a 'blood and thunder' literature, as simple as the thunder of heaven and the blood of men.'

For us today, then, Chesterton's message remains clear: give us more blood and thunder – and no censorship!

Villains in Particular

Comic Villains

Four hundred years ago the Jacobeans saw no contradiction between wickedness and humour. Far from it: they delighted in black humour. Jacobean villains were stage villains, outrageous and shocking, and they performed their perfidious acts within touching distance of the audience. It was inevitable that the shocked spectators would laugh at their perfidy. How else could they react? A gasp, a startled cry: both are easily disguised with a laugh. For the performers performing dastardly acts within inches of the audience it was both more rewarding – and probably safer – to encourage laughs rather than hostility from their voluble and close-by judges. With exaggerated and hammy villainy the actors drew hisses, catcalls and chuckles – all of them good-natured – and frequently they were egged on by the delighted audience to even more outrageous villainy. Those were bloody, brutish days; actors today find it harder to raise a laugh by gouging out an eye or raping a fair maiden – though let's not forget that Hannibal Lecter raised the biggest laugh in the film in its final moments, when he promised to dine on his victim's entrails (with Chianti).

We are not concerned in this section with those whose outrageous behaviour would appal us in real life. This is fiction, not real life. Fiction's villains include many whose behaviour we ought to condemn but, because of the villains' likeable nature, we forgive. Villains who, despite their misbehaviour, have encouraged us to laugh include:

Villain	*Traits*
Blackadder	Alternatively toadying and sarcastic coward who reappears through the ages.
Basil Fawlty	Hotelier from Hell.
Flashman	MacDonald Fraser's superb development of Thomas Hughes's schoolboy bully.
Follywit	Buffoon-like villain who robs his grandfather and marries a whore.
Captain Hook	Pantomimic Pirate Chief who wants to run his sword through Peter Pan.
Horner	Horny libertine who beds *The Country Wife*.
Long John Silver	One-legged pirate cum ship's cook on the trail of Flint's treasure.

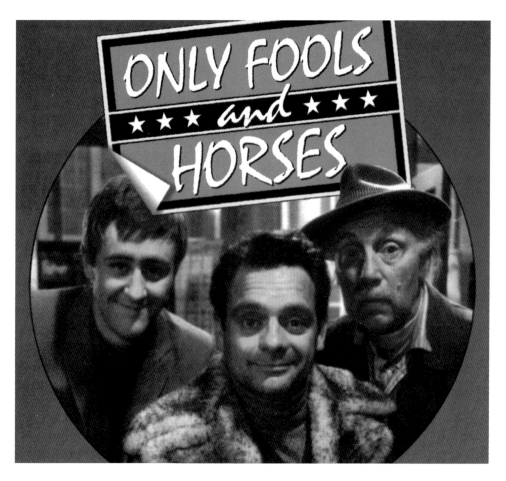

Rackrent family	Uncaring and largely absentee landlords in 18th Century Ireland.
'Del Boy' Trotter	TV's most incompetent and likeable would-be rogue.
Uncle Oswald	Said to be 'the greatest fornicator of all time'.
Volpone	Cunning old merchant who gains much by pretending to be dying.

The Undead

Werewolf and vampire stories are part of myth. Vampire tales are popularly assumed to have begun with legends about the real-life historical Vlad the Impaler, a ruler given over to unbridled blood lust and cruelty, though in fact they predate him, and the earliest werewolf tales are to be found in Ovid and Herodotus. These supernatural villains stand out largely because they are both near-human: the werewolf being, for most of the time, an apparently normal man, but one who transforms at each full moon into a ravaging half wolf, half human creature; the vampire being someone denied the peace of death but condemned instead to an eternal half-life, neither dead nor alive, never to find that 'better place' that humans find. The vampire cannot be killed (other than by a silver bullet or by a stake driven through the heart – or in occasional variants, by fire) but has nevertheless to sustain his travesty of life with regular infusions of mortal blood. To kill a werewolf is almost as difficult: impervious to sword or bullet he can be killed only by a weapon that has been blessed in a chapel dedicated to Saint Hubert. (And is there one of those near where you live?)

Though occasionally pitiable because he cannot prevent his regular transformations, the werewolf is a creature of horror who on the nights of the full moon feasts upon the flesh of villagers unwise enough to stray from safety. The vampire's nature has gradually developed from that of the historic Vlad to become more complex. In one of the earliest written variants, John Polidori's *The Vampyre* (1816), the vampire is reported initially not as a slayer but as a tempter and corrupter of young women. When Aubrey, the hero of the story, first hears of the mysterious **Lord Ruthven** (the vampyre (sic) of the title) he could be forgiven for assuming him to be merely a sponger on their wealth:

She told him the tale of the living vampyre, who had passed years amidst his friends, and dearest ties, by feeding upon the life of a lovely female to prolong his existence for the ensuing months.

From *The Vampyre, A Tale* by Polidori

But at the climax of the tale Aubrey discovers that it is rather more than their money that Ruthven extracts:

At the desire of Aubrey they searched for her who had attracted him by her cries; he was again left in darkness; but what was his horror, when the light of the torches once more burst upon him, to perceive the airy form of his fair conductress brought in a lifeless corpse .. There was no colour upon her cheek, not even upon her lip; yet there was a stillness about her face that seemed almost as attaching as the life that once dwelt there: – upon her neck and breast was blood, and upon her throat were the marks of teeth having opened the vein: – to this the men pointed, crying, simultaneously struck with horror, 'A Vampyre! A Vampyre!'

From *The Vampyre, A Tale* by Polidori

The horror that climaxes Polidori's tale – the sucking of blood from her neck and breast – is a physical act perpetrated upon a beautiful woman, and violence upon a woman is an eternal sexual fantasy. It is this element of the story which will be emphasised in later tales.

The bed in that old chamber is occupied. A creature formed in all fashions of loveliness lies in a half sleep upon that ancient couch – a girl young and beautiful as a spring morning. Her long hair has escaped from its confinement and streams over the blackened coverings of the bedstead; she has been restless in her sleep, for the clothing of the bed is in much confusion. One arm is over her head, the other hangs nearly off the side of the bed near to which she lies. A neck and bosom that would have formed a study for the rarest sculptor that ever Providence gave genius to, were half disclosed.

From *Varney the Vampire* by James Malcolm Rymer

Thus is the scene set for the climactic scene in many a vampire story, with the innocent, half-dressed maiden left unprotected and alone. But in dramatic terms the picture is incomplete without the intrusion of a man, a man who can gain access to and enjoy these luscious maidens, who can, in effect, rip out their virginity and make them his. In most of the stories the maiden invites the vampire in, unaware of what will happen to her. This is a potent fantasy, but one by no means confined to men. That the sucking of blood is a symbol for rape – and on occasions, consensual sex – is too obvious to need spelling out.

In almost all the stories the girl's bare neck, interestingly, is a more erotic zone than the untouched bosom.

With a sudden rush that could not be foreseen – with a strange howling cry that was enough to awaken terror in every breast – the figure seized the long tresses of her hair, and twining them round his bony hands he held her to the bed. Then she screamed – Heaven granted her then the power to scream. Shriek followed shriek in rapid succession. The bed clothes fell in a heap by the side of the bed – she was dragged by her long silken hair completely on to it again. Her beautiful rounded limbs quivered with the agony of her soul. The glassy horrible eyes of the figure ran over the angelic form with a hideous satisfaction – horrible profanation. He drags her head to the bed's edge. He forces it back by the long hair still entwined in his grasp. With a plunge he seizes her neck in his fang-like teeth – a gush of blood and a hideous sucking noise follows. The girl has swooned and the vampire is at his hideous repast!

From *Varney The Vampire* by James Malcolm Rymer

One might have thought, after Rymer's *Varney* (1846) that there was little that could be added to the story. But then came Bram Stoker, with the most famous vampire story of them all. For the bulk of that story, see under **Dracula**. But for sensuality, here's a taster:

I suppose I must have fallen asleep; I hope so, but I fear, for all that followed was startlingly real – so real that now, sitting here in the broad, full sunlight of the morning, I cannot in the least believe that it was all sleep.

I was not alone. The room was the same, unchanged in any way since I came into it; I could see along the floor, in the brilliant moonlight, my own footsteps marked where I had disturbed the long accumulation of dust. In the moonlight opposite me were three young women, ladies by their dress and manner. I thought at the time that I must be dreaming when I saw them, for, though the moonlight was behind them, they threw no shadow on the floor. They came close to me and looked at me for some time, and then whispered together. Two were dark, and had high aquiline noses, like the Count, and great dark, piercing eyes, that seemed to be almost red when contrasted with the pale yellow moon. The other was fair, as fair as can be, with great, wavy masses of golden hair and eyes like pale sapphires. I seemed somehow to know her face, and to know it in connection with some dreamy fear, but I could not recollect at the moment how or where. All three had brilliant white teeth, that shone like pearls against the ruby of their voluptuous lips. There was something about them that made me uneasy, some longing and at the same time some deadly fear. I felt in my heart a wicked, burning desire that they would kiss me with those red lips. It is not good to note this down, lest some day it should meet Mina's eyes and cause her pain; but it is the truth. They whispered together, and then they all three laughed – such a silvery, musical laugh, but as hard as though the sound never could have come through the softness of human lips. It was like the intolerable, tingling sweetness of waterglasses when played on by a cunning hand. The fair girl shook her head coquettishly, and the other two urged her on. One said: –

'Go on! You are first, and we shall follow; yours is the right to begin.' The other added: –

'He is young and strong; there are kisses for us all.' I lay quiet, looking out from under my eyelashes in agony of delightful anticipation. The fair girl advanced and bent over me till I could feel the movement of her breath upon me. Sweet it was in one sense, honey-sweet, and sent the same tingling through the nerves as her voice, but with a bitter underlying the sweet, a bitter offensiveness, as one smells in blood.

I was afraid to raise my eyelids, but looked out and saw perfectly under the lashes. The fair girl went on her knees, and bent over me, fairly gloating. There was a deliberate voluptuousness which was both thrilling and repulsive, and as she arched her neck she actually licked her lips like an animal, till I could see in the moonlight the moisture shining on the scarlet lips and on the red tongue as it lapped the white sharp teeth. Lower and lower went her head as the lips went below the range of my mouth and chin and seemed about to fasten on my throat. Then she paused, and I could hear the churning sound of her tongue as it licked her teeth and lips, and could feel the hot breath on my neck. Then the skin of my throat began to tingle as one's flesh does when the hand that is to tickle it approaches nearer – nearer. I could feel the soft, shivering touch of the lips on the supersensitive skin of my throat, and the hard dents of two sharp teeth, just touching and pausing there. I closed my eyes in a languorous ecstasy and waited – waited with a beating heart.

from *Dracula* by Bram Stoker

In the fiction of the undead, Bram Stoker's *Dracula* is the archetype and remains supreme. It is Stoker – in the guise of his vampire hunter, Van Helsing – who, in faltering English summarised below, spells out the essential characteristics of the vampire:

He is known everywhere that men have been .. He cannot die by mere passing of the time .. He can fatten on the blood of the living .. But he cannot flourish without this diet; he eat not as others .. He throws no shadow; he make in the mirror no reflect .. He has the strength of many in his hand .. He can transform himself to wolf .. He can come in mist which he create .. He can see in the dark – no small power this, in a world which is one half shut from the light .. He can do all these things, yet he is not free. Nay; he is even more prisoner than the slave of the galley, than the madman in his cell. He cannot go where he lists; he who is not of nature has yet to obey some of nature's laws – why we know not. He may not enter anywhere at the first, unless there be someone of the household who bid him to come; though afterwards he can come as he pleases. His power ceases, as does that of all evil things, at the coming of the day.

from *Dracula* by Bram Stoker

The first female vampire was **Carmilla**, in the book *In A Glass Darkly* (1872) by Le Fanu, and we should remember that the word 'vamp', nowadays applied to a seductress (usually beautiful and irresistible) who sucks the spirit out of men, is a shortening of 'vampire'. Whether one sees a vamp as a villain, though, depends on one's sexual preference.

Villains Against James Bond

As if Bond himself were not magnetic, and as if the Bond Girls wouldn't keep men returning to the cinema, the villains that James Bond confronts would justify an encyclopaedia to themselves – especially since the villains in the films are not always the same as those in the books. Here are the **film** villains:

Mr Big, in *Live and Let Die:* played by Yaphet Kotto.

Ernst Stavro Blofield, in *From Russia With Love* played by Anthony Dawson.

Ernst Stavro Blofield, in *You Only Live Twice:* played by Donald Pleasance.

Ernst Stavro Blofield, in *On Her Majesty's Secret Service:* played by Telly Savalas.

Ernst Stavro Blofield, in *Diamonds Are Forever:* played by Charles Gray.

Ernst Stavro Blofield, in *Never Say Never Again:* played by Max von Sydow.

Elliot Carver, in *Tomorrow Never Dies:* played by Jonathan Pryce.

Le Chiffre, in the 2006 *Casino Royale:* played by Madds Mikelsen.

Sir Hugo Drax, in *Moonraker:* played by Michael Lonsdale.

Aurie Goldfinger, in *Goldfinger:* played by Gert Frobe.

Gustav Graves, in *Die Another Day:* played by Toby Stephens.

Dr Kananga, in *Live and Let Die:* played by Yaphet Kotto.

Kamil Khan, in *Octopussy:* played by Louis Jordan.

Elektra King, in *The World Is Not Enough:* played by Sophie Marceau.

Rosa Klebb (of SMERSH), in *From Russia With Love*: played by Lotte Lenya.

General Koskov, in *The Living Daylights:* played by Jeroen Krabbe.

Aris Kristatos, in *For Your Eyes Only:* played by Julian Glover.

Emilio Largo, in *Thunderball:* played by Adolfi Celi.

Maximillian Largo, in *Never Say Never Again:* played by Klaus Maria Brandauer.

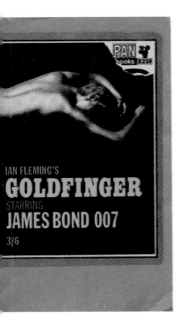

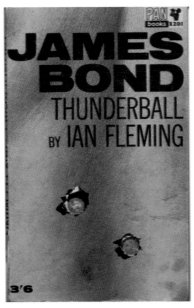

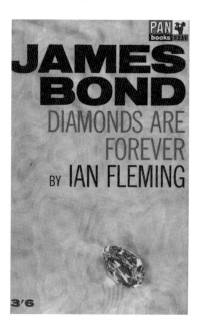

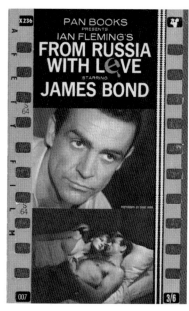

Colonel Moon, in *Die Another Day:* played by Will Yun Lee.

Dr Julius No, in *Dr No:* played by Joseph Wiseman.

General Orlov, in *Octopussy:* played by Steven Berkov.

Franz Sanchez, in *Licence To Kill:* played by Robert Davis.

Francisco Scaramanga, in *The Man With The Golden Gun:* played by Christopher Lee.

Karl Stromberg, in *The Spy Who Loved Me* played by Curt Jurgens.

Alec Trevelyan, in *Goldeneye:* played by Sean Bean.

Mr White, in *Casino Royale:* played by Jesper Christensen.

Brad Whittaker, in *The Living Daylights:* played by Joe Don Baker.

Viktor Renard Zokas, in *The World Is Not Enough:* played by Robert Carlyle.

Max Zorin, in *A View To A Kill:* played by Christopher Walken.

But those are the film villains. Here are some differences you'll find in the stories written by Ian Fleming:

• In *Diamonds Are Forever* Bond's adversaries are The Spangled Mob, comprising Jack and Seraffimo Spang, Mr. Kidd & Wint.

• In *From Russia With Love* more emphasis is given to the sinister Russian agency SMERSH, and Red Grant has as important a role as does Rosa Klebb.

• In the short story *For Your Eyes Only* the villain is Von Hammerstein.

• In *Thunderball* more emphasis is given to the secret agency SPECTRE.

• Adversaries in *The Spy Who Loved Me* include Mr. Sanguinetti, Sol 'Horror' Horowitz, and 'Sluggsy' Morant.

• In the short story *Octopussy* Bond confronts Major Dexter Smythe.

Villains Against Sexton Blake

Since Blake was possibly the longest-lived detective in crime fiction – certainly his adventures have exhausted more words of fiction than any other – it is not surprising that in his time he has met with many fiendish adversaries. Here are a few.

- Prince Wu Ling – Chief of the Brotherhood of the Yellow Beetle
- Dr Huxton Rymer – doctor of death
- Waldo the Wonder Man.
- Mademoiselle Yvonne – glamorous enough to romantically entrap our hero.
- Zenith the Albino.

Sexton Blake films date from 1914, and a series of silent movies in the Twenties starred **Langhorne Burton** in the role. By the Thirties **George Curzon** (who became the radio Blake) had taken over, to be followed in turn by **David Farrar** in the Forties.

ITV ran *Sexton Blake* from 1967 to 1971, with **Laurence Payne** as Blake, **Roger Foss** as boy wonder Tinker and **Dorothea Phillips** as their Baker Street landlady, Mrs Bardell. BBC TV serialised *Sexton Blake and the Demon God* in 1978, with **Jeremy Clyde** as Blake and **Philip Davis** as young Tinker.

Villains Of The Silver Screen

Cinema

Strongly-delineated villains are more prevalent in films than in printed fiction because films are more dependent on story. Fiction doesn't have to tell a story – how often have you read a book which, in the end, didn't seem to have been about anything much at all? That's an accusation you can make less often about the cinema. Films tell stories, and a good story needs a conflict. The ultimate conflict is between good and evil, and in such a conflict there must be representatives from both sides: heroes and villains. Hence cinema needs villains to set against its clean-limbed heroes.

To give a comprehensive listing of cinema villains would require a book the length of Halliwell, but a selection of the finest British screen villains is given below:

Film	Villain	Played by
A Clockwork Orange	*Alex, a gang-leader in the dystopian near future.*	*Malcolm McDowell*
The Blue Lamp	*Tom Riley, young criminal with a gun.*	*The equally young Dirk Bogarde*
Brighton Rock	*Pinkie, a heartless young thug.*	*Richard Attenborough*
The Day of the Jackal	*The Jackal, a ruthless mercenary.*	*Edward Fox*
Dracula	*Count Dracula, Transylvania's least desirable export.*	*Bela Lugosi set the tone. Christopher Lee then made the role his.*
Far From The Madding Crowd	*Sergeant Troy: but try telling a woman that he's a villain.*	*– Especially when he's played by Terence Stamp*
Frankenstein	*Dr Victor Frankenstein, creator of 'the monster'.*	*Colin Clive in 1931 but Peter Cushing is the one that we remember.*

Film	Villain	Played by
Kind Hearts and Coronets	*Louis Mazzini, ninth in line to a dukedom. So that's only eight people standing in his way.*	*Dennis Price*
Oliver Twist	*Fagin, a pre-OFSTED teacher of impressionable boys.*	*controversially portrayed by Alec Guiness*
Richard III	*King Richard, cinema's greatest Shakespearean villain.*	*Made unforgettable by Laurence Olivier*
The Third Man	*Harry Lime, dealer in diluted and thus ineffective drugs.*	*Orson Welles, making the most delayed entrance in cinema history*

TV Villains

Television abounds in villains. Its schedules are crammed with dramas, and dramas need an endless supply of villains. TV soaps, even when they start out as gentle sagas, drift inexorably into tales of conflict and into each of them creeps a villain. Whereas in a single play or TV film, seen once, the villain must make a real impact to be remembered, in a TV soap, seen weekly and sometimes almost daily, the villain can become a part of the viewers' imaginary life.

You must remember these:

TV Show	Villain	Played by	Characteristics
Bad Girls (1999) *Stories of women prisoners in Larkhall. Violent, sleazy and way over the top. Hence its popularity.*	Wicked women banged up included Shell Dockley Denny Blood Corrupt staff included: Jim Fenner Sylvia Hollamby	Debra Stephenson Alicia Eyo Jack Ellis Helen Fraser	Bisexual murderess Dockley's mate Wicked warder Wicked wardress
Bergerac (1981) *Amiable series set on Jersey about an ex-alcoholic cop with a limp.*	Few of the show's villains were really nasty, and certainly his one-time father-in-law Charlie Hungerford wasn't, but he did stay the course.	Terence Alexander	Dodgy businessman, sympathetically portrayed
Blackadder (1983) *Four comic series, beginning (shakily) in the Wars of the Roses and ending superbly in the First World War.*	Edmund Blackadder. Blackadder and his setting reincarnates through time but he remains amusingly cowardly but superior. Melchett Baldrick	Rowan Atkinson Stephen Fry Tony Robinson	A villain throughout history, played for laughs Supercilious rival. Would be a villain if he had the brains.
Callan (1967) *Landmark series about a 'disposable' agent in British Intelligence*	Toby Meres. Rival agent, supposedly on the same side as Callan	Anthony Valentine	Privately educated, affectedly superior, unblinkingly vicious. Irresistible.

TV Show	Villain	Played by	Characteristics
Coronation Street (1960) *The ultimate TV soap, set in the imaginary Manchester suburb of Weatherfield*	Richard Hillman	Brain Capron	Disguised himself as Aiden Critchley so he could kill Maxine Platt. He later drowned.
	Ernie Bishop	Stephen Hancock	Shot dead in wages snatch Bigamist
	Arnold Swain Alan Bradley	George Waring Mark Eden	Thug, run down by a tram
	The Battersbys	Bruce Jones, Vicky Entwistle, Jane Danson, Georgia Taylor	Neighbours from hell
Dick Barton – Special Agent (1979) *Star radio series, much less successful on TV*	Melganik	John G Heller	Evil and (of necessity for the series) indestructible.
Doctor Who (1963) *Intended originally for children, the series hooked gener-ations of parents, and has proved to be as indestructible as the Doctor himself. Doctor Who has been played by: William Hartnell Patrick Troughton Jon Pertwee Tom Baker Peter Davison Colin Baker Sylvester McCoy Paul McGann Christopher Eccleston David Tennant Matt Smith (McGann was in a 1996 one-off TV film)*	Daleks are in top spot among the Doctor's adversaries, though others include:	Unnamed players	Looking like portable tin heaters, they should have been risible but became a legend. They are mutants from the extinct race of Kaleds.
	Davros	Michael Wisher, David Gooderson & Terry Molloy as time progressed	Evil genius who created the Daleks in the first place. Has the best mask in the series.
	Cybermen	Unnamed players	Mechanical marchers from Earth's twin planet Mondas.
	Ice Warriors	Unnamed players	Cold devils from Mars.
	Sea Devils	Unnamed players	Earth's earlier inhabitants, from beneath the waves.
	Silurians	Unnamed players	Reptilian cousins to the Sea Devils.
	Yeti	Unnamed players	Furry robots, who you shouldn't try to cuddle.

TV Show	Villain	Played by	Characteristics
	Zarbi	Unnamed players	Giant ants.
	The Master	Roger Delgado, Anthony Ainley, Eric Roberts (TV Movie only), John Simm	A Time Lord, like the Doctor, but intent on universal domination.
	The Rani	Kate O'Mara	Female but more terrible version of The Master.
EastEnders (1985) *BBC TV's answer to Coronation Street. Set in the imaginary Walford in London's East End, the series is rougher, bleaker and more shocking than its northern rival*	Dennis Watts (Dirty Den)	Leslie Grantham	The most notorious of the show's wrong 'uns, mainly from his vicious self-interest but partly from the fact that the actor playing the part had served time for murder.
	Cindy Beale	Michelle Collins	Sorted out a child custody battle by having her husband shot.
	Max Branning	Jake Wood	The world's worst father and husband. Has slept with his son's girlfriend, while ignoring his own pregnant wife. Even when Tanya poisoned and entombed him, Max still came out alive.
	Nick Cotton	John Altman	Son of long-running character Dot Cotton and her attempted murderer, he successfully killed Reg Cox in episode 1.
	Little Mo Morgan	Kacey Ainsworth	Tried for attempted murder.
	Grant Mitchell	Ross Kemp	Shaven-headed hardman, involved in too many scams to recap here. Slept with his wife's mother, but see below.

TV Show	Villain	Played by	Characteristics
	Phil Mitchell	Steve McFadden	The other of the show's two balding baddy brothers. This one slept with his brother's wife. Has had a long fight with alcoholism too.
	Billy Mitchell	Perry Fenwick	Chip off the old block.
	Steve Owen	Martin Kemp	Let Matthew Rose take the blame for killing Saskia – but was then himself burned alive in an exploding car.
Emmerdale Farm (1972) *Began life as a rural saga, a kind of TV 'Archers', but toughened up in the 1980s – and went too far, some fans complained. Because Emmerdale Farm had metamorphosed, it was renamed* **Emmerdale** *in November 1989.*	Cain Dingle	Jeff Hordley	Rural bad boy, spent time in jail and had affair with local policewoman. Also fathered a child on Charity Dingle. (Don't ask.)
	Rosemary Sinclair, nee King	Linda Thorson	Arch schemer, thought to be the murderer of her own husband, Tom King. Tried to poison her daughter-in-law. Appeared at one point to have arranged her own fake murder, setting up Mathew King as her supposed killer. Finally committed suicide – or did she?
	Nicola de Souza	Nicola Wheeler	Irresistible to men – despite the fact that she keeps trying to murder them.
Fawlty Towers **(1979)** *Comic masterpiece, perhaps because there were so few episodes, with Cleese superb as the most British of hoteliers.*	Basil Fawlty	John Cleese	Hotelier who hates his job, his life, and everyone.
	Cast also included:		
	Sybil Fawlty	Prunella Scales	Basil's wife
	Polly Sherman	Connie Booth	Their all-purpose maid
	Manuel	Andrew Sachs	He's from Barcelona

TV Show	Villain	Played by	Characteristics
The Fixer (2008) *Villain released from jail to work for the secret service.* *Yes, that old plot but rather better done.*	John Mercer	Andrew Buchan	We first meet him in jail, so he must be a villain, mustn't he?
	Lenny Douglas	Peter Mullan	or is this man, a shadowy figure from the unnamed service, the real villain?
Forsyte Saga (1967 – remade 2002) *The first was a compulsive filming of Galsworthy's classic. The second looked at only the first two of the nine book series.*	Soames Forsyte (1st)	Eric Porter	A 19th century man of property and business.
	Soames Forsyte (2nd)	Damian Lewis	Seen as a villain by those about him, though not by viewers or readers of the books.
Garry Halliday (1959) *BBC TV children's serial about a plucky pilot*	The Voice	Elwyn Brook-Jones	Deskbound and hence overweight master criminal, as likely to kill off his assistants as to kill heroes. Temporary henchmen included Kurt and Trauman
GBH (1991) *Hard-hitting political drama written by Alan Bleasdale for Channel 4. Set in an unnamed, therefore fictional, Liverpool – though a former Deputy Leader of the council (Derek Hatton) almost sued.*	Michael Murray	Robert Lindsay	Freshly elected as leader of the city council, his mix of left-wing maliciousness, vendettas and personal venality causes havoc. He doesn't realise that he himself is being manipulated from both left and right extremes.

TV Show	Villain	Played by	Characteristics
The Jewel in the Crown (1984) *Based on* The Raj Quartet, *four novels about India in 1942-7 by Paul Scott*	Ronald Merrick	Tim Pigott-Smith	Sadistic, racist and viciously ambitious police officer who seeks to resist the emancipation of India. Among his manipulations is the framing of Hari Kumar for the rape of Daphne Manners.
The Master (1966) *No relation to The Master in* Doctor Who, *but the eponymous villain of an ITV children's adventure series*	The Master	Olaf Pooley	150- year-old power-crazed extra-sensory scientist living on Rockall, who intends to hold the world to ransom – unless a boy, a girl and a dog can stop him.
Only Fools and Horses (1981 – 2002) *A comic masterpiece concerning the many failures of the Trotters of Peckham Rye* '*only fools and horses work':* *proverb anon.*	Derek 'Del Boy' Trotter	David Jason	He'd love to be a rogue but it's a step beyond him.
	Rodney Trotter	Nicholas Lyndhurst	Put-upon younger brother.
	Aubrey 'Boycie' Boyce	John Challis	Second-hand car dealer, a rogue, but less sharp than he thinks.
	Cast includes: Raquel Slater / Trotter	Tessa Peake-Jones	
	Cassandra Parry/Trotter	Gwynneth Strong	
	Granddad Trotter	Lennard Pearce	
	Uncle Albert	Buster Merryfield	
	Marlene Boyce	Sue Holderness	
	Trigger	Roger Lloyd Pack	

TV Show	Villain	Played by	Characteristics
Till Death Us Do Part (1966) and later **In Sickness and in Health** (1985) *Bigotry, ignorance and foul language (for its day) divided viewers into appalled critics and devoted fans. (Most viewers were fans, of course.)*	Alf Garnett His non-villainous family comprised: Else Garnett Rita Garnett Mike, the 'Scouse Git'	Warren Mitchell Dandy Nichols Una Stubbs Anthony Booth	Extreme caricature of an extreme East End bigot. An ex-docker, Alf sits at home and fumes at his patient wife, liberal daughter and dim but well-meaning son-in-law. His unflinching portrayal on screen should have made Garnett an object lesson but the nation took him to its heart.

A Timeline of Villainy

1682 Birth year of Jonathan Wild, duplicitous thief-taker (making him the first bent copper?).

1702 Jack Sheppard, jail-breaker, born in Stepney.

1706 Dick Turpin, highwayman, born in Hempstead, Essex.

1739 Dick Turpin hanged.

1748 *Clarissa* introduces us to Robert Lovelace.

1753 Bow Street Runners founded.

1764 Birth of Ann Radcliffe, who became the supreme Gothic novelist.

1765 The first Gothic novel: *The Castle of Otranto*. (**Manfred** is the villain)

1780 Price of a novel is around 2/- a volume.

1794 *Caleb Williams* published.

1816 Supposedly the first literary manifestation of a vampire, *The Vampyre, A Tale*, introduces the leech-like Lord Ruthven.

1818 *Frankenstein* is published.

1821 Price of a novel is fixed at an eye-watering 1$\frac{1}{2}$ guineas.

1828 Trial of William Corder for the murder of Maria Marten.

1829 London Metropolitan Police founded.

1838 *Oliver Twist* first serialised, introducing two of Dickens's most famous villains, **Fagin** and **Bill Sikes**.

1841 *The Murders in the Rue Morgue* published in *Graham's Magazine*.

1848 WHSmith establishes its first book and news stand, at Euston Station.

1850 Pinkerton National Detective Agency formed in Chicago.

1872 *In A Glass Darkly* published. It is the first novel about a female vampire – Carmilla.

1878 CID formed at Scotland Yard

1886 *The Strange Case of Dr Jekyll and Mr Hyde* introduces the innovatory Mr Hyde.

1887 *Beeton's Christmas Annual*

brings the first appearance of Sherlock Holmes, in *A Study in Scarlet*.

1888 The Jack The Ripper murders terrify London's ladies.

1890 Britain's first literary agents set up. Conan Doyle's *The Sign of Four* published.

1891 First *Strand Magazine* Sherlock Holmes story: *A Scandal in Bohemia*.

1892 Anarchist bomb outrages in Paris.
'Death' of Sherlock Holmes at the Reichenbach Falls at the hands of **Moriarty**.

1897 *Dracula* published, as was *The Prince of Swindlers* featuring Simon Carne, fiction's first gentleman thief.

1901 Oscar Wilde and Queen Victoria die.

1903 Sherlock Holmes returns! in *The Adventure of the Empty House* in *Strand Magazine* Wright brothers' first air flight.

1905 An Irish printer founds Sinn Fein. First Edgar Wallace novel: *The Four Just Men*.

1908 The FBI founded, within the US Dept of Justice.

1910 Dr Crippen arrested at sea.

1911 Siege of Sidney Street. First Father Brown book: *The Innocence of Father Brown*.

1912 Brides in the Bath sensation

1914 August: First World War begins.
The last full-length Sherlock Holmes novel: *The Valley of Fear*.

1916 Easter Rising in Dublin. Lloyd George becomes Prime Minister.

1917 *His Last Bow* appears to be the end of Sherlock Holmes. America joins the First World War.

1918 Neville Heath is hanged. In November the First World War ends.

1920 Prohibition introduced in America.

The Old Fleet Prison.

Newgate Prison.

Irish Home Rule Bill passed. IRA killings escalate. *Bull-Dog Drummond* is published.

1921 Larson invents the lie detector

1923 Hitler addresses first Nazi rally. German currency collapses.

1931 Moseley forms fascist 'New Party'. *Frankenstein*, filmed by James Whale, stars Boris Karloff as the monster. *Dracula*, filmed by Tod Browning, stars Bela Lugosi.

1933 Birth of the Kray twins.

1934 'Bonnie & Clyde' killed in America. Charlie Richardson born.

1935 First Penguin paperback: cost 6d.

1936 Germany occupies the Rhineland. Jarrow March. Abdication crisis. Tod Slaughter takes the title role as *Sweeney Todd*.

1939 First screen appearance of Basil Rathbone as Holmes: *The Hound of the Baskervilles*. World War Two declared in Europe.

1945 World War Two in Europe ends.

1947 Al Capone dies in America.

1949 Haigh executed for the Acid Bath Murders. The film *The Third Man* introduces Orson Welles as one of cinema's greatest villains. *1984* published.

1950 Graham Greene's book of *The Third Man* follows the film. *Eagle* comic introduces *The Mekon*. Donald Hume trial. Klaus Fuchs jailed for selling atomic secrets to USSR.

1952 First stage production of *The Mousetrap*. First James Bond novel: *Casino Royale*. Identity Cards abolished in UK

1953 John Creasey founds the Crime Writers' Association. The murderer Christie is hanged.

1955 'Rock Around The Clock' riots in UK. Ruth Ellis is the last woman to be hanged in Britain. ITV launched in September.

1956 The Suez crisis. Hungarian uprising crushed by Soviet Union.

1958 Christopher Lee first appears as Dracula.

1960 First TV screening of *Z-Cars*, which continued till 1978. *Lady Chatterley's Lover* brought to trial.

1962 Cuban Missile crisis. Marilyn

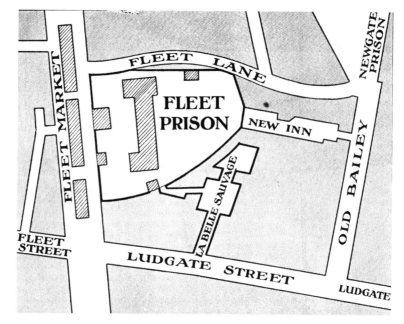

Monroe dies of overdose. London Airport Bullion Robbery. First screening of *Z Cars* First Bond film: *Doctor No*. Publication (relatively unnoticed) of *A Clockwork Orange*.

1963 The 'Profumo affair'. Kennedy assassinated. Great Train Robbery. *Doctor Who* first screened.

1966 Ian Brady & Myra Hindley jailed for the 'Moors Murders'. England wins soccer World Cup.

1967 Charlie Richardson gets 25 years.

1968 *Doctor No* is the first Bond film.

1969 Mad Frankie Fraser gives Ronnie Kray a character reference at Old Bailey. Krays found guilty. The first *Flashman* book appears: *Flashman: From the Flashman Papers 1839-1842*

1971 Kubrick releases his sensational film of *A Clockwork Orange*.

1972 Nixon re-elected as US President. Vietnam war approaches its end.

1973 Ceasefire in Vietnam. The Watergate affair. Edward Fox stars in *The Day of the Jackal*.

1974 Lord Lucan disappears. Nixon resigns.

1975 First screening of *The Sweeney*. Margaret Thatcher becomes first woman leader of Conservative Party. Inflation reaches 25%.

1976 Britain's hottest summer of the century. Punk Rock hits the charts. Agatha Christie dies.

1979 Margaret Thatcher becomes Prime Minister. Iran Embassy siege. *Sweeney Todd* becomes a musical.

1980 Mugabe becomes PM of

Zimbabwe, and Nixon President of USA.
John Lennon is shot in New York.

1982 IRA bomb Horse Guards. Iraq bombs Iran.
Britain wins Falklands war.

1984 IRA bomb Tory party conference.
An inevitable but effective TV version of *1984*.

1986 US bombs Libya.
Chernobyl nuclear disaster.
Jeffrey Archer resigns.

1987 King's Cross underground fire disaster.
'Black Monday' shares disaster.

1989 George Bush succeeds President Reagan.
Tiananmen Square protest.
Berlin Wall comes down.
Georges Simenon dies, in Lausanne.
Blackadder series ends without a laugh.

1990 The first Gulf War begins.
Eddie Richardson gets 25 years for cocaine smuggling.
BBC TV's *House of Cards* sends our opinion of politicians to new depths

1992 Phil Collins plays Great Train Robber Buster Edwards in *Buster*.

1995 26-year old Nick Leeson brings down Britain's oldest bank, Barings, losing £620 million.
Death of Ronnie Kray.

1999 NATO air attacks on Serbia.
First screening of *The Vice* and *Bad Girls*.

2001 9/11 attack on Twin Towers.
First screening of *Messiah*.
P D Cornwell 'identifies' Jack the Ripper.

2003 US-led invasion of Iraq.

2004 Asian tsunami kills 300,000.

2005 UN authorises International Criminal Court to try Darfur war criminals.
July: London bus & tube bombings.
Hurricane Katrina hits New Orleans.
BBC TV has a surprise hit with a 'soap opera' version of *Bleak House*.

2007 BBC TV's most recent serialisation of *Oliver Twist*.
Saddam Hussein executed.
Tony Blair finally resigns.

2008 Gordon Brown finds the job harder than he expected.
Mugabe reveals himself as The Great Dictator.

2009 World's bankers become the real villains.
This book published.

The Condemned Cell
at Newgate.

'Thus have we endeavoured, and we hope not unsuccessfully, to
compleat this work, in conformity to the proposals originally offered
to the public. We trust we have not omitted any trials of great
importance, nor inserted many of a trifling nature.

Those who wish well to Society will be pleased to see vice exposed
in every shape, and reprobated under all the variety of forms it may
assume. Too much cannot be said to discountenance its propagation,
or to enhance the charms of true religion and virtue.

To advance these important purposes should be the aim and end of
every publication. The book that does not tend to make people wiser
and better is a nuisance to Society, and a disgrace to the Press.'

from the original Concluding Note to
The Malefactor's Register or New Newgate and Tyburn Calendar

Acknowledgements

Much of the information in this book comes from a lifetime spent reading books my mother would not have approved of. (Actually, she *would* have approved. It was my father who... But that's another story.) As well as plundering books and magazines in my own far too large collection, I owe thanks also to the following reference books:

Boys Will Be Boys by E S Turner (Michael Joseph, 1948).

Companion to Literature in English edited by Ian Ousby (Cambridge, revised 1992).

Companion to Popular Literature by Victor Neuburg (Batsford, 1982).

Imaginary People by David Pringle (Grafton Books, 1985).

Movie and Video Guide by Leonard Maltin (Plume 2002).

The Oxford Companion to English Literature edited by Margaret Drabble (OUP, 2000).

Penguin TV Companion by Jeff Evans (Penguin 2003 revised edition).

Penny Dreadfuls by Michael Anglo (Jupiter Books, 1977).

Popular Literature by Victor Neuburg (Penguin, 1977).

Print and the People by Louis James (Allen Lane, 1976).

The Reader's Encyclopedia by William Rose Benet (Thomas Y Crowell, various editions).

Sequels compiled by M E Hicken (London Assoc. of Asst. Librarians 1982).

Most of the pictures in this book are from my own collection, but I would like to thank the many publishers who have allowed me to use their book jackets for illustrations. Also I'd like to give a special word of thanks to my editor, Fiona Shoop, and to the diligent production team at Pen & Sword Books in Barnsley. Despite their efforts, any errors and opinions in the book are, of course, my own. Every effort has been made to trace the appointed owners of the material still covered by copyright, but where any accidental infringement has occurred please contact the author care of the publishers.

INDEX